A Diabolical Plot

Guy Fawkes: Demon Hunter

Benjamin Langley

Published by Shadow Spark Publishing, 2023.

For the plotters, the pantsers, and all those that love to see it through to a finish.

Prologue

Guy Fawkes Arms, Scotton. False panel behind the bar.

Jamie stares at his scrawled note, written as soon as he'd left Sidney's bedside. The promise of proof made Jamie immediately book a table for dinner at that restaurant, The Guy Fawkes Arms. The thought of investigating a hidden panel recalled the thrill that drew him to a career in journalism, back when he believed it would involve secret codes and clandestine conversations inspired by the spy novels he'd read in his youth.

At home, Jamie plays through different scenarios that will allow him to access the panel. His excitement evaporates the second the last of the blisters on his neck erupts, the blisters he'd won as a prize for dragging Sidney from that bonfire, an act that started him on this journey through Guy Fawkes' life as a demon hunter. A trickle of pus oozes inside his shirt and onto his collarbone. He rushes to the bathroom to grab some tissue and wipes away the mess before dabbing at the stinging wound. He remembers Michael's guidance and washes his face and neck, dabs it dry, and reapplies the cream. Maybe the best thing to come out of all this is meeting Michael and having someone to talk to again. Life has been lonely since leaving the comfort of his regularly paying desk job at the newspaper.

In the hours he has to kill before leaving for the restaurant, Jamie completes the usual routine of checking his emails for responses to pitches, seeking leads on all the usual sources, and jotting down notes on potential articles based upon the news of the day. No inspiration strikes. His head is full of demons. Instead, he gets back on the Guy Fawkes research trail, part of him hoping to find a nugget of information to illuminate Sidney's story. When everything he reads only serves to fit Sidney's narrative (in terms of times, people and places—the demons are absent), Jamie can't help but feel a knot of anxiety tying itself further inside him. If Sidney's story is true, what does that mean for the world?

He opens another website fronted by more news of the Prime Minister's broken promises. It may be a poorly taken or edited photograph, but Jamie swears the Prime Minister's eyes look ringed in yellow. Beside Alistair Bar-

clay-Fitzwilliam is his advisor, Kristian Byrne. As always, his teeth are showing.

As Jamie drives into Scotton, he gazes at the houses, seeking the oldest buildings in the village, wondering if Guy Fawkes ever walked past any of those
places. The darkness coupled with a light fog leaves houses hidden, so he can
only guess the location of Percy House. If not for the changing gradient, he'd
not know hills surrounded him. He wonders on which side Guy tended his
sheep in those naïve days he believed he had a chance of peace. Jamie remembers Sidney recounting Maria's death, unable to believe something so horrific
could have happened here.

He parks and exits his car, the night's chill hitting him hard, stinging
his wounded face. Inside, Michael is already waiting, so Jamie hurries to the
table and sits. The Guy Fawkes Arms is a typical British village pub, partially converted into a restaurant, a mahogany bar splitting the diners from the
drinkers, with a low ceiling, exposed beams, and a roaring fire in a grand
brick fireplace.

Michael winces when he sees the side of Jamie's face, and after a brief
and slightly awkward interchange in which Michael recounts burn aftercare
instructions, Michael approaches the subject of their presence at the Guy
Fawkes Arms. "So, what are you going to do, wait until their backs are turned
and ransack the bar?"

Jamie smiles. "That's one option, but we should probably try something
less forceful."

Michael tilts his head and scratches behind his ear.

Jamie raises his eyebrows and leans in. "After dinner, we'll chat with the
bar staff and simply *ask* if I can look behind the bar."

"It's hardly cloak and dagger, but I guess it's a good starting point."

Jamie glances over his shoulder and lowers his voice. "I'll give you the signal if we need to knock people out."

Michael smiles, but something about it seems false, and a fog of silence
descends upon them. Jamie's eyes go back to the fire.

When the waitress approaches to take their order, she also succeeds in hitting the reset button. Michael reaches for his coat, which he'd placed on the back of his chair, and pulls out a piece of paper. "I made a few calls. I can't share specific details or any names, but..."

Jamie takes the paper and scans the list of events at fireworks displays, all involving burns, mostly to the hands. They go back years.

"Are these all..."

Michael nods. "I can't say for sure. There are always injuries at these events. Always burns. But there's plenty of anecdotal evidence. These aren't sparkler injuries or touching bits of fallen fireworks. Everyone who's worked at these events has a story about the time a man ran for the bonfire. It's him. Every time."

Jamie gazes past Michael, to the bar.

"He's a troubled man, Jamie." Michael's eyebrows draw together as he holds eye contact. "Are you sure you want to get involved?"

As much as Jamie understands Michael's point, he can't stop glancing at the bar, considering what might lie within.

Their meal arrives, and they eat, taking the conversation away from Sidney, away from Guy Fawkes, but he's always present, like an uninvited guest that has pulled his chair to their table to watch them eat. They decide against dessert in favour of venturing to the other side of the bar. They order drinks, and while the young barman pours them, Jamie asks, "So, why is this place called The Guy Fawkes Arms?"

The young man shrugs, but another barman plods over. He's older, heavy-set and speaks with a strong Yorkshire accent. "I can tell you all about that." He nudges the young barman aside. "Away with you, lad."

The barman tells the tale of Guy moving to Scotton when his mother remarried, moving on a few years later.

Jamie leans in and takes a chance. "I've heard a rumour..."

"Aye, go on."

"That there's an old artefact hidden in this bar."

The barman folds his arms, his mouth tightening into a scowl. "Associate of Sidney, are you?"

Jamie turns to Michael, who gives him a blank stare, then back at the barman. "We met recently, yes."

The barman sighs. "We don't want that trouble again."

"What trouble?"

The barman stares at Jamie. "Kept pestering our patrons with his stories. We barred him."

Jamie raises his open hands. "We don't intend to do anything like that."

"The missus caught him prying a panel off here one night." He ducks behind the bar and, a few seconds later, places a small wooden box on a bar mat. "If you're in contact with Sidney, be my guest and take it back to him."

Jamie takes the lid off the box. Inside is a small bone whistle.

The next day, Jamie waits outside the hospital until visiting hours. He's got the box in his bag. He dares not touch the whistle; it looks so brittle that it might crumble upon his touch.

When allowed onto the ward, he finds Sidney sitting in his bed. Some of his dressing has been removed, including that around one hand, which shows the scars of previous burns. Sidney stares at the bag. "Did you find it?"

Jamie chuckles. "I didn't so much find it as the owner handed it over."

Sidney's eyes narrow. "But you have it?"

Jamie nods.

Sidney clears his throat, the effort drawing a rattle from his chest. "I'm going to need a favour."

"Okay." Jamie pulls up a chair and sits. "Finish the story, and I'm all yours."

Chapter 1—In Which Guy Fawkes Returns to Calais

Almost three and a half years had passed since Guy boarded the English Ship Castor in Gillingham alongside Kit Wright. In that time, he'd reunited with Jack Wright, Ralph White, and Oswald Tesimond. He'd travelled through France, the Holy Roman Empire, and the Austrian Kingdom of the Hapsburg Monarchy before spending time in Spain, Venice, Genoa, and the Papal States. He'd fought alongside Ottoman Turks, Oromo people of Ethiopia, Portuguese Jesuits, and anyone else willing to raise a sword against a demon. And in April 1596, he found himself in Calais once more, but not to venture back across the North Sea. No, he would not return to England yet; his purpose was to deliver a group of Jesuits to a ship bound for England and take out the demon scum that infested the port town.

With the sea in view across the fields of an abandoned farmstead and the noise of war blasting nearby, Guy brought his horse to a halt. The warmer European climate had lightened his hair to a sandy colour; only a trace of the red so prominent in his youth on those rainy days in York remained. A full beard protected much of his face from the Mediterranean sun, which had turned his skin tawny. Like his companions, he wore a black hooded cloak, for often their party operated away from the forefront of battle, carrying out illicit operations under the cover of darkness. Guy drew his sabre, his weapon of choice for the last two years since winning it in a drinking game from a soldier of the Polish-Lithuanian Commonwealth he'd befriended in Prague. He studied its length and reminded himself of its weight. It wouldn't be long before he'd point it in anger once more.

He stopped alongside General Bartolomé de Sevilla, a Spaniard under the command of Colonel Bostock, another Englishman fighting against the country of his birth. Alongside Guy stood his old friends, Kit and Ralph, and a comparatively new one, an Ethiopian Oromo named Abuna Samra. In his early thirties, Samra had been fighting in Europe for a decade. He'd lost his left hand, swiped off in his youth by the claws of a hulking demon. This loss drove him to study demonology to give him the power to combat evil. Books had provided him with knowledge, and he used his skill in weaponry to develop a crossbow to attach to his stump.

In the distance, the Spanish troops lay siege to Calais, the sound of cannon fire and crumbing stone accompanying the rising smoke. With the sun an hour from setting, the group dismounted their horses and moved into the stables. Ruin had fallen upon the building, though most of the roof remained intact. Guy waited for a gap in the blasts of cannons and approached Bartolomé. "Bart, what's our plan?"

Bart slapped Guy on the back. "Guido, trust that we have it all in order."

Guy's brow furrowed, and not in annoyance at his nickname to which he'd grown accustomed. "So, tell me."

Bart grinned and turned to the west, shielding his eyes from the low sun with one hand. "When darkness falls, we enter the citadel."

Samra approached. "The citadel wall will not hold out against the cannon fire much longer. When the walls crumble, there we shall enter."

Bart looked at Samra and shook his head. "*El Caballero del diablo!* The devil knight, Michel Patras de Campaigno, will expect us to enter through the breach."

"Then where?" Samra asked with a shrug.

Bart beckoned Kit and Ralph over.

"Oh no!" said Guy, moving between them. "I'm not following another of Kit's plans."

Bart held up a hand to quiet Guy. "Kit and Ralph have been to the citadel before. They know the subterranean passages."

Guy put a hand to his head, and Ralph reached into his robe to pull out a scroll.

Kit placed his hand in his pouch full of runes which had hung by his side since childhood. "It's simple, Guy. Darkness coincides with low tide. We can drop into the river south of the citadel and swim toward the s dock. We can capture it from the inside."

"Ralph, can you verify that?" Guy asked.

Ralph unfurled the scroll to reveal a map of the citadel.

Kit's eyes grew large. "Why do you need Ralph to verify it? Don't you trust me, Guy?"

"Kit, I know you too well to follow you blindly down a dark passage. This time, you expect me to do it underwater?"

Kit crossed his arms. "Name one time I've led you in the wrong direction."

Guy stepped closer to Kit. "How about three? Sicily, La Coruna, Lübeck."

"Strictly speaking, Lübeck wasn't my fault. And what about Guimarães? We never would have escaped that snake-headed demon if we didn't take *my* route through the tunnels."

Guy pushed up his sleeve to reveal a jagged scar on his forearm. "Aye, I have this memento of that adventure."

Bart moved between Guy and Kit, his hands held out, pushing the two apart. "Stop! We don't have time for your petty squabbling! Ralph, show Guy."

Guy moved to Ralph's side, who pointed out the route on the crudely drawn map.

"See!" said Kit, turning away and sighing noisily.

Bart cursed in Spanish.

"I don't like it." Guy rolled up the map and returned it to Ralph. "Samra, when you were last here, you said demons came from the water?"

Samra tightened the straps holding his crossbow to his arm. "Mermen with gills. Half-skin, half-scales. Dead eyes like those of a shark."

"And you could kill them?"

"Like any other demon." Samra loaded a bolt into his crossbow.

Guy turned his attention back to Bart. "So, once we take the city, we return to the Ardres Lake to get the priests and escort them to the boats?"

"Correct."

"And on the other side? When they get to England?"

Kit cut in once more. "Jack's going with them. He'll see them safe."

Cannon fire sounded once more, followed by crumbling stone.

Bart sat and leant against the wall. "Guido, sit. Rest awhile. Eat. It won't be long now before we are called into action."

Guy drew his sabre once more to glance at the blade before sitting in a circle with the others, men he'd need to count on over the next few hours if they were to escape another demon encounter unscathed.

At sundown, Guy and his companions slipped between buildings with their hoods up, the darkness their ally. During a prolonged assault, cities fell into an uneasy rest after sunset. From experience, Guy knew that movement through a city under siege required caution. Cannon fire ceased, but defiant residents remained a constant threat. Many hid inside the citadel, but others stayed in their homes, the doors barricaded. They peered through windows with a bell in hand to ring in case of anything suspicious. Vigilantes disobeyed curfews, eager to see off the invaders through any means necessary. But on this night, only a single sentry stood between the party and entry to the city, and he fell silently to a flash of Bart's Toledo sword. The group sneaked through the city, staying close to the walls, moving in single file until they reached the river. They closed on the citadel with minimal exertion, avoiding detection and only having to knock one brute out, who lurched at them from the shadows. When they reached the river, they peered in. Guy had to admit that the water level was low, and Kit had been right about the tides. That didn't make dropping into the freezing water any easier as he plunged in up to his waist.

A candle flickered in a window overlooking the river. Guy stilled in the shadows, waiting for it to pass once more before following Bart and the rest of the party, half swimming, half wading as the river bent towards the citadel. As the fort came into view, blocking out the moonlight, Guy noted the water's warmer temperature.

"Anyone else feel that?" Guy whispered.

"Aye," Ralph called.

"It reminds me of when the mermen came," Samra said. "The place they rose from... the sea boiled."

Bart held out his arm to stop the others and pushed himself a little further through the water. He turned back. "The water glows red under the citadel."

"Then we find another way in." Guy glanced back along the river for a place to climb out where no eyes would fall upon them.

"We continue." Bart urged everyone onward. "If *El Caballero del Diablo* is summoning creatures from the depths, we must stop them. They will fall upon our army if we don't. In this darkness, against an undead foe, they won't stand a chance."

Taking on enemies at home in the water in darkness wasn't Guy's idea of a sensible plan. But Bart had a duty to the Spanish Army. While Guy had fought for them for some time, he didn't share the same affinity. His mission was different: stay in the game long enough to get an audience with Philip II to push the Spanish King on to claim the English throne. Through this plan, Guy hoped to save the country from the demon scourge. In his time in Europe so far, he'd made good progress, working under numerous commanders who had grown to trust his judgement. An audience with royalty had been spoken of, and with each successful mission, Guy knew his opportunity approached.

Guy peered at the familiar hellish red light. What choice did he have? Turning back would not impress Bart, which in turn would upset Bostock, which would keep him further away from King Philip II. And there were five of them, well-trained soldiers familiar with the foe. He'd had worse odds.

"How deep is the water at the dock?" Bart asked.

Ralph answered. "They've dug it out, so it's deeper there."

"So, we won't be able to stand?"

"No, but before that, it's at its most shallow. It's why they don't bring boats in at low tide."

"Shallower than here?" Bart glanced at the water lapping at the top of his hips.

"Aye," Ralph said, and Kit nodded in agreement.

Bart drew his sword. "We approach that point, and if they're raising undead sea creatures, head them off there and enter the citadel after."

"Sounds simple." Guy dropped back to fall in line with Samra. "Tell me more about these demon mermen."

"What more is there to say?"

"How tall are they? What reach do they have? What need we be wary of? Claws? Teeth? Anything else?"

"They're bigger than the average man, and..." Samra gasped, and then, with a splash, he disappeared, pulled underwater.

Guy reached out, but too late to grasp the arm of his friend.

A tentacle slapped the water, sending a tidal wave rushing towards them.

Guy shielded himself with his arm as the wall of water hit him. Beside him, Kit fell. Guy lunged forward and grabbed his arm, dragging him back to his feet as the last follow-up waves crashed over them.

Guy splashed through the water. "It got Samra! Quick!"

A bulbous head covered in orbs protruded from the water. Several tentacles breached the surface, reminding Guy of the worst day of his life, when a tentacled creature had killed his wife and his son. He froze as the moment came alive at the forefront of his mind.

A cry from Samra as the tentacle lifted him from the water brought Guy back to his senses, with the creature huge and wild before him, a many-eyed demon octopus, each tentacle of uniform length, nothing like the monstrosities that had destroyed his life that night so many years ago.

The creature tipped back its head, and a hollow appeared, not so much a mouth, but a void into blackness.

Samra screamed again as the tentacle whipped him up in the air and let go, sending him towards that gaping maw.

Samra reached across and released the bolt from his crossbow. The creature jolted back and Samra splashed into the water at the dock only a few yards from the creature's bulk.

The adage came to Guy again—if it flinches, it's afraid of pain, and anything afraid of pain can be beaten. Inspired by Samra's actions, Guy increased his pace through the shallower water, racing towards the dock, with Kit, Ralph, and Bart close behind.

Together, Guy, Kit, Ralph, and Bart raised their weapons and summoned strength into them. Power surged through Guy's sabre, jolting into his shoulder as the blade doubled in length and blue flame danced at its edge.

"Stay where it's shallow to take it on where you have a sound footing," Bart cried. He splashed forward, swinging at a lunging tentacle which reeled back.

Kit and Ralph followed, swords ready to strike.

Guy crept forward, keeping the creature in his eye-line. He watched the movement of the hellish octopus, studying the pattern of its moving tentacles. On the far side, Samra swam away with an awkward and lopsided paddle. A tentacle snaked toward him. If it grabbed his legs and dragged him under, he wouldn't have a chance. He'd dropped all but the loaded bolt when the first tentacle had grabbed him, so he had no further ammunition.

As Guy made for the dock, he slapped the surface of the water with the flat of his hand, hoping the octopus would sense the movement and focus on him. The tentacle that had been closing on Samra twitched. A couple had been drawn to Bart, Kit, and Ralph as they splashed through the water and clambered onto the stone dock. The body of the beast plunged into the water and emerged once more, closer to the dock, five tentacles slamming onto the stone. The trio of demon hunters leapt away, caught only by the cascade of water.

Another tentacle made for Guy as he continued to slap the water. A pair of the creature's eyes remained on him while the others focused on its attackers on the dock. Guy took a step and struck the surface of the water in the same place, and when the tentacle darted forward, he twisted and sliced upwards, severing it in two. The end plummeted into the water, and as the octopus twisted its body, a tidal wave rushed toward him. To avoid being struck by the gushing water, Guy plunged under. The force of the water twisted him round but with far less power than if it had struck above the surface.

The creature's tentacles rose into the air, flapping in agitation. Guy scanned the dock. Bart and Ralph stood at its edge, slicing whatever came within reach... and Kit? It took a second before Guy saw his blade flash. An instant later, he plunged it into the octopus's head. Of course, he'd leapt onto it. It was the most Kit-like action imaginable. As the remaining tentacles dropped into the water and the body surged under, another wave came. Guy ducked once more, emerging a few second later beside a bedraggled-looking Samra.

"You okay?" Guy asked.

Samra placed his hand on one hip and drew in several deep breaths. He managed a nod, though no words would come.

"That was one hell of a shot from there."

"Had to." Samra put his hand to his chest. "It would have swallowed me whole if I missed."

Guy wanted to argue, to say he had his back, but it would have been a lie. The demon-hunting game took no prisoners, afforded no one a second chance. One wrong move, one misstep, one missed strike, and the demons had you. It didn't bear thinking about.

"Come on," said Guy. "Let's get out of the water. We've got a citadel to storm."

Chapter 2—In Which Guy Fawkes Finds Trouble Deep Within the Citadel

Guy Fawkes had learned many things on his jaunts across Europe tackling demons including the fact that witches usually created gateways to draw evil creatures from the netherworld. Rarely would a witch drag evil from the cracks in the earth, as Guy had experienced in his younger years. The red glow in the water flowing under the citadel of Calais indicated one of these hell-gates, and if the devil knight could draw through a creature like that demonic bastardisation of an octopus, he'd have the strength to draw out a legion to confront the gathering Spanish army.

Guy, Kit, Ralph, Bart and Samra reunited on the stone dock, shaking as much water off themselves as possible and regaining their breath. Samra had rescued his quiver from the water and found most of his bolts still in it. He placed it back across his body and plucked a bolt from it to rearm his weapon.

The red light that shone from the water had receded, with only a glimmer emerging at the perimeter.

"Why has the light moved?" Guy asked as he peered into the water.

Ralph joined him, placing a hand on his shoulder. "The river splits. The bulk runs to the sea beside the citadel, but the maps showed a tunnel..."

"A subterranean river?"

Ralph scratched his head. "The old maps showed a cave system beneath the citadel. Nothing suggested water."

"So why has the light shifted?"

Bart joined them at the water's edge. "When *El Caballero del Diablo* called that creature, *monstruo pulpo*," he waved his arms, mimicking tentacles, "part remained in *Infierno*. Now the link has been," Bart chopped with his arm, "cut, the link dies. The red is another light. He summons creatures within the tunnels."

Guy turned to the steps that led from the dock into the citadel. "Will that lead us into the caves?"

Kit pointed into the water at the most intense point of the glow. "We're already wet. Why not take the direct route?"

13

Guy sighed. Kit was right. As he prepared to leap into the water, Bart put his hand across his chest to slow him.

"You go with Kit and Ralph. Take it on at the source. Samra and I will head into the citadel and raise the flag, signal our soldiers to join us."

Guy turned to brief Kit, but Kit had already leapt in the water, swimming for the red light. Without pause, Guy plunged in, too, with Ralph following a second later.

Kit was a stronger swimmer than Guy. Guy's muscles burned as he pushed himself to catch his friend. Even with the water stinging his eyes, the red light gave off enough of a glow for Guy to follow Kit's path, breaching the walls of the citadel. The red light remained somewhere below, but further in towards the heart of the building. After no more than a minute, which Guy's bursting lungs would have sworn felt much longer, he followed Kit to the surface. Reaching up, Guy brushed the cave roof. He craned his neck to gulp in air. Ralph emerged behind him and gasped at the air, too. The three of them treaded water, taking a moment to regulate their breathing. With only a small pocket of air available, Ralph prodded Kit's shoulder. "What now?" He failed to hide the panic in his quivering voice.

"I'll lead," Kit said. "I'll keep a slow count in my head. If I reach sixty, and there's nowhere else to get air, we return to this point."

Guy turned to Ralph, who nodded, and they followed Kit once more. The level didn't drop as they swam in further, and Guy always monitored the roof above, hoping for some kind of break. He'd lost his count a little after twenty, and so long had passed since. Still, Kit continued before them. His body twisted as he turned to dive deeper. As soon as Kit had shifted from his immediate view, Guy understood why—a rock wall stopped any further forward movement. Surely, they needed to retreat. If they got to the other side of the rock and found nowhere to draw breath, coming back the other way would sap too much energy... but he couldn't let Kit continue alone. He had to trust Kit's instincts. Guy's arms protested with each stroke, and his lungs cried out, desperate for air. Even if he needed to, he wasn't sure he could make it back.

A needling concern gave way to momentous worry, before growing to all-out panic. He no longer battled only the ache in his arms and the pressure in his lungs but the beating of his heart that threatened to burst out of his ribcage.

But then the jutting rock gave way.

Ahead of him, Kit twisted once more to head upwards, and Guy followed, pushing himself harder still, begging fate to be kind and to provide a breathing space above. He could no longer see the dark of the rock, that had to mean something. Seconds later, when he burst from the water, he had the thrill of air sucking back inside him, and the instant realisation of what a world of Hell they'd emerged into. When Ralph burst from the water beside him, he had to resist the urge to cup his mouth. Ralph needed to gasp at the air, but Guy feared his gasp would alert those they'd stumbled upon.

Red light bathed the chamber. On the opposite side, the water lapped against carved rock, and steps led into the water where the red light glowed with intensity. At the top of the steps, several lanterns illuminated a group of men, dressed in the lurid colours of French nobility. At their centre, over a flaming pit, stood a man in armour. Two misshapen horns protruded from the top of his helmet. His open visor revealed his face. His dark words carried across the water, the unmistakable universal language of evil. This could only be *El Caballero del Diablo,* the devil knight. He held a red gem, no doubt the artefact which imbued him with his power over the legions of Hell. A number of the demon mermen Samra warned them about stood on the lower steps, from where they towered over their human counterparts. They had wide heads and a reptilian neck frill to protect their gills.

The water bubbled as more of the creatures emerged.

"We have to close the gate," Guy said. "We can't let them keep summoning those creatures from Hell." He looked from Kit to Ralph. Both nodded their heads, but neither moved.

"Any ideas?" Guy asked. He expected Kit to make his usual suggestion of dashing into the thick of the action.

Kit remained silent.

From the other side of the water, a whistle blew.

The devil knight turned, pointing to the steps that led into the body of the citadel behind him. A couple of the nobles hurried up the steps, and a wave of the demon mermen followed.

"It's Bart and Samra. The guards must be onto them," Ralph said.

With no time to waste, Guy eyed the water opposite. "We can climb up there." He pointed to an area to the left of the steps, a natural slope from the water out of the immediate view of the mermen. "Get the jewel from the devil knight and destroy it. Seal the gateway."

"And the mermen?" Kit asked.

"We deal with them the same way as we always do."

Guy turned and swam for the slope, taking a curved path that kept him as far away from the red light of the hell-gate as possible. He reached the spot a second before Kit, and in tandem they pulled themselves out of the water, staying low and hiding in the darkness. The water rippled as Ralph swam towards them. Another movement caught Guy's eye: a barbed and scaly arm breaking the water. Something swam towards Ralph. It had to be one of the mermen.

Not wanting to alert the others to his presence, Guy beckoned Ralph on with a sweeping motion of his hand, but Ralph remained focused on the slope he swam toward.

Guy nudged Kit and pointed. The shape became clearer as it swooped through the water at a pace much greater than Ralph's. It would get to him first. Blessing their weapons would be useless—the second they jumped into the water to attack, they'd extinguish. Kit glanced down and grabbed a rock, hurling it into the water in front of the merman. The creature diverted from its path, avoiding the projectile. Following Kit's lead, Guy did the same, again causing the demon merman to alter his path. A few strokes separated Ralph from safety. As Kit clutched the last of the decent-sized rocks, Guy made for the slope and crouched, ready to help Ralph ashore.

As soon as Ralph's arm came to rest on the rock, Guy grabbed it. As he took his friend's weight, Ralph's body jerked, becoming too heavy to pull in. Ralph cried out, spluttering water and almost choking.

Kit threw another rock, and with it, the resistance Guy faced disappeared, and he dragged Ralph the rest of the way up.

Ralph glanced down, checking his footing before turning to look back into the water, trying to spy the merman who'd so nearly dragged him back into the water. Ralph rubbed at his side, and gritted his teeth.

"Is it bad?" Guy bent to check the wound, but Ralph covered it with his hand.

"It's not the worst," Ralph said, the strain in his voice suggesting otherwise.

"Draw your weapons," Kit called.

Ralph's agonised cry had given away their location, and three of the mermen strode along the rock path towards them. More glided through the water.

"Stay against the rock so they can't lunge from the water," Kit said. He took the lead on the path, checking the distance behind him to the slope.

"Get in the middle," Guy said, manoeuvring Ralph between him and Kit, with the path too narrow for them to stand more than one abreast. This way, Kit could take on whatever threat appeared before him, and Guy could attack whatever emerged from the water, giving Ralph time to recover his strength and assist whoever needed it most.

Kit glanced over his shoulder. He turned back, charmed his weapon, and slashed at the first of the creatures. A splash alerted Guy to a merman landing on the bank on all fours. It stood, and Guy saw one up close for the first time, towering above him. The red glow of the hell-gate reflected its shark-like eyes. Two rows of jagged teeth filled its cavernous mouth. It brought its hands together, the long claws clashing together. Barbs stuck out of its scaly arms, those on the elbows protruding a couple of inches. Devoid of human emotion, it darted for him, the animal instinct to hunt and to feed controlling every movement. Guy spoke the words that brought flame to his weapon. The creature continued to stomp forward with no fear.

Guy proved the creature foolish not to fear the blade as flame sliced through its midriff. With a foot, Guy pushed the body into the water. Another took its place. From behind, Guy heard the familiar rush of flame. He glanced over his shoulder, leaning to one side to let Ralph lunge with his rapier, plunging it into the merman's chest. Guy kicked that one into the water, too.

Kit had felled the three before him. The devil knight continued to stand over the brazier, chanting his evil incantations.

The two nobles that stood beside him drew their swords.

Guy turned to Kit. "Rush them?"

Kit grinned, and both took off into a sprint. Guy's enemy dropped his sword with the first strike. As Guy lunged for him, he leapt back out of the way, the blade slicing only through cloth.

The noble gasped, turned, and fled for the steps.

While Guy could give chase, he prioritised stopping the demon incursion. Ralph had fended off a couple more of the mermen. Kit continued to battle against the other noble, and he had him against the rocks.

Guy turned his attention to the devil knight. His eyes glowed, fixed not upon this world but that plane between life and death, that special place Guy could tune into if he focused his mind, that place he'd spent most of his life trying to ignore, fearing the voices from beyond would drive him insane.

More of the devilish mermen strode up the steps in front of the devil knight. Guy rushed forward and kicked out, knocking the flaming brazier to the ground, spilling hot coals which sizzled as they hit the steps before plunging into the water. Next, Guy swung his sword, slashing at the arm that held the gem. Blessed with its own demon protection, the armour proved impenetrable, and Guy's sword bounced from it.

Back in the plane of the living, eyes blazing with anger and evil, the devil knight turned to Guy and spat at the ground before nodding his head to bring his visor down. He kicked out, and Guy leapt back, avoiding the strike. Guy slashed out at a couple of the nearby mermen before glancing at Ralph and Kit to ensure they were holding their own. Ralph stood before a couple of felled bodies, and while he moved awkwardly, he could shift into defensive and attacking positions where necessary. After dispatching the noble, Kit slashed through mermen on his way back to Guy. The devil knight squeezed the gem harder. The bubbling in the water become more ferocious, steam rising off it as the temperature rose. Guy swung his sword again, but once more found the armour impervious.

Water lapped higher up the steps as a frothing roar echoed around the chamber.

As Guy glanced to identify the source, the devil knight swung his sword. Guy only had time to lift his weapon to deflect the strike, the blade flashing down, tearing through his breeches, and scoring the flesh on his shin.

Guy planted that foot and swung the rest of his body round, lifting his elbow to crash it into the devil knight's helmet. Bludgeoning pain spasmed from his arm, but it did the trick, causing the knight to stumble, giving Guy a chance to scan for a gap in his armour.

As the knight staggered back and raised its sword, Guy noted something else, too, and stepped back.

With his helmet twisted, the devil knight had no vision of his left-hand side. Kit brought his blade down toward the knight's wrist.

At the last second, the knight pulled his hand back. Kit's sword struck the gem, knocking it from the grip of the devil knight.

El Caballero del Diablo cried out, turned, barged into Kit as he raised his sword to strike again, and ran.

Guy struck with his sword, but his blow bounced off the back of the devil knight's armour, and the villain fled, racing for the steps leading into the heart of the citadel.

Water lapped at Guy's feet, and waves crashed into the walls all around him. He turned to Kit, who'd grabbed the stone. "Destroy it."

Water hit Guy's leg, stinging the cut there.

A humming drone echoed from several discreet parts of the chamber, the call of the demon mermen. Where they'd fallen back, with the rising water, they came forward again.

With water splashing at his hips, Kit smashed the jewel into the rock wall. First, it cracked before shattering, bathing the chamber in an intense red light before it extinguished. The red glow in the water faded too, closing the hell-gate. Darkness consumed the chamber.

The humming grew louder, accompanied by the clicking of the claws of the demon mermen and the smacking of their lips. The only light shone from the trio's illuminated weapons as Guy, Kit, and Ralph waded through the waist-deep water to meet in front of where the hell-gate had been.

"We have to get out of here," Ralph said, pointing with his blade towards the steps that led into the citadel. "We have to stop that damned demon knight."

As they made their first movement, mermen descended upon them. The trio flashed their blades one way, then the other, taking out the first wave of half-a-dozen, leaving heads and arms bobbing on the rising water.

The trio retreated towards the stairs as a surging wave crashed upon them, knocking them off their feet and extinguishing their weapons as they plunged beneath the water.

They grabbed for each other's limbs and struggled back to their feet. A hint of light came from above, where the steps led into the citadel. There had to be a lantern burning in the corridor there, but the disorientation caused by being knocked underwater, made the location of the first step unclear.

The clicking of claws and the smacking of lips came again as the demon mermen closed in. How close was impossible to tell in the near darkness. The water had risen to midway up their chests. Guy, Kit, and Ralph moved back-to-back. Each charmed their weapons again to bring light. The creatures surrounded them, the shape of the flaming blades reflecting in their dead eyes. The three of them slashed at the mermen, but no sooner had their weapons felled the demons than they extinguished in the water. A ripple indicated movement as another came forward. Guy swung with his blade, trying to keep it out of the water, but instead of slicing through demon flesh, without the flame, it struck the armoured scale.

Behind him came a rush of water as Kit disappeared. Ralph yelped, and with a great deal of splashing, Ralph dove in after him. Guy kicked at the beast in front of him, knocking it back into the water. Its claws scratched at his leg. He charmed his weapon once more, holding it high, out of the water. At least a dozen of the creatures remained. It would do no good to take them all on, not as the water continued to rise. He glanced behind him to the steps, calculating the odds of getting there before a vicious pod of demonic mermen sploshed into them. Ralph had dragged Kit back to his feet, and they slashed at the water to keep the demon mermen at bay.

"Kit, go for the stairs. We'll cover you," Guy called. He swung his sword above the water level to keep the demons back. Ralph kicked through the water at a nearby merman and thrust his sword. While he could not pierce the creature's scales, the force knocked it back. Kit dived and pushed himself through the water.

Guy lunged his sword in the general direction to deter any merman, and seconds later, Kit stood on the steps. He charmed his sword and urged his friends to join him.

"Go on!" called Guy as he sliced the scalp of the merman that had occupied Ralph.

Ralph made for the steps, while Guy turned his back on them to head off any last invaders. He swung his sword to the right as one dove under the water. He couldn't slash at it, but he couldn't let it grab Ralph, either. Guy lunged with his other hand and grabbed the creature's leg. Its barb dug into Guy's hand, forcing him to let go. Guy glanced at the steps. He'd done enough. Above him, Ralph clambered up the steps.

Kit splashed down a few steps, back into the water up to his waist. "I'll cover you."

As Kit's sword flashed, Guy dove underwater emerging seconds later at the bottom of the steps.

Ralph sat halfway between the rising water and the doorway at the top of the stairs, struggling to draw in breath.

Kit reached out and hauled Guy to safety, then stabbed at another lunging merman.

They bolted up the stairs, toward the light above, stalling only when voices signalled people approaching. Kit helped Ralph back to his feet, and Guy sighed. What choice did they have, face the enemy above or plunge back into the watery domain of the mermen with no weapons that worked against them? Guy gulped and headed through the doorway at the top of the stairs.

Chapter 3—In Which Guy Fawkes Says Goodbye to Friends and France

Perseverance, resilience, tenacity, whatever kept Guy Fawkes going despite facing a constant glut of enemies, despite the ravages on his body, despite the low odds of success, he again blessed his sword and prepared to fight.

At the top of the stairs, lanterns illuminated the fallen bodies of soldiers and the bloodshed of an ultimate battle for the citadel. The armour of the devil knight made him immediately identifiable as he clashed swords with another. The second he called out, Guy recognised Bart, for the Spaniard's battle cries had taught him a glut of Spanish profanity in recent years. Each blow came with an insult disparaging the mother, the father, and the heritage of the devil knight.

With no immediate need to fight, Ralph sunk to the ground again, and Kit bent over him.

"Help Bart," Kit cried, "Then we need to get out of here."

Guy hurried along the corridor, sword at the ready.

El Caballero del Diablo lunged forward, forcing Bart back. In his retreat, Bart stepped on the wrist of a fallen soldier. His ankle turned, and he threw out an arm to regain his balance. The devil knight laughed and swung his sword.

Guy was still too far away to intervene. Everything about the sight before him suggested he'd soon see another friend fall in battle, and Bart did fall, but not to the devil knight's blow. He threw himself to the ground, into a forward roll, out of the way of the devil knight's blade, which clattered against the wall. From his prone position, Bart twisted round and thrust his sword up, finding the gap in the armour at the inner thigh.

The devil knight cried out and released his sword. He dropped to his knees, thumping Bart in the chest with his heavy gauntlet.

Injured, *El Caballero del diablo* didn't hear Guy coming.

Guy grabbed the horns of his helmet and wrenched it off, pulling the devil knight back.

Before he could right himself, Bart struck. When *El Caballero del diablo* tried to gasp in breath, only a guttural choke came. Blood gushed from the open wound and slewed out of his mouth as he spilled his life on the citadel floor.

Guy helped Bart to his feet and looked back down the corridor. Kit remained sitting over a prone Ralph. Samra had joined the pair. The sound of battle had ceased. Relief washed over Guy as he staggered to a stop, the need to fight gone. His allies surrounded him. Now, the gash in his leg ached. The chill in his bones from being submerged in cold water sent him into a fit of shivers. His muscles spasmed in protest at the intense workout they'd suffered.

"The citadel is secure," said Bart. A deep slash ran through his leather jerkin, and spatters of blood covered his face and stained his sandy hair. They hobbled along the corridor, back to their friends. Samra held his hand to his head, failing to stem the flow of blood that ran down one side of his face.

Kit had lifted Ralph's top to reveal the cause of his woes. A bloody wound, a barb sticking two inches out of it.

"We've got to get him out of here," Kit said, looking from Guy to Bart and then to Samra. "Should we pull it out?"

Samra, who had some medical skills from his time as an Ethiopian Army surgeon, rushed to his side and shook his head. "If you pull that out, he bleeds to death before he steps foot outside."

Ralph winced as Samra checked the wound.

"What, then?" Kit asked.

Ralph grimaced as Samra covered the wound again.

"Infection is setting in. They have some medical supplies at the camp, but..." Samra left the inevitable unsaid.

Guy knew Samra's usual course of action for infection: amputation. Trouble is, you can't amputate someone's side.

"What about fire? Seal the wound?" Guy suggested.

Samra shook his head. "You'd only be sealing the bad blood in. If there are leeches, we can draw it out, but..."

"But we need them yesterday. Got it." Kit sprung to his feet and helped Ralph up. Without prompting, Guy moved to his other side.

At least they could leave the citadel by the front exit.

By the time they reached the lakeside camp and dismounted their horses, Ralph had lost the ability to move his legs, becoming reliant on Kit and Guy. He said a few mumbled words, finished conversations from bygone days. Samra had hurried ahead to prepare all the required equipment and medicines.

Guy and Kit rushed Ralph to the marquee where Samra waited by a rudimentary bed. As soon as they lay Ralph down, Samra checked his pulse. He dipped a cloth into the bucket of water and placed it on Ralph's forehead.

Samra shook his head. "His temperature—he's burning up."

"What can you do?" Kit asked, his eyes red from the strain of holding back tears. Since their time at Saint Peter's School, wherever Kit had gone, Ralph had been by his side.

"We can try to draw out the infection."

Samra tore away Ralph's clothes to reveal the wound. The lantern glow gave Ralph's skin a red hue, except for the area around the wound. Blood covered some of it, but other parts had turned a silvery blue.

"What is it?" Kit asked.

Samra touched it and some of the blemishes flaked away. "It looks like scales."

Guy shook his head. "It's the barb in him. It's a demonic infection." Guy glanced at his hand. Where a merman's barb had caught him, the flesh felt hot. The wound, an inch long across the crease of his palm, had closed up. It would leave a scar, but he found no sign of the corruption spreading. He'd rinse it in holy water, nonetheless, and put some of the salves the priests made on it. None of them worked as well as the concoction his sister, Anne, made, but she lived far away, in Yorkshire. His thoughts drifted home before Ralph yelled out dark words in the language of evil, dragging Guy back to the awful present.

Samra tossed the removed barb onto the ground while another covered the wound to stop the flow of blood.

From a second bucket, Samra plucked a fat leech. He placed it close to the wound. Some of the colour drew back from Ralph's chest, but after a few seconds, the leech dropped off, petrified.

Samra urged over an assistant and bade them stitch the gash on Ralph's side.

As Samra reached for another leech, a shadow moved over them.

Colonel Bostock leant over Ralph and stared into his eyes. "This man doesn't need a physician, damn it. He needs a priest."

"If we can draw out the infection..." Guy started.

"He's a hell of a soldier, and between you, you did good today, but the mission isn't over until we get those priests on the boat heading for England."

Kit looked round. "Is Jack here already?"

"He's with the Jesuits now, briefing them on what will happen when they reach England."

"I hear you needed a priest?" A familiar voice turned Guy around.

Now in his early thirties, Oswald Tesimond looked almost unrecognisable from the boy who had been there when Guy encountered his first demon, the boy who had saved his life and taught him so much in his younger years. But Oswald had taken another path, eschewing the sword for the textbook and the cross. As a Jesuit priest, he made it his duty to spread God's word and share God's divine justice, something that would have to be done in a clandestine manner back in England where demonology had a firm grip on the upper reaches of religious order and within the monarchy. Now dedicated to spreading the word of the Knights Templar, still alive in the spirit of the demon hunters, he'd found a degree of contentment. When Oswald left Guy back at Saint Peter's School, he was a young man on the verge of oblivion. His sunken eyes showed the horrors he'd witnessed and how close they'd come to destroying him. His years in Europe lifted that gloom, the hint of colour in his face restoring him to the land of the living. While still thin, Oswald had put a little meat on his skeletal frame. He leant over Ralph and drew the sign of the cross over his forehead.

"What more can we do, Father?" Samra asked.

"Exactly what you are doing: your best. But if God has a greater purpose for him on the other side, it may not be enough."

The second of the leeches fell off. Samra placed two more leeches and squeezed the rag to dribble water into Ralph's mouth.

"Guy, come," Bostock called.

Guy followed from one marquee into another which Bostock used as a headquarters.

Inside, Jack awaited. As soon as Guy entered, Jack embraced him. It had been several months since they'd last been together, with Jack having been back in England preparing for the arrival of the Jesuits. After a briefing from Bostock, he left them alone. Soon, their conversation turned to England.

"Any news from Scotton?" Guy asked.

Jack sucked air between his teeth. "Your step-father remains keen to help. He says he can keep more people safe there."

Guy shook his head.

"I know you don't want it to bring your family into danger, and so far, I've resisted adding to his burden."

The implied "but" made Guy suck air between his teeth.

Jack put a hand on Guy's shoulder. "Both Anne and Elizabeth are married now."

Guy had last had word from Anne shortly after her wedding. She claimed to have married a good man, which pleased Guy. He had not heard from Elizabeth.

"Has Elizabeth chosen well?"

"By all accounts. A gentleman farmer with a glut of land in Scotton."

The thought of Elizabeth having plenty of land to oversee and plant as she wished brought a smile to Guy's face. "And your family? How's Martha?"

Jack frowned. "She's doing her best, but your friend Thomas Percy and she rarely see eye to eye."

Guy sighed. Thomas Percy had never seemed likely to settle, but he had hopes that a family would anchor him and bring him some kind of joy.

"I spent some time at Cowdray House."

Jack's expression told Guy the news wouldn't be good. "Married life not treating the Viscount well?" Guy recalled his time with Anthony Browne, the way he'd gobbled up stories of demon hunting and nearly lost his life in the fight against devilry on more than one occasion.

"Married life suits him well. Alas, he lost his first born. Young Anthony Browne passed away in his mother's arms."

A pang of hurt hit Guy, a mix of the impossible desire to be with his friend to bring him comfort and his own memories of the loss of his son, John. He took a second to compose himself. Jack's expression told him something remained unsaid. "And Catesby, is he well?"

Jack shook his head. "No longer at Cowdray House. Left with Tresham to be closer to London. They had some kind of plot and didn't want the Viscount involved."

From the look on Jack's face, there was something else. "There's more bad news. Get it over with."

"It happened a few years ago now, but I doubt anyone told you. It's Marlowe."

The name brought the beginning of a smile to Guy's lips, one fear kept from fully forming. "Hasn't got himself locked up, has he?"

Jack swallowed noisily. "Worse."

Guy gritted his teeth. "How?"

"Bar brawl."

Guy pictured his playwright friend throwing a tankard of ale over another. "So, he died doing what he loved. Crazy fool."

"But his play, *Doctor Faustus*, was an enormous success."

Guy's eyes grew large. "You saw it?"

Jack puffed out his cheeks. "Aye."

"You? In a theatre?"

"Spying on Her Majesty."

Guy shuddered as he recalled the demonic troupe accompanying the queen when he'd last served her party in the Rose Theatre. "All still rotten there?"

"Cecil has wormed his way in. He's by her side always, he has her ear, and he has her mind."

"Any hope for change?"

Jack raised his eyebrows. "Aye, in Scotland."

"Scotland?"

"King James VI—rumours say he's in the witch-hunting game in Scotland."

Guy puffed his cheeks. "An ally in Scotland?"

"Aye, and some speak of him as heir to the throne."

Guy blinked several times. "Cecil won't have it."

"Cecil can't change blood. He's the logical heir, and since the Council of the North has had less sway since Walsingham's demise, it's what the north whisper of."

"Still no open debate?"

"Please! Her Majesty refuses to hear talk of succession as if she plans to reign for eternity."

Guy scratched the side of his head. "You don't suspect she's…"

Jack shook his head. "There's no corruption there. She's holding onto that throne by sheer force of will alone."

The canvas of the marquee parted and Oswald entered.

"How's Ralph?"

Oswald gazed at the floor. "He's under the dark hold of henbane now. It'll ease his suffering. I hold little hope he'll rise again in this plane."

Guy ventured from one tent to the other to check in on his friend. Samra still sat by his side, but the look of devastation revealed his lack of hope.

Ralph's eyes were closed, his face motionless. With his wound covered, he looked at peace.

Kit returned and embraced Guy. "I fear he is lost."

As much as Guy wanted to say something positive, he had nothing to offer.

"We can only be glad for the time we knew him," Kit said.

They stood together over Ralph, telling stories, including him in their conversation, asking their silent companion if he remembered certain events until they saw a glimmer of light on the horizon through the gap in the tent.

Together they returned to Bostock's marquee, Kit wiping his face with the back of his hand before entering. Inside, Colonel Bostock addressed the gathered group of half a dozen Jesuits, Oswald among them.

A few minutes later, they rode towards the dock, Kit, Guy, Jack, and Bostock accompanying the priests. After a couple of hundred yards, Guy fell in alongside Oswald.

"I always seem to be explaining to you why I'm leaving," Oswald said.

"I get it this time. You're still a part of the fight, still saving souls, but in a different way."

"That's one way to perceive it."

"Stay out of their reach." Guy recalled some of Walsingham's torture devices. Given his experience with Cecil, he could only imagine that the queen's spymaster had devised equipment even more barbarous.

Oswald offered his hand. "Look me up when you return home."

"I'm sure I'll know a man who'll know a man, who'll know where to find you."

"Have faith that we won't need to hide much longer."

Guy wished he could share Oswald's confidence. But faith made Oswald a good priest, leaving those that lacked it, like Guy, to get his hands dirty.

As the distant lights of Calais grew nearer, they quietened, half expecting to hear the sound of cannons. But the Spanish army held the city in an uneasy peace.

Upon their arrival, Jack approached the ship's captain. They greeted each other before inviting the priests onboard and hurrying them below deck. Jack leapt off the boat, heading over to Guy first. "Until we meet again, friend, on friendly shores or on the battlefield."

"Take care."

Jack broke the embrace and went to his brother.

As Guy stared at the lapping waves, turned golden by the rising sun, a hand rested on his shoulder.

"I've decided to grant your wish, Fawkes." Bostock withdrew his hand from Guy's shoulder. "It's time to report our success to King Philip, and I'm giving you the honour of presenting him with the good news." Bostock handed Guy a scroll.

Guy thanked Bostock and waited for Kit. The accompanying party did not wait for the boat to sail into the distance. When the crew hauled the anchor in and untied the boat, they made their way back to the camp.

As soon as they returned, Kit dismounted his horse as close to the medical tent as he could get. He hurried inside.

Guy waited outside, wanting to hold onto hope for a moment longer. He wanted to believe that when he entered the tent, he'd see Ralph sitting up, boasting about another scar he'd have to show, how fate still had another purpose for him.

When he emerged a moment later, Kit's grief-stricken expression told Guy all he needed to know about Ralph's fate.

Chapter 4—In Which Guy Fawkes Dines with Royalty

For six weeks, Guy Fawkes spent the bulk of his days on horseback, travelling south to Madrid, the journey eased by having Kit, Bart, and Samra alongside him. They shared stories of Ralph's bravery, focusing on the past in fear that their hopes for the future were too intangible to grasp. Bostock made Bart the official leader of the trip, for King Philip II would afford a fellow Spaniard greater comfort. From Calais, the journey measured some 800 miles. Alas, this distance grew every time the party had to bypass a town hit by the bubonic plague. The only other delays came when some opportunistic highway robbers picked the wrong target, not realising four deadly soldiers with little coin were a poor choice. Bart had no qualms about putting such men to death, and Samra enjoyed the target practice, alarming them by shooting off their hats.

April gave way to May, and heading south brought better weather, so the party often slept under the stars, finding orchards and vineyards in which to spend the night. It was June by the time they reached the Spanish capital, and late afternoon when the Royal Alcázar of Madrid came into view. The Golden Tower, crowned with a slate spire, dominated the horizon, vast compared to the fledgling capital's other buildings. King Philip II had made Madrid his capital city some thirty years prior when he shifted the court to the city, and since, those seeking opportunity had flocked there.

Bart gazed at the building, muttering, "*la torre dorada.*"

"You're dumbfounded, friend?" Guy asked as he rode next to Bart.

"Every time I see it, I am captivated by its beauty. I see it again as if for the first time. Is there anything as magnificent in your hometown?"

Guy thought of the majesty of York Minster and how he used to gaze at that place in wonder in his youngest days, but it had become associated with devilry and corruption, and reminiscence brought only heartache. "No."

A farmer working the field turned to them and spat on the ground.

"Not the welcome I expected," Kit said.

"They hear people speaking English, and they don't like it," Bart said in a low voice before calling out to the farmer in his native tongue.

The farmer bowed his head.

"What did you tell him?" Guy asked.

Bart grinned, the shining sun making his teeth sparkle. "That I'm taking you English pigs to the dungeons."

Guy stared back at the gleeful farmer.

They stopped at the city gate while Bart spoke to the guards on sentry duty. Soon, the sentries ushered them inside the walls.

As mistrusting eyes fell upon them, Bart turned to Guy. "There's little love for the English here. To them, you are godless heathens. They have heard how your country has turned from the church, how they have cast out the Pope."

Kit chimed in. "Aye, but that wasn't specifically us."

Bart continued. "Then your Queen not only rejected our King's gracious offer of marriage, but she had the audacity to sink his ships in the English Channel."

Guy squirmed in his saddle. "As loathe as I am to defend my demon-infested isle, Her Majesty has a right to defend her country."

Bart shrugged. "And yet the insult stands."

The Royal Palace loomed before them, the streets widening as they neared.

"How does your king react when he has visitors from England?" Kit asked.

Bart sucked air between his teeth.

"They put Bostock on the rack," Samra added.

"That's only a rumour," Bart said.

Samra raised his eyebrows. "He told me himself."

"But I'm sure it will be different this time." Bart nodded. "You have the letter. We are bringing tales of glorious success."

Kit drew his horse to a stop. "Will he read that before or after he slings us in the dungeon?"

"It will be fine. I am certain." Bart urged Kit onwards with a nod of his head. "Besides, the dungeons here are exquisite."

Before they had time to continue their conversation, the main portcullis opened, and five white horses trotted out carrying armoured soldiers. Half a dozen soldiers bearing muskets followed them out.

"Don't flee," Bart said, staring at Kit. "Stay here while I speak to them."

Guy, Kit, and Samra manoeuvred their horses close to one another. Guy resisted the urge to reach for his sabre.

Bart rode over to the soldiers, speaking in Spanish. In his time in Europe, Guy had picked up some of the language. He'd learned the word for 'friends', which gave him some hope. The word *tortura,* however, left little to the imagination and drew sweat from his brow that he couldn't blame the Spanish sun for.

Eventually, Bart stopped talking, and one soldier tugged on the reins of his white horse, steering it over to Guy.

"Guido," called Bart, "show him the letter."

Guy reached into his horse's saddlebags. He noted the soldier's hand on the hilt of his sword, ready to fell Guy if he made any sudden movements. Guy pulled out the scroll and handed it over. The soldier broke the seal and unfurled it. He took a moment to scan the contents.

Guy tried to read his face as the soldier's eyes skimmed the letter. Guy studied the soldier's lips, looking for a twinge in the lips to indicate a coming smile or scowl.

After reading Bostock's message several times, the soldier laughed. He handed the scroll back to Guy and slapped him on the back before returning to the palace.

"Come," said Bart. "Follow. I told you it would not be a problem."

As Guy followed the soldiers, he caught sight of Bart puffing out his cheeks.

Flanked by guards, Guy, Kit, and Samra strode into the Royal Alcázar of Madrid, following Bart as he conversed with the general leading their welcoming committee. They passed under the portcullis, through a gatehouse where more soldiers loitered, and into a courtyard paved with marble. Here, the floor gleamed, with not a hint of the dust that they'd travelled through on the roads into Madrid. The sun shone on the marble, dazzling the party as they crossed the courtyard. Guy shielded his eyes from the sun and cast glances in every direction. The opulent marble-tiled courtyard served another purpose: the reflective floor blinded any visitors, with noble intentions or sinister ones as they moved into the open space. The high walls on either side contained narrow windows, perfect for archers to pick off any confused intruders. Guy had heard of the cunning of King Philip II, and this demonstrated the truth of that claim.

When the group reached the end of the courtyard, no longer dazzled, Guy admired the pillars on either side of the grand doors leading into the body of the palace. The meticulously patterned ironwork of the doors appeared not only beautiful but provided another measure that would make the inner palace difficult for invaders to breach.

They moved further through the building, passing thick walls and barrable doors, before arriving in the king's throne room. Philip II sat not upon his throne but at the head of a long table. Wrinkles aged his long face, particularly around his eyes, making the king look every one of his sixty years. A wiry white beard covered his cheeks, trimmed short and neat. He wore a thin linen cloak. Other men around the table also appeared senior in years, many wearing far more lavish clothes—robes decorated with golden thread, colourful silks, and tight-fitting doublets.

Philip nodded toward the approaching party and rose from the table, beckoning someone to follow as he exited through a door to the right.

Another man, dark-haired with a handlebar moustache and a goatee beard, rose and approached the party. The red and white pattern of the Spanish flag emblazoned the arms of his otherwise beige tunic. He approached Bart, and they shook hands.

Bart turned to his companions. "Gentlemen, this is Carlos de Balbao, the King's military advisor. He thanks you for your service."

Carlos bowed, turned, and left.

Bart approached his friends. "We are to dine with royalty tonight and quarter in the east wing. Our friends will show us the way."

An hour later, Guy sat in the royal banqueting hall, a room containing two rows of great stone pillars. Like in many other great halls Guy had visited, tapestries hung on the walls. Unlike in England, these contained decorative patterns rather than telling elaborate stories. Between each of those tapestries, grand weapons hung on the walls, enormous shields, crossed spears, and various types of swords, including unusual styles such as the Egyptian khopesh, and a pair of Assyrian sickle swords. The swords impressed Guy to such as extent that he didn't notice a server place a plate of cold meats in front of him. Only as the server walked away did he notice he stood at a mere four foot and walked with a strange gait. Looking across at the other short servers, he noted how oddly they walked. When he caught sight of one of their faces, Guy realised the servers weren't even human. Trained chimpanzees served the food. Guy gasped. His friend Thomas Percy had told him about the trained animals back when he'd worked a single shift as a server on an eavesdropping mission at King's Manor. Guy had assumed this invention or pure fancy on behalf of his friend, but how could he deny the evidence of his eyes?

After the meal, in which the chimpanzees proved themselves more than capable of delivering and collecting plates, many of the gathered guests left, leaving Guy, Kit, Samra, and Bart with Carlos, King Philip II, and the gentleman the king had earlier departed with. Carlos introduced the stranger as Juan de Velasco. Unlike his peers, Juan eschewed the beard. With receding hair, equal parts black and grey, and a smooth face, he looked different from the courtiers back home. His piercing blue eyes and his striking deep black eyebrows suggested an alertness, giving Guy the idea that his primary interest resided in himself. They gathered around a single table.

"My friend here tells me you wished to speak to me about a topic of some importance," Philip said, indicating Bart as he gazed across the table at Guy.

Guy nodded in respect. "Your Highness, I'm aware you once had the title of King in my home country."

Philip muttered something in Spanish.

Carlos intervened. "His Majesty would prefer if you spoke not of that time."

Kit bit his lip as he made eye contact with Guy.

Guy struggled to find a more direct way of getting to his point before setting on showing his own displeasure with his homeland. "England is a foul, demon-infested land."

King Philip spat on the floor, his face sour.

"Here, in Spain, you have shown you have the strength to deal with the demon scourge." Guy glanced at Kit, who gave an encouraging nod.

King Philip took the compliment with a shift of his lips, a lift of the cheekbones, the very start of a smile. He reached across the table for a ready-peeled orange. He popped a segment into his mouth.

Kit mimicked the King and did likewise.

Guy considered the time for pleasantries over. "England needs you."

King Philip II chewed slowly. After swallowing, he licked his lips. "I, however, do not need England."

Guy glanced at his friends.

Kit shrugged.

Samra stared at his plate, avoiding eye contact.

"Now if you'll excuse me..." King Philip nodded across to the door. A human servant rushed over, and as King Philip II stood, accompanied him from the room.

Silence descended on the table until the King had left.

"That went well," Kit said.

Carlos cleared his throat. "The years in England hurt His Majesty. Subsequent encounters rubbed salt into those wounds. Juan takes charge of most of the king's dealings with England."

Juan leant forward, those magnificent dark eyebrows closing to indicate his seriousness. "England remains in His Majesty's sights. How he'd love to curl his fingers around her and pull that land into his glorious empire."

Treacherous worms wriggled in Guy's belly.

"Prove your worth," Juan continued. "Show the King he has English friends on whom he can count, and invasion may enter his mind again."

With that, Juan and Carlos made their excuses, leaving Guy and his friends with the remainder of the food.

Alas, Guy had lost his appetite.

Kit, however, happily ate Guy's share as well as his own.

Chapter 5—In Which Guy Fawkes and Friends are Sent on a Mission

Months passed. Guy grew familiar with the King's foibles and found Carlos an essential ally in translating King Philip's cryptic comments and moods. Juan de Velasco, however, often proved his foil, talking of diplomacy and healthy foreign relations that negated talk of an invasion of England.

Carlos made use of Guy, Kit, Bart, and Samra, often sending them on missions alongside his soldiers. Sometimes they ventured as far as the south coast to endear themselves further to His Majesty. Much to Bart's chagrin, those missions never took them close to Seville, for he longed to show his friends his home and introduce them to his father.

One day in September, after returning to the Royal Alcázar with the head of a demon-loving traitor and his rat familiar in a sack, Carlos urged Guy and friends into the royal chamber with the promise of good news.

"So, the King will send a force to England?" Guy asked as Carlos raced to his seat at the table.

Carlos gave a wan smile.

King Philip II entered and took his seat, with Juan walking beside him. "I thank you once again for your service to me."

"As always, it is a pleasure, Your Majesty," Guy said, bowing.

"A pleasure," Kit mimicked, also bowing.

"Do you believe I am now in a position to take on the forces of England?" King Philip II smiled.

Guy turned to Kit, hoping he wouldn't speak before Guy digested the question. The King never did anything so directly. A sub-question, the one he truly sought to answer, always lurked in the depths of his words. Kit stared at Guy, waiting for him to take the lead.

"Your army is strong, Your Majesty."

"You have not answered my question." King Philip showed his teeth.

"While I believe you would give them a good fight, I sense you need something to give you the advantage."

"A fool would have flattered. A foolish King would have swallowed it. I am glad neither of us is a fool. Let us take a walk in the garden."

Guy left his friends behind and followed King Philip and Juan through the corridors of the palace to emerge into a walled garden at the rear. Fan palms and olive trees grew, with the flowers of a daphne bringing colour.

Halfway around the garden, King Philip II spoke: "You want me to invade England?"

Guy considered for only long enough to realise a pause may be insulting. "That's correct, Your Majesty."

King Philip II showed the palm of his hands. "And I want to invade England."

"I'm glad to hear it."

"And Juan here reminds me the queen grows old—opportunities may present themselves."

Juan nodded. "My growing network of spies tells me of discord."

King Philip II placed a hand on Guy's shoulder. "But something holds me back."

Guy recalled their first meeting, to the offence the king had taken when he spoke of the past. "History."

King Philip II increased his pace before stopping at an olive tree. He plucked a black olive and stroked it between his fingers, exploring its roundness. "What do you know of gunpowder, Guy?"

In Guy's time fighting for the Spanish, he had seen powerful explosives used to breach walls and sink ships. While never in control of it, he understood its use. "It is a powerful substance."

"Do you know what you need to make gunpowder?"

Guy saw no need to disguise his ignorance. "I do not."

"Sulphur, charcoal, and saltpetre."

Guy nodded.

"I can access all three here in Spain." King Philip II threw the black olive at Guy's head. "Juan, does England have such resources?"

"All but saltpetre they have in their kingdom. The saltpetre they trade for."

The King continued walking. "We must stop the English firing their cannons."

Guy studied the king's harsh expression before responding. "You seek to cut off the English supply of saltpetre."

King Philip II smiled.

Guy glanced from King Philip II to Juan. "With whom do the English trade?"

Juan opened his mouth, but King Philip II put a finger to his lips before turning to Guy. "First, swear to me, that you are willing to betray your country."

Again, those treacherous worms wriggled inside him. "I swear."

"Prove to me that you can cut off the supply, and I shall commit my forces to achieving both of our desires."

"Where do you need me to go?"

Juan locked eyes with his king, waiting for confirmation that he could speak. "Morocco. You shall sail south across the Mediterranean. You will visit the great Sa'di Dynasty and put a stop to this supply of saltpetre."

While Guy had pledged fealty to the Spanish king without so much as a second thought, he realised his folly in doing so without speaking to his companions first. He returned to the king's chamber, only to find his allies had deserted it. He hurried to Kit's room. Guy knocked on the door, and his friend answered without pause.

Guy jumped as Kit threw the door open. "Were you waiting at the door for me?"

Wide-eyed, Kit pounced. "So, will he do it? Will he invade England?"

"May I come in?" Guy peered into Kit's room. If not for Kit standing by the door, the room would have appeared unoccupied, for not a single artefact, not a single item of clothing could be seen. Kit bade Guy to enter and indicated the pair of comfortable chairs by the small table. The Royal Alcázar's guest rooms were all of sufficient size to welcome guests, and no doubt many a political move had been discussed at such tables in this and other rooms.

"Before the king commits to such action, he needs us to carry out a mission for him."

Kit sighed and slapped a hand down on the table. "Have we not already proven ourselves with these demon hunts all over Spain?"

"Aye, to test us. This task is related to the planned invasion."

Kit leant forward. "What does he need us to do?"

"The English get their saltpetre, which they need to make gunpowder, from the Sa'di Dynasty. King Philip needs us to go to Morocco to halt that trade."

Lines of concern decorated Kit's forehead. "Morocco? Where even is that?"

Guy only had half an idea. He'd studied maps of Europe, but beyond that, much of the world remained a mystery. "We must travel south across the Mediterranean Sea."

"So, it's in Africa?"

"I guess so, yes."

"Then let's speak to Samra. He'll know more about it." Kit stood.

Guy gazed up at his friend. "So, you're in?"

"Of course. If you say this is the action we need, then it's what we do." Kit flew from the room.

When Guy reached the corridor, Kit pounded on Samra's door.

Samra opened the door and before he had time to greet Kit, he'd already squeezed past him into his room.

"We need to know all about Africa." Kit folded his arms, looking serious.

Puzzled, Samra turned to Guy and welcomed him to his room.

Kit sat in one of the chairs, while Samra and Guy stood inside the door. "'Africa' is a word of Greek origin, meaning 'without cold'. An older name for the land, though, is Alkebulan, meaning mother of mankind. But I think you are not here for either a history or an etymology lesson. I can no sooner tell you about the whole of what you speak of as 'Africa' than you can tell me, in sweeping blows, of 'Europe'. It is made up of many parts and always changing. Perhaps, if you afford me some context, I can accommodate you?"

Guy explained King Philip's proposed mission.

"Then we shall venture into the mountains. Did you know, the Greeks thought them so magnificent, they could be only the body of the great Titan Atlas, collapsed and petrified, but again, it is not the mythology of the place you desire."

Kit's eyes had grown large.

Guy put his hand on his friend's shoulder. "While fascinating, it's the political situation that would serve us better."

Samra perched on the edge of his bed and indicated that Guy should sit on the chair beside the one Kit had already taken. "The land known as Morocco has been sought by many over the years. Its Mediterranean cities have great history, but the Wattasid Dynasty let it slide into decline. They are no more, and as part of the Sa'di Dynasty, the Sultan of Morocco promises to restore the glory days to the land. Ahmed al-Mansur is a powerful man in charge of a great army."

Guy had heard the name from Juan. "It is he that signed the alliance with the English. Will he and his followers be our greatest threat?"

Samra grimaced. "It is a long time since I last set foot in those lands. I hear whispers from my friends back home about another threat, one who seeks to spread ill throughout the land: Zidan al-Saqar." Samra shook his head. "I shall speak no more of him and his Children of Mizraim. To speak their name is to summon them, and I want no part of their evil."

Guy tried to lock eyes with his friend, but Kit's gaze remained on the floor. "We would benefit from your expertise and your courage if you chose to join us, but I understand if you wish not to."

Samra looked up. "No, I must not be afraid. We must confront great evils if we are to purge all our lands of them."

While planning for the mission began immediately, October had arrived before Guy's ship landed in Africa. Guy often thought of his friend Christopher Marlowe, and his talk of subtle subterfuge, while on the voyage as he considered the best way to discover and intercept shipments of saltpetre leaving Morocco for England. Juan had further briefed Guy on the relationship between England and the Sa'di Dynasty and the nature of the goods they traded. England had allowed them to arm themselves better in the seas, turning them into a constant source of concern for King Philip II on his southern coastline. No wonder King Philip II wanted to complicate the relationship between England and Morocco if the two plotted against him together.

Prior to their departure, the party of four had grown to five. While Guy, Kit, Bart, and Samra were always going to make up the group, Bart had made a friend who he chose to bring along on the voyage. Alongside the chimpanzees trained to deliver food, the animal keeper at the Royal Alcázar had a small number of capuchin monkeys. They were far too small to deliver plates of food for a banquet, but King Philip liked the expressions on their faces, so his animal keeper trained them to take him grapes. One had taken a liking to Bart. The capuchin's keeper granted permission for Bart to take the creature on the voyage. He named him Silas.

They landed in Casablanca, a city under the control of the Spanish. The saltpetre would make its way from Morocco to England via the port city of Safi in the west, a place unsafe to sail into under a Spanish flag. Guy had been given maps of the region, and the party pored over them in the dockside tavern as they considered their options.

Samra pointed to Safi. "The simplest way to stop the supply is to steal it before it leaves Morocco."

Guy shook his head. "But that only stops one shipment. We need to impair the supply for as long as we can—if possible, bring it to a halt altogether."

Bart pointed at Kit and Guy. "Go to Fez. Play the part of English nobles and call off the agreement."

Guy and Kit frowned in unison. "Not our style," Guy said. If only Thomas Percy were with them. He'd be able to pull it off. Not that Guy wanted to mention Thomas in Kit's presence, not with the difficult marriage to his sister, Martha.

"If we want to cause mayhem," Kit said (and Kit always chose the plan with the most mayhem), "we have to go to where they mine it. Destroy the operation there, and no more saltpetre for the English."

Bart's brow furrowed. "I agree, but we cannot very well do that without better understanding the operation—how they mine it, how they ship supplies, otherwise our sabotage may be ineffective."

Kit ran his hand through his hair, then looked up accusingly at the blazing sun. "We're here for a while, then."

Samra grinned. "Not finding the climate to your liking?"

Kit turned, raising an arm to shield himself from the brightness. "I'll have to get used to it."

And while Kit had plenty of time to get used to it, he never felt at ease under the sun's burning rays. 1596 gave way to 1597 while the party studied the process in Safi. Acts of piracy weren't beyond them, but as they'd already established, stealing one shipment would be of little benefit. The level of control city officials had over the docks made spying difficult. Ahmed al-Mansur's men checked every incoming and outgoing shipment. They did not allow ships bearing unfamiliar flags to dock; they fired the dockside cannons often as warnings to travellers who failed to reveal their identity. Perhaps Ahmed al-Mansur was right to be mistrustful. Rumours suggested the Portuguese longed to re-establish themselves in North Africa, and the Ottoman Empire gnawed at the edges of the Sa'di Sultanate as it tried to expand its influence over the continent.

Samra had helped to find out about the level of control the Sultan held over imports and exports. Being multilingual, he listened in to conversations which the Europeans couldn't follow. This way, he discovered the location of the mines, as he expected, deep within the Atlas Mountains.

Once Samra had ingratiated himself to those with knowledge, he brought his friends into the fold. He sat with friends, new and old, in a bar close to the market, a place where sailors often dropped in while docked to tell tall tales of their travels.

"What more do you know about the mining of saltpetre?" Samra asked.

"You don't want to get involved," Samra's new friend said.

Bart smiled. "Too late for that."

"You won't be smiling for long if you go to the mines, believe me." The official rolled back his sleeve. Three burn marks, each the length of a finger, lay across his wrist.

Guy examined the familiar marks and shook his head. Once more, they'd have to deal with all manner of devilry.

Chapter 6—In Which Guy Fawkes Goes Demon Mining

It took weeks to travel into the Atlas Mountains before they were anywhere close to the mining operation. Travel by camel allowed the party to take all the provisions they needed, though the experience proved strange for those who'd grown up riding horses, leading to much cursing on the journey. When not listening to the expletives of his European companions, Samra explained how miners obtained saltpetre, paraphrasing what he had learned from those in Safi. The process sounded like dark magic to Guy, and given the destructive power of what it created, it seemed likely the substance was connected to evil.

When the mountains came into view, Kit's jaw dropped. "Guy!" he called, trying to draw his camel up to Guy's. Alas, Kit had yet to master his beast: it refused to slow by Guy's camel, so they conversed at a volume that sent lizards skittering for cover. "Those Atlas Mountains," he called, "they do look like a fallen God."

Guy scanned the horizon, looking at the shape and the sudden appearance of those mountains in an otherwise flat landscape. "Aye, I see it too." What Guy failed to add was that to him, it looked less like a God had fallen there and more like a place God had forsaken.

As night drew near, they set up their tent, the mountains dominating the horizon. While they sat around the fire preparing food, Samra explained what he'd learned. "They venture deep into the mountains and drag black earth out. Some say the dirt has been enchanted by creatures that lurk deep within the darkness."

Intrigued, everyone stared at Samra, even Silas.

"Others say it gets its power from bat shit..."

Kit stood. "No. I am not going into a cave full of bat poop." Kit moved away from the fire.

Samra smiled. "This earth is no good. They have to work the saltpetre out of it. So, they put it in huge vats, they add water, and they boil it."

"And they do this in the caves?" Guy asked.

Samra nodded. "As far as I'm aware."

"So, it's going to be as hot at Hell in there too, great." Guy glanced at Kit, loitering on the other side of the tent, and avoided temptation to join him.

"They mix this with ash, and they have the saltpetre."

"How do they get the ash?" Guy asked.

Samra shrugged. "They burn wood to boil the vats. I guess they use that."

The setting sun left only an outline of the mountains visible. Guy scanned the landscape. "Where on the horizon do you see trees growing?"

Samra looked around. He shrugged.

"So, they have to bring in the wood. There are two ways we can help stop this process."

Bart pointed into the mountains. "Close off the road. Stop the wood getting to the mines."

Guy nodded. "And seal the caves."

Kit returned to the group. "It won't be that simple. There's no way we're going to end this without going deep into the caves."

Samra shook his head. "I'm sure that won't be necessary."

Kit threw out a dismissive hand. "Oh, it will be more than necessary. We'll have to go deep into those caves. We'll have to traipse through bat shit. No doubt we'll have to fight off hideous bat creatures, too."

Samra moved round to face Kit. "We have a plan. It won't be like that."

Kit huffed. "Guy, tell him."

Guy's brow furrowed. "What?"

"Tell him it's *always* like that."

"Maybe this time..." Guy laughed at his foolish optimism. "Who am I kidding? It is always like that."

"I'm getting some sleep. It'll probably be the last decent night's sleep I'll have without the haunting stink of bat poop." Kit huffed into the tent.

Bart leant on Guy's shoulder. "You two go back a long way?"

Guy recalled their first meeting at Saint Peter's when they were seven. Within months of meeting, they'd got into a scrape with their first demon. "As long as I can remember."

"Is he always like this?"

"Not always, but... we've been in some situations together."

"And, Guido, you always end up in the shit?"

Guy smiled. "Aye. Always."

Three more nights passed, with days of difficult travel, the terrain proving demanding for novice camel riders. On the road, they met a convoy of wagons returning from delivering wood to the mine, but none leaving with a shipment of saltpetre. When they reached the road that led to the mine, they found a secluded spot to make camp and secure their camels. Next, they diverted from the path, scurrying up the rock to get a better vantage point.

The miners had excavated the site to open an area outside of the cave, shifting rock to provide sufficient space to deliver wood to the mine and to take shipments of saltpetre from it. A tent outside suggested guards, with nothing to stop access into the mines. Who in their right mind would wish to enter?

Kit peered over the rocks. "Rush the tent?"

Guy put a hand on his shoulder. "Perhaps we need to be a little more subtle."

Kit rolled his eyes. "You always want to go for something more subtle. What's your great plan then?"

Guy shrugged.

"I've got it!" cried Bart as he reached into his pocket for a treat for Silas.

Moments later, they were in position. Under Bart's order, Silas scurried into the tent and made a call. Once Bart saw movement inside, he whistled, calling Silas back out.

A guard wearing a white robe and headscarf hurried out of the tent, following the monkey. Samra swung his crossbow, catching the man on the back of the head.

Guy, Bart, and Kit rushed into the tent, catching the two remaining guards cold. Within minutes, Kit had tied the three of them up and gagged them.

The guards wore light robes, like those the quartet wore. Knowing the miners inside would confuse them with guards, the gang approached the mine.

"So, we're going in?" Kit said.

"We can't collapse it with innocent people inside," Bart said.

"Besides," added Samra, "We've nothing to collapse it with. There must be gunpowder inside. With that, we can seal the mine and shut off the road. They'll be out of operation for months."

Kit stood with his arms folded.

"I'm sure we won't need to venture in far," Samra said. He put his arm around Kit, and they walked into the mine together.

Guy lingered at the entrance to the cave. Something more than the odour of burning wood came from inside, a scent all too familiar, a scent associated with many of his worst memories, a scent that indicated a place where the barrier between Hell and earth was thin: the stench of sulphur hung thick in the air. This strong stench suggested more than mixing in sulphur to make the gunpowder—this reeked of devilry. And Kit was right: when were these things ever easy?

Guy turned to Bart. "So, we're all going in?"

"Make out we're sentries, checking on the process. Don't go hunting for anything specific. Try to get an idea of how it works, and where they might store the gunpowder."

Silas climbed back onto Bart, hiding within his robes, and the four of them explored the large open cavern. Wafts of hot air blew from within, and several small fires illuminated certain parts of the cave. When he moved closer, Guy realised these fires were under the enormous vats. His nostrils twinged when a blast of air hit him: smoke, and the hellish scent of sulphur. A pungent odour hung in the air too, no doubt from the damp earth, drenched in the bat poop the miners dragged from the depths of the caves. These scents comingled to suggest something evil, something they merely blocking access to the cave wouldn't stop.

The smell came time and again, in gusts as if massive bellows were blasting it from the depths of the cave. Guy approached a vat. A man in dirty rags wandered between each, supervising them, but paid no heed to any of the extra visitors. He left a long stirring paddle sticking out.

The pungent smell grew stronger as Guy approached the vats, but this wasn't the source of the sulphuric stink which flowed from deeper in the mines. Further along, Guy heard exertion. Now and then, someone would come out of the mine, pushing a cart full of dirt. Some of the vats were busy with activity as men skimmed a substance from the top. Fresh dirt brimmed in others. Whatever the process, the miners knew what they were doing.

A whistle came from Guy's right. He turned to where Kit beckoned him over. Kit had discovered an alcove, in it, several barrels. "Here we have the saltpetre," he said, pointing at a stack of barrels on one side. He pointed at another barrel on the other side. "And there's enough gunpowder in there to bring this to rubble."

Guy moved over to the barrels. On the side of each, charred into the wood was a symbol, a five-pointed star, a spear running horizontal across it. "Kit, there's something else."

Kit shook his head. "Oh, no, Guy. We've got what we need here. We can wait it out until dark, until everyone goes home, and we can blow the passages."

"That might not be enough..."

"It will. If we blow the tunnels, we'll trap whatever horror is in there. We don't have to go exploring the depths of the earth. We don't have to pick a fight with whatever evil lives there."

Guy put his hands on his hips.

Kit scrunched up his face. "We do, don't we?"

"You're normally the one who loves exploring these tunnels and rushing headlong into danger."

"That may be, but we've never had to deal with *bats* before." Kit pinched his nose. "And that smell!"

"Of all the things we've dealt with, you're concerned with a bad smell and a few bats?"

"Aye." Kit flapped his arms like wings and stuck his top teeth over his bottom lip. "They're all wings and teeth and that horrible squealing sound."

"And that's better than being up to our knees in filthy water with rats dropping from above?"

Kit flapped again. "Aye, because these are like rats with wings! But I get your meaning. We have to shut this place down good and proper."

Together, they shuffled the gunpowder out of the cave entrance into the guards' tent. They checked on their prisoners. One had worked loose his gag, but had only succeeded in talking the ears off his two mumbling companions. All three had their gags temporarily removed so they could take on water before Kit re-tied them, much more securely.

Samra and Bart emerged from the cave shortly after.

"There's more going on here than saltpetre mining," Bart said.

Kit sighed. "And we're going in when the shift is over to face danger once more."

Samra smiled. "You're not enjoying your time in Africa, Kit? You don't usually get so..." Samra searched for the word, "frustrated by it all."

Kit mopped his brow with the back of his hand. "Why does it have to be so bleeding hot?"

"You know where it's cooler?" Bart asked.

Kit stared at him with mistrust.

"In the caves."

"Oh, but not those caves. There's heat radiating out of them. They've probably got a hell-gate in there, and they're letting the demon furies out to play."

"There's only one way to find out..." Guy smiled at his friend.

Bart nodded towards the cave. "There's movement."

They backed inside and watched the miners make their way from the cave and head along the road.

"Nothing strange about that," Guy said, having seen no sign of the usual demon-controlling nobles that caused problems in such areas.

They waited a few moments for anyone else to emerge. Once clear, they headed for the cave once more. With the fires beneath some vats left burning, a little light remained in the cave. The sound of mining activity from below, however, had ceased.

Kit examined the entrance again, touching the rock at the sides. "Are you sure we can't seal this with the gunpowder?"

"If you'd rather stay here and set the gunpowder ready to blow it up, that will be fine," Bart said.

Kit shook his head. "I'm going with Guy."

"Okay, I'll remain here. The road won't be too hard to block, either, with a blast on the mountainside."

Kit helped Bart move the barrel of gunpowder before joining Guy and Samra. Silas had scrambled onto Bart's shoulder and sounded off a goodbye as the others left.

It didn't take many steps into the deeper mines before the sulphurous smell grew stronger still. Guy pulled the end of his sabre from his scabbard. The dull blue glow indicated the presence of something demonic.

"Ready your weapons." Guy unsheathed his sword and imbued it with life with his incantation. Kit did likewise, and Samra put a blessed bolt into his crossbow. The second it clicked into place, a high-pitched squeal came from deeper within the mine. Other squeals joined it, growing in pitch, causing the trio to clench their teeth. A gush of air, bringing with it that stench of rotting eggs, came as the first of the bats flapped past them. Samra shielded his face while Kit and Guy dropped low, covering their heads with their arms. All became quiet again as the three stood, peering into the darkness.

"Bloody bats," Kit said.

"The question is whether we startled them or if something deeper within did," Samra said.

The trio crept in further, relying less and less on the glow of their weapons as a red light radiated from around the corner.

"That's not good, is it?" Samra asked.

Guy and Kit shook their heads in unison.

"What is it?" Samra asked.

"Only one way to find out." Kit took a few more steps around the corner. A few seconds later, he turned back, holding his nose.

"What is it?" Guy asked.

Kit gagged. "The devil's jordan." Kit stuck out his tongue and pulled a sickened face.

Samra's brow furrowed. Ever the scholar, and looking to improve his English, he had to ask. "Jordan?"

Guy gazed at Kit, still pinching his nose, and answered. "Toilet."

Guy removed his headscarf to cover his nose and headed around the corner. His eyes watered, burning with the level of sulphur in the air. Even with his nose covered, the smell crept inside, making his nostrils twitch and his stomach quiver. He persisted longer, venturing farther than Kit until he didn't only have the stench to contend with, but the sight of it too.

The tunnel widened into a chamber where they had been mining. Some way in, a source of light revealed more, a flaming hell-gate spewing forth brown filth. Had a witch opened the gate partway into a river from Hell, a river flowing entirely with demon effluent? Various implements showed how they operated. They used great rakes to drag filth from the demon turd stream onto the banks where it would mix with the soil and dry out. With this noxious mixture the miners created gunpowder. No wonder it was so explosive when it contained the contents of a demon's bowels!

Guy hurried back around the corner to where his friends awaited, glad of the fresher air once he turned his back on the filth stream. Silas stood beside Samra, pointing and squealing.

"What is it?" Guy asked.

Samra grabbed Silas who climbed round to sit upon his shoulder, continuing to squeal. "I'm pretty sure Bart sent him in to warn us. Someone's coming!"

Chapter 7—In Which Guy Fawkes Encounters Zidan-al-Saqar and the Children of Mizraim

All too often, Guy found himself in situations that only ever grew worse. Again, he expected he wouldn't escape the mine without some new trauma, and scars either mental or physical, both if he were unfortunate.

"We've got to get out of here," Kit said.

Samra shook his head. "They'll be coming this way."

Kit peered along the passage towards the noxious fumes of the devil's effluent river. "We can't go that way."

"Cover your face with your headscarf. It's not so bad," Guy lied. The sooner they got moving, the sooner they'd find somewhere to hide. It was the only way to avoid immediate detection. The large, open chamber had lots of other passages leading from it. Aye, a hell-gate stood right there, and the worst denizens of Hell were using it as a water closet, but the alternative risked meeting an unknown threat in a narrow tunnel.

Guy led the way with Kit gagging behind him. Samra composed himself well in his first encounter with the stink, but Silas squealed and hid within the folds of Samra's robe.

"Around here," called Guy, pointing to an alcove about as far away from the stink as they could get without disappearing into a tunnel which led into the depths of the mountain. Several of the elongated rakes rested against the wall, their heads at the trio's feet. Guy dared not look at what the miners had dragged them through.

But no sooner had they entered the alcove than the sound of screeching drew their shoulders up to cover their ears, and a flock of bats swooped down through a crack above, and past them, heading out of the cave.

"Great idea, Guy!" called Kit, shuddering.

"Quiet!" Guy whispered, raising his finger to his lips. "With a bit of luck, the bats will have disturbed whoever's in the tunnels and they won't have heard."

Kit mopped his brow and gazed at the ground. Samra shuffled in front of him, peering back the way they'd come.

From this position, Guy considered how long the mining operation had been going on. The partially excavated space on the other side of the river of filth suggested they'd started there. Later, the witches relocated the hell-gate to alter the path of the river to cover a new layer of soil. With careful operation, they could harvest the organic material needed to make gunpowder for eternity.

As Guy scanned the cavern, light came from the tunnel that they'd entered, followed by chanting in a language unknown to Guy. It sounded unlike any of the Afro-Asiatic languages he's heard since landing in Africa, but likewise lacked the harshness of the demon tongue he'd heard at summonings.

Samra gasped as the voices grew nearer. Guy turned as his friend crouched lower.

A group all wearing dark robes spread out. As they weaved around one another, it proved difficult to calculate their number, but Guy estimated upwards of thirty in the party, all adults.

They came together in a circle and chanted.

Samra tugged on Guy's sleeve.

Guy crouched. "What is it?"

"Bad news. That's Zidan al-Saqar. This operation belongs to the Children of Mizraim."

"The who?" Kit asked. Clearly, he'd not been listening when Samra warned them of this particular threat.

Samra sighed. "Demon-loving crazies."

"What are they doing here?"

Samra nodded towards the hell-gate. "They must draw from its power."

"What do you know about them?" Kit asked, interest piqued only when the threat closed on them.

"You read the Christian Bible?"

"Aye."

"You know the story of Noah's ark?"

Kit threw up his hands. "Don't tell me they're going to call demons through that gate two-by-two."

Samra shook his head. "God brought the flood to purge the world of evil, right?"

Guy and Kit answered in unison. "Aye."

"But evil still exists in the world."

"Aye."

"This mob believes evil survived through Noah's son, Ham. Noah's descendants populated large parts of Egypt, where they got into all kinds of dark magic. Their symbol is the speared star."

Kit stared at Guy. "We saw that on the gunpowder."

"They must have some dark purpose here. In this situation, I'd expect some ceremony, but I see no sacrifice..."

No sooner had Samra spoken than the tunnel leading to the chamber lit up again. Another group of black-robed people, further members of the Children of Mizraim arrived, two of them holding torches, the other pulling along their prisoner: Bart.

"We can't let them..." Kit chirped before Samra dragged him down.

"There's no point in us being thrown into the pit alongside him. We have to think smart."

"You've worked with us long enough to know that's not how we operate," Kit said.

"Shh!" called Guy. "I've got a plan. Take one of these." Guy handed Kit a rake.

"What are we going to do?"

"We mine."

Guy edged out of the alcove. The Children of Mizraim remained gathered in a circle, with Bart dragged ever closer. Guy had studied the path of the river and considered the mining operation. One of the passages would offer salvation, so he took slow steps towards it.

The tunnel arced round as Guy had expected, leading to a chamber that had previously been excavated of filth-enriched soil. Light ebbed from another tunnel, further along, one which led back into the chamber where the Children of Mizraim performed their ritual.

"How long do we have?" Guy asked as he wormed his way out of his robe.

"Five minutes, maximum," said Samra.

Guy nudged Kit. "Rake the soil." He faced Samra. "What's most likely? Do they spill Bart's blood or toss him into the hell-gate?"

"The hell-gate. For a standard sacrifice, they wouldn't come," Samra gazed at the ground in disgust, "here."

Guy threw his white robe into the slop Kit had raked up, manoeuvring the tool with efficiency with one hand as he held his headscarf across his face with the other.

"Samra, how many bolts do you have?"

"A couple of dozen."

"Okay, cover them in that muck."

Guy opened his robe to see how filthy he'd made it.

"That's not—" Kit started.

Guy nodded. "Decoy demon."

"You remember what happened the last time we tried the decoy demon?"

"That was the practice run."

Samra leant in. "It went badly?"

Kit placed his hand on Samra's shoulder. "Oh, very badly."

"Aye, but this time we'll have fire bolts, and it's the best plan we've got."

Kit sighed and fingered the hilt of his sword. "Okay, let's go for it."

They headed along the other tunnel, curling back round to the main chamber and appearing on the other side of the river of filth. The chanting from the Children of Mizraim had reached a fervour. One robed man, standing a clear foot taller than any of the others, read from a book, calling above the level of the background chants. His eyes lit up with a bright yellow as he spoke with intensity.

"That's him," Samra whispered. "That's Zidan."

Zidan had thick, dark eyebrows and sideburns that came down and ran all along his jawline, but not meeting at the chin. His hands were large enough to crush a skull. As soon as he finished his speech, he pointed to the two men who held Bart captive. They pinned his arms behind his back and held curved blades to his throat.

Guy had prepared his decoy, a contraption that required both him and Kit to control it, using a pair of filth-encrusted rakes pushed through holes in Guy's robe (leaving Guy only in his underclothes). Samra, meanwhile, loitered beside them, Guy's flint in one hand, ready to ignite his bolts before he fired them. Remaining as best they could in shadow, they crept closer to the hell-gate.

Zidan cast his arms out as he read another line from the book to the cheers of his followers.

Guy and Kit knew they had to burst forth at the right moment to convince the demon worshippers that they were what had been summoned. If they could cause confusion for long enough, they could grab Bart and escape.

The two men holding Bart edged him forward, their eyes glowing red as they stared into the hell-gate.

"Now!" urged Guy.

Samra struck his bolt, and it ignited. He fired it from an angle so that it appeared to come from the hell-gate. The bolt flew towards the roof of the cave, sparkling and fizzling as the filth burnt away, leaving a red trail in the air which drew the eyes of the cult.

Raising the robe and clawing out with the rakes, Guy and Kit rushed forward, stomping through the river of filth. The second they touched the flow of effluent, the leather of their boots sizzled.

Samra's first bolt had embedded in the cave's roof and dripped sparks. He ignited and fired another bolt, aiming for a spot above where most of the cult gathered, repeating the process over and again, creating a fiery rain.

The men holding Bart panicked as the filth creature flapped towards them, making strange yipping noises as it raised its weird hands in the air. They hurled Bart forward, turned, and ran.

Guy and Kit curled the robe, wrapping Bart in it, and tried to retreat.

Bart lunged with flailing limbs, a fist deflecting off the top of Guy's head.

As more fiery rain dropped, the Children of Mizraim retreated to the rear of the chamber. With their hubbub, Guy feared not being heard. "Bart, it's us."

Another arm struck Guy, but Bart pulled the strike at the last second, mashing Guy on the forehead.

A great whoosh came from somewhere behind them. Once more, the Children of Mizraim erupted into panicked wails, this time fleeing the chamber and heading for the exit.

"We did it!" Kit called. "We scared them off."

That woosh came from behind them again.

"I'm not sure *we* scared them," Samra called as he turned round to face the hell-gate and the creature oozing through it.

Guy scrambled to his feet, realising most of his boots had dissolved where he'd stepped through the filth. His feet felt hot, but that was the least of their concerns.

Pulsing through the gate, came a giant scarabaeiform larva. The spherical and smooth brown head wriggled from side to side as each section of its body squeezed through. Its translucent body revealed a central channel which pulsed with a red glow, as if lava passed through its central core. With six legs at the front of the body, it continued to pull itself through the gate. From that position, Guy found it impossible to tell how long the creature was. Each of its sections seemed to pulse out of the hell-gate and grow after it squeezed through, dominating the space it entered.

"Run!" Bart called.

The larva twisted its head toward him and revealed a mouth, from which came gushing a scarlet substance that steamed as it splurged onto the rock below. It flew out in a stream, cutting off the path to the exit.

Kit and Guy summoned strength into their blades.

"You're not going to suggest rushing this one?" Guy asked.

Kit nudged Guy with his arm. "I've already lost my boots walking through demon shit. I reckon maggot spew would rot my feet to the bone."

The head turned their way.

"You're right." Guy turned to the others. "Into the tunnels."

Bart followed behind as Guy and Kit used their swords to illuminate the ground to avoid the rivulets of lava vomit. Samra bent to grab something from the ground and rushed to catch the others. Seconds later, they were back where they'd raked the filth.

"Is there another way out?" Bart asked as they came to a stop.

Guy pointed around the corner.

"That takes us back to the chamber..." Samra said, out of breath.

"Aye, wait for it."

A squelch came from behind them. The larva had followed and struggled along the narrow passage, contracting its body and forcing itself through.

As the mouth opened, ready to spew out my toxic sludge, Guy yelled, "Run!"

The quartet (plus Silas clinging on to Samra and refusing to emerge from within the folds of his robe), sped back into the main chamber. The larva wriggled, trying to back out rather than manoeuvre through the tunnels.

"Careful of the ground," Guy called. The larva's lava vomit had solidified in places, and steam rose from it. They each leapt over the streams to stable ground, trying to move at pace from the chamber.

The larva, feeling the vibrations of its fleeing prey, reacted in the only manner it could while facing the wrong way. Its rear end contracted, lifted slightly, and a jet of filth sprayed out. The quartet continued to flee as slurry covered them, stinging as it contacted their skin.

"I hope you prepared the gunpowder before the Children of Mizraim caught you," Guy called as the moonlit chamber came into view.

"I had," Bart said. "We have to hope they didn't disturb it when they left."

Within seconds, the party realised their hopes were intact. Where Bart had set the gunpowder, it remained in place.

"Okay, fire it up." Guy and Kit raced to one side, while Samra and Bart hurried to the other. They lit their charges and sped away from the entrance.

The larva squirmed into the chamber, wriggling towards the moonlight, but before it reached the exit, the first explosion set off, setting rock tumbling into the open cave mouth. A few seconds later, the second sent more rock crashing to the ground, which set off a wave of other collapses.

The four of them stood there, Guy only in his underclothes, boots dissolved, covered in rancid waste, with a thick dust cloud settling over them.

Kit turned to Guy, holding eye contact, his face the epitome of annoyance as he flicked slop from his own hair. With his cleanest finger, Kit reached into his ear to clean that. He shook his head.

Silas emerged from Samra's filthy robe, not so much as a drop of the filth on him.

Samra stroked the creature's head. "Did we trap it?" Samra nodded towards the collapsed rock.

Bart shrugged. "Either way, no one's getting any saltpetre from that mine for some time."

"Next we block the road?" Kit asked.

Samra rubbed at his neck. "First job is to find water. We need to get this muck off before it does lasting damage." He held out the book he'd grabbed from the floor of the cavern. "But we've got bigger problems to worry about."

Chapter 8—In Which Guy Fawkes Seeks the Cult of the Children of Mizraim

It took a week for Guy Fawkes and his party to return to Safi. What joy they felt to see the ocean once more lashing against the rocks, the sea mist so refreshing after days travelling through the dust. Relief that the mountains were behind him filled Guy. He hoped he'd never return to such a place, to face such a foul beast. They had left the mine, finding a stream a couple of miles away where they could bathe the stinking larva mess from them. Samra had been right to suggest it could do lasting damage—a week later, their skin still suffered with dry patches and pustules where contact with the demon sewage had been most prevalent.

By the time they returned to the mine and set off the explosives to block the road, the sun was rising. The cave mouth remained blocked, meaning that awful demon maggot remained trapped. With a little luck, it would render that mine useless and destroy the hell-gate in the process.

Samra had spent much of the journey back solemn and sullen in the company of the occult tome he'd salvaged from the cave. With each page, he looked more troubled. The strange and archaic language of the text meant even an experience scholar of the occult like Samra could only translate parts where loan words were used. Each of those brought greater woe. In Safi, he sought the wisdom of others he hoped could dismiss his concerns. Samra had a contact he knew from his days as a student, a man named Jabir, who he arranged to meet in the hammam. While not alien to Bart, the concept of a public bathhouse felt peculiar, to say the least, to the filthy denizens of England for whom dunking heads in a trough of water fortnightly was sufficient. Patrons filled the hammam, their voices echoing around the dome-shaped building. Around the perimeter, in three separate sections, were the baths, a yard and a half deep, each decorated with mosaic tiles of blue, white, and yellow in intricate patterns. When the quartet sat down, the water lapped at their shoulders.

Samra didn't bring the book into the bathhouse (for obvious reasons); he wanted only an initial meeting to ascertain what knowledge Jabir had. Samra liked to meet acquaintances at bathhouses. They were places of great honesty and trust for even the most ingenious would struggle to conceal a weapon while bathing.

A lean man in his mid-forties, Jabir had a tidy beard and short, dark hair. His eyes, too, were dark, and his expression one of absolute seriousness. He spoke first in Samra's native Oromo language (though Samra corrected him on a couple of pronunciations) before greeting Bart in Spanish. After a brief chat, Jabir turned to Guy and Kit and spoke in English. "A pleasure to meet denizens of the Demon Isle who don't want my head on a stick, for once."

Guy shuddered at the reminder of the gory decoration of York's city walls. "I apologise if any of my countrymen have sought to do you harm."

Jabir smiled. "You do not have to answer to their crimes. Now, if you'll excuse me, I need to speak to your associate."

Jabir and Samra waded across to the opposite corner of the bath, partially hidden by pillars.

Bart ducked under the water, emerged, and rested his head against the tiles.

Guy and Kit sat awkwardly in the water with their arms folded.

"Every time someone calls England 'Demon Isle', I feel I need to defend it," Kit said.

A heaviness weighed down Guy's eyelids. "Aye, but it can't be defended."

Kit sighed. "Still, it's our home."

"And one day it could be great again." Guy raised his eyebrows, trying to shake off his burdens. "That's why we're doing this."

Conversation faltered. They gazed around the baths studying the unique patterns made by the tiles. Guy glanced across at Samra and Jabir, who sat close, intense expressions on their faces.

"Looks serious," Guy said.

"I don't like it. Can't we dash back to Spain now we've halted the saltpetre operation? We need King Philip II to save our country."

"We'll get there, Kit. If we've found the seeds of something sinister here, we can't leave people to suffer."

Kit smiled. "Sometimes, you sound like Oswald. All that time you spent with him over the last few years paid off."

"Aye, I appreciated the chance to work out what it all means. Sometimes you have to get it out of your head."

Kit tapped Guy on the forearm and nodded to the corner.

Samra and Jabir climbed out of the water.

"We've got movement. About time we got out of this bath. It's weird."

"You won't be seeking to open such an establishment when you return to England?"

Kit's mouth formed a troubled 'o'. "Can you imagine half the people of York in here? You wouldn't fancy getting in the water with them, would you?"

Guy chuckled. "Aye, there's a long way to go before England's ready for a bathhouse."

Thirty minutes later, Jabir had led the group to a place where they could eat and discuss the situation further. The exotic mix of spices delighted Guy, tantalising his senses to the extent that he failed to notice the low ceiling and knocked his head against the stone. He continued with caution, but could hardly resist focusing on the smells that made his mouth water. Once seated, he relaxed, that is, until the conversation took a turn for the unsettling.

Samra leant across to his friend. "Jabir, tell them what you know of the Children of Mizraim."

Jabir's forehead wrinkled as he spoke. "Deeply unpleasant chaos seekers. They intend to bring the order of the world into ruin."

"And Zidan?" added Samra.

Jabir shook his head. "Pure evil. He'd rather let the ashes of a city fall from his hand than to see it in the grip of another."

Guy's brow furrowed to match Jabir's. "What were they doing at the mine?"

"I'm working on theories based upon the text they dropped. It's an Egyptian Plague Grimoire. One of two things is possible."

"Go on."

"First, they are part of a legitimate operation. They called out demons to help fertilize the ground to make rich saltpetre."

Guy nodded. "But the chaos thing..."

"Yes, the... chaos thing... makes it unlikely they'd partake in business activities without a secondary agenda."

"Then?"

"Sabotage the saltpetre."

Kit leant forward. "So, we were working with the same intent?"

"It's impossible to tell exactly what incantation they read, but they had a different purpose. They wanted to put something into the saltpetre, not shut off the supply."

"What?"

"I can't be sure, but I fear they're trying to infect the supply with plague spores."

Kit interjected again. "Are you talking about the Black Death?"

"Some kind of mutant version of it, yes."

Kit scratched the back of his neck. "There's a stone in the church at Heyton, where I lived as a child, with a cross etched on it for every person who died of the plague. Me and Jack tried to count them once. We got nowhere near finishing."

Guy let Kit's words hang in the air for a moment. "But we've got the book now. That'll stop them, right?"

Jabir shook his head. "This book is a reproduction."

"Okay, but we shut off the supply. We collapsed the cave, so it hasn't got out there, has it?"

Jabir shrugged. "We do not know for how long they've been doing this or what other means they use to spread infection."

Guy glanced over at Kit. "We have to track them down. We have to stop this."

Kit nodded as Bart chimed in for the first time. "That's fine, but do you have any idea where to find them?"

"We have some knowledge of them within my department at the University of al-Qarawiyyin. I have written also to colleagues at Al-Azhar University. It's likely that between us we shall be able to locate them."

"So, what do we do, wait here until news comes?" Bart pulled a dagger out of his boot and picked at his fingernails.

"It will take months to get news from Egypt. By then, they may have moved on. It would make sense to head for Fez. It may be they are close to that city if they hope to spread their ill."

"Aye, and it makes sense not to be at a port town when Queen Elizabeth sends someone after the saltpetre supply," Kit added.

Jabir gazed at the floor. "When I left Fez last week, people spoke of a spreading sickness. It's as good a place as any."

The city of Fez lay in a fertile region over three hundred and fifty miles from Safi. Kit had spent the first day of the journey looking back toward the sea, no doubt favouring a return to Europe over seeking plague spreaders in foreign lands. Fez itself was an unappealing city. Jabir explained the recent history, which had left large parts in ruin. The city had been the centre of a power struggle, with the Portuguese, the Wattasids with the help of the Ottoman Empire, and finally the Sa'di dynasty all controlling the city for a time. While there had been twenty years of peace, destruction, caused in an instant, takes many generations to reverse. What's more, the Sa'di sultanate focused much of their attention on Marrakesh, leaving Fez to fester.

As they closed on the city, one building stood out in particular.

"Borj Nord," Jabir said. "A fort."

Guy noted the similarity between it and many of the fortifications in Spain and Portugal, but as he got closer, something more sinister became apparent. "Why do the cannons face into the city?"

"When they built the fort, they feared not invasion from outside. Civil unrest, however, troubled those times." Jabir pointed towards the centre of the city.

"They fired cannons at their own people?"

"I warned you the city remains in partial ruin."

Kit rode alongside Jabir. "What kind of welcome can we expect?"

"The city has had a period of stability."

Guy's eyes lingered on the cannons until he had to move on once more.

Jabir continued to stare at the fort and urged his camel to move faster. He muttered something under his breath.

Guy caught Samra's eye. "What is it?"

Samra pointed at the top of the fort. "No flag."

By the time Guy reached the fort and the entrance to the city, Jabir stood clutching the bars of the gate. A crude sign hung from the iron bars, a word scratched into the surface with a rock.

"What does it say?" Guy asked.

Samra gazed at the ground. "Plague."

Jabir gazed through the bars. He muttered words Guy couldn't understand, but he understood that look, the knowledge that everything he knew and loved remained trapped on the other side of the gate ransacked by plague.

A hand slammed against the bars, rattling the gate. A pustule-covered face came into view with dark and heavy bags under the eyes. When he grinned, his gums were almost white. He made a play of opening the gate.

From above came the familiar sound of cannon fire followed, a second later by crumbling stone. A cloud of dust floated up over the city.

The sound of the blast continued to ring in the party's ears. "The mad bastards!" Jabir cried. "They're firing into the city."

Guy and Samra took several steps back to better see the top of the fort.

"Stop!" Guy cried, waving his arms. If people fled the city, and they carried the disease, it would spread in no time.

Another blast sounded. More dust plumed.

Guy scanned for an entrance to the fort, but guards had sealed the rear door. The other entrance stood within the city's walls, behind that locked gate guarded by the infected soldier.

Guy glanced up again. A figure moved into view.

Samra wasted no time dispatching a bolt which embedded in the soldier's skull. From above came a thump as he collapsed onto the roof. "We have to hope he worked alone."

Jabir shook his head. "But what hope is there now? They have polluted the city. We'll never catch them."

"They won't be in the city," Guy said. "But if they truly desire chaos, you can bet they'll be close enough to watch it fall apart."

Trauma weighed Jabir down. The heaviness of each word made speaking an effort. "But they could be anywhere."

Bart scanned the length of the city walls, stepping back to get a better view. He turned to Guy. "Do you think..."

"Aye. Jabir, your city, the river runs through it?"

Jabir gave a pained nod.

"We follow it to the source. That's where we'll find them."

Chapter 9—In Which Guy Fawkes Seeks to Track Down and Destroy the Children of Mizraim

The party travelled southwest, following the river into the Saïss Plain, stopping when they reached a small community of stone huts. Irrigation channels ran in to water the crops, but no one tended the fields. As they closed on the first abode, an ox lowed. The closer they got, the more urgent the calls of the beast became. Guy approached its pen. Its water trough was dry, and it had no food.

Guy scanned the area. "Be careful. The plague may be here too." He patted the creature on the head, but it butted him away and lowed once more.

"It's unlikely they're here," Bart said, eager to move on.

Guy hurried into the shack next to the pen, locating dry hay piled in one corner. Guy gathered an armful and threw it to the poor creature before opening the gate so the ox could find a new life for itself.

Kit had returned from a quick check of the buildings. "Signs over all the doors."

"Plague," Samra added.

"No sound from inside."

Guy rubbed the back of his neck. "We should continue to follow the river. If they poisoned the water supply, it would explain why these folk suffered too."

"So next set of buildings we see—" Kit started.

"Aye, could be them. We'll approach with caution."

Jabir reached into his bag. He took out a long cylinder and held it to his eye. "There's another set of buildings farther along the river."

Guy held his hand over his eyes to block the glare of the sun and peered into the distance. "Where?"

"Try this." Jabir handed him the object.

Guy mimicked Jabir's actions, peering into the end, his head jutting forward. As the image inside came into focus, Guy yanked it away from his eye and gasped. "What devilry is this?"

"Let me see." Kit held out his hand, and Guy passed the contraption to him.

Guy stared into the distance again, then back at the device. "It sped me through the land... I stood immediately before a distant abode."

Kit peered into the end of the cylinder and likewise pulled it away from his eye in horror.

"You don't have these in England?" Jabir smiled.

"Nothing like it." Guy stretched onto his tiptoes to try to see further.

Jabir took back the contraption. "It's a telescope. It uses curved glass to alter the way you see."

"Like a magnifying glass?"

Jabir smiled. "Yes, like a magnifying glass in principle."

Guy held his hand out once more, and Jabir returned the telescope. Guy looked into it again. "That's our next port of call."

A few minutes on camel-back brought the buildings into view with the naked eye. While the previous habitat had been a recently operating farm, this one showed far greater signs of neglect, with crops dying in the fields and fences broken.

They stopped behind a cluster of rocks.

"It might be another farm. The plague may be rife here too, so touch nothing, and keep your face covered." Bart demonstrated by pulling his head-scarf round to cover his mouth and nose.

"But it might also be where this cult positioned themselves to poison the city. We'll flank the buildings to give us the best chance of pinning them in. Jabir, I'm going to ask you to remain here."

Jabir closed his eyes and exhaled as if he'd been holding his breath for a long period. "I'll leave the experts to the assault, but if you need me..."

"We need you to protect our provisions."

Jabir saw no reason to argue.

"Samra and I shall approach from this side." With the point of his sword, Bart drew out the buildings in the dust, adding an arrow leading to it from one side.

"And you want us to wade across the river and approach from the other side?" Kit asked.

"That's right. Stay low. Use the land for cover and scope out the situation. Don't run into danger. If they're inside, we work on a plan to take them out together."

Guy and Kit hurried away from the rocks to the river. They stood at the side and watched the water flow. The river, a dozen or so yards wide, meandered past a series of islets and rocks, no doubt used by the farmers to access both sides without having to track back to the bridge.

"We don't know what's in the water. They could still be poisoning it." Guy stared down, noting the way the water rushed between some rocks and splashed over others.

"Aye, Guy, I know better than to go slurping the water."

"Sorry, I don't mean to tell you what to do."

Kit smiled. "But we've got to look out for each other."

"It's how we've made it so far."

Guy hopped onto the first rock, and then onto the larger islet. Kit hopped across to join him. They studied the remaining rocks that would take them to the other side, noticing the way some shifted a little when the water passed.

"Stay in the middle of the rocks," Kit called in a loud whisper.

Guy glanced back and smiled. He leapt from rock to rock, building momentum to make the final longer leap onto the bank on the other side without too much trouble. Kit followed, making the task look simple.

"First job done. Now onto the fun part." Guy adjusted his belt and shifted his scabbard, testing the hilt of his sabre. Aye, it was ready.

There were five buildings, two on the same side as Guy and Kit, and three on the other. They passed through a field on the way to the first, noting the way the crops hung limp. The irrigation channels were dry. Guy following the channel back to the river where the earth had been compacted to stop it running down the channel, Someone had filled them in, no doubt to keep most of the water flowing along the river.

As they got closer, it became more apparent that not all the buildings were dwellings: a store for crops, another for feed, and a ramshackle structure offering shade for livestock.

Kit whistled to get Guy's attention, pointing to what he'd spotted. The field made it obvious that no one farmed the land, but the six camels sheltering under a canopy in the paddock indicated the presence of people.

The other building was much larger, the size of a family home. It dwarfed the two properties on the other side of the river. Staying low, Guy and Kit rushed to the building, pausing beneath a window. A scratching sound came from inside. Guy peered through the window. A robed man sat at a desk, copying text from one book to another. Another grimoire?

The entrance was around to the left. Guy and Kit headed in the opposite direction, crouching to avoid detection. The next window revealed nothing but empty beds, and an untidy pile of rags. In the next room were more beds. The other side of the house revealed a large, open area. Various implements and weapons lay against the walls between scattered barrels and sacks. At the far end, stairs led downward.

"There's a basement. We'll have to check that out."

They continued around the building but found nothing else of interest until they were close to the entrance. From behind them came a whistle. Bart and Samra crouched behind a pile of straw behind a building. A narrow bridge ran over the river, connecting the buildings. Guy checked his surroundings before heading across the bridge to join his friends, with Kit not far behind him.

"They're here," Bart said. He wiped his sword clean in the hay.

"How many?" Guy asked.

"We took out four in the buildings. Any on your side?"

Guy nodded towards the large building. "There's one copying from a book in the corner room. Lots of supplies in there too, and steps lead into a basement."

"Okay, we go in quiet. Take the one at the desk but keep him alive. After that, we check out the basement." Bart gave his sword another wipe, and they made their way back across the river.

The house had that familiar smell of demon waste. So, they had been to the mine before to salvage some of their product. Guy needed no further proof that they caused the infection in Fez.

Bart signalled to Samra to wait at the top of the stairs in case anyone emerged from the basement. The chanting coming from below indicated a number of people were present, but whatever unsavoury act they conducted meant they were less likely to come upstairs.

From the supplies littering the room, Bart grabbed a length of rope and a partially empty sack. He poured the contents, some kind of grain, on the table before stretching the sack to check its size.

"I'll lead with the rope; you grab his hands." Bart flexed the rope as they crept towards the door. That's when Guy saw what he'd missed when he'd peered through the window, a Pharoah eagle-owl on a perch the height of the desk. As Bart lunged, the owl hooted, and the man leant forward, avoiding the rope.

Guy completed his task, flying in and grabbing hold of the man's right arm.

Kit, however, had a fresh concern as the owl flew from its perch, screeching, talons twisting toward him. He deflected the bird with his arm.

The man, meanwhile, twisted round, throwing an uppercut into Guy's jaw. Guy lost his balance and slumped into the desk, spilling a pot of ink over the paper.

As Kit continued to tangle with the owl, Bart unfurled the sack and pulled it over the man's head. He swung a fist, blind, but connected with nothing. Guy punched their adversary in the stomach, forcing the wind out of him as he crashed back into the chair.

Kit had hold of the owl's wings. He hurried to the window and hurled it outside.

Bart grabbed the rope and wrapped it several times around the man, tying him to the chair.

The trio took a moment to gather their breath and allow their heart rates to settle back to normal.

"That bird may have been his familiar spirit," Bart said.

"What could I do?" Kit stuck out his tongue and picked a small feather from it. "I couldn't let it free in here."

"I'm not blaming you, but it means we have little time. He'll convene with another, and they'll be on to us."

Kit nodded in the general direction of the basement stairs. "We better get moving."

"No, Kit, you stay here. Make sure he," Bart put pressure on the tied man's shoulders, "doesn't escape."

"But..." Kit glanced towards the stairs, knowing he'd miss out on the action below.

"We need you up here," Bart said.

Kit frowned and touched Guy's shoulder. "Be careful."

"As always."

Guy and Bart joined Samra in the main room. He looked from Guy to Bart until one gave him a brief explanation.

"And what about the basement?"

"Doesn't sound good. Some kind of ritual. I heard a yell. They must have someone down there."

Bart led the way, sword drawn, with Samra and Guy flanking him, both with weapons at the ready. A flaming brazier illuminated the room, the blue tinge to the fire worse than unnatural. A dozen robed men bowed while another held a gleaming red stone. He led the ritual, a man of similar height to Zidan. A man and a woman, both naked, hung from their arms, which were tied together and placed on hooks in the ceiling.

As the man holding the red stone clenched it tighter, the flame leapt up, licking at the legs of the hanging sacrifices, dragging screams from them as the worshippers gasped in awe.

"Rush them," Bart said. "I'll go for the leader. Guy, cut those people free. Samra, pick off as many as you can to clear a path."

Guy couldn't believe Kit remained upstairs when his favoured order was issued: run into battle, sword swinging. As Guy ran down the stairs, he surveyed the situation. The cultists weren't ready for battle. That would give him a chance to get to the centre and release the prisoners. Of course, by then they'd surround him. The alternative—hacking his way through—would take longer to reach the tortured couple, but it would make escaping much easier.

As the cultist leading the ritual yelled and tightened his fingers around the stone again, Guy made up his mind. Flame licked out of the brazier. Both the man and the woman screamed as they lifted their legs away from the flame. Alas, it dug into the poor man's flesh as if the fire had hooks, dragging a strip of his flesh down and into the flames where it sizzled.

When Guy reached the bottom step, the first of the cultists spotted them. With a crazed look on his face, the cult member rose to his feet and called out. Guy shoved his down, then leapt, landing on one cultist's back, before launching onto another. As the man beneath him tried to stand, Guy's balance shifted. He leapt away, but his ankle turned as he missed the spine of the second and slid to the ground. His enemies were still coming to terms with their assault, giving Guy time to kick at a cultist still on his knees while others scrambled into action. Material whirled in front of him as the cult members rose to defend themselves. With the whoosh of crossbow bolts, more fell and chaos descended upon the basement alongside its ever-present companion, panic. Guy closed on the brazier. The hooks were too high for him to cut the rope, so he kicked the brazier over. The fire roared, and as the coals spread over the stone ground, tiny flame fists rose and shook at him until they realised the most glorious opportunity.

No longer in agony but in desperation, the two prisoners squealed at their unexpected chance of salvation. That salvation, however, depended on getting rid of a dozen cult members who had time to draw their swords. One fell in front of Guy, a crossbow bolt sticking out of the back of his head. Across the room, Bart clashed swords with the leader of the ceremony. He slashed, and the cult leader fell, dropping the red gem.

Guy lunged at the nearest cultist, spearing him with his sword. "Destroy the stone," he cried, aware that the flaming coals had some kind of life of their own, and with it, malevolent intent. Guy took several steps back, slashing at anyone who approached. If they were to coordinate their assault, he wouldn't have a chance. All strategy evacuated his mind as the hellfire attacked. Coals rolled to where the robes of the cultists touched the floor. Flame spread, stirring the cultists into a panicked frenzy, but the more they moved to put out the fire, the more flame leapt from robe to robe.

The fire spread before Guy. He took a second to read the risk, slashed at his robes and shook them to the floor. As fire consumed the end of it, he kicked it towards a group of his foes, sending them fleeing the flames.

"Destroy the stone," Guy cried again.

Bart smashed the hilt of his sword onto the gemstone to no avail. He grabbed it and hurled it at the ground. It shattered, and the malevolence left of the fire. The fire did not, however, lose its lust for life or its intense hunger, and continued to feast on everything around it. Cultists ran for the stairs. Others continued to run around without purpose. Samra picked off a few as they approached, and Bart chased after the rest.

The ground of the basement had filled with smoke as robes and rugs burned. Guy coughed and approached the pair hanging by their arms. He grabbed the woman's legs, taking her weight so she could lift her arms from the ropes. Guy placed her down, and she struggled for the stairs. Helping the man proved more difficult. The wound on his leg meant he flinched every time Guy tried to grasp it, and his greater weight, and the fact blood lubricated his leg, made manoeuvring him difficult. The prisoner's desire for survival helped him fight through the pain barrier, and, when Guy took a firm hold of his legs, he twisted his arms free from the hook. Freed, he hobbled towards the stairs. His wife had moved slowly, concern for her husband restricting her speed. Reunited, moving as one, they travelled upstairs with purpose, the need to survive this horror and start anew a possibility so distant only a moment earlier.

Kit had dragged his prisoner (chair too) outside as soon as he caught a whiff of smoke, and guarded him against any attempt to free him by fleeing cultists. Most were more interested in self-preservation than aiding their so-called ally. Soon, with the last of the cultists either dispatched of, or fled, the quartet reunited outside, with the grateful couple speaking frantically in a language Guy couldn't understand.

Kit took a moment to survey the situation. One glance at Guy made his brow wrinkle. "Why have you taken your robe off again?"

"Nasty habit. You're not going to leave the lady without attire, are you?"

Realising the couple stood naked, Kit unwrapped his robe and handed it to the woman. He took off his headscarf and gave it to the man. "Better than nothing, I suppose."

Both nodded their gratitude.

Bart turned his attention to their prisoner. He pulled the sack from his head and grabbed his face, his fingers digging into the meat of his cheeks. "Your books burn inside. It's over!"

The cultist laughed.

Bart cuffed him in the face with the back of his hand.

Guy leant in close to him. "What have you done? How do we stop this plague?"

The cultist's eyes narrowed as he tried to comprehend what he heard. "Englander?" He spoke with a strange accent. "Your island is doomed."

Bart struck him again and spoke in Spanish.

This time, the cultist's reply came in Bart's language, and caused Bart to strike him again.

As they continued their discussion, Samra fetched Jabir. He spoke with the couple and expressed their thanks, translating the brief tale of how the cult overran their home, and murdered their children.

After several minutes of silence, Bart stood over the cultist, breathing hard, his knuckles bruised.

Jabir approached him. "The lady wishes to know if you are done with the prisoner."

Bart threw a dismissive wave at the cultists. "He's no use to us."

Jabir nodded at the couple.

The woman crouched, grabbed a rock, and ran towards the chair. She smashed the stone upon the cultist's head. As blood poured down his face, she raised the rock and struck him again. She saw no reason to stop her assault, not until no discernible face remained.

Chapter 10—In Which Guy Fawkes Finds Fresh Trouble in Spain

Months passed. Guy's party returned to Safi to track past shipments from out of the mine, but given the illegal nature of the operation, few accurate records were held. As Guy cursed the poor record keeping, he sensed the ghost of his father—as professional an administrator as possible in his role as an ecclesiastical lawyer—staring over his shoulder, a sense of pride that at least the need for proper administrative processes had rubbed off on him. At least the operation hadn't resumed, with rumours of significant problems in excavating the entrance to the cave again.

Bart travelled first to Spain (leaving Silas in Samra's care), pained by the mocking tone of the cultist who revealed that countless barrels were already on the way to his home country. Guy and Kit did what they could remotely, sending letters to their families, warning them of the coming plague. Guy wrote also to Anthony Browne of Cowdray House, hoping the Viscount could use some of his power to put pressure on the authorities to investigate shipments of saltpetre from Morocco to stop the demon plague from taking hold.

The authorities in Fez had acted swiftly. While deaths were in the hundreds, putting the city into lockdown stopped the spread into other cities, and strict curfews stopped inter-household contagion. The cannon attack on the city had been the work of a rogue soldier, infected and rash. But where the plague had taken hold, the cost was near absolute, whole families wiped out within days.

Largely, they spent those months hunting members of the Children of Mizraim, destroying any saltpetre they discovered, and periodically revisiting the mine to sabotage any potential attempt to restart the operation. Zidan, however, remained elusive. Signs of his mighty destruction trailed behind him, with lives ruined and habitats decimated by plague.

Early in 1598, Bart returned from Spain and reunited with his friends in Safi. Together, Bart, Guy, Kit, and Samra dined, sharing news about the events of the last few months.

"King Philip II would like you to return to Madrid," Bart said.

A sense of relief washed over Guy. Chasing the Children of Mizraim had proven a frustrating experience. Each discovery uncovered another pocket of worshippers performing acts of mutilation as they summoned horrific hellbeasts of every form imaginable, providing Guy with a gruesome and extensive mental trophy cabinet.

Kit's sat more upright, his eyes growing wide. "Does it mean he has England in his sights once more?"

"He did not give me details."

Kit turned to Guy. "This could soon all be over. We've waited so long. Maybe soon we can go home."

Samra placed his elbow on the table. "I'm staying here. There is still so much work to do, and with Jabir's contacts, I'm sure we can purge this land of the plague threat."

Guy wanted to grab his friend, to drag him onto the ship with them. Alas, Samra would not leave. His study of demonology, his time in the military, and his years fighting hideous creatures had given him great power, and he intended to use that to do good. No, Guy had to be satisfied with a brief embrace and promises that they would meet again in a better place.

They said their goodbyes and made for the docks, where Bart had a ship waiting. They were to sail for Portugal and travel by land back to Madrid.

A combined sense of relief and dissatisfaction hit Guy as he boarded the ship. Undoubtedly, his work had stopped a great evil from spreading, but the thread ran and ran. The idea that such a disease existed in mankind left him empty. He could understand the motivations of many of the evil men he'd encountered in the past—the desire for power, for wealth. However, the desire for chaos, for the utter destruction of order, he could not comprehend. How could you tackle someone who believes in nothing, whose destruction is the one thing they'd welcome if it meant something else was destroyed along with it? Guy could not appreciate that ideology, and to see it so prevalent pained him.

On that first night aboard the ship, when he lay in his sleeping quarters, afraid sleep would never come as he tried to process the Moroccan mission, a glow came from the end of the bed.

It had been a long time since the skull of Thomas Percy had paid him a visit.

"Guy Fawkes." Percy drew out the name, speaking in a long whisper.

"Thomas Percy," Guy mocked the skull's speech.

"Despair not about the events of the last year."

Guy shuffled into an awkward sitting position. "How can you not despair when you face evil like that?"

"Remember York."

Guy had so many memories of the place of his birth that he couldn't fathom the relevance of Percy's reference.

"What of it?"

"After Margaret Clitherow, what rose from the horror of that day?"

Guy heard Margaret's bones break as the reluctant volunteers placed heavy rocks on her body. "Hope."

"Hold on to hope, Guy Fawkes. It will drag you through the dark days ahead."

"The dark days ahead? What dark days ahead?"

The luminesce left the room, with Guy more troubled than before. A place of great trouble lay behind him, but what hope had he of leaving all of his problems behind, for Percy had hinted at yet more heartache before him. Percy, annoyingly, had a terrible habit of being right about such things.

The trio spent several weeks in the port city of Faro in Portugal, checking shipments as they came in and listening to stories of travellers. Some spoke of passing through towns with great sickness, but it never took hold to the extent that Bart feared. When the time came to move on, they purchased horses. They were not in a desperate race for Madrid and stopped for some weeks in Seville to recuperate in Bart's family home, where his father still lived, alone after the death of his wife some ten years earlier.

In May, they set off again, but trouble soon found them in Cordoba. They were some distance out of the city when the first signs of ill appeared. They followed the Guadalquivir River on the south side, with Bart claiming they'd be able to cross the great Roman bridge when they reached the city itself. However, on the other side stood a crucifix. Each peered at it, their expressions turning to horror as they realised that a dead body was tied to it.

The way the birds had feasted on the flesh reminded Guy of the heads placed on the gates in York he'd walked through so often as a child. Past horrors echoed through the years, reminding Guy of Percy's warning. And this act appeared far more barbarous than using the head of the dead as a warning. The living, those who had sinned against the state, were left to die, pinned to a cross.

Guy and Kit turned to Bart. "Is this... normal here?" Guy asked.

Bart stared across the river at the spectacle. He shook his head. "Never in my life have I seen something like this..."

Further along the river, closer to the city, stood a similar shape. Guy pointed. "There may be another."

"What would make them do this?"

Bart spoke through gritted teeth. "When the King hears of this outrage, there will be a great reckoning."

Guy considered Kit's question. What would make people do this? Pure evil.

By the time they reached the bridge, crucifixes appeared on both sides of the river. Rotting fruit surrounding them suggested an additional humiliation suffered by the crucified.

At the opposite end of the bridge, a crowd had gathered.

Guy gazed along the road running on the right of the river, where it veered away from the city. He wondered if a simpler path lay that way. "Do we have to cross?"

"We have to find out what's going on. Don't say anything that may draw negative attention to us." Bart pulled on his horse's reins and started across the bridge.

Guy and Kit looked at each other and trotted behind Bart.

Once they were almost across the bridge, the situation became clearer. Two factions squared off, a distance of a couple of yards between them as they hurled abuse at each other. Guy's rudimentary grasp of Spanish allowed him to understand many of the religious slurs, one side making ungodly accusations, while the others suggested devilry in their neighbours.

Guy examined the crowd as they approached. The people bore no sign of the plague he'd seen in Morocco. Something unified the group who faced the bridge. Their eyes burned with zeal as they called out the heresies of the other side. They shouted with passion, brandishing crosses and holding rosary beads so tightly their knuckles were white.

Given the accusation, Guy grew concerned that devilry resided in the population of Cordoba, but as the crowd parted to allow them through, he witnessed no taint in their eyes, no frailty that suggested the presence of familiars. Division had come between the people of the city, and each side believed they were right.

Bart called out. "Who is the authority here? Who allows such civil unrest?"

A middle-aged gentleman, tall and slender, wearing a black doublet and large white ruff stepped out from the side facing the bridge. He raised his voice to speak over the opposing mobs. "Who are you to come here accusing our city of not operating within the laws?" The bags under his eyes belied the confidence of his voice.

"I am in service to King Philip II."

The gentleman bowed his head. "I am Gonzalo Alfonso, Duke of Cordoba, and I welcome you at this time in which God shines truly upon us."

"Of what do you speak?"

"Come! Bear witness to the miracles of Cordoba and report back to his Highness. Blessed day! To the convent!"

The crowd's fervour grew at the mention of the miracle, but those facing the bridge turned away, marching into the centre of town while their opposition followed, again accusing them of darkness.

The trio dismounted their horses. Bart turned to Guy and held out his horse's reigns. "I am sure the cause of this dispute will be simple to resolve at the convent," Bart said. "Follow the crowd."

A weight grew heavier in Guy's chest. Whatever this so-called miracle, Guy knew it would bring trouble.

Chapter 11—In Which Guy Fawkes Encounters a Resurrected Nun

Guy and Kit hung back while the Duke walked with Bart towards the Convent of Santa Isabel de los Angeles.

Guy checked no one paid attention to their conversation before he whispered to Kit, "Did Oswald ever tell you the tale of the possession of Magdalena?"

"The virgin birth miracle that turned out to be demon possession? Didn't she give birth to some kind of giant caterpillar thing?"

"Aye." Guy turned round again. "That happened here."

Kit sighed. "Well, maybe they're due a genuine miracle. Maybe we're going to enter and find it raining sugared almonds from Heaven."

Guy smiled. "Do you honestly believe there's a chance of that?"

"Of course not. The only rain we'll get is blood and guts. Isn't it always the way?"

The procession stopped several doors from the convent. The duke called out to his people, and many of them dispersed, some turning to the opposing pack of followers to recommence the old argument.

Bart edged through the crowd to join Kit and Guy. "They will allow us in, but remember, this is a holy place and a place of God. Intense spiritual awakenings are occurring inside. The duke has asked us to do nothing to affect their worship."

The trio tied the horses to the post close to the convent and joined the Duke.

Duke Gonzalo took in a deep breath and straightened his back, standing an inch taller. "When our king was but a child, his mother sent for cloth from this convent in which to wrap him. We were blessed then, and now the Lord has blessed again."

Kit leant in close to Guy. "He means the caterpillar cloth. They wrapped the king in a special caterpillar cloth."

Gonzalo's eyes narrowed at Kit.

Duke Gonzalo led them into the convent. It took a second for Guy's eyes to adjust to the darkness. All the windows had been covered, dark material draped over some, wood nailed across others. The only light came from the many candles. Smoke hung heavy in the air and mingled with the scent of wax. The entrance opened into the temple. At the far end the altar stood. On the floor, to the left, nuns in habits crawled along a pattern of coloured tiles. In each alcove, on both sides of the temple, a woman sat. The first woman on the left sat in quiet contemplation. Opposite, a woman held a candle. She poured hot wax onto her hand, suppressing any audible reaction.

Further along, two women sat opposite one another, both wearing crowns of thorns. A trickle of blood had run from the woman on the left's temple to her cheek.

A scraping noise came from near the altar. Bent over with the weight, a nun dragged a huge crucifix towards them.

Kit stared at Guy, inaction driving him to frustration. Guy turned and tried to catch Bart's eye, but he continued to stare forward, fingers curled into an ever-tightening fist.

Before they reached the altar, the duke led them out of a door on the right, back into the open air of the cloisters. A covered walkway framed the garden. Herbs grew in beds around the perimeter, and in the centre, a woman dressed in the traditional garb of a nun, lacking only the white parts, tended to a plant. As her hand stretched out from the folds of her clothes, the skin sizzled. Undeterred, she snapped a vine from the plant. As she moved it towards the basket at her elbow, it withered and dried, all the green disappearing as it turned dark brown.

Once she had harvested several vines, she retired to the shade, weaving her harvest into another crown.

Duke Gonzalo urged the group to turn back to the temple. "One day last week, the jujube plant appeared. Nothing had grown there, not since she left. But the next day, she returned, too." Gonzalo glanced at the ground and audibly swallowed. "She brings hope and prosperity back to our city."

"But..." Kit started, but didn't know how to address his concerns. Silence descended once more as they passed back through the temple. The nun dragging the crucifix struggled through the nave, straining under its weight. In the alcoves, the four women remained, one with a drip of blood hanging from her chin.

The crawling nun stood and adjusted something within her habit; the protrusions in the material at her knee suggested she had placed a string of beads there, which would push against the bone as she crawled, further penance for the sins of mankind.

Once outside, Duke Gonzalo spoke again. "And after she returned, people flocked to the church. You have seen the extent of their dedication to spiritual devotion. You see how they suffer on our behalf."

Bart grabbed Duke Gonzalo by the arm. "Is there somewhere we can talk in private? There are many ears on the streets, and I don't wish for anyone to believe I speak for the king."

Gonzalo nodded. "Meet me at the city hall in thirty minutes."

"We stable our horse somewhere close to the edge of the city," Bart said once Gonzalo moved out of earshot. "We may need to leave swiftly."

Within thirty minutes they were outside the city hall having stabled the horses and refreshed themselves with a drink at the tavern. Bart had remained tight-lipped, and every time either Guy or Kit tried to speak, he silenced them, raising a finger in the air and making his eyes large. Guy understood his concern. The stranger's arrival had divided the city. Almost every instinct in Guy's body indicated the devilry at play, and she had to be stopped. He ghastly appearance, her effect on the plant—it all pointed to evil. Some refused to see it, blind to the obvious wrong of the situation. Guy's other impulses urged him to get back on his horse and ride away as soon as possible. Whatever power she had, she drew worshippers and turned the town against those that opposed her. The faces of the women in the convent disturbed him most. They lacked the demon-infected glow behind the eyes poisoning them; they showed no anger that fuelled their actions and deformed their expressions. The blank look terrified Guy, as if they had become empty vessels in the presence of whatever evil lurked at the convent, and vessels in that scenario are so often filled with vitriol.

Duke Gonzalo greeted his guests at the foot of the steps leading into the city hall, eying other folk and loudly proclaiming what joyous times they lived in before beckoning Guy and friends into his central office, a well-decorated room with terracotta tiles and heavy furniture. The duke sat behind a desk with several scrolls stacked on it. Two armchairs sat on the opposite side of the desk. Guy brought a third from the side of the room and sat facing the duke alongside Bart and Kit. A cool breeze blew in through the open window, but noting it, Gonzalo gulped and pushed it closed.

The four of them sat in silence.

Gonzalo stared across the table at Bart.

Bart looked from Guy to Kit, and back to Gonzalo again. "You understand you have a problem here?"

Gonzalo glanced at the window. "What can I do?" His hands touched the side of his head. "This lady turns up at the convent, and people called her Magdalena de la Cruz, announcing her return a gift from God like they don't remember how her story ended."

Bart again glanced at his companions. "We almost believed you celebrated that... thing."

"You saw the crosses. Horror awaits any who question her."

"Have you not sent for help?" Bart asked.

"I cannot get a message out of the city without her eyes falling upon it. So, I have been playing nice, praying for help to come." Gonzalo smiled.

"And here we are." Bart placed his arms around the back of Kit's and Guy's chairs.

Guy leant forward. "What more do you know? What have you seen her do?"

"You saw what happened to her skin in the light. She uses that strength, takes the pain and somehow brings new life to that plant."

"Yeah, what was that all about?" Kit asked.

"It's a jujube plant. The one from which they made Jesus's crown of thorns. Some think it a sign of her purity."

"Not her evil?" Guy asked.

Gonzalo only sighed.

"And nothing grew there before?" Bart asked.

"It's long been barren."

Bart rubbed his temples. "And the nuns? Has she corrupted them?"

"That convent *had* no nuns. The church closed it after her last corruption. She betrayed God. The first nuns appeared from nowhere; they flocked over the bridge, a dozen of them. Others are women from the town, drawn to this new worship. More join her daily."

Kit shook his head. "What's her purpose?"

Guy ran his hand through his hair and massaged his scalp. "The same as ever. Chaos. Satan finds souls sweeter if they're claimed from God, that's why he corrupts the holy. For him, sinners are readily available, but when he can turn someone's piety to devotion to him, they taste thrice as good."

Kit raised his eyebrows. "Oswald's influence on your thinking, again?"

"Aye, but it sounds about right."

Bart stroked his chin. "She cannot have risen from the grave herself. Someone must have summoned her. Has anyone suspicious visited the town?"

Duke Gonzalo grimaced. "We had a great many visitors to the town, one month ago, when the young prince passed through."

"Prince Philip?" Bart asked.

"The very same. People came from all around to be in the presence of royalty. He stayed only three days during a time of great festival."

"Anyone could have used the opportunity to plant the seeds of discord," Bart said.

"But why would someone choose to resurrect *her*? People remember what happened, don't they?" Kit asked.

Gonzalo sighed. "I have been a duke for a long time. I have attempted to do what's right, and you quickly learn people have short memories for some things, and long memories for others."

"So, they'll remember Magdalena?"

"You are correct. But not entirely. Mention a name from the past and some people will smile about the good times. They forget how the story ends."

"And that's what it's like here," Guy added. "Demon fog. It messes with the memory. When they hear 'Magdalena', they remember the old folks' stories. People talk on the streets of the miracles and the good times."

"Only few recall the corruption and the decay," Bart added.

Gonzalo stared across the desk at the three strangers again. "I don't suppose you have any experience dealing with situations like this?"

Kit laughed. He tipped his chair back so far, he almost lost balance.

Chapter 12—In Which Guy Fawkes Investigates the Miracle of Magdalena De La Cruz

Having left Duke Gonzalo at the city hall, Guy, Kit, and Bart stopped at the nearest tavern and hid in a shady alcove away from prying ears.

"Someone must have summoned her," Guy said. "It's the only way she could have been resurrected."

"And that's another thing. Is it her body or something else mimicking her?" Kit added. "She's been dead for 35 years, so the body has to be..."

Guy looked across at his old friend and finished his sentence. "Fragile."

Kit jutted out his chin in contemplation. "Perhaps something more like, mushy. Or gooey."

Bart's brow furrowed. He took a sip of his beer, but a grimace remained on his face.

The door to the tavern flew open as a middle-aged woman burst in. She cried out in frantic Spanish and left. Guy only picked up the name Magdalena.

An old man, frail with a long, wispy, white beard, leant out from his chair and cried, "*Maldita mujer*!"

"What did she say?" Kit asked.

Bart cleared his throat. "Sister Magdalena summons all worshippers to the convent tonight."

"What for?"

"She didn't say." Bart slumped back in his chair. "One can only assume it is something that will drive her worshippers into even greater adulation and drive a deeper wedge into this divided city."

"I guess we should attend to find out what's going on?" Kit reached into his pouch to fiddle with his runes.

"I tell you what's going on." The old man dragged over a chair and sat at the table. His voice was gravelly and his English fractured but easy to follow.

"All this," he threw a dismissive hand back. "I see it all before."

"You were around the first time?" Guy attempted to work out the old man's age based upon Magdalena's history.

"I work at the prison. I hear her confession."

"What did she say?" Guy asked.

The old man shook his head. "This come after her..." he made gestures with his hands, holding them to his body and pulling them away.

"Exorcism?" Guy suggested.

The old man nodded. "She was so sorry. Demons, she said, led her astray."

"Which demons?"

"I met with the great Saint Ignatius Loyola. He doubted her, always, even when they most," he paused, reaching for the word, "worshipped her. He spoke of two. Balban and Patorrio. I won't follow this ungodly show. Not now." He gazed at the door. "And that *ramera*, Sofia, can go to Hell with her."

Bart leant forward. "Guy, do you recognise those names?"

Guy recalled the training he'd had on the great demons. "No, but they could be regional names, Spanish versions of who we know as Balam or Pyrotoro. What did they look like?"

The old man shrugged. "They never describe them to me."

Guy sighed.

"Perhaps it is in his book, though."

"Loyola's book? Where would we find that?"

"Ask the Duke. He has records at the city hall." The old man stood. "Me, I won't go anywhere near it."

"A wise choice," Guy said. "And what of the messenger? You don't seem in favour of her, either."

The old man glanced at the door again as his face screwed up. "Sofia Serrano. *Escupirle.*" He stuck out his tongue as if he'd tasted something bitter. He babbled in Spanish and left.

"What did he say?" Guy asked.

Bart puffed out his cheeks. "She wears her piety like a medal and pours scorn on all that don't meet her lofty ideals."

"No wonder he won't be attending the convent tonight."

"We're not going to be as wise?" Kit asked.

A rush of memories, foolhardy decisions that led to dangerous situations, hit Guy. "When are we ever? Let's head back to the city hall. We have time to investigate before tonight's show."

Duke Gonzalo urged the trio back inside, and when they spoke of Loyola's records, he sent an assistant to seek them out in the archives. He couldn't keep the smile from his face at the prospect of finding a way out.

"Will you be answering the call and visiting the convent later?" Bart asked.

Gonzalo looked drained of all vitality, all emotion. "What choice do I have? I must retain this outward show of acceptance of the miracle."

"What do you expect?"

"Another display of devotion. Perhaps an ascension from one of her followers. Whatever it is, I must witness it to understand my people. I need to know what's driving them, so I can stop any further deaths."

"Can you not put a curfew in place? Declare the convent out of bounds?"

Gonzalo clicked with his tongue and sucked air through his teeth. "If my actions put me in direct opposition to her, she will turn her supporters on me. Who will fight to stop me from being raised on the crucifix? No, if I follow, I can propose the rule of law needs to be maintained. I can hold on to a sliver of control until we can send her back to Hell."

"Sir?" The servant had returned with a small stack of books.

Gonzalo invited him to set them on the table.

Guy took the first one. "Scan for references to demons."

Kit grabbed a book and flicked through a couple of pages. "But it's all in Spanish."

"That's okay. Scan for the names Balban or Patorrio. They're more likely to be written in the Spanish form. Bart can translate any passages we find."

"And *diablo*," added Bart. "Look for the word *diablo*."

They spent several minutes scanning through the books.

"Here's one," said Bart. They all stopped and waited for him. He skimmed it again before paraphrasing. "This tells of her first encounter with the demon. Loyola writes of how at five years old she saw the man for the first time—a tall man surrounded by a shimmering mist. She falsely identified him as Jesus, angering him. Here, the possession began."

Kit's brow furrowed. "So, a shapeshifter?"

The quartet continued to scan the texts. Kit stopped them next. "There's something here." He handed the book to Bart.

Bart scanned the page, flipping it over, before turning back. "He says that Magdalena described Balban as a terrible beast. Flat nose, twisted horns, no teeth." Bart puffed his cheeks. "Does that help?"

Guy shook his head. "It's not Balam. Maybe a translation of Balaam, a diviner whose name is often used for any magician."

"What about Botis?" Kit added. "He can transform and the books say he has horns. Always depicted with teeth, though."

"Okay, keep looking." Bart handed Kit his book again.

"Patorrio is mentioned here." Kit stopped them again moments later. He returned the book to Bart.

Bart scanned the page and sighed. "Fire-breathing bull. Sounds about right."

"And this tells of the exorcism," Gonzalo said, pointing at his book.

Guy leant over the page. "What did they do once they extracted the demon?"

Gonzalo scanned the page and shook his head. "It doesn't say. They exorcised the demon and," he paused, scanning further, "Magdalena repented her sins."

Kit closed his book. "So, they didn't deal with it. They purged the demons, and they slipped off."

"They've probably been loitering in the ether ever since, waiting for an opportunity to bring havoc once more." Guy, too, closed his book.

"Someone came here when Prince Philip passed through and sensed the sickness hanging in the air. He brought them back. Perhaps as a sick joke, he encouraged the demons to take on the form of Magdalena." Bart shook his head.

Gonzalo continued to flick through the pages of his book. "Is there going to be anything else? A spell to keep us safe from her, from the demons? Does it tell you how to defeat them?"

"It doesn't have to tell us," Guy said. He glanced at Kit.

"No." Kit smiled. "We whack them hard with a blessed blade. That normally does the trick."

Gonzalo looked from Guy to Kit and back again, puzzlement spreading across his face.

Bart stepped beside him. "Oh, they're serious."

Gonzalo glanced at the spring-driven clock on his desk, a large ugly silver-encased block with an ornate pattern obscuring the roman numerals. "It is time to make for the convent. I hope your swords are ready to do some whacking."

Unlike their earlier procession to the convent, this journey was alongside excited crowds, eager to witness Magdalena's message. She had yet to speak since her return and the promise of hearing the wisdom of one who had been at God's side until recently swayed some unbelievers to attend in support rather than opposition.

A chill wind blew through the darkening streets. The temperature had dropped several degrees, warning Guy about what they were about to walk into.

People packed themselves into the temple of the convent, shoulder to shoulder, leaving insufficient room to draw a blade. The alcoves where worshippers had previously tested their devotion were now vacant, candles taking the place of suffering women. The area around the altar remained clear, ready for the spectacle to come.

A woman in a habit stepped to the front; red rivulets of dried blood decorated her face, the white of her habit stained pink in places.

"That's her!" Kit pointed. "The one who ran into the tavern."

"Sofia," whispered Gonzalo. "Once in my household staff."

Sofia scanned the crowd, her lips pursed, her eyes boring into every member of the congregation. Someone coughed, and Sofia's eyes darted to them.

Once quiet descended upon the temple, Sofia spoke, and Gonzalo translated. "When Our Lady, Magdalena de la Cruz, stands before you this night, you will witness the blessing Our Lord has brought us."

The gathered crowd stood in anticipation, quiet, waiting for a sign of Magdalena's approach. Footsteps came from the cloisters, and through the door, four nuns entered. They stood, two on each side of the altar, and removed their habits. With iron-tipped whips, they whipped their own backs, all working in coordination.

Sofia stepped forward and spoke again.

Gonzalo resumed translation duties: "They cleanse not only their sins, but the sins of all gathered here, so you are pure enough to witness God's miracle."

Magdalena entered, tottering towards the altar, turning one way then the other for all to see as she cradled her swollen midriff. Sofia's steely gaze brought gasps to a halt, and when Magdalena stopped before the people of Cordoba, they quietened. Magdalena raised her habit to show her pregnant form to the gathered city folk. Her hair flashed from black to blonde as her hand circled her abdomen. The skin there was tight, but the hand that circled it looked wrinkled and ashen. When her hair flashed blonde, her eyes changed too, the irises turning intermittently black.

Magdalena dropped the habit and exited.

Sofia stepped forward again. No sooner had she finished speaking than the crowd pushed toward the exit. Not until they were outside, letting floods of people move past, did Bart reveal what she said. "Spread the word. Gather the unbelievers and meet at the bridge at sunrise."

Chapter 13—In Which Guy Fawkes Wakes Early to Witness Fresh Horrors

While time permitted more sleep, Guy woke early, his nerves fraught. Even as they'd left the convent, he'd heard suggestions of acts of wickedness to non-believers. He knew enough Spanish to pick up the misdeeds. They'd debated long into the night, but what could they do to stop them? If they raised weapons against these people under the influence of Magdalena, the mass of her followers would swamp them. Duke Gonzalo's predicament became clear. He could only play rather than to act against an unstoppable tide. Guy figured he couldn't let himself get washed away before he'd taken some time to learn how to brace himself against the waves.

Having woken before the proposed breakfast meeting, Guy wandered the streets of Cordoba. Signs of struggle were everywhere: smashed windows, doors wrenched from their hinges, and bloodstains on the streets. Some houses had words and signs painted over the doors, and many of those houses were safe from the abuse the others had suffered.

While Guy did not know where Gonzalo lived, he passed the city hall to check it had not been attacked. The building remained free of any signs of struggle, though it lacked the marker many other buildings had.

A small chapel had avoided the ravages of the night. While none ventured near a place of worship not associated with the cursed nun, desecrating it was a step too far, and as such, Guy slipped in with no one paying heed to his movements. He needed a moment of quiet reflection, and perhaps he'd be able to tune in a voice that could guide him in the right direction.

When Guy joined his companions for breakfast, he did not have a huge appetite. Thomas Percy had come to him, but only to warn of great danger and potential loss. Kit sat with a plate full of food, which he had a few mouthfuls of, before placing his cutlery back on the table and fiddling with his runes once more.

Only Bart ate with gusto.

"Do you not share our concern for the day?" Guy asked.

"Are you joking? This is my third breakfast. There's nothing better to do than eat as a distraction."

Kit plucked a rune from his pouch, checked it, and placed it back. "This one might be bigger than we can handle. Maybe we should return to Madrid and inform the king. Carlos may send a force that can deal with it."

"You might be right," Guy said.

Kit feigned dismay. "What's this? Guy Fawkes agreeing with me for once?"

"Aye, but I often disagree as you're the one urging us into peril."

Bart swallowed a forkful of egg. "I, too, agree."

"So, we go this morning to assess the situation, meet with Gonzalo to find out how he wishes to progress, and then speed for Madrid," Guy suggested.

"And if we're stopped leaving the city, we say it is our duty to spread word of the Resurrection of Magdalena de la Cruz and the Miracle of Cordoba."

Guy glanced at the hilt of his weapon. "We only draw our swords if our lives are at stake. To them, we must come across as believers."

"Almost sunrise. We should depart." Kit pushed his plate forward and stood.

Bart snagged a piece of bacon from Kit's plate and did likewise.

Guy took a moment before standing and following the other two out in the early morning.

The streets were already busier than they had any right to be at so early an hour. People moved towards the bridge at a uniform pace.

"It is like they are under some kind of thrall; they act as her minions," Bart whispered while falling into step with the others.

Guy leant in close. "Perhaps that is part of the plan: enslavement of the people through worship."

They fell into a quiet walk until they reached the bridge, where dozens of people gathered. Most came in silent obedience, looking on with wonder, but not a shred of malice. Others, however, had followed Sofia's instruction. She ushered those to the front. They held their unwilling prisoners, some of whom continued to struggle; others had resigned themselves to their fate and fallen to their knees. One who had not given up the struggle, despite two grown men having hold of his arms, was the old man with the long, white, wispy beard who had sat with Guy in the tavern the previous day.

From the distance, growing louder each second, came a scraping sound.

Guy craned his neck, but over the crowd, he could not see what was going on until the people shifted to allow the new procession through.

Magdalena headed the group, her belly bigger and rounder than the previous evening. She wore dark gloves, and a thin black veil hung over her face. Behind her came a congregation of nuns, dragging crucifixes behind them. Guy scanned the procession, counting two dozen as they moved to stand on the bridge.

Sofia followed at the rear, her hands joined in prayer. When she reached the front, she scanned the crowd, focusing on those that had brought prisoners. She addressed Magdalena, who nodded, her gaze hanging on the condemned. She turned and made her way back through the crowd. People held out their hands to touch her as she moved through them. Those who were successful fell to their knees and crossed themselves, or burst into tears of gratitude, swelling with absolute love.

Sofia spoke, and Bart whispered her words to Guy and Kit. "So many have shown your faith in Our Lady. So many of you are here with love today. Our cross-bearers were willing to show their devotion to Her; they were willing to be placed on the cross, but your dedication to weeding out the faithless element means they don't have to. True sinners will pay penance on the cross, and Our Lady's congregation can continue their work seeking absolution to make this city pure..." Cheers momentarily paused Bart's translation, "in preparation for the arrival of the miracle birth."

As Sofia continued to talk, those bringing sacrifices dragged their quarry toward the crosses.

"Our Lady has asked everybody to do their part to place the prisoners on the crosses."

The surge of bodies pulled Guy, Kit, and Bart into it, sucking them towards the bridge, towards the rows of crucifixes.

"We can't go along with this. We can't stand by and watch them crucify innocent people," Guy said.

Kit glanced around. "We can't fight off all these people."

Bart, too, checked the crowd. "We do what we can. Tie loose knots. Give these people a chance to escape. Only one needs to be free and they can release all the others once the crowd leaves."

Together, they pushed through the crowd towards the front, heading for the old man. The two that had him pinned were struggling to wrap the rope around his hands as he kept squirming free.

Bart spoke to the men in Spanish before moving over to take hold of the man's hand. The old man's expression showed his horror at this absolute betrayal, and the fight left him. Bart turned to the two gentlemen and pointed at the old man's legs. Kit and Guy lifted the old man. He weighed so little, his bones barely holding his wasting flesh. They didn't need two to hold him, but their presence stopped the men who had rounded him up as an unbeliever from doing a competent job. Bart tied both arms in such a way that they would not come loose with him hanging from them, but a little manoeuvring of the elbow would allow them to slip loose.

Next, they placed the crucifix against the bridge and tied it in place.

The old man groaned as he shifted, and his arms bore the weight of his body.

Guy tried to make eye contact with him, tried to indicate that it would be okay, but the old man's eyes were full of bitter scorn.

Still, others struggled to erect their crucifixes. Guy, Kit, and Bart moved farther along the bridge, where they could lend more assistance.

A couple were taking the more sensible approach of tying their victim to the crucifix while grounded, but the young woman kept snatching her limbs away, making it impossible to tie her to the cross. The couple yelled at each other as they attempted to complete the job.

Kit rushed to them and held one hand in place. The man took the rope and moved to wrap it around the girl's arm, but Guy grabbed the other end as he weaved it through, tying a runner knot that would come loose with the right pressure.

The man yelled and pointed at the knot.

Bart intervened, pointing, and shaking his head, but the furore had caught Sofia's attention.

Sofia approached, and a circle formed around them.

Guy understood enough Spanish to pick up his accusation of sabotage.

Noticing Guy, Kit and Bart were under accusation, the pair that had captured the old man moved over to him. They tugged on the rope which dangled in the old man's reach, and the knot unravelled, leaving his arm to drop free.

Sofia stood before them, her eyes burning with hatred. "You seek to let these sinners go free?"

"They are not sinners," Bart said.

"They are worse; they are unbelievers. You, though, you who seek to undo our plan, you who defy God's order, there is a greater price for you to pay."

Sofia whispered to a group of strong volunteers, and they held a brief debate. A few seconds later, she stated her order: "Take them to Magdalena."

Chapter 14—In Which Guy Fawkes Forces Magdalena de la Cruz to Show her True Colours

A few seconds passed in which it would have been possible for Guy, Kit, and Bart to draw their swords. How many of the crowd could they defeat? Even if they each slaughtered a dozen members of the public, it would not be enough to stop the tide against them. So, in those brief seconds, Guy and Kit shared a glance and understanding passed between them. There would be another opportunity, one in which the blood of innocents would not be shed.

Without a struggle, Guy allowed two people to take hold of him, one locking each of his arms to their bodies, while pushing on his shoulder with their other hand, applying enough pressure to show they knew how to cause harm.

A dozen followed them to the convent, leaving the bulk behind to oversee the crucifixions. Boos rang out as they walked through the streets. The party following behind them hurled abuse, only parts of which Guy understood. The early morning sun brought a glimmer of sweat to their brows. Guy tried to remove himself from the moment, trying to focus on the confrontation to come. He needed the townsfolk to see Magdalena for what he believed her to be. If they struggled free from their captors and struck her down, it could turn her into a martyr. There would be a whole city of souls left behind, perfect for demonic manipulation. But the long game was no longer an option, not when innocent people were being tied to crosses and left to die. Not with their sabotage detected. They could wait no longer to let evil show its teeth. Perhaps a face-to-face confrontation would force evil's lips to part, and they had a small audience. If he could get to the vial on his belt, there was hope. Thomas Percy had to have urged him to fill it for some reason. If he could break the illusion with that group, it might open the door for it to crumble for the rest.

As soon as they reached the convent, their captors forced them through the deserted temple, and into the cloisters, where Magdalena tended to her jujube plant. She turned to her guests and her eyes narrowed, the irises growing darker, becoming indistinguishable from the pupils.

One member of the crowd moved forward.

Magdalena turned her head on its side and waited for him to speak.

"These men are your enemies." Guy understood that part, and the Spanish word for 'crucifixion' was close enough to the English that he understood the context of the rest of the man's message.

Magdalena cradled her belly. Once more her hair lightened, and her face took on a youthful look. Did the crowd only see this version of Magdalena? Guy saw through the façade. Cracks formed in her skin, the dirt clung under her fingernails, and when she opened her mouth, the jagged points of teeth and the fork in her tongue showed.

As she spoke, Magdalena pointed to a door on the opposite side of the cloisters.

Their captors shoved Guy, Kit, and Bart forward once more. They meant to cross the centre of the garden. They meant to pass Magdalena. As Guy closed on the jujube plant, he made himself stumble, placing his left foot in front of his right, which he planted on the ground. One of his captors, as he expected, shoved him. His knees buckled. He slipped from their grip, and he twisted onto his side. The hubbub of the gathered people meant they didn't hear the crack. Shards of glass embedded into Guy's side—a price worth paying for leaving a pool on the ground.

The two members of the mob grabbed Guy. He feigned weakness, delaying the moment they dragged him back to his feet, allowing more of the liquid to drip from his clothes into the shallow puddle he'd created. Magdalena stood close, staring at him as he passed. She lifted her habit, despite the early morning sun causing a gentle smouldering of her flesh. Perhaps, seeing the suffering of the prisoners nourished whatever spawn grew inside her.

Guy twisted his neck as far as his captor's grip would allow. "Stomp the puddle, Kit."

Even if anyone gathered spoke English, the message was too obscure to act as a warning.

Kit could not have known the small pool on the ground before him consisted of spilt holy water. Maybe Kit was the sort to be unable to resist splash-

ing into a puddle, or perhaps something about Guy's voice suggested how important—nay, vital—this act was to their ongoing existence.

Kit took an awkward half-step to better position himself, then stomped
forward, the front half of his boot hitting the water and sending a few
droplets into the air.

It splashed up higher than probable, the highest droplet touching Mag-
dalene's lip. She screamed long before it hit there, though, for several drops
splashed onto her bulging abdomen. Her forked tongue darted out between
her lips as she hissed. She tumbled to the floor, clutching her belly, a look
of innocence on her face as she glanced up, horrified, from the bed of herbs
she'd fallen into. The captors rammed their trio of prisoners to the floor, pinning them under their knees, face down.

Guy's captor pushed his head into the stone, but Guy didn't feel the cold
rock pressing against his cheek. He barely noticed people marching beside
him, though he heard a shout: "Mátalo!" a word called with such venom, it
had to be an execution order. No, Guy paid little heed to those things, because on the ground in front of him, Magdalena lay, transforming before his
eyes.

Magdalena's hair dried to the texture of straw. Her face turned grey and
cracked like mud baked by the scorching sun. Her pointed teeth gnashed together, and with her clawed hands, she tore her habit away, revealing her pulsing belly. Red scorches marked where the holy water had struck her.

Pressure lifted as Guy's captors fled. As he stood, his arms brushed
against the jujube plant, its fruit dead, its branches crumbling.

Magdalena gave a pained cry, and a crack appeared on her belly. As if an
earthquake tore her open from inside, her body shook, and the crack opened
wider. The body of Magdalena became thin, flesh departing from her limbs,
pulling away as if she were deflating.

The crack in her belly opened wider as her former followers fled. Two
red hands from within her pulled the chasm open wider, impossibly so, as
if it were folding back the earth itself. A deep rift split the garden. A beast
climbed out: flat nose, twisted horns, no teeth. The brute stood eight foot
tall with bulging muscles. It stared at Guy, its mouth curling into a toothless
grin. Drool slopped to the ground as it chuckled.

"So, if that's Balban, where's Patorrio?" Kit asked.

What remained of Magdalena pulled together, curling up like a ball before stretching out and wriggling like a larva before growing rapidly into a heaving black bull, its whole body aflame. It stood before them, snorting, dragging one hoof across the paved path of the cloisters as it prepared to attack.

"You had to ask, didn't you?" Guy said.

"I wouldn't want it to be too easy."

Guy and Kit drew the weapons, blessing them with the properties to kill demons, extending their length and sharpening the blades.

Bart muttered a prayer before drawing and blessing his weapon, too. "Plan?" he yelled.

Patorrio scrapped his hoof with greater vigour while Balban flexed his muscles.

"Whoever summoned them isn't present, which means we have to stop them." Guy eyed the two demons and scanned the cloisters, hunting for a plan. "Run for the temple. Patorrio won't be able to get through the door."

Kit glanced at Balban's hulking mass. "And he will?"

"Aye, he's a shapeshifter. I'll draw Patorrio away and join you as soon as I can."

"No," called Bart. "Let me deal with the bull."

Needing no further encouragement, Kit reached into the herb garden, grabbed a clod of earth, and tossed it at Balban. It erupted as it struck his chest and sprinkled to the floor. It had the desired effect of getting his attention. Balban strode towards Guy and Kit, who headed for the temple door.

Guy turned back as Bart circled Patorrio. He remembered hearing Bart's tales of bullfighting, but he'd not have faced any beast as fearsome as this. If it could buy them time to take out Balban, together they could fell the bull.

Kit made it to the door first; he hurried through, then turned back at the altar, waiting for Balban.

Guy slid in beside him with the red skin of Balban visible on the other side of the door. Its body shifted, becoming leaner, shorter, allowing it to move through the door. Once through, it started to shift to its original shape. Kit and Guy jumped in tandem, slashing at the creature which deflected the blows by raising the tough skin of its arms. This action had consequence, as

Guy and Kit hacked at the excess flesh, mid-shift, letting it fall to the floor where it quivered like jelly.

Guy and Kit had encountered shapeshifters before, and they'd learned something useful about them. Their form was unlike other demons, and catching them as they changed decreased their mass. Once lopped from them, their residual jelly flopped away, unable to reattach to the whole, offering no greater threat than a slip hazard.

The best strategy, therefore, involved tempting a shapeshifter to shift shape. Give them a reason to need to squeeze through a tight spot, reach a little further, and strike. As they shrunk, the threat decreased. Guy considered running back through the door to force it to shift once more. As if he needed a reminder of the foolishness of that thought, the walls shook as Patorrio crashed into them somewhere in the cloisters. Guy hoped Bart had sidestepped it without a problem.

Guy and Kit fell into a familiar rhythm, drawing Balban into the centre of the temple and circling it, remaining at opposite sides. When the creature's eyes lingered on one, the other would strike before darting back to safety. It didn't take long for the creature's frustration to grow, shifting to make its reach longer. But it constantly stretched for the wrong target, and an undefended hack led to more of the jellified creature being hacked away. The smaller it became, the greater its need for extended reach, and the more frequently it shifted, curving snake-like arms towards Guy and Kit.

The process changed again. Guy allowed an arm to strike his leg, inviting it to wrap around, to pull him closer. As it put greater focus and more mass into that arm, Kit struck, lopping off that limb close to the body. The useless limb flopped to the ground. Too little of the creature remained for it to be a threat. Together, Kit and Guy slashed at it until they'd turned it into tiny cubes.

No sooner had they dispatched with Balban, than the wall beside them crumbled, the horns of Patorrio sticking through. It shook the rubble free, glared at Kit and Guy and launched forward again. Guy and Kit split, heading in different directions across the temple. Patorrio had selected Kit as his target.

Guy scanned the rubble for Bart: no sign. He hurried toward the collapsed pile of stone to search for his friend. Taking his eyes off his path proved a mistake as a globule of Balban lay beneath his foot, and when he stepped on it, his foot slid out, and pain exploded in his knee.

As Guy fell to the floor, Kit leapt onto one of the alcoves and off again, over Patorrio, who slammed into the stone. The stained-glass window cracked, and panes slid out, smashing when they hit the floor.

Patorrio backed out of the alcove and turned. His eyes locked on Guy.

Guy tried to scramble to his feet, but that pain in his knee came again. Bile bubbled in his belly, and he crashed back to the floor.

Patorrio's hoof scraped on the stone floor of the convent temple. He snorted, smoke billowing out of his nostrils, and the fire on his hide rippled. He charged for Guy.

Guy got on his good leg, hopped away, but the demon bull had him in his sights.

"Olé!" came a shout.

Bart shoved Guy to one side and leapt the other way. The bull flew between them, crashing into the altar.

Kit ran across the temple, and before Patorrio could turn, slashed with his sword, the charmed blade slicing through the rear leg.

Patorrio huffed and tried to turn, but Bart joined in the assault, hacking at the creature's middle, and all fight went out of it, the flame extinguishing as the creature collapsed to the ground.

Kit moved over to Guy and helped him to his feet.

Guy tested his leg: he could place no weight on it.

Bart moved towards the entrance, hoping to let in the light of the day, to tell the people of Cordoba that their nightmare was over.

Sofia stood on the other side of the door. She screamed and plunged a dagger into Bart's chest.

Guy cried out and collapsed to the ground again. Kit ran toward Bart, and Gonzalo burst in, knocking Sofia to the ground and pinning her.

Kit raced over to Bart.

Kit's sickened expression told Guy all he needed to know.

Chapter 15—In Which Guy Fawkes and Kit Wright Travel Far and Wide Before Returning to Madrid to Face Fresh Challenges

Guy and Kit abandoned the plan to head for Madrid the second Gonzalo confirmed Bart's death. Having spent weeks in the hospitality of his family home, the only right course was to return to Seville. Guy couldn't walk without support. He sat awkwardly in the saddle, but forced himself to ride out the pain to accompany Bart's body back home.

For three weeks they remained with the extended family of Bartolomé de Sevilla, sharing his father's home once more, celebrating his life, and trading tales of his daring. His was a life truly lived, a life that enriched so many others and saved so many more. A life ended too soon.

When it came time to leave, Guy's knee had healed. A twinge of pain came if he twisted too quickly, but time would heal it in full.

Guy and Kit found leaving Seville for the second time even harder than the first. Bart's father considered Guy and Kit as a connection to his son, and Guy and Kit saw Bart's father as a connection to their friend. Together, they kept his spirit alive. In leaving, they said a final goodbye.

Instead of following a path that would take them back through Cordoba (though Gonzalo had begged them to stop by on their return), they took a different route, avoiding major cities. They passed through Sierra Norte, meeting the Guadalquivir River as it cut through woodland. They traversed a dry region where no other humans resided. The great forest brought tranquillity, and they arrived back in Madrid many months after their intended return. The calendar read October 1598 by the time they approached the Royal Alcázar of Madrid, looking like the wanderers and weary travellers they were.

Again, as they approached the Alcázar, the portcullis rose. Five armour-clad soldiers rode out on white horses, followed by a group of foot soldiers bearing muskets.

Guy smiled at Kit. "Some things never change." He turned to the guards and raised his arms. In Spanish, he spoke, "We come in peace with news of King Philip's mission to Morocco."

The lead guard drew his sword.

Kit mirrored Guy, raising his hands too.

"May we speak with the king?" Guy asked.

The guard shook his head. "The King sees no one."

"Then can we speak to Carlos de Balbao?" Kit asked.

"He is dead." The guard indicated to the others that they were to seize the prisoners. Guy and Kit dismounted their horses and surrendered their weapons. The guards, with heavy hands on their shoulders, guided them through the portcullis, which closed behind them. Instead of being taken across the courtyard where they had ventured into the palace so many times, the guards marched them into the nearest tower; howling came from below, potentially that of a human. Rather than being taken closer to that hideous sound, they were slung together into a cell at ground level.

"At least we've not been consigned to the lower dungeon," Guy said as he took a seat on the stone floor.

"They'll send someone to speak to us pretty soon, though, right?" Kit sat too.

"What do you think happened to Carlos?"

Kit shrugged. "Some military campaign gone wrong."

"Might be why they're taking extra precautions."

"Aye, they'll be having a chat about us. Word will get to the king, and we'll be free. They won't leave us in here all night."

Hours later, as darkness descended on the cell, Kit's proclamation sounded foolish.

Guy woke in darkness, Kit snoring beside him.

From the corner of the cell, a speck of light grew until it revealed the skull of Thomas Percy.

"If you're here to tell me to be cautious before returning to Madrid, we realise that. Last night would have been an ideal time to stop by when we were outside gazing at the stars, enjoying our liberty."

Percy drifted from side to side. "So, I have caught Guy Fawkes in an irate mood."

Guy rolled his eyes. "Aye, you have."

"Trust no one here. Much has changed."

"Aye, again, last night, had you told me that, we may have approached with a touch more caution."

Percy spun round and disappeared, leaving Guy to cup his ears to block out the sound of Kit's snoring and get back to sleep.

Guy did not rest easy, though he did fall into a deep sleep, the kind that one descends into when there's nothing else to do and the body tunes out everything. Guy didn't hear the key in the lock or the cell door creaking open, and when a guard placed a hand on his shoulder to wake him, he was lost inside his head, and that pressure on his arm became Sofia, dressed in white leaning over him with a knife.

Guy braced himself for an impact that never came, and when he opened his eyes, he looked upon a well-dressed courtier.

"The King will see you now," said the young man. Guy did not recognise his face from his previous time at the Alcázar.

The guards led them back into the courtyard and through the familiar entrance.

As they reached a crossroads in the corridor, Guy glanced down the passage to the left as a woman in a white dress passed: Sofia! Guy grabbed Kit's arm, but by the time he turned, she had disappeared.

"What is it?" Kit asked, continuing to peer down the empty passage.

"I thought I saw Sofia."

Kit shook his head. "She's locked up in Cordoba. What would she be doing here?"

Guy sighed. "She looked so real."

Kit brushed Guy's shoulder. "I see Bart everywhere, too, now we're around people again. Being back here, it's bound to bring back memories."

The courtier cleared his throat, and they continued through the familiar passages into the royal courtroom. That's where the similarities stopped. Kit gazed at the throne and said, "That's not..." before his better judgement stopped him. Indeed, the king sat upon the throne, but not the same king they'd left. The former prince, elevated to the position of highest power, now reigned as King Philip III. At only twenty years of age, some eight years Guy's junior, naivety painted the new king's blemish-free face. His oversized ruff hid most of his face. His cheeks bulged into it, making him look cherubic, if not for the grand handlebar moustache. History tells us Philip started growing his moustache when his father became ill, some two years earlier—a great decision, for this single feature established him as an adult. And yes, King Philip II had known of his sickness when he sent Guy to Morocco, but he did not believe he would pass before their return.

Guy and Kit bowed to their king, who nodded. King Philip III turned from them to converse with the gentleman standing next to him, a gentleman Guy took an immediate dislike to. He had an untrustworthy appearance, something animalistic but not in the way of a familiar. His build was not feeble, as familiars often were, and he lacked the rodent look. Guy knew he'd think twice before ever turning his back on the man.

He turned away from the king and approached Guy and Kit. His doublet and hose were a terracotta colour, with gold decorations at the cuffs and collar. He had very little facial hair—a small, black beard in the Balbo style—minimal growth on his chin, a stalk leading to his lower lip, and a pyramidal moustache. It looked altogether like too much work to maintain. His eyes were piercing, with something in his manner of staring that reminded Guy of the Queen's advisor, Robert Cecil. His short hair was covered in something that gave it the appearance of a shimmering black pool.

He stretched out a hand.

As soon as Guy shook it, a wave of revulsion hit him. How he wished Thomas Percy had told him more.

The man shook Kit's hand too. Luckily, he had made eye contact with Guy again and did not notice Kit wiping his hand on his breeches.

He spoke in good English with an accent difficult to place. "I am Fernando de Andalusia, chief advisor to His Majesty. I offer my apologies that you were treated as strangers upon your arrival."

Kit grumbled and Guy nodded, forcing a smile.

"One of our commanders here tells me you travelled with Bartolomé de Sevilla. Had you returned with him, perhaps we would not have had such confusion."

Guy bowed his head. "Alas, you are not the only ones to have suffered a loss."

Fernando wrinkled his lips. "I am sorry to hear that. While in Morocco?"

"We were on the road back to Madrid when we encountered some unpleasantness."

"In Cordoba," Kit added.

Guy noted a twinge in Fernando's eye when Kit mentioned the name of the city, something he shook off by putting a hand on Guy's shoulder.

"Now I understand certain promises may have been made." While Fernando spoke in a low voice, a sinister hiss hung on some of his words.

Guy shook off the advisor's hand. "Aye, when we cut off the supply of saltpetre, King Philip planned to invade England."

Fernando sighed. "We are assessing our diplomatic relations with a number of states."

"Is Juan de Velasco still in charge of your foreign affairs?"

Fernando's mouth narrowed. "He still has some say, yes. He has come round to his new king's way of thinking: war is no good for the long-term prosperity of a nation."

A stone plummeted from Guy's heart and settled heavy in his gut. All their effort for nothing.

"Don't look so despondent. There may yet be an opportunity for you. Prove to the new King, as you proved to his father that you are worthy, and he may yet decide your course of action is what's best for the world."

"And how would you like us to do that?"

"We are having a little trouble maintaining control in the Netherlands."

Back to Northern Europe. Back to where they'd spent so many years trying to establish trust. Guy and Kit spent every second of their journey north cursing the new king's chief advisor.

Chapter 16—In Which Guy Fawkes Finds New Hope in the Netherlands

After many weeks of travelling, relief came when the fortification at Eindhoven appeared on the horizon. The city itself had no walls, having been destroyed during the ongoing conflict. Seeing no need to protect the people, the city's fortification had not been rebuilt. Instead, the Spanish had built a separate fort from which they controlled the area, sending out troops to skirmish with the Dutch, pushing further into their territory.

Access to the fort came with less difficulty than getting into the Royal Alcázar of Madrid. A soldier greeted them, his accent suggesting a native of Yorkshire. "More recruits, aye? Head through there," he pointed. "You'll be under the command of Sir William Henry." Guy led the way into the main area of operations, a large room dominated by a table with a map of the region unfurled across it.

Sir William Henry was a much older man than Guy expected. He wore black leather armour, the kind Guy had only seen before in portraits. Perhaps in his mind Guy had pictured a carbon copy of Bostock, still in his prime and so solid that blades bounced off him. Henry's stature differed: tall, thin, and all too angular, as if built entirely from broken swords. Even his long grey beard ended in a point that looked capable of doing harm. The bags under his eyes suggested a life of struggle, hanging low, giving the impression they weighed down his whole face.

"New recruits?" He spoke in English, glancing at them for only a second.

"How could you tell we were English?" Guy asked.

Henry grumbled. "Got that look."

Kit peered into Henry's eyes. "What do you mean, got that look?"

"That down-trodden, dragged-through-the-shit, you-won't-beat-the-fight-out-of-me look."

Kit turned to Guy and nodded. "Aye," they said in tandem.

"Fresh out of England, are you?"

"We've been in Europe for some years." Guy struggled to remember how long.

"Africa too," Kit added.

At that, Henry's eyebrows raised a fraction. "Got a bit of experience in European war?"

Countless battles flashed through Guy's mind. "You could say that."

"Gunpowder? Any experience with that?"

Kit shuddered at the memories of the caves of Morocco. "You could say that, too."

"So, what drove you out of England? Taxed to shit and gone broke? Poked with a stick for talking about God the wrong way?"

"Mostly the demons," Kit said without giving it a second's thought.

Henry thawed a little, and Guy tried to kindle his fire. "You know how bad it has become in England?"

Henry shook his head. "It's been many a decade since I set foot on the isle I once called home. We tried to fight back. 'Rising of the North', they called it, mostly so they could mock us because of its failure."

"At Brancepeth Castle?" Guy asked.

Henry's brow furrowed as he peered at Guy. "Aye, you know of it?"

"You knew Thomas Percy, I take it?"

Henry's face further creased. "You must have still been shitting your pants when he died."

"He died before my birth."

Henry titled his head slightly. "So, what know you of Thomas Percy?"

Guy turned to check that no one other than Kit listened in. "He comes to me."

Henry rolled his eyes. "Ah, one of them, are you?"

"I guess I am."

Henry turned his attention to his map. "Looks like I've finally got some capable recruits. Get yourself settled in at the barracks and we'll talk strategy."

Over time, Guy came to know his commander well. Like Bostock, Henry grew up as an English Catholic who later turned on his country as result of persecution. The conflict in the Netherlands was on theological grounds, and as such, Henry spoke of it with disdain. The newly formed Dutch Republic promoted ideas of freedom of religious thought. England supported the Dutch, officially hoping to make Protestantism the primary religion, while the Spanish considered any step away from Catholicism to be heathenry of the highest order. Of course, the participation of the English Government suggested devilry, and William Henry's role involved keeping on top of the creeping threat of evil, a task he'd attended to with considerable success.

From their very first conversation, Guy understood the man, and expected they'd get on well.

As predicted, time passed with a degree of contentment. 1598 became 1599, became 1600. In those early months, Guy wrote to Duke Gonzalo of Cordoba to check that everything had settled and with a brief query about the young king's advisor. When Guy received the response, he discovered that Fernando de Andalusia had indeed been with Prince Philip (his title at the time) when they passed through the city. Alas, no one would consider this sufficient evidence to prove Fernando's demonic leanings. Guy's other hopes also seemed to be waning. Philip III's war policy maintained hostility towards England, but another invasion attempt had been all but ruled out for the time being. Another troubling report stated that Sofia had indeed been transported from Cordoba's jail to Madrid, to stand trial. Perhaps Guy had seen her in the Royal Alcázar? How Guy wished he too had a contact in the Royal Alcázar of Madrid who could monitor events. Sir Henry had a spy there, a young man named Ricard, but his strict orders forbade him to correspond with any but Sir Henry who had little interest in the potential whereabouts of who he called, "some know-nothing religious zealot."

Guy however, re-established communication with Samra. With a continuous base for an extended period, the exchanged several letters, though they made not for pleasant reading. Samra still hunted Zidan and the Children of Mizraim, who continued to contaminate water supplies to spread their infection. He commanded a small band, and with Jabir, he sought an end to the cult's blight.

Guy also had access to plenty of news from England and Scotland, for Henry had a fine network of spies with whom he would regularly correspond. After proving their worth by taking out an infestation of demons who had infiltrated Dunkirk early in their time in the Spanish Netherlands, Henry confided in Guy and Kit. With Queen Elizabeth in her mid-sixties, and with no heir, talk of succession dominated discussion in elite circles. The Queen gave Robert Cecil the duty of choosing a successor, for she refused to name one. Given Cecil's meddling in the Catherine Stanley affair, Guy suspected his plots would be malevolent. Henry's opinion differed.

"They say he is considering Scotland's boy king." King James of Scotland held on to the moniker of boy king thanks to taking the throne of Scotland at thirteen months. Even at thirty-four, it stuck. As a great-grandson to Henry VII, he had lineage in his favour.

"If he succeeds," Henry said, "our land may finally be purged."

"How so?"

Henry produced a book and held it before Guy.

Guy read the title: *Daemonologie, In Forme of a Dialogue.*

"And it opposes witchcraft?"

"Aye." Henry nodded. "Strongly."

A smile spread across Guy's face. "So, why do we need to continue our mission here? Why need we the Spanish King to take the crown when a legitimate king of England can liberate us?"

"You're what, thirty years old, Guy Fawkes?"

"Aye."

"Then you should know better than to put all your hope in one man."

Myriad disappointments from Guy's past rushed to punch him in the face.

Henry placed a comforting hand on Guy's shoulder. "Philip II devoted his life to keeping Spain demon-free. His son, we hope, will do likewise. If James becomes King of England, he's going to need a powerful ally to help him rid England of the sickness."

"So, we keep fighting."

"Aye, we keep fighting. And on that subject," Henry grinned, "I'm going to be sending you to the coast."

"Where?"

"Nieuwpoort."

"What's going on there?"

"Not sure. Nothing more than whispers right now, but I got a letter here saying an ancient church rose out of the sea."

"We'll make our way before dawn breaks."

"Thank you." Henry nodded in appreciation. "Oh, and Guy."

Guy turned back to his commander.

"Take this with you for a bit of reading material."

Guy took the copy of *Daemonologie.* The words of Francis Ingleby, Guy's mentor, Kit's uncle, the man who had died fighting for what he believed in at Durham, rang in Guy's ears: Hope lies in Spain. Aye, that remained true, but a new hope grew, and of all places, it came from Scotland.

Chapter 17—In Which Guy Fawkes Battles Towards the Hell Cathedral of Nieuwpoort

Guy and Kit arrived in Nieuwpoort at the beginning of July with a small force of Henry's soldiers, many of whom had experience battling demons. The territory lay within the Spanish Netherlands, so there would be no great force of Dutch to worry about. Henry had suggested they were likely to discover a small troupe of witches summoning creatures to cause mayhem.

The group passed through the city, untroubled by anything more severe than whispers. Speakers of the native languages liaised with the locals, who all spoke of a great need to visit the beach and see for themselves what devilry had come to Nieuwpoort.

Even before reaching the sea, they saw the pointed spires, an affront to the horizon. A few more steps and two more towers came into view. They stood on the sand, the whole hellish structure standing before them, a demon cathedral of black stone with four spired towers like giant daggers assaulting the sky. A rocky path led to its front door. The sea did not crash against it but bent away from the structure, refusing to break there, choosing the familiar sanctity of the beach every time.

The cathedral looked like something out of Dr Johannes Faust's *Praxis Magica Faustina,* a grimoire obtained by Christopher Marlowe and shared with Guy during that period in which they lived together.

Through the window of one of the towers, a red light glowed. The sky darkened and a fierce blast of wind spat sand in their faces. Guy and Kit blinked their eyes clean and scanned the beach. Sand eddied in ever-increasing circles, growing taller, thicker, until a column as tall as Guy came spinning their way. They shielded their eyes as it exploded over them. Again, the red light in the cathedral window shone.

Kit pointed to it. "Someone must control an aerial power from up there."

Another sand column closed on them. Further away, a greater formation of sand came together, growing as it neared.

Guy and Kit burst forward, shoulders first, breaking through the column and sending sand scattering behind them. Sir Henry's soldiers likewise braced themselves. The next swirling column towered before them. This had gathered compacted sand, heavy with the weight of water. Guy leant into it, but as it collapsed upon him, he fell to the ground with it, leaving him giddy.

Kit dragged Guy back to his feet. "We've got to get into the cathedral. We've got to stop whoever's controlling that thing."

A shower of sand fell upon them. Guy looked to the skies and cursed.

They turned towards the cathedral, where the path of rocks led into the sea and into that hellish building. More sand, gathered by the corrupted, demonic forces of nature, compacted to make a giant fist. Guy raised his hands in defence, but it still had the power to knock him into Kit and leave the two of them struggling for balance.

"Keep going!" Kit cried. "When we get to the sea, it'll struggle to carry the sand over it."

They braced themselves against several more barrages, and Sir Henry's men suffered the same, following behind them. After the fifth blow, the assault ceased.

Again, the red light in the window shone. Guy and Kit hurried forward, until the sand stirred before them, rising, creating an ever-thickening wall.

"Men!" cried Guy. "Shields up. To the wall!"

The small band of men rushed to the sand, pushing their shields into it.

"Twist your shields into the sand, create a break in the wall."

Once the soldiers forced a breach into the sand wall, Guy and Kit bolted for it, aiming for the gaps created by the shields. While they were much larger than those spaces, they had to hope that with some of the sand diverted away, they could break through. As their shoulders pushed through to the other side, the weight of sand pressed against them. The narrow sand-wall's resistance broke. Sand collapsed all around them, its weight diminishing as collective control failed and each grain fell once again under the force of gravity.

"Here we go," called Guy as he stepped onto the first of the rocks and made for the cathedral.

While Kit's theory about being safe from the sand proved correct, the wind had a new weapon now, splashing them with vast waves that broke as they hit the rocks, threatening to take their feet out from beneath them. The waves came in rhythms, so a second before they broke, Guy and Kit planted their feet, ready for the blast of water.

The aerial power changed its approach, going back to the swirling circles it had used with the sand, creating waterspouts it could unleash at its will. When they saw them coming, Guy and Kit parted, knowing it could strike only one. When the water attacked Guy, Kit stood aside, waiting to grab his friend and hold him steady. Guy did the same for Kit.

Between blasts, they leapt from rock to rock, but the cathedral never grew closer. Drenched, weighed down by waterlogged clothes, and exhausted from running, dodging, and leaping, Guy and Kit pushed on. A great rumble came from far below. Guy jolted as the rock beneath his feet juddered. Kit grabbed his hand to steady his friend.

"We've got to get there quick, or we won't make it." Guy turned back to the cathedral and leapt across the next three rocks before bracing himself to be struck once more. As the water hit him, he found Kit next to him again, holding him safe. He blinked the water from his eyes. For a second, he thought the cathedral was further still away, but as an immense wave rippled towards him, riding over the rocks, he understood: the cathedral was sinking back into the sea. "Back!" he cried.

Kit, too, saw the disaster unfolding before him. He turned and leapt from rock to rock, but the shoreline lay out of sight. For how long had they travelled along the path; for how long had the cathedral retreated, drawing them nearer? And the quicker and the deeper it sank, the greater the size of the wave behind them grew.

"Jump!" Guy yelled as the water pushed at his back.

He leapt from the rock, twisting his body into a dive, but the wave caught him, hitting him with immense force, turning him over and dragging him down. He gulped, taking in water. His head rushed with the pressure hurling him forward.

If it were not for the immense wave, the tsunami generated by the sinking of the cathedral, neither Guy nor Kit would have had the strength to swim back to shore. Instead, the force of the angry sea carried them.

If there were cliffs, or even a few rocks on Nieuwpoort's beach, the chances of a cracked skull as they collided with them would have been high indeed. Fortunately, Nieuwpoort's long and sandy beach offered no such threat. Beyond it lay the dunes, also free of mutilating obstructions that would cause mortal wounds. The sea carried them onto land, scraping them against the sand, lifting skin from every place not covered before leaving them on soft grass, coughing, spluttering, but very much alive.

Guy and Kit shuffled into seated positions. The rest of Sir Henry's party gathered, having retreated when they saw the almighty wave coming.

The salty water stung their raw, sand-scraped faces as it dripped off them.

Still wheezing, Guy turned to Kit. "At school, did we ever learn of a sinking cathedral?"

Kit shook his head. "No, friend. We must have skipped that day."

Both smiled, despite the additional pain it brought to their faces.

They peered out to where the cathedral had stood. Dark clouds gathered over the waves. The sea, so calm upon their arrival, continued to churn with enormous waves that crashed against the sand and retreated with a hiss.

Then the ships came. Great galleons appeared on the horizon, twenty of them or more, the English flag flying from the mast of each.

Guy and Kit struggled to their feet. Guy surveyed their small bank of soldiers: they could not hold back an invasive force.

"Take your fastest horse and ride from this place," Guy called, dismissing his party, telling them to spread news on invasion, to get people to the nearest fort or to fortify their properties.

Kit brushed his hand through his hair, flicking saltwater onto the grass. "Don't tell me you plan to take a stand against twenty ships, Guy Fawkes?"

Guy unsheathed his sword and used it for balance. "Don't tell me you're suggesting a plan other than running in headfirst, Kit Wright?"

"I do love your company, Guy, but damn if it isn't painful sometimes."

"Nonsense! You wouldn't have it any other way."

Kit glanced at Guy, smiled, then looked at the grass. "Aye, you're right. As long as I'm fighting beside you."

The thought of raising his sword made every muscle cry out in protest. Kit's chest heaved. Guy shook his head. "We're in no condition to fight."

"I'm glad you're aware."

"No. We watch who disembarks from those ships, and we get that intelligence back to Sir Henry. Further along the coast, they must have seen these ships sail by, but if we can give an idea of numbers, they'll send a force to push them back into the ocean in no time."

They both leant on their weapons as the ships closed before seeking somewhere to take cover, somewhere they could watch without being seen. Having been gifted with one of Jabir's telescopes, they at least had a greater chance of doing so. They returned to their horses, and Guy took the implement from the saddlebag. They found a position within the dunes where the grass grew high on a bank of sand which they could hide behind.

The galleons dropped anchor close to the beach. There would be no need to launch rowboats. They would storm through the shallow waters.

Guy peered through the telescope, expecting to see ropes drop from the side, for troops to descend into the water. That didn't happen. He watched another ship. That, too, had dropped anchor a similar distance away. When the fifth ship dropped anchor, Guy noticed movement on the first, a figure moving towards the starboard into the bulwark, and tumbling over the side, splashing into the shallow water.

At first, Guy suspected an accidental fall, the stereotypical drunken sailor finding the cessation of the boat's movement too much and losing his legs. Then a second followed, tumbling over the side, and plummeting into the water. Then a third. Guy handed Kit the telescope and pointed in the right direction. With his naked eye, he could make out similar movement on the other boats.

"They're getting up." Kit handed Guy back the telescope.

Sure enough, those that had tumbled from the starboard walked through the sea in a manner suggesting they weren't without physical injuries. Dozens of them now wandered onto the beach, planting their feet on the sand like toddlers in desperate need of a nap. Guy held the telescope limp in his hand.

Kit snatched the implement and gazed at the invaders. "What's wrong with them?"

"There's only one way to find out."

Guy raised his head, plotting a course to intercept an invader.

"Wait!" Kit pushed Guy's head back down. "There's someone else. He's sliding down the rope."

Kit handed the telescope back to Guy. Sure enough, on each ship, one person had full control of their actions. When they landed, they charged forward, getting in front of their less nimble crew. One of these more agile men raised his weapon, and it glimmered yellow-green. They wore some kind of covering over their faces, which from a distance, looked like sacks.

"They're some kind of demonic horde with witches leading them." Guy held out the telescope for Kit.

Kit didn't take the telescope. He stared out to sea. "We should get on a boat."

Guy agreed. They loitered in the dunes until most of the shuffling horde had left the beach, hoping Sir Henry's men had got the warning out in time and the people of Nieuwpoort had found safety.

They scooted across the beach, staying low. It seemed unlikely the ships would be left abandoned, so Guy and Kit prepared to fight. In this case, they suspected one or two sentries to await them rather than an entire legion. They picked the nearest ship and listened: no sound of any great hurrah, no conversation. Kit, the nimbler of the pair, scaled the rope first, stopping a little way from the top to listen once more. A second later, he pulled himself the rest of the way up and landed on the deck without a sound. He scanned the area, then beckoned Guy to join him.

As they hunted around the deck, the sound of whistling grew louder, coming from the quarters below. They moved to either side of the door. Guy pulled out his boot knife, and the second the sailor passed, he held the knife across the man's neck.

The sailor threw back an elbow. Guy, exhausted from the earlier sea trauma, was not as alert as he should have been and let the man squirm out of his grasp. He hadn't wagered on a second assailant though, and Kit dispatched him, thrusting his sword into the man's chest.

Guy puffed out his cheeks.

"I know you wanted to question him, but once he wriggled free, I couldn't take the risk."

"Thank you. You think there are any more?" Guy listened at the door.

"Only one way to find out."

Kit moved through the door first, peering in every direction, taking caution, listening after every board creaked in case it alerted anyone. If anyone else remained on board, they were likely on the lower deck rather than with the cannons, but something else caught Kit's eye. He beckoned Guy over to look at a barrel. He reached for a candle from the wall, lit it, and held it closer to the barrel. "Is that symbol familiar to you?"

Guy gazed upon the symbol: a five-pointed star with a spear running across it.

Chapter 18—In Which Guy Fawkes Seeks Assistance from Madrid

As Guy and Kit clambered from the boat, they speculated that one of two things had happened. Either the ship had sailed from England unintentionally carrying plague-infected gunpowder, and the crew had become sick en route, or someone with malevolent intent had infected the crew with the plague and unleashed them upon an unsuspecting population. Given that there was at least one person on each boat who had control of the rest, the second theory seemed most likely. Despair swirled around Guy's head. What kind of depraved individual would weaponise a virus and unleash a plague upon innocent people? The face of Robert Cecil entered his mind before his thoughts turned to staving off the threat.

How could they save Nieuwpoort? They hoped residents had barricaded themselves in houses and fortresses, but if this demon plague spread like a sickness, it threatened everyone. The important thing was to stop it from getting out of Nieuwpoort. That meant visiting neighbouring communities and shutting off the roads, creating blockades, and isolating the infected area until someone found a way to cure or purge the sickness. No, they would fight again another day for Nieuwpoort, it's abandonment a short-tern necessity to halt a greater threat. Guy still felt like a coward as he and Kit galloped away.

Guy and Kit travelled due east and started rousing volunteers to spread the word. From each of those communities, Guy urged the people to fortify what parts of their land they could, and to send riders to neighbouring towns and villages.

By the time they returned to Eindhoven, Sir Henry had already received word from the troops Guy had first sent back.

"You know how they've used that damned cathedral, don't you?" said the old man.

Guy shrugged.

"If you don't know, you're a bigger fool than I took you for. It's a beacon. It brought the ships to the shore, and it could appear anywhere else along the coast."

Guy ignored the insult. There was no point in challenging Sir Henry. "We have to stop it."

Sir Henry held out a hand to stay Guy. "Hold, you hasty buffoon. This is something which requires great care. You think you can stand there and stop this unstoppable wave of evil. It would wash over you in an instant."

"What do we do?"

"Make for Madrid."

Guy threw his hands up and stood. "That'll take weeks."

"Aye, it will. Same to come back again. I'll have Kit link with Bostock to build a force against them here. We'll brace the other coastal towns and keep our eyes open for that cathedral. But the more men you can rouse in the south, the stronger our force will be."

Guy gazed at Kit. "But..."

Sir Henry huffed. "None of your nonsense. I need Kit here, and I need you to use your powers of persuasion with royalty." With that, Sir Henry gave them a dismissive wave.

Kit and Guy stood outside.

Kit spoke first. "You better take care of yourself. You'll struggle without me watching your back."

Guy smiled. "Aye, and who's going to stop you running headfirst into danger without a second thought?"

Kit plunged his hand into his pouch of runes. "I'll have to stop and ask myself, what would Guy do?"

"And do your own thing, anyway?"

"It's normally the best idea." Kit plucked a rune from his pouch, and without looking at it, handed it to Guy.

Guy took it and turned it over, admiring the two lines carved into the stone.

"What does it mean?" Guy asked, holding it out for Kit.

Kit glanced at the stone. "Uncle Francis never got around to explaining them all to me." He peered at it again. "But I'd say those two lines represent you and me. It means we'll stand together again one day."

"Aye, I hope you're right."

Heavy footsteps stomped behind them. Sir Henry cleared his throat. "You called this invasion a dire emergency. There's no time to stand about."

Guy and Kit glanced at each other and moved for their horses.

"Guy," called Sir Henry. "I'm sending a Spaniard to join you. Might help smooth the translations."

Guy rode, for weeks on end, in the opposite direction of Nieuwpoort, away from great peril. Alongside him rode Jose Iglesias, a Spanish general. At least, Guy hoped, there would be easier communication and a much-reduced chance of imprisonment upon arrival at the Royal Alcázar of Madrid.

They passed through the same landscapes and towns as Guy had a few years earlier, with little having changed except for the speed at which they travelled. Only when they reached the Alcázar, did they notice any significant difference. No longer did the welcoming party that passed under the portcullis ride on white horses. No, they were on black stallions with black armour. Still, when Iglesias spoke with them, they urged the visitors inside and to the court.

Immediately noticeable was the way King Philip III's face had thinned. He no longer looked like an infant sitting on the throne, but a man who had silenced his troubles. His eyelids looked heavy, but he had a content expression. "What troubles you, friends?"

Iglesias started to explain the situation, but King Philip held up a hand to stop him. He leant across to one of his guards who dashed off.

The King remained seated, his jaw moving as if chewing on something.

Moments later, Fernando appeared at the door, alongside a woman. She left him at the door and returned whence she had come. There was no mistaking her face: Sofia Serrano, murderer of Bartolomé de Sevilla and an accessory to the horrors of Cordoba, a demon's aide.

Fernando glanced at Guy and Jose and elected to conduct his business in English. "I'll thank you not to bother His Majesty with your trivialities." He urged them to sit at the long table at the other end of the court, which had been moved further from the throne than it had been in King Philip II's day.

While King Philip III had grown thin and a languid air hung about him, over the years, Fernando had bulked out. He retained the Balbo beard and the triangular moustache, but where before it made him look as if he were playing a role he couldn't comprehend, now it suited him.

Guy's business was the demon incursion in Nieuwpoort, but he couldn't let Sofia's presence go unchallenged. He pointed towards the door. "What's she doing here?"

Fernando glanced at the door, but Sofia had left. He turned back to Guy and held his gaze. "That's no way to speak of my wife."

Guy's jaw dropped. "But she's—"

"Sofia was as much a victim of deception in Cordoba as anyone. Her devotion to God made her believe in a potential miracle. Can you really bear a grudge because of a person's faith?"

"She killed my friend."

Jose shuffled in his chair.

Fernando's eyes blazed. "Unless you wish to spend some time cooling off in the cell, I suggest you turn your attention to whatever triviality brought you here."

Guy swallowed back bile. Fernando's choice of companion only gave him another reason to dislike the man, but he had to keep that distaste down and prioritise. "What's happening in Nieuwpoort is far from trivial."

Fernando leant back in his chair. "Please, elaborate."

Guy handed Sir Henry's letter to Fernando. "Give this to your highest commander. It outlines what Sir Henry needs to counter the threat."

Fernando plucked the letter between thumb and forefinger and placed it on the table. "Is this genuine?"

"Very much so. The plague will destroy all life in those towns, and if we can't stop it spreading from one to another, it will cause chaos in the region, and, over time, further afield."

"And this threat comes from England."

"The ships had the red and white flag of England."

"Someone could use that as a ruse, of course, to create animosity between England and Spain."

Guy rolled his eyes. "There *is* animosity between England and Spain, ever since King Philip II..."

Fernando leant forward, eyes blazing. "He is no longer king! We will not carry out any rash action."

"When we boarded a ship, the barrels had the same symbols as those from the mine in Morocco. As I'm sure you're aware, there is a trade agreement for saltpetre to make gunpowder between the English and the Moroccans."

"A trade which I believe you were supposed to bring to a close."

"Aye, but how much of this contaminated saltpetre is already out there? The English may have been working for years to find out how best to ferment the evil in this stuff and use it to cause most harm."

Fernando linked his fingers. "So, what do we need to do?"

Guy nodded at the letter. "You have Sir Henry's request for troops."

"We shall supply them and get them mobilised as quickly as possible. I'll send riders out the second I leave this table, but we cannot send all the men Sir Henry desires."

"Why not?"

"I have no reason to disbelieve your words. Similarly, I received a letter from Bilbao this morning. It reports of a great black cathedral rising from the sea to the north."

Guy's mouth dropped.

"So, what would you do, Guy Fawkes? How do we strike against this threat?"

"If we can destroy the cathedral, you can stop the ships from arriving."

"How would you like to visit Bilbao?" Fernando smiled.

Something in the movement of his mouth, in the way his lips twitched, urged Guy to question him further. "It's not a city I know well. Is it much like Cordoba?"

Fernando's brow wrinkled. "Now, why would you mention Cordoba?"

"It's one of the few Spanish cities I have had the pleasure of staying in for any length of time."

"Bilbao, Fawkes, is not much like Cordoba at all. Though I'm not sending you to enjoy the cuisine or the sights. Will you go there? Will you do as you say and tear down this aquatic cathedral?"

Guy puffed his cheeks. "I'll try." Any task that took him away from the Royal Alcázar appealed. A sickness hung in the building, one that could rot and corrupt worse than the plague on the beaches of Nieuwpoort.

Chapter 19—In Which Guy Fawkes Gains a New Spanish Companion and Assaults the Cathedral in Bilbao

Fernando sent Iglesias to liaise with Spanish commanders and to lead a force north, insisting they wouldn't follow the orders of an Englishman. Similarly, Fernando had no intention of giving Guy any authority in Bilbao.

"Let me introduce you to the Inquisition." Fernando led Guy to the tower, past the cell he'd once spent a night in, and into the gloom of the dungeons. Guy peered into an empty cell, but from the room opposite came screams to suggest its regular occupant was otherwise engaged.

"It is because of the Inquisition that I came to see Sophia's side of the story—she's a victim of the devil's trickery, like Magdalena a generation earlier."

Guy had no intention of conversing with Fernando about the salvation of Sophia Serrano and their subsequent love story. Instead, he scanned the dungeon. The torture equipment, the racks and the wheels, and the whips and flails on the walls took Guy back to the horror of Durham castle's dungeon. In reaction, he took a step back from Fernando, giving himself enough room to unsheathe and swing his sword.

Fernando continued at pace, ignoring the desperate pleas groaned by the prisoners in each cell. When he reached a door at the far end of the dungeon, passing a gaoler who held a branding iron over a brazier, Fernando knocked three times, stepped back and waited.

A tall man stepped out wearing a long red robe emblazoned with yellow crosses. He closed the door behind him, glancing over Fernando's shoulder to meet Guy's gaze with his small, piercing eyes before he greeted Fernando. Guy noted the sword hanging at his side, the black-jewelled hilt poking through his robe.

After a brief chat, the man returned to the room to recommence whatever torture he'd been performing.

Fernando urged Guy to turn and walked alongside him back toward the stairs. "Iker Delgado—he has superior knowledge of the arcane to any in

Spain. He shall lead you in Bilbao. Do not get on his wrong side or you'll find yourself in the sanbenito like the rest of the heretics."

As Guy considered the potential dangers of this mission alongside men he didn't trust, he'd never missed Kit more.

The next morning, they were on their way, Guy standing out from Iker and his six companions, all dressed in red, also members of the Spanish Inquisition. He spoke to his allies in quiet Spanish, insistent on keeping a divide between Guy and the others. Not one for conversation, he feigning limited English, though his twitching face whenever Guy spoke aloud belied his claims and exposed his keen ear.

Unlike Nieuwpoort, cliffs lined Bilbao's coast. Like Nieuwpoort, the cathedral had risen out of the water, the black stone glistening in the sun. Again, a rocky path led from the cathedral to the beach, but it would be pure folly to traverse it, knowing the cathedral could descend and leave them stranded.

Guy, Iker, and the others stood on the cliff, gaping at the accursed cathedral. Guy pointed and explained his concerns to Iker, deliberately downgrading his language, talking down to Iker, as if he believed Iker had limited English.

"We need a boat." Guy used gestures to aid the conversation. "We sail north of the cathedral and approach from behind."

Iker stared at him for a moment. More went on behind those cold eyes that Guy hardly dared comprehend. Instead, he took in the day: mid-afternoon, warm, blue sky, and the odd cloud drifting on the calm breeze. Nieuwpoort had seemed similarly calm. As soon as they got close, all that would change.

The group took the path that led from the cliffs toward several small beachside abodes. A short jetty had a couple of rowing boats tied to it. Using the king's coin as a persuasive tool, Iker boarded one of the boats. The owner had no intention of sailing out onto those waters while that building scarred the coast. Had Iker used a different approach, a simple request and a warm smile, Guy believed the owner would have lent the boat. Iker, however, rarely used gracious smiles and kind words.

Four of Iker's men took control of the oars, leaving Guy and Iker ready to leap off to the cathedral. The rowing boat would stay in the vicinity ready to rescue them when they left, having vanquished whoever controlled the cathedral. These plans always sounded so simple...

At first, the ocean ignored them. The waves continued to roll; the sky remained calm. But the second they turned the boat, a wind picked up, splashing them with droplets of water, before the breeze grew in strength to chill them as it licked their wet faces.

Next, the water became choppier, the crew having to duck under waves that caught the back of the boat. The pace of the tide changed, too, the waves coming in greater regularity. This force sped them towards the cathedral, but with each wave, more water poured over the side, or leapt into the air and cascaded upon them, so bailing out water became a constant necessity.

"Turn!" Guy called, the cathedral getting close.

"Are you mad?" Iker leant in close, eyes blazing.

One of the crew spoke in Spanish. Iker turned to him, raised a fist, then nodded.

"Get ready!" Guy cried.

The crew turned the boat. The next wave, instead of breaking over them, carried the boat closer still to the cathedral.

"Row!" cried Guy.

As the crew paddled away, the boat turned further, still drifting towards the cathedral, sped there by the waves, but switching to an angle so it could pull away.

"Jump," cried Guy. He leapt first. Before he hit the water, Iker followed. A couple of strokes brought him to the rock, where he pulled himself up. Iker joined him a second later. A wave came crashing in.

The water struck the rock first, splashing up and crashing into the pair, robbing air from their lungs, knocking them back, threatening to throw them off the back of the rock. The water withdrew, attempting to yank them back into the sea the other way.

Iker spluttered as he regained his footing. "Some plan!"

"We're here, aren't we?" Guy stared at the cathedral door.

"Get inside before the next wave knocks us off." Iker pointed to a huge wave rushing towards them.

Guy glanced beyond it, to Iker's companions in the rowboat. They'd powered safely away from the danger of the rocks and waited in calmer waters, highlighting the fact that the sea targeted Guy and Iker.

A grand arch led into the nave of the cathedral. On either side, staircases led to the towers, and at the far end, the pattern matched. Guy drew his weapon and blessed it, bringing the blue flame to life along the blade. Iker huffed, keeping his weapon sheathed as he moved inside the cathedral. Tiles covered the floor, but a mass of seaweed disguised their pattern. Stained-glass windows depicted great blasphemies, and the walls ran with a dark red substance.

Armed only with their swords, Guy realised the ridiculousness of their task. Yes, they could take down whoever resided inside, but destroying the cathedral would be impossible. Perhaps that would be a task for later: sail a boatload of gunpowder for it and set it alight with a flaming arrow. Aye, the best ideas always came at the most impractical of times.

At the end of the nave, steps led into the crypts, water lapping at their tops. To Guy's relief he could conceive no good reason to venture down there. He thought of Kit. He'd dive down those steps in an instant if he thought it would help.

"One of the towers?" Iker suggested.

"At Nieuwpoort, that red light came from the one on the left." Guy pointed. "So, we should go up those stairs."

"I'll check the other side," Iker said, marching for the steps.

"We should stick together," said Guy with little enthusiasm as Iker disappeared up the other set of steps.

Guy considered turning back and following him before deciding otherwise. He felt safer alone. Iker gave the impression that he'd stab someone in the back if it suited his needs, and Guy didn't want to be that someone. As he took each step, he realised that people he didn't trust surrounded him: Iker's eyes constantly burned on the back of his head and Fernando too had that sinister look. With the way King Philip III sat drooling on the throne, unable to make the simplest decision without his advisor, the crown slid toward Fernando's head.

At the top of the tower a door stood, a red light ebbing from underneath it. As much as he didn't want to be with Iker, he missed Kit's presence. "I'll barge the door; you follow in a second later," Guy whispered to himself, imagining his friend by his side. He took a couple of preparatory breaths, then ran at the door, twisting his shoulder to take the brunt of the blow. Wood splintered as the door flew open. Guy's momentum carried him inside, trying to look everywhere at once to spot his enemy.

Red light bathed the otherwise empty room. The light shone in through the window, coming from the opposite tower.

Guy stormed down the stairs. While he didn't trust Iker, he had no intention of letting him face a threat alone. The plan to speed down one set of stairs and storm up the second changed the second Guy heard the strange gurgling from below.

As he emerged into the nave of the cathedral, splashing into the water that had risen to lap at ankle height, he saw an enormous beast, its head huge, scaly and fish-like, with great black eyes on the side. A mouth the size of the boat they'd rowed in on dominated its face, full of teeth the length of sabres. Flopping in front of that, coming from the top of the head and hanging in a fleshy cave, burned a red flame. A body like that of an elephant, leathery, grey skin, and enormous, powerful legs supported the strange fish-like head.

Iker stood by the wall next to the other staircase, arms spread out as if he could disappear into it.

Flanking the creature, with a couple on each side, were skeletal demon mermen, each dripping wet.

With the floor of the cathedral now covered with a couple of inches of water, Guy had no intention of slowing to wait for Iker, but he at least gave him the courtesy of announcing his plan: "Iker, run!"

With that, Guy bolted for the door.

The elephant-fish demon stomped towards them, and the skeletal mermen did likewise, but they were too far away. Guy reached the arch and ventured out on the black rock. The second he did so, a demon merman leapt out of the water and landed on the rock in front of him. The creature lunged forward with a trident. Guy dodged, but his feet skidded on the wet rock. He grabbed for the door to right himself. When stable, Guy caught sight of Iker running blindly for the door with his head turned to look over his shoulder. He crashed into Guy, knocking him to the ground.

A demon merman gurgled above him and thrust his trident down.

Guy shuffled to the side, the trident scraping his arm. Guy grabbed the weapon and pulled it, sending the merman off balance to fall into the water.

Iker grabbed Guy's arm and pulled him to his feet.

Mermen climbed onto every rock. The wind and sea gathered against them too, bringing higher waves crashing onto the rocks, splashing out, threatening to drench them with the wind attempting to upset their balance and topple them into the sea.

"Back inside," called Iker, his voice weak as it fought against the raging storm.

For a second, when Guy looked into his eyes, he thought Iker planned to stab him, but Iker turned and hacked at one of the skeletal mermen, crumbling its bones to dust. Whatever enchantment he had on the curved blade of his weapon worked.

The hybrid elephant/fish demon thundered across the nave, mouth opening ever wider.

Guy and Iker dived out of the way of its charge.

It turned and came again, the red flame hanging in front of its mouth jiggling from side to side, glowing brighter with each swing.

While Iker dived one way, Guy stayed on his feet, slashing at the creature's hide.

Before Guy could strike again, a pair of skeletal mermen came at him in tandem, carrying tridents covered in algae. With pain scorching his arm, Guy struggled to deflect their blows, each one sending jarring spasms through his agonised muscles.

The mammal/fish demon turned from Iker battling one set of foes, to Guy battling another.

Guy kicked out, knocking the leg bone of one of the skeletal mermen away. He hacked at the other, separating head from neck. He braced himself, ready to dive out of the way of the enormous demon, but had a last-second re-plan, shoving a skeletal merman into the beast's path.

Only when the elephant-sized fish-demon chomped on bones did Guy move away.

He turned to Iker. More enemies approached him. "Behind you," Guy cried.

Iker ducked under the lunge of a demon merman and leant into him before lifting his head, flipping his enemy into the onrushing mouth of the gargantuan beast. Another merman stood before him. He grabbed its trident by the shaft and swung him round. The merman spun and fell, joining his kin in the gaping mouth of one of Hell's weirdest residents. A great chomp and the sound of splintering bone signalled its demise.

The cathedral shook. The water level had risen to Guy's ankles. "Iker, lure more of them in!"

Iker poked his head out of the door. "There's a dozen on the way." He slashed at another one, splitting its guts and spilling them into the water.

The body of the almighty demon rumbled. Its body pulsed, and it spat out a series of bones. Iker raised his hands to block them, but couldn't stop a tibia striking his forehead, causing him to stumble.

"Iker, clear the path as best you can. I'm going to lure that thing to the back."

Iker staggered toward the door.

Guy grabbed a few of the semi-digested bones. He backed away from the creature and hurled a bone at it. After its meal, it moved sluggishly. It turned to Guy and hung its head low.

Guy flung another bone. This one struck the top of its head. It shook its head from side to side, causing the flaming lantern to swing. Guy threw another bone, and it stomped toward him. Guy glanced past the beast. Iker finished off three of the demon mermen and the remaining skeletal one.

Guy had wanted to lure the creature to the back of the nave to give them time to escape it, but the distance he had would have to suffice. Besides, the water had risen to his knees. They didn't have much longer.

Guy raced across the nave, lifting his knees high to pick up as much pace as he could. Iker had felled two more of his adversaries by the time Guy got there, leaving only a couple more. Guy lunged his sword into the back of one, and kicked the other to the floor, leaving Iker with the simple task of lopping its head off.

"Let's go," Guy cried.

Iker bolted for the door where one merman remained. Iker leant to the side, dodging its trident lunge, grabbed its arm, and slung it behind him, directly into Guy. Guy lifted his arm to stop the creature, knocking him to the floor, but pain erupted in his wounded arm again. Blindly, Guy kicked out, striking the creature on the knee, knocking it off balance. The rumble behind him told him the hideous abomination grew close. Guy reached forward, his fingers sliding into the gills of the demon merman, and he flung him into the path of the charging beast. As teeth clashed on bone behind him, he raced for the door.

With the cathedral having started its descent, Iker would be unable to summon the rowboat in time. What other option had they than to sprint along the rocks? Focusing on their footing as the wind tried to blow them off and the waves tried to knock them into the ocean, they leapt from rock to rock, the cliffs getting closer and closer.

Guy glanced back. The majority of the cathedral remained in sight. In Nieuwpoort, it had descended slowly at first, only to rush into the ocean at the end. It had been that rush which had caused the tsunami that swept them onto the dunes. No such safety existed this time, only the deathly solid rock wall of the cliff.

As Iker's feet touched the sand of the beach, he slowed. Guy moved past him and headed for the incline that twisted around the cliff face.

"Where are you going?" Iker asked.

A wall of water emerged from the sea, threatening to sandwich them all between it and the cliffs.

Iker ran too, stretching forward, his fingers falling on Guy's shoulder, intending to pull him back. Guy grabbed those fingers, and squeezed them together. Iker cursed, and the pair continued running to higher ground.

Only when at the top did they look back as the water slammed into the cliff several feet below. Spray rained on them, and a great drag of wind attempted to suck them in, but as they threw themselves to the ground, they knew they were safe.

Guy waited to get his breath back before he spoke. "What the hell?" He stared at Iker.

"Hell indeed." Iker half smiled.

"Not in the cathedral. Your actions."

Iker shrugged. "What do you want from me?"

Guy's hand explored the metal of his hilt. "You pushed one creature into my path, and you tried to drag me back on the incline."

Iker shook his head. "I didn't so much think of you, only what I needed to be safe."

Guy gritted his teeth. "What did you find in the tower?"

Iker pulled a damp wad of paper from within his robes.

"What's that?"

"All the evidence we need." Iker grinned.

If not for Iker's position as trusted friend to the man running the country, Guy would have wiped the smile off his face with extreme violence.

Chapter 20—In Which Guy Fawkes Takes a Long Journey North

Iker remained tight-lipped about the contents of the documents, and Guy would not beg the man for a hint. He'd wait until Iker issued orders and from them, read between the lines.

When the rest of Iker's Inquisition arrived, he gathered them into a huddle.

Again, Guy thought of Kit. He wouldn't have attempted to throw Guy to the demons. Iker had smirked when Guy had struggled on the rocks. Again, he considered the perilous situation in which he'd found himself. But with the cathedral sunk and no sign of ships in Bilbao, he considered his duty over. If he could find a way to split from Iker's party and return north, he'd feel so much safer.

Iker finished his conference. A couple of his men mounted their horses and rode off.

Iker approached Guy. "The plan is to head north along the coast."

"I may go ahead—speed back to Nieuwpoort to lend a hand there."

Iker scowled. "Your duty is to King Philip III."

Guy's brow furrowed. "I'm sorry?"

Iker fingered the hilt of his weapon. "I have sent some of my men west to spread word along the coast and to prepare vessels. I need you with me."

"For what purpose?"

"We cannot travel with diminished numbers given what we may face."

Guy took a few steps toward Iker and stood a blade's length from him. "So, why did you send some of your men away?"

"To counter the cathedral. If we station ships packed with explosives at our ports, should the cathedral rise, we can destroy it."

A jolt of pain hit the back of Guy's head as if Iker's fingers had darted into his mind and plucked out his idea.

Iker grinned. "We shall travel along the coast to the north, spreading the word."

"Did those documents give you that idea?" Guy nodded to the letters in Iker's hand.

"They reveal the plot to strike all along the coast, so it made me aware of the danger. But, no, it reveals the names of the traitors, men believed faithful to the King who have proved to be anything but."

Guy stared into Iker's eyes. "Name them."

Iker laughed. "You have not gained my trust, Fawkes."

Guy turned his back on Iker, walking away to gaze out over the sea again, anger roiling inside him with great ferocity.

That night, as they camped ten miles further along the coast, Guy found a quiet spot to rest. He lay twigs nearby, so he'd hear one snap should anyone approach. He didn't trust Iker enough to sleep a sword's length from him. More than anything he needed sleep, and he hoped for the wisdom of Thomas Percy.

Disturbed by dreams of another rising cathedral, sleep brought little comfort. This demon cathedral resembled York Minster, forcing past traumas upon him. He woke when they became too intense, first thinking the light of morning had roused him before he recognised the radiance as that of Thomas Percy.

"So, you're still there," Guy said, relief washing over him as he bathed in the skull's luminosity.

Percy's skull drifted closer. "I'm always here."

"You weren't. Not when Walsingham invaded."

Percy's glow grew brighter. "I remained. You lost the ability to speak to me."

Guy swallowed hard, concerned to ask his next question. "Is there anyone else in there with you?"

Percy drifted back. "What do you mean?"

"Like before, when Walsingham planted his seed in my mind. Iker stole an idea from me."

"Consider ideas as living entities. They want to come into being. When you have an idea, it's because that idea came to you. At the same time, it's spreading spores, trying to seed in other people's minds."

Guy nodded, confirming Percy's revelation. "So, he's not in my head."

Percy swooped down and circled Guy. "No, Guy Fawkes. It's pretty lonely in here these days, and that's the way it should be."

"Good."

Guy's relief waned as Percy swooped toward him. "You're right to be wary of Iker. Great malevolence radiances from him."

"Believe me, you're not the only one who can sense that."

Thomas Percy faded away, and Guy blinked until he woke properly. He sat, vigilant, waiting for Iker's party to rise.

Over the weeks they travelled along the coast, they visited many places, including Donostia-San Sebastian, Saint Jean de-Luz, Arcachon Bay, La Rochelle, Brest, St Brieuc, Barfluer, and Le Havre. In each place, the message remained the same: stock a ship full of gunpowder and watch for a mysterious black cathedral rising from the sea. They were still days away from Nieuwpoort when Iker let down his guard.

They were close to Dieppe, passing through places familiar to Guy from his earliest days in Europe. Days of driving rain and plummeting temperatures necessitated taking shelter rather than wild camping, as had often been the preference. With a local festival in the town, there had been no rooms available at the inn, no matter the weight of coins Iker placed in the barkeep's hand. Instead, they found an abandoned farm. The house itself was inhabitable, the thatch roof destroyed by fire. The barn, however, had a watertight roof and a door that closed.

Any night in a barn always reminded Guy of his days living with Uncle Thomas, sleeping in the hayloft, and to keep his distance from Iker, who had only become more odious with greater familiarity, Guy elected to sleep in this barn's hayloft and leave the others on the ground floor.

Iker, obviously, had to make this appear his decision. He climbed the ladder, cautious to avoid the weak struts, and barked at Guy, the same stuff he said every day. As he remonstrated, hands gesturing, pointing in the rough direction of the sea, Guy let his frustration spill and yelled, "Shut up!"

Iker took out the papers he'd protected so well and pointed at them as if they gave him some kind of authority. In his agitation, he didn't notice one sheet of paper fall from his stack, coming to rest on top of some loose hay.

Guy apologised; he felt no remorse, but he wanted Iker gone. Iker barked more nonsense and headed down the ladder.

Iker cursed at the bottom of the ladder as a strut gave way. A second later, the ladder disappeared from the top of the hayloft. Guy paid no attention to the sound of the ladder being chopped for firewood. He had something more important to read.

Guy lit his lantern and scanned the text, translating it as best he could.

The language choices made it difficult to make out much—a mention of ships, and the word for demon occurred frequently. The name 'Bostock' featured in the letter which caused some discomfort, but the signature at the bottom caused greater alarm: Gonzalo Alfonso.

Guy shoved the letter between two slats of wood. He sat in silence, waiting for the same to come from the ground floor. Only when that silence transitioned to snores did he take out the letter to read it again. He drew air between his teeth. First, Guy tried to find some kind of falsehood, but the names were there in ink on the page. Guy recalled their time in Cordoba. Gonzalo went along with the whole Magdalena thing. He had a good reason to go along with it to protect himself and his people, but all the same, maybe he had been involved in summoning her. Maybe he'd played Guy the whole time. Bostock, though, he trusted. Worse, Kit continued to fight alongside him, and if Iker planned to take out Bostock, he'd have no qualms about destroying anyone who stood in his way. As much as Guy wanted to be rid of Iker, now he had to keep him close to protect his friend.

Troubled, he settled into a shallow sleep, waking as the first hint of sun came through the slats in the barn. He clambered from the hayloft without the ladder, showing no sign of his anger at Iker.

"Iker," Guy called. "We need to talk."

The wiry Spaniard's eyes darted to his sword, not at his side but sheathed by a barrel. He turned to Guy. "What is it?"

"In the cathedral, you found those letters. You told me you couldn't trust me with the knowledge. We have travelled together for some time since, and I have given you no reason to mistrust me."

"Have you given me a reason to trust you?"

Guy swallowed back vile words. He'd not sliced through his neck, which had taken remarkable restraint: surely, that earned him some credit?

"You dropped this." Guy offered the reclaimed page of the letter.

"So, you already know." Iker turned to check the supplies.

"Not everything." Guy took a step closer to Iker. "Gonzolo Alfonso signed the letter. What is his involvement in this?"

Iker stood. "I'm sure King Philip's gaoler will have got it out of him."

"You had him arrested?"

Iker rolled his eyes. "I sent men to him as my first act upon finding those letters."

"And what of Bostock? How is he involved?"

Iker spat at the floor. "Like most English dogs, he cannot be trusted."

"Liar," called Guy, his hand worrying at the hilt of his sword.

"He's a traitor. He plays both sides."

"That's a lie."

"It's clear if you read the letters." Iker made no attempt to disguise his disdain.

"Only part of one. What do the rest say?"

Iker sighed. "If I tell you, will you drop this angry mongrel act?"

Guy sat upon one of the less rotten piles of straw.

Iker pulled the rest of the papers from his doublet. He thumbed through them. "So, it's the last page of the Duke's letter you read?"

"Aye?"

"You didn't see the first page. It's addressed to Johan van Oldenbarnevelt."

"But he's..."

"An enemy of Spain? Liaising directly with the English? Yes, that's why the Inquisition seek him. The Protestants cannot gain influence in our country."

Guy recalled Gonzalo's actions in Cordoba. His actions were those of a devout Catholic. Guy vowed to return to Madrid to clear Gonzalo's name when this ended. There were other courses to pursue before that became possible.

"And what of Bostock?" Guy asked.

"There are a couple of letters here between your so-called friend Bostock and one Walter Devereux. Have you heard of him?"

Henry Hastings' distant relative, an Englishman directing military strategy in Europe.

"Aye, I know of him."

"Would you like to read the letters?" Iker flicked through the pile and handed one to Guy. "This one is in English."

He scanned the information. Aye, he saw Bostock's signature at the bottom. He addressed Devereux several times. The information within told of troop movements within the region. One mentioned where Jesuit priests hid in England. Guy scanned for the name Oswald, and the location Scotton, but both were absent.

"Is that convincing enough?"

Guy's jaw clamped. He swallowed back bile then stared Iker in the eye. "Tell me again where you found these letters."

Iker sighed. "What will it take for you to trust me? I ran up the tower and barged the door. The man inside, no doubt in control of the cathedral, held a red jewel. We fought. After I slayed him, I took these papers from a table we smashed in our skirmish."

"So, who commanded the cathedral to sink back into the sea?" Guy asked.

"Perhaps his death, or the power of his stone, triggered the event. How am I to know?"

"You didn't destroy the stone?"

Iker held his hands out wide. "Should I have done?"

Guy rolled his eyes. "It would have stopped the aerial powers. The summoned creatures may have disappeared. It would have made our escape from the cathedral easier."

Iker stepped forward and gave Guy three gentle taps on the cheek. "What does it matter? We escaped with not so much as a scratch, did we not?"

Guy remembered the wound on his arm, which had only recently healed. "With little help from you."

Iker jabbed a finger into his chest. "I destroyed the witch controlling the tower. I'd wager it's why it has yet to rise again."

Guy half turned away from Iker, ready to terminate the conversation. "So, why are we on this journey?"

"We're closing on Calais. There, we'll deal with the traitor, Bostock."

Guy faced Iker once more. "He's not a traitor," Guy said, his eyes flaming with anger.

"Be careful on which side you fall, Fawkes. One as low as you wouldn't be afforded the luxury of questioning. We'd lop your head right off."

"I'd like to see you try."

Iker turned to his men. "Confiscate his weapons and prepare to depart."

Guy drew his sword.

Iker grinned. "Is this how you want your life to end? So be it."

Each of Iker's men drew their swords and formed a circle around Guy.

The odds were far from being in his favour. While he understood the appeal of a glorious death in battle, his plan did not include dying a fool and rotting in anonymity. He tossed his sword to the ground and raised his hands. He'd accompany Iker now, further north, whether or not he wanted to.

Chapter 21—In Which Guy Fawkes is Reunited with Colonel Bostock

Iker ordered his men to kill Guy should he flee. Given they were armed with not only swords but also bows, escape was impossible. Instead, Guy rode behind Iker, with the remaining members of his party following behind.

Something about the whole situation made little sense. Luckily, Guy had plenty of thinking time. Starting with the premise of Bostock's innocence meant that the letters had to be forgeries. Given the details about troop movements, someone could have doctored a genuine letter. Bostock may legitimately have shared the information with another colonel. All it would take is altering the recipient. This could easily be done. Guy had heard of the wonders of lemon juice to hide parts of messages.

The remaining questions of note were who and why? Had Iker forged them himself? Iker may have arrived at the cathedral with them already tucked in his doublet. He may have written them himself, or they could be part of a more elaborate plot. An ally of Fernando surely desired to stir confusion. Purging so-called traitors who were good men would allow Fernando to have a greater grip on Spain and further manipulate King Philip III. Alternatively, Iker told the truth: the witch brought the letters to the cathedral. Did they mean to weaken the Spanish by tricking them into executing honest men? Had the English orchestrated it? Whatever the scenario, Guy saw no end to its ramifications, not without serious bloodshed.

As he continued on the journey, he pondered something more difficult. What could he do about it? The answer lay in Fernando. If Guy could remove his toxic influence from King Philip III, the king would regain control and get back to working on removing devilry from his court, something his father had done. Alas, Guy's path took him ever farther away from Fernando and King Philip III. But Iker served Fernando, a symptom of his diseased control. Whether Fernando had manipulated him, or whether he was evil, Guy knew not. He suspected the latter, though that would also mean no witch in the tower. So, why did they visit the dark cathedrals at all? The forged letter ruse? Perhaps Iker was in earnest, but a fool. He believed Fernando's lies. In the tower, he defeated a witch and found the letters. He trusted every word of them. Fewer gaps remained in this story, but it didn't fit with a narrative that gave Guy a genuine reason to lop Iker's head off. Of course, he'd need to get his sword back to do that. Aye, this indeed was a complicated knot, far from being untied.

To complicate matters further, one rider Iker had sent forth to scout Bostock's abode reported back that they'd need to continue. Colonel Bostock fought in Nieuwpoort, in charge of the final push to run the plague demons out of the city.

"Does this not show you Bostock is on the side of good?" asked Guy.

"It could be part of his game, Fawkes. Show valour to gain greater respect, greater responsibility, and when the time comes, cause a greater betrayal."

Guy clicked his tongue. "Bostock's not like that."

Iker rolled his eyes and turned to his men. "We will return Guy Fawkes' weapon when we reach Nieuwpoort. We're going into the thick of the fight, and we'll need all men at arms."

Days passed before they reached Nieuwpoort. The smell of smoke hung in the air long before the light of the flaming buildings came into view. Guy recognised the buildings they passed as they left the city. Those a significant distance from the centre appeared untouched, though the residents had fled. The infection they'd kept rooted to the heart of the community, and now a final push would purge it.

The group edged through the ruined city, listening for the chorus of wails that came from the plague demons or from the sound of battle. It wasn't until they neared the centre that they heard anything: the action focused on a cluster of houses to the west of the town centre.

Iker raised one hand to bring his team to a halt. "Slaughter any demons and round up human survivors. Send them here. They may carry remnants of the plague, but God shall protect you from its burthen." Iker turned to Guy. "Fawkes, you're with me." Iker made a show of withdrawing Guy's sword from his horse's saddlebag and flinging it to the ground.

Guy dismounted and collected his weapon. He withdrew it from its scabbard to check it over, allowing a fantasy of inserting it into Iker's throat play out in his mind.

As they walked back across the town square, Guy wondered if Kit would be among Bostock's forces. He dug Kit's rune from his pouch and traced the two lines with his finger. Guy and Kit, together again. He hoped it forecast the truth.

Iker approached the first house from where he could hear wailing and accompanying that, a repetitive bang.

With his men behind him, Iker entered. Guy followed at the rear. Guy entered as a man fell, his face melted by the effects of the plague, an axe by his side. On the other side of a battered table stood a couple of weary soldiers. "Thank you," one said, lowering his head.

"Stand down." Iker cried, holding his sword aloft. "Move to the town square and await further instruction. Spread the word: the Spanish Inquisition has authority here now!"

As they sped to the next building, Guy once more questioned Iker's approach. Had he not just slain a demon in earnest and let the soldiers go free?

With little time to ponder, they entered the next house, in which Guy needed to draw his sword. He pulled a cloth from his side and held it over his mouth as he hacked into three the plague demons, who offered little resistance. Their attention remained on the stairs that the survivors had barricaded, their drive to infect whoever his up there.

Once the last plague demon fell, Iker called out. "Salvation has arrived. You are free to come down and gather in the town square."

Outside, Guy called to Iker. "Are you not concerned about being in a room with those beasts? Do you not fear catching the plague?"

"Providence protects us."

The next house offered a greater threat. A dead soldier lay in the doorway. Two others continued to fight. Not only did they have a dozen plague demons to contend with, but also a red-skinned demon, some low-ranking official from Hell. It had the face of a lion, with a matted mane encrusted with filth, and it bore curved blades in each hand. Another dead body lay at its feet.

From the floor above came chanting and a snivelling giggle, the telltale signs of a witch and its familiar.

As Iker and his men poured forward, some thinning the number of plague demons, some fending off the larger beast, Guy ran out of the front door. A hellish glow came from the upstairs window. Aye, as Guy suspected. A stack of barrels stood by the house. Guy climbed onto them and peered through the window. At least five people were inside, though three looked to be there involuntarily, huddled in the corner. The thin shape of one man gave him away as the familiar. Guy shattered the window with his elbow and climbed in. The familiar barely had time to turn before Guy sliced him through from shoulder to hip.

"Stop!" cried the other man who had to be the demon master. His complexion pale, his cheeks hollow, the corruption of drawing powers from demons for countless years had taken its toll. Still, his power came from his words, and to stop him from calling anymore, Guy thrust his fist into his face. He crumpled to the floor.

Guy beckoned those over that cowered in the corner. "Get his arms."

He scanned the floor, but finding nothing suitable, had to hack material from the fallen familiar's clothes. He shoved it into the witch's mouth to stop him summoning anything else while the former captives held him down.

Guy ran down the stairs. Iker and his men stood over the felled plague demons. Some glared at the space in which the demon had stood.

"I've captured a witch upstairs and felled the familiar to rid us of the demon."

Iker stomped up the stairs, with Guy following behind. He pulled out his sword and slashed at the witch's face, splashing those that held him with blood. As they gasped, Iker plunged his blade into the demon master's throat.

Iker stood inches from Guy. "Thou shall not permit a witch to live."

Guy stepped back, wiping spittle from his face.

Iker's chest heaved with the effects of exertion. "You allowed the demon to return to Hell instead of letting us vanquish it."

Guy wanted to tell him that his men's puny weapons had no chance against Hell's own children, that he would have to pick chunks of his men from his robe for hours but thought better of it. At least Guy had seen Iker's dedication to fighting demons.

A crash came from somewhere nearby.

Guy raced outside. The building next door had smoke billowing from the upper windows. Dust cascaded from the front door, suggesting something had collapsed inside.

Smoke whirled around the building, gathered, and flew in through the window.

"Aerial power!" Guy cried.

Iker held his arm out to stop Guy racing into the building, indicating that he should follow behind.

Guy let them go first, giving himself time to survey the scene. Again, dust and debris danced along the floor, collected by the ill wind. Inside, the bodies of several soldiers lay, many missing limbs. Dust filled the room from the collapsed ceiling. The sound of clashing swords came from above.

Iker ran up the stairs. "This is the Spanish Inquisition. Cease all demonic activity and come with me."

The sound of laughter echoed around the building. Guy took the stairs. From the position of the rubble on the ground floor, he knew to avoid the back room. The fighting came from a bedroom near the stairs.

Air rushed past Guy, battering his face with stones and sand. A figure backed out, slashing as he made his retreat. Even though it had been years, Guy recognised Bostock.

Bostock turned and ran into another room. A figure made entirely of sand shuffled after him. Behind it came several small furies, those born in Hell and dragged through cracks in the earth.

Guy lunged, his flaming blue blade penetrating the centre of one of the small creatures. He kicked another away as he twisted his body to swing his sword again and bisect another.

From another room came the sound of swords swinging, demonic wailing, evil cackles, everything Guy expected from a night on the town.

He dashed into the room with Bostock.

"Colonel Bostock," Guy called before he noticed the flames attacking the far wall and claws of smoke reaching for it.

An inhumanly tall man, his head bowed to avoid touching the ceiling, held a large red jewel, squeezing it as he pointed at the flaming wall, summoning balls of flame to fly at Bostock.

"Guy, you bastard. Do us a bloody favour and knock the stone out of the hand of that prick."

The tall man's eyes lit up, glowing with an intense white light. His voice, so full of bass, shook the floor. "Man's dominion on this soil is over. We'll dine on your souls. We'll decorate our armour with your skin."

Bostock raised his shield to block another fireball. "Shut your mouth, you stinking helmet. No one wants to hear it."

"Your blood will run through Hell's great river."

Bostock glanced at Guy. "Guy, do you want to hear it?"

Guy clenched the hilt of his sword tight and ran toward the lanky demon. "No, Colonel!"

The creature twirled around, losing form as Guy passed through him. It reappeared at the doorway.

Bostock took several heavy breaths. "He keeps doing that." Annoyance misshaped Bostock's face. His brow shimmered with sweat. "With a bit of help, we might pin him down."

"Iker," Guy called, hoping to enlist the assistance of the Spanish Inquisition. Still, swords clashed elsewhere in the building, dealing with either low-level furies or plague demons.

"Head towards the back room. He'll likely appear there," Bostock called.

"It's collapsed."

"Aye, don't go in there, ye daft bastard."

Guy rushed towards the room. The air glistened, dust particles rushed past him, and the shape shimmered in front of him. Guy lunged, but the shape dematerialised once more.

"Wait until it's solid before you swing," Bostock called.

Bostock ran back into one of the bedrooms.

From downstairs came a shout. "Colonel, are you in here?"

Guy recognised the voice. "Kit," Guy yelled back. "Upstairs, but be careful."

Kit ran up the stairs with his usual vigour. A thick, dark slop hung from his clothes. "Guy! You're here!"

Bostock gritted his teeth. "You can 'ave a bloody kiss and a cuddle when we fell this pillock."

"Right, sir." Kit scanned the room before drawing his sword.

The figure started to form from sand in front of Guy again. He waited until he could no longer see the darting flames through its clothes, but as he swung his sword, a ferocious gust blew out his sword's flame, and it bounced off the creature's limb as if it were stone.

"We've got a problem," Guy called.

The demon raised its hands, calling the wind to feed the fire, making the flames dance higher, spreading from the rear wall to lick at the ceiling, taking told, spreading further across it.

Bostock burst into the room with Guy. "Okay, Kit."

Bostock flung a flaming dagger.

Prepared for a strike, the demon had no time to call a gust to extinguish it. Instead, it dematerialised, the dagger flying through the cloud of swirling sand to hit the rear wall and knock a flaming plank to the floor.

Guy raced for the other bedroom. The creature shimmered in front of Kit.

Kit raised his sword, ready to swing.

"Wait!" called Guy.

"I've got this." Kit held his sword before the ever-solidifying creature. "Get the jewel."

Kit sidestepped and swung his sword, slicing through the top of the creature's arm.

With its other arm, it slashed out while screeching, pushing Kit back against the wall.

The creature's disembodied arm twitched. Its fingers closed around the gleaming, red stone.

Guy darted forward and turned his sword over, ready to bash the stone with the hilt. A rush of air passed him. Guy dived at the rock, smashing it with the butt of his sword, shattering it in two.

The aerial power's final gust rushed into the flame, and the fire fed on its last offering.

A fireball burst upwards. A beam cracked and fell.

"Kit, watch out!"

The beam above his best friend crashed down, pulling parts of the roof with it.

Heeding the warning, Kit dived to one side.

The beam smashed to the floor, cracking the weakened floorboards. Another crack came, and they gave way. The floorboards beneath Kit snapped. Panic spread across his face, but before he could shift his weight, they fell. He reached forward while falling, but only succeeded in bringing more floorboards down on top of him as he plummeted to the ground floor. The rear wall collapsed into where Kit had fallen, followed by part of the roof.

"No!" cried Guy. He turned for the steps, but as he reached the top, Iker appeared.

"We've got to help Kit!" Guy cried.

Iker continued up the stairs. "That's not why we're here."

"Who's this?" Bostock asked.

Iker smiled. "The Spanish Inquisition."

Bostock's face contorted, first showing confusion, then fear.

Once on the top step, Iker stretched, joints crackling. "You weren't expecting us?"

He pushed past Guy.

Guy made to go down the stairs, but more of Iker's men came up.

"Go back!" Guy called. "We have to help Kit."

Bostock's eyes were on the men climbing the stairs.

"Seize him," called Iker.

Bostock raised his hands, too heavily outnumbered to fight them off.

Two men still blocked the stairs. Guy turned the other way, heading back into the far bedroom. Flame continued to lick at the walls and much of the roof had collapsed. He sought a route to the ground floor, and this would suffice.

He turned back as Iker plunged his dagger into Bostock's chest. What aid could Guy offer the colonel, now? He jumped, instead seeking Kit. One leg landed on a pile of rock, the other on a piece of wood, which snapped with the force of his landing. His ankle rolled and a stabbing pain shot from his leg—not from his ankle, but from the piece of wood sticking out of his calf.

Stirring the kindling wood sparked the flames, making them rise once more.

Guy threw himself from the pyre, rolling on the floor to extinguish the flames and simultaneously wedging splitters of wood further into his flesh.

All around him were the bodies of fallen soldiers and defeated demons. He stood up and hopped past the stairs, making his slow way to the other side of the building, to the collapsed pile of stone and wood that hid his friend.

Fire rained from the ceiling as flaming thatch and bits of beam and floorboard fell from above. Guy dropped to his knees before the pile of debris; Kit lay somewhere among it and he couldn't leave him trapped there. But as he shifted his weight, a great groan came from beneath him. The questionable stability of the floor made Guy move with greater caution, though he dared not slow his attempts to rescue his friend.

Flame spread across the top of the largest beam, but one side had not taken. Guy placed his hands against it and pushed. Immense heat radiated from the wood, sapping the strength out of his arms. His ankle didn't have the strength to support his weight, affecting his pushing strength.

"Do you require some assistance?"

Iker's voice sent a shiver down Guy's spine.

"Help!" Guy cried, gulping at the air. As much as he despised Iker, he needed him.

"Go on!" Iker yelled over the sound of another crash. "Lift it as high as you can, and I'll clear some of the debris from beneath it."

Guy gritted his teeth and cried as he pushed all the strength of his body into lifting the beam and all the strength of his mind into ignoring the pain.

But Iker did nothing.

All that exertion and Iker moved not a jot to help.

Guy turned a fraction of an inch, ready to chastise Iker, as the leader of the Spanish Inquisition plunged a dagger into his back.

Chapter 22—In Which Guy Fawkes Recovers

Darkness surrounded Guy Fawkes. Whether he was sitting, standing, or lying, he couldn't tell. When he tried to shift his body, a strange sensation hit him. He expected pain. Why, he couldn't remember. Instead, nothingness overwhelmed him—he felt no movement in his joints or friction from whatever he moved on, no sensation of passing through the air. And yet, he was moving, closing slowly on a distant light.

Next, Guy felt cold, hard rock beneath his feet. He stretched out his hands and touched rock there, too. The light in front of him grew brighter still until he recognised his location: Saint Robert's Cave! But how? That was back in England. Many years ago, an anonymous rider had taken him there after fleeing the demons that destroyed his home and killed his uncle. Had someone done likewise to speed him from danger in Nieuwpoort?

He remembered waiting in Saint Robert's Cave until Kit had run in, bouncing with excitement after a night battling demons.

Thinking of Kit hurt. Again, Guy couldn't recall why.

He had to get to the altar where light shone from the true skull of Thomas Percy.

Movement caused pain, and movement achieved nothing. Guy made all the motions to move his legs, but they moved only downwards, the cold of the rock creeping further and further through his legs. He tried to reach out for stability, but that same cold spread deeper and deeper into his arms. With movement impossible, Guy recalled the ways Oswald had helped him to relax. He needed to focus. He drew in a breath, but his chest expanded with the cold of rock. Exhale, he told himself. Nothing. Exhale. Still nothing. If this continued much longer, he'd cease to exist.

For a moment, he did nothing, clearing every thought, every concern from his mind. He breathed once more. The solidity left his limbs. The altar grew closer, though he couldn't feel himself moving towards it.

On the altar, the eyes in that ever-present skull came alive.

While the mouth did not move, Guy heard Thomas Percy's voice. "Place your hands on me."

Such a simple command. Guy lifted both hands, but when he looked, his hands remained by his side. He turned his arms in a full circle. The movement in his shoulders felt right, but still, his hands remained stationary.

He closed his eyes and visualised wiggling his fingers. He pictured them on the skull, imagining the texture of the bone, but when he opened his eyes, his hands remained by his side.

The skull repeated the instruction.

Guy stared at one hand. He watched it as he put all his strength into working the muscles to move the hand. Guy closed his eyes and pictured energy flowing from the centre of his body into his arm. His fingers tingled.

Finally, pain came, not in his hands, but in the back of his head. As Guy continued to try to move his arm, the tingling spread to his hand, and the pain in the back of his head intensified. His hand darted out and came to rest on the skull. His head throbbed as if it were going to explode.

"Other hand," Percy called.

Guy repeated the process, fighting to switch off the pain. When the palm of his hand tingled, his brain pulsed, expanding, ready to leak out of his ears. Still, he continued to push himself until the second hand rose.

When Guy's fingers touched the skull, the pain in his head grew to a new intensity before a hook smashed into the back of his head and dragged down, pulling that pain into the centre of Guy's back, to the spot where Iker's knife had plunged in.

Guy gnashed his teeth together, and scratched at the skull, trying to dig his fingernails into the bone, so he could feel something other than pain.

"Why?" he cried.

The light faded. "Pain is better than the absence of everything."

The death of the light left Guy in darkness once more. For a long time, darkness alone kept pain company.

When Guy opened his eyes into the conscious world, confusion overwhelmed him. Pain remained, but more too: the tightness of bandages around his middle, the damp sweat in his hair, the weight of linen bedsheets. Had Guy ever slept in a bed so fine?

Guy took in the surrounding details. A fire burned in the hearth. He'd awoken in a large bedroom. His vision slowly improved to reveal a tapestry hanging on one wall.

He tried to shuffle into a sitting position. Pain struck him again, and his vision blurred, darkness threatening to take him back into its embrace.

A woman entered carrying a bowl and some cloth. Her wavy, chestnut-coloured hair hung at shoulder length, and when she saw Guy's open eyes, her mouth formed an O. She put the bowl on the mantelpiece and hurried to the door where she spoke in a language Guy didn't understand. It sounded like Dutch, a language of which he had only the most basic knowledge.

The woman returned.

"Where am I?" Guy croaked. Talking pained his throat.

She held a finger to her lips, and left the room again, returning a second later with water. She held the cup to Guy's lips, and he leant forward ever so slightly to drink.

"Thank you," Guy muttered, his throat a little soothed.

Again, she held a finger to her lips. She fetched the bowl and took a sponge from it with which she mopped Guy's brow. The cool water eased Guy's pain.

The woman took the cloth now. Guy understood she meant to change his bandages.

"Lucia!" someone called from the corridor.

Guy recognised the voice even if he didn't recognise the name. The voice could only call from the depths of his mind, words coming from a distant age, calling him back to the world of his dreams once more.

The woman hurried out of the door. Did that make her Lucia? If so, did that make the impossible voice real?

Kit Wright stormed into the room. "You're awake!"

Guy's heart raced, and he couldn't stop his body from shaking, despite the pain it caused as he sobbed. "You're alive?"

Kit sat by Guy's bed. "You too, which is the bigger shock."

"How? What happened?"

"I'll tell you the quick version. Lucia wants to change your dressing."

"Who's Lucia? Where are we?"

Kit couldn't keep still, his head turning from Guy to the door, and when he looked at Guy, his eyes flitted between his face and his torso. "You're asking questions that come at the end of the story. You're supposed to be resting, so lay back and be quiet for a moment."

Guy leant back on the bed and waited for Kit to regale him.

"Before the day you arrived in Nieuwpoort, we'd been hacking at the edges of the town, shrinking the infected area. It's funny how you turned up after we'd finished the bulk of the work." Kit smiled. "In the first few houses, we came across more of those plague demons. The way they shuffle about, they're no real threat unless they trap you somewhere. Anyway, we cleared a couple of houses full of them..."

Guy smirked, and Kit stopped speaking.

"What's that smile for?"

"You still tell stories like you're ten years old, and everything is the most exciting event to ever happen in the whole world."

"Is there any better way to tell a story?"

"I don't believe there is. Please, continue."

"Anyway, we cleared a couple of houses of them, and in the next one, there's this hulking demon."

Kit held his arms out and beat his chest, mimicking the demon. "The others hadn't dealt with anything like this, so they sent me against the beast. It had a head a bit like a horse's—the eyes on the side of the head and a long face. We were fighting for a bit. Sometimes I had the upper hand; sometimes, he did. I got a good whack in, left it spraying out demon blood, but it swiped out with a hoof in revenge and knocked me onto the ground. Then it spun its hands and opened a hell-gate, and you won't believe what came out."

"What was it?"

"You know those half-horse, half-men creatures?"

"Centaurs?"

"Aye, one of them, but the other way around."

"What, a horse's head on a..."

"On a man's body. Only a full-sized horse head was too heavy for a small man's body to take, and it fell over. I stared at it, bemused, and the demon did too. I don't think he meant to summon that."

Guy pictured the ridiculous creature. "I don't imagine he did."

"This shout comes from someone in the back room. It's only a bloody demon master and his familiar. They'd backed themselves into a corner. While the demon continued to stare at the abomination that had come through the hell-gate, I threw a knife at the familiar, and the demon," Kit spread the fingers of one hand, "gone."

"And the demon master?"

"Some men ran in to take the glory, banging on about the Spanish Inquisition, and they killed the demon master, didn't even question him."

"Sounds familiar."

"Then comes the bit you know. I ran into the house. You and Bostock were playing hide and seek with that disappearing-reappearing sand demon, and you needed me to sort it out for you."

"Aye, we did. Get to the next part. I saw you fall through the floor and the roof collapsed on you."

"When the floor collapsed, I kept going. I hit the ground, it cracked beneath me, and I fell again, into the basement."

Guy tried to sit forward but found himself forced to cough.

Kit offered water.

Guy took a sip. "A basement?"

"Aye, luckily. I hit the floor, landed awkwardly on my ankle. My leg felt like it had exploded. Next, more debris dropped through with me rolling on the floor in agony. It blocked the hole above me."

Guy shook his head as far as he dared. "I tried shifting that beam, got a knife in my back for my efforts, and you weren't even trapped under it?"

"Well, I was under it. A whole 'nother floor under it."

"Did you have any idea what was going on above?"

"Not at the time. The basement stairs were at the opposite end of the building. The ceiling glowed red with fire, and I had to dodge flaming chunks of wood. With my ankle done in, I wasn't moving at much of a pace. I climbed the stairs and emerged in that back storeroom. I tried the door, but I couldn't shift it. I smashed a window and got out that way."

"Why did you come back?"

"Looking for you. They dragged Bostock out, letting his blood run all over the square. I didn't want to mess with them again, and as you weren't with them, I assumed you were still inside. They took off, beckoning all the soldiers they'd located to go with them. When I crept back in, you were lying on the floor, a knife sticking out of your back, and fire all around you. The second I stepped inside, the floor creaked. If I weren't careful, I'd end up back in the basement, and there wouldn't be any getting out the second time."

"But you were careful."

"How do you know?"

"I'm here, aren't I?"

"Right, so I'll skip the part where I heroically plucked you from the flames, ignoring the immense pain of my busted ankle as fire rained from above and the floor gave out beneath me. I'll leave out the death-defying leaps I made from one flaming floorboard to another to grab you—and your damned sword—and rescue you from the building, shall I?"

Guy struggled to hold back a smile. "Aye, that bit sounds boring. Skip right by it."

Kit's eyes narrowed. "So Nieuwpoort was deserted. Those that were left were with that Spanish Inquisition lot, so I headed for the beach. I slung you in a rowboat and rowed to the next town over."

"Is that where we are now?"

"No, we've moved on since. This place belongs to the family of Bostock's wife. Lucia, who's been looking after you, is his niece."

"How long have I been under?"

"You've been coming and going for weeks. You wouldn't live if they pulled the blade out wrong, and you wouldn't live if they left it in. It's a bloody miracle what these medical men can do these days."

Pain burned in Guy's back. He arched it slightly.

Worry lines aged Kit's face. "Is there anything I can do to help?"

"It sounds like you've done enough." Guy turned to study Kit. "And you? Is your ankle healed? No lasting damage?"

"It's okay. Listen, I should let Lucia check your bandages."

Guy waited until Kit left before he attempted to wiggle his fingers and toes. Something told him he was lucky to be able to do so.

Chapter 23—In Which Guy Fawkes Says Goodbye to Kit and Answers the Inevitable Call

Recovery came slowly. Guy had no comprehension of how his body worked—or didn't, in some cases. He had no idea that turning at the last second because of his mistrust of Iker saved him from death. The blade had missed Guy's spine, but as his body healed, the nearby scar tissue compressed his spinal cord, causing a variety of motor issues. The strength of Guy's grip in his sword arm had diminished, and he walked at a slower pace.

Lucia remained by his side, and the more time they spent together, the greater the affection grew between them. She was five years younger than him. She'd never travelled so far as five miles from the radius of her house, so she found Guy's accounts of raging seas, mighty mountains, and thick, verdant forests fascinating. Guy enjoyed teaching her words in English, and she laughed at his struggles to shape his mouth right to pronounce words in Dutch. While Guy felt not the all-consuming passion and overwhelming love he had for Maria, he experienced a great deal of contentment when by her side.

Kit remained close. He re-joined Sir Henry and visited Guy to regale him with tales of assaults against waves of demons whenever he could. He shared news of how his allies had destroyed the great cathedral using the exact plan Guy had suggested somewhere near Dunkirk. Samra continued to send communications to Eindhoven, which Kit brought to read to Guy. Samra's chase for Zidan had ended in failure in some ways, for he'd lost all trace of the Children of Mizraim, but success in others, for the land had been purged of the plague. Sometimes, Kit came with news from England. When he arrived in the Spring of 1603, he brought news of drastic importance: Queen Elizabeth was dead, and the crown of England had united with that of Scotland, the kingdom ruled by James I.

Spending so long in bed had given Guy time to read James I's treatise on witchcraft, *Daemonologie*. This gave Guy great faith that the new king could cleanse England of demons. But the dream of a union with Spain, a joint effort to rid the land of demons, became less likely as a result of the demonic fingers grasping control in Madrid. Sir Henry's spies in the Spanish court, reported Fernando's dark influence over King Philip III and his control and misuse of Iker's wing of the Spanish Inquisition.

That spring day had brought a backwards step for Guy, his grip failing when practising with his sword. He'd have to fight with his left, but to stop using his right hand felt like a betrayal. How does one give up on a part of their body?

When Kit arrived, it brought Guy pleasure.

They sat in the garden under the shadow of a blossoming apple tree.

Kit told a grand tale of fighting demons on the River Seine before jumping to a letter from Jack with news of another plague outbreak in England. While Kit's stories often leapt around, on this occasion their jumbled nature indicated Kit's troubled disposition.

"Kit, tell me what's upsetting you."

Kit stood, wiped his hands on his hose, and sat again. "Things aren't going so well in Madrid." Kit pulled a rune from his pouch. He checked it and handed it to Guy. "Remember when you asked me about these? One of our first conversations at Saint Peter's."

Guy took the rune, once more enjoying the weight of it in his hand, and its smooth texture. "Kit, what's happening in Madrid?"

"King Philip III is not in control of the city."

"Kit..."

"Fernando's pulling the strings."

"Kit..."

"And he's sending Iker to do all these things, which are a clear abuse of power."

"Kit..."

"Sir Henry has his spy reporting all of this back."

"Kit, tell me something I don't know."

"That spy needs an ally." Kit stared at the floor. "Sir Henry wants that ally to be me." Kit stood again and wiped his hands once more.

"I will come with you!" Guy said, reaching out to touch Kit's arm.

Kit stared at Guy's sword, propped against the table.

"I have been practising with my left hand." Guy swallowed hard, but the lie wouldn't pass. He knew he couldn't accompany Kit, but could he allow Kit to put himself at risk like that? "Are you not worried that Fernando will recognise you?"

"Many years have passed since we sat at the same table. And I'm cutting my hair short. Different style of beard. I'll have a low role, so we'll never be in the same room."

"That's such a risk, Kit! I wish I could go with you."

Kit sat again. "Guy, nothing thrills me more than when we fight side-by-side. I long for a day when we can stand together once more, but..."

Guy thought of Kit's rune with the two wavy lines. "I'm too weak." Guy kicked out, knocking his sword to the floor.

"Half of Guy Fawkes is still worth a hundred witches. It's not even that. People don't consider me smart. People say I act first and think later, if at all, but I notice things."

Guy looked his friend in the eye. "Kit, no one says that about you."

"They wouldn't dare! But they believe it."

Guy shook his head. "No."

"It's not the point, here. I see the way Lucia looks at you. I notice the way you stare at her. Is there a chance for you to be happy?"

It would be a lie to say that Guy had not considered staying put. He had grown comfortable in his time with Lucia, and making the arrangement more lasting had crossed his mind. It wasn't the same vision as the one he'd lived with Maria—how could he to replicate those feelings when it brought too much pain to even try? For once, though, Guy saw himself sitting across a table from Lucia, holding her, sharing a life.

"You might be right, Kit."

"I hope I am. I've never felt that way. I've never had the desire to settle down or to have a family."

"You will one day."

Kit sucked in a breath between his teeth. "No, Guy, I don't think I will. I don't hold any desire for it. Affection like that doesn't exist in me. I don't picture myself walking through golden fields hand in hand with anyone."

A twinge of guilt hit Guy for having had that vision of himself with Lucia.

"What is it you desire?"

Kit gazed at the sky. "The thrill of the adventure. But it's always better when you're by my side. Those are the moments I've treasured. Those are the moments I will treasure again."

"If you need me, Kit, for anything, get word to me. If you need me, I'll come for you."

Both men stood, Guy hiding his struggle to step toward Kit.

"I know you will," Kit said as they embraced.

Time passed. The affection Guy held for Lucia only bloomed once Kit gave him permission to live that life. He made his feelings clear to Lucia, and she too had grown fond of him. Her desire to help Guy recover developed from looking after his physical recovery to sharing a mutual mental stimulation. Unlike every member of her family, Guy did not protect her from the horrors of the world. He shared news from the rest of Europe, and even though she rarely left the house, her world became so much larger.

Kit's duty involved writing to Sir Henry, and Sir Henry made it his business to visit Guy to keep him up to date. In the Spring of 1604, one of Sir Henry's visits brought an end to Guy's peace.

"The quiet life is serving you well, Fawkes," Sir Henry said when he joined Guy, sitting out in the garden overlooking the rolling hills.

"It's not a bad life." Guy hardly dared say how much he enjoyed the tranquillity of his life with Lucia in case he jinxed it. Perhaps he always understood the fleeting nature of his contentment.

"I've had word from Jack Wright."

As much as Guy loved to hear from his friend, these moments were always difficult. Sir Henry left a gap between announcing who he'd heard from and the content of their message. This gap allowed Guy to run through the whole gamut of hideous possibilities: imprisonment, dismemberment, betrayal.

"Things have taken a turn in England."

All hope was fleeting, not only his but that of his nation, too.

"The boy King has proved false. Talk of ridding the country of witches is code for ridding the country of his enemies. Jack has had to put additional measures in place to keep the Jesuits safe. That tome of his, *Daemonologie*, is corrupting the minds of folk nationwide. It's turning neighbour on neighbour, with cheers ringing out every time some poor healer dances with the noose."

Guy took a moment to digest the news before responding. "Do you suspect there has been a change of heart, or has his talk of demons always been false?"

Henry waved his hand dismissively. "There are stories that he relies on your old friend, Robert Cecil. The Queen's Secretary of State and Spymaster has the same position for the new king."

Memories of Cecil burned Guy's mind. "Aye, and Cecil has the taint of devilry all over him."

"Worse still, there are rumours of a peace pact between England and Spain. With the rulers of England and Spain manipulated by demon-loving malcontents, it doesn't bode well for either country."

"What says Kit of events in Madrid?" Guy asked.

Sir Henry sighed. "Now, Kit Wright, I've not heard from."

More severe possibilities passed through Guy's mind: torture, possession, death.

"It could be nothing more serious than the courier being delayed on route. He may have been too slow to turn back on the road when coming upon a plagued town and placed in quarantine, but truth is, that communication is already a week later than expected."

Guy's mouth filled with saliva. He swallowed hard. "I will go to Madrid."

"You're not the soldier you were, Guy. Even the journey would ruin you."

Guy felt a twinge in the centre of his back. "I made a promise."

"I've lived too many years to waste my words trying to persuade a determined man against his decision. Me calling you a fool won't do no good either, but you're a damned fool, all the same."

Guy knew he needed to speak to Lucia, but he sought guidance elsewhere first.

Once he'd seen Henry off, he returned to his chair in the garden and closed his eyes. The restless dead murmured, as always. He imagined the sound of church bells that intensified those voices, and he pictured Thomas Percy's floating skull. He imagined the feel of the bone, the sound of his voice, and then, the old rebel manifested before him.

"I know what you're going to say, but I need you to tell me all the same," Guy said.

The glow around Thomas Percy's skull intensified. He swooped down and circled Guy, but spoke not.

"You have no wisdom for me?" Guy asked.

Fire burned in Percy's eyes. "You have all the knowledge you need."

Guy gazed at his shoes. "My destiny is not to remain here."

Percy moved closer to Guy. "You have, I fear, other ideas?"

Guy winced. "If I ignored the call, if I stayed here, with Lucia, for how long could we stay out of it all?"

Percy swung from side to side. "I know on which path you must eventually travel, but I cannot forecast for how long you can avoid your fate."

"But eventually it would come for me, and Lucia would be consumed in the act."

"I cannot see the events that push you back on the path, but you know your history."

"If I leave, is there a chance for Lucia?"

Percy's head bobbed, the equivalent of a shrug, albeit a shoulderless shrug.

"You need not answer. If I stay, eventually, she'll suffer some kind of horror. That's a certainty. Then I leave, with hope that our time together has not already doomed her."

"You grow wise with age, Guy Fawkes. Until we speak again."

Percy disappeared, but Guy remained seated. He wanted to savour the view, the feel of a comfortable chair, and the warmth of an unjudgmental sun for but a few minutes more.

Clouds moving in front of the sun roused Guy. He stood and walked inside, casting one glance back at the view. He ambled through the house, letting his fingers linger on furniture, his eyes taking in details from the tapestries that might bring comfort in dark days.

After this walk, performed as a slow march towards the scaffold, Guy met with Lucia in the bedroom.

She read his face as he stood at the door. "My aunt told me life with a soldier caused constant worry: the next visitor could speed your love away."

Guy glanced at the floor. "I have a duty to my friend."

Lucia stood. "And no duty towards me?"

Guy remembered the horrors that had stolen his family when last he attempted to avoid his duty, when last he chose peace. He couldn't let Lucia suffer in the same way. "Lucia, my life over the last year has been a dream. Ever since I woke from that horrible, still darkness, and you entered to care for me, I've been in this fantasy land, born into a new world, a caul covering us, protecting us from the outside."

Lucia turned away from Guy and spoke in a low voice. "Then you let the outside in."

Guy moved round to face Lucia and took her hand. "I wish I could make you understand how much I hate leaving you."

"Then don't."

"I must." Guy released Lucia's hand. "I was always going to. That's the trouble with dreams. You have to wake up."

Lucia turned her back on Guy again, taking a step closer to the bed so he couldn't circle around her. "It was never the same for us. You woke into this world and thought you were dreaming. This has never been your reality. *It is mine.* I lived the same life every day, and Kit dragged you bloody and drooling to our door. My reality became something else. I made you drink when you were barely awake. My reality involved changing your bandages. My reality meant helping you get out of bed to walk again, and then, my reality became loving you. You opened my eyes to a different world. You talk about waking from a dream and having to leave to go back to your awful reality. Now I have to sleep and return to the nightmare of the void. A life of nothing. With no one." Lucia turned to face Guy. "Go on, Guy Fawkes." She slapped him, hard, on the face. "Take that to remember me by."

Guy had no words left. He'd earned the sting in his cheek. An apology would be only empty words, no weight, no matter. No action could show he meant it. A promise to return would also be pointless, the equivalent of resting his head in a fine bed once more, only knowing he had to climb out again. Another slap on the face would knock his head from his shoulders. Guy knew his fate. Since his earliest days he had known his path: a path that led to his doom.

Chapter 24—In Which Guy Fawkes Returns to Madrid

Guy Fawkes had often travelled great distances alone. As he made that long journey south, he couldn't help but recall some of those other journeys. That desperate trek to Durham when still pained by his injuries from defeating Master Leonard and Edwin Sandys in York Minster. That, too, had been to ride to catch up with Kit, but Kit had not welcomed his presence. A meandering journey had led south from Scotton to Oxford University and then on to Cowdray House when he sought a new life, carrying Walsingham's demon seed. Later, he'd journeyed from Cowdray House to Gillingham, avoiding the authorities as Queen Elizabeth wanted him to answer for the death of Catherine Stanley. At the dock, he'd found Kit waiting for him, and Kit had been beside him on many of his travels since.

The solo journey gave Guy time alone with his thoughts—the last thing he needed. Over the years, Guy had found ways of dealing with his inner demons when they tried to speak ill. At these times, he sought a place to rest. If he got his head down, he could at least attempt to converse with the spirit of Thomas Percy. The old rebel offered little new: speculation on the end of Guy's days in Europe, talk of a return to England to find a new purpose, but it stopped the self-accusations and the needling guilt. It stopped the longing for an impossible life with Lucia.

Guy arrived in Madrid unscathed. He took a room at an inn some distance from the palace. Sir Henry had given him the address where he would find Ricard, the spy that worked at the Royal Alcázar. There were several hours before that meeting. Guy changed out of the clothes that had seen him through the last part of his journey, peeling them off his sweat-drenched body. As he sat at the end of the bed, he examined himself. He twisted his arms and legs, analysing every stretch of exposed skin. His right arm had become thin, and the skin hung loose and wrinkled except parts blemished with scar tissue from various puncture wounds and scratches. Some practice with the sword in his left hand had maintained the bulk there, but burns scarred that arm. Similarly, his legs had their share of scars, a range of gashes, puncture wounds, and burns decorating them. Slashes covered his chest.

An ugly puncture on his shoulder puckered like an angry anus. Luckily, he couldn't see his back. A matching wound where the crossbow penetrated him would be there, and of course, close to the spine, he'd find Iker's mark. What more scars would his body gain before the end he felt creeping ever closer?

Guy lay on the bed, hoping for the restorative power of sleep, but some wounds, particularly those in his head, were too deep to heal.

Ricard's house lay in a part of Madrid where nobles rarely walked. Nonetheless, he moved with caution, walking among crowds, taking unusual routes, and staying in the shadows.

When he knocked on Ricard's door, however, he found the gentleman to use not a hint of caution, welcoming Guy in and asking him to sit before Guy even introduced himself.

Ricard was in his late twenties and had long, blonde hair and a tiny beard. "What can I do for you, friend?" Ricard spoke in Spanish.

Guy responded in his own language, knowing Ricard spoke fluent English from his conversation with Sir Henry. "You have surprisingly little caution given some of your contacts."

"He who opens his door with caution appears suspicious to everyone on the street. Have I a reason for caution with you?"

"I come from Eindhoven." Guy remained guarded in his speech, naming Sir Henry's home town rather than giving away the name.

"From Sir Henry, I'll wager?"

Guy smiled. Ricard intended to remain direct in his responses. "What know you of Kit Wright?"

"Did Sir Henry send you to replace him?"

While Ricard's question was again plain, a tower of unanswered questions lay stacked against it, the weightiest one, what had happened to Kit that meant he needed replacing. Guy, too, took the direct approach: "What happened to Kit?"

Ricard sighed. "In the dungeon at the mercy of the Spanish Inquisition."

"What happened?"

"Accused of spying when loitering in the King's court too long. News of the London Treaty must have intrigued him."

Guy rubbed the back of his neck. "What's this London Treaty?"

"I imagine you crossed paths with my messenger travelling to inform Sir Henry. A party from England are here to sign a peace agreement."

"From England? Led by whom?"

"Robert Cecil."

Hearing the name sent a shudder along Guy's spine.

"Would you like a drink?" Ricard said, rising from his chair. "You look pale."

Guy rubbed his temple. "I wasn't expecting to find myself in the company as one so odious as he."

"You couldn't have chosen a worse time to be in Madrid."

"And yet here I am. My most pressing matter is how to get to Kit." Guy remembered his first visit to the Royal Alcázar, with the soldiers on horseback and those wielding muskets. They retreated beyond a portcullis, beyond which lay the courtyard open to the mercy of the archers.

"While it is a bad time to be in Madrid, the Alcázar will be busy. They will guard the entrance, but inside they will be too occupied to pay much heed to another person."

"Aye, the problem lies in getting access. I can get myself slung into the prison, but from experience, there's little I can do once I'm locked in there. Will this peace treaty be celebrated with some kind of banquet?"

"Indeed, but the palace guards know all who bring them supplies. As much as the sun has coloured your face, they'll know you're no Spaniard."

"Is there another way in?"

"All palaces have escape routes. King Philip II built the Royal Alcázar to withstand a siege, but it would be foolhardy to rely on that alone. Did you ever meet the former king?"

"Aye."

"He was no fool. There is a secret passage from the royal bedroom that leads to the basement of the Church of Saints Justus and Pastor."

Ricard shared his knowledge of the secret passage that led to the Royal Alcázar, including the best route through to the dungeon, and which members of staff were trustworthy. Soon, the conversation led to those of importance in the Alcázar.

"Is Juan de Velasco still a frequent visitor?"

Ricard nodded. "Yes. He is there at the moment, integral to the peace negotiations."

"Do you consider him a good man?"

Ricard gritted his teeth. "Good is," he paused, "difficult to define. I think he is honest. His desire for peace is true."

"I don't wish to offend you by asking of your king."

Ricard closed his eyes and his mouth tightened.

Guy sighed. "So, you too believe he is under the control of Fernando."

"One day, I hope we can see our king truly rule. Now he is confined to his chair with that man whispering in his ear."

"Is a woman still present, Sofia?"

"Fernando's wife?"

Guy's heart sunk to hear she still had influence at the Alcázar. "What do you make of her?"

"Let's say she and Fernando are a good match, and when I say good..." Ricard let the thought trail off before changing subject and offering Guy sustenance.

After a fine meal, darkness fell. Equipped with leftovers and a skin of wine, Guy made for the church for evening mass. A strong congregation of eager worshippers flocked inside. The priest, an older man with a wisp of white hair on the top of his head gave his sermon with enthusiasm. He closed his eyes as if to better communicate with his Lord and Saviour, which made Guy feel less guilty about slipping from the pew and edging into the shadows of the semi-transept. The service lasted an age. Without seeing the priest, Guy found following the service difficult. While Guy had learned a great deal of Spanish, ecclesiastical language in another tongue remained unfathomable.

When the service ended, Guy pushed himself farther into a corner. The shadows hid him if anyone glanced into that part of the building. After the congregation left, the priest extinguished the lamps and silence fell on the building.

Guy waited a little longer, beyond the time the priest closed the door as he left. Staying away from the windows, he ventured into the basement. There, he dared not light his lamp in case the glow caused anyone to investigate. Given that he would have to remain in the tunnel overnight (unless he wanted to spring into the King's bedchamber while the king slept), Guy took his time to identify the location of the secret door. Ricard's instructions had been vague, for he had not been into the church basement to verify it.

As Guy crept around the basement, vermin squealed. He appreciated the company. Ricard had told him to head down the stairs and turn to the left to find the passage hidden on the west wall—which made perfect sense as the Royal Alcázar lay a short distance to the west of the church. There Guy sought a bookcase, the bottom half of which hid a passage.

Guy stumbled, arms stretching in front of him. The grit of a place long abandoned for anything other than dumping relics in—a place where more goes in than ever comes out—crunched beneath his feet. His toe stubbed a box, but his slow pace meant it caused no pain. He diverted around the box and continued for the wall. Sure enough, he located the heavily laden bookcase. These were not fake books attached to a mechanism. The tunnel hid behind the bookcase, with the bottom panel removable. If one were escaping the Royal Alcázar, they would reach the end of the tunnel, slide the loose panel to one side, and push all the books forward so they could shuffle out.

Guy wished to leave no sign of entry to the passage, which took greater care. He removed the books, leaving them where he could pull them back into place from inside the tunnel. He slid the rear panel to the side and dropped into the tunnel with a splash. In places, the water came an inch up his boots. Finding a place to rest for the night without getting soaked would prove a problem. First, he grabbed the books and replaced them on the shelf. No one would study them so closely to know they weren't in the same spot. Next, he slid the panel back into place. He made his way along the tunnel, counting his steps. He had no desire to be too close to the palace until morning. An unusual sound might send someone scurrying into the secret passage after him. But by Guy's calculations, he had reached a point somewhere beneath a street, somewhere no one would listen for him.

Drier ground meant he could sit and rest, and when sleep refused to come, Thomas Percy's company stopped his mind from wandering into dangerous territory.

Chapter 25—In Which Guy Fawkes Infiltrates the Royal Alcázar of Madrid

After several hours of waiting in the dark, walking back and forth and flexing his muscles to avoid cramp, Guy set off again for the King's bedchamber. He knew this escapade would be brief indeed if he had timed it incorrectly. While he didn't doubt that he could fight off King Philip III if he remained in the state he had been when he last saw him, the knock-on effects of regicide would make it impossible to reach Kit.

Ricard promised to do his utmost to make sure the King's maids would not go to the bedchamber too early, but it was near impossible to try to coordinate times. More than anything, he depended on dumb luck. At the end of the passage, several steps led up. At the top of the steps, a solid piece of wood separated Guy from the king's bedroom. Guy explored it for a catch with his fingers. He found it embedded into the wall, stiff after having not been used for so long. Guy wedged his sword into the gap, lifted the catch, and the piece of wood shifted. Whatever lay on the other side felt bulker than expected, for it ground against the tiled floor, scrapping with every inch that Guy shoved it. If anyone occupied the rooms nearby, surely, they'd investigate the strange noise.

Guy gave it another shove, continuing to push as the scrapping noise grew louder until he'd forced a gap wide enough to squeeze through. He paused. No one came running in to investigate. From the other side, he lifted the fake door, hidden within a bookcase like its twin in the church, back into place. The scuff marks on the floor would indicate someone had opened it and arouse suspicion, but with a bit of good fortune, no one would have reason to come into the King's bedchamber until nightfall, and by that time Guy planned to be some distance from Madrid.

While Guy had been a frequent visitor to the Alcázar during the latter years of King Philip II's reign, he'd never been in this part of the building, far beyond the throne room, and about as far away from the dungeon as possible. Ricard had advised that the palace would be busy as result of the visiting dignitaries and the importance of the documents to be signed, but there would be no need for those visitors, especially those looking dishevelled after spending the night in a dank tunnel, to be in this part of the building. This meant it should be possible to move away from the King's bedroom without encountering anyone else, but it magnified the consequences should he run into someone. They'd ask questions for which Guy would have no sufficient answer other than his sword. He reached for his weapon, but grasped nothing, before remembering he wore the sheath on the other side. It would be better if he saw no one at all.

He headed for the door and listened. The absence of footsteps or voices gave him the confidence to open the door. A long corridor ran along the south side of the palace, with multiple doors on either side. What chance had Guy of avoiding detection if someone were to walk the other way? Halfway along the corridor a staircase rose to the upper floor. From there came voices, a familiar English one among them. A second later, he came into view. Sneering as he issued orders to his servants, Robert Cecil, King James's Secretary of State and Spymaster, took the steps hunched further forward than Guy had ever seen him before.

Guy backtracked to the King's bedchamber. Ricard had told him of another way, one he should only use if desperate, for it could have dire consequences for the lowest members of the palace society—the staff. But the King's chamber had a door to the servants' passages so they could deliver food from the kitchens and deliver other such supplies around the castle without disturbing their masters.

So dependent were many of the staff on the King's coin, that they would sell Guy out sooner than listen to his reasons for being there, and the maids were among the most desperate. The kitchen staff, if Guy were to make his way there, though, were supposed to be an absolute delight, always smiling despite the demands of their masters.

If Guy followed the passage to bypass the long corridor, that would be sufficient. From there he would be in familiar territory, and he knew some of the shady corners, some places to avoid, some places where he'd come face to face with a musket if he wasn't careful.

At the end of the servant's corridor, it split in two, a path leading back out into the main corridor, and another path taking him towards the kitchen. He didn't need to find the kitchen, though. A servant approached from that direction, marching with purpose but staring at the floor. Guy listened at the door. Only when certain no one loitered in the corridor, did he make his way out. Some way ahead, Cecil's party disappeared around the corner.

Guy had little choice but to follow. They headed off towards the throne room, and Guy took the corridor in the opposite direction, leading toward the courtyard. From another corridor that bisected the passage another face familiar to Guy approached, Juan de Velasco, King Philip's advisor on foreign affairs. The closer Guy got to the heart of the Alcázar, the easier it became to blend in. Men delivering goods, no doubt for a banquet to celebrate the peace agreement, wandered back and forth. The guards at the gate would have searched and questioned each on entry, but as Ricard suggested, once inside, they moved about freely between the banqueting hall and the court-yard, where boxes, crates, and sacks lay piled on top of each other.

Guy fell into step behind a couple of Spaniards as they hurried back to the courtyard to collect another box. From there, he moved to the side, close to where a beautiful array of flowers had been delivered. When he sensed the eyes of guards upon him, he shifted a box from one place to another and their attention waned.

On the other side of the courtyard, leading into the tower, a guard sat outside the cell Guy and Kit had once spent a night in. Beyond him, the steps led into the dungeon. Guy spotted an unattended wooden crate and grabbed it.

From inside came a trill and the sound of ruffling feathers. Guy shifted the box away from his body and resisted the temptation to replace it. Such movements would rouse suspicion.

As he headed toward the tower, a familiar woman entered the courtyard. Guy stopped as Sofia approached the flowers, bending over them to take in their scent. She closed her eyes to focus her senses, but their scent failed to shift the shape of her face from a frown. When she opened her eyes, they were almost entirely black, nothing other than the pupils visible, no other colour, no sign of human life. She took a bunch of flowers and walked out of the courtyard, back toward the banqueting hall with not a jot of urgency. Was she, too, under Fernando's influence? She'd spoken with such passion about God's miracle in Cordoba. Had Iker's intervention with his Spanish Inquisition broken her, too? An unwelcome wave of pity washed over Guy.

Still, he didn't have time to empathise for long. Loiterers looked suspicious. He strode towards the guard, holding the box close to his chest, running imaginary conversations through his head, testing his knowledge of Spanish.

The guard by the stairs raised his head as Guy neared. He looked like he'd had a busy morning. At least a half dozen people, many bringing goods for the banquet, stood, sat, or lay in the cell, some arguing with each other, some calling for his attention.

"Where are you going?"

Guy held the box towards the guard. "For the gaoler."

"What's inside?"

Guy shuffled the box to bear the weight on his left arm, and prised off the lid. The trilling came again as Guy gazed at five quails.

"What does he want with them? Or don't I want to know?" The guard grinned, showing blackened teeth.

From within the cell, another argument started, one man pushing another against the bars.

"Oi!" called the guard. He hopped off his seat, indicating the stairs to Guy as he turned his attention to his prisoners.

Guy took the stairs, readjusting the box to balance it better. He didn't know how concerned he should be that the guard hadn't probed further about the quails. Exactly what went on down there?

Chapter 26—In Which Guy Fawkes Seeks Kit in the Dungeons

At the bottom of the stairs, the area opened up, with several cells visible. Guy recalled his previous visit with Fernando, when he'd met Iker Delgado for the first time. The head of this branch of the Spanish Inquisition had been carrying out some hideous torture in the far room. Kit had to be there somewhere, and Guy suspected the far room the most likely location. A nagging doubt gnawed at the back of his head: *if he's still alive.*

Guy glanced into the nearest cell. The withered man inside suggested they didn't give the prisoners the release of death without significant trauma first. That gave him some hope for Kit.

The dungeon had only one exit (unless it, too, had a secret escape), so if he let no one pass, they couldn't report his presence. The danger came from someone else entering the dungeon.

If the gaoler were present, he'd have keys. He'd take them, free Kit, and then things could become difficult. With all the activity above, though, there had to be a way out of the palace. He'd figure that out when the time came.

He placed the crate on the floor. In a moment of inspiration or folly, he took off the lid and placed the box on its side. Freed quails trilled and strutted along the damp, stone floor, heads bobbing.

The withered man in the nearest cell muttered something, but he couldn't lift his frail frame from his bed.

Guy moved to the wall on the right, hiding in the shadows.

It didn't take long for other prisoners to spot the quails, some reacting with shocked gasps, others getting up, trying to beckon the birds into their cells. One man screamed.

It had the desired effect. Voices called out. As far as Guy could tell, there were at least two people of authority present. Heavy footsteps on the stone indicated one coming his way.

From deeper in the dungeon came an annoyed rasp, the footsteps growing in pace. Wings flapped and the quails' noise increased. The man must have spotted the box, for he hurried towards it. Guy waited with sword drawn, holding it in his uncomfortable left hand. The angle of the strike differed, which required a surprising amount of thought after years of letting his instincts dictate his movements.

The man crouched over the box. Not trusting himself to make an instant, killing blow, Guy kicked him. The man toppled onto his side and rolled onto his back.

Guy jabbed the point of the blade into the man's throat. Holding the hilt with both hands, he pushed down before the man could protest.

The withered man in the cell continued to stare. After a renewed effort, he clambered from his bed, dragging himself onto the floor with his hands and crawled along to the bars. He wore only rags to cover his genitals. He had so little muscle that each distinct rib stood out. The skin on his face hugged the bone. He'd seen more flesh on heads on spikes, back in York as a child, even after the crows had struck. But his eyes retained a glimmer of hope.

Guy approached the cell. "Gonzalo?"

Gonzalo's lips crept up at the corners, movement threatening to tear his paper-thin skin. "Guido Fawkes," he said in a frail voice barely distinguishable from his raspy breath.

"Is Kit here?" Guy asked.

"Kit Wright." Gonzalo pulled himself into a standing position.

"Yes, is he here?"

"Guido Fawkes and Kit Wright. Saviours of Cordoba."

Gonzalo's mind was too far gone to separate the past from the present. "I'll get you out," Guy said. He turned his attention back to the rest of the dungeon.

Guy checked the body of the man on the floor. He had no keys—more likely a lackey than the gaoler. How long before someone came after him?

Guy glanced along the corridor, then back at the body on the floor. The dark corridor hid many sins. With the lackey being of Guy's size, Guy could walk along the corridor, and the gaoler wouldn't question his presence, not until he got close. As he walked, Guy noted the quails gathered in a spot against the wall, pecking at something spilled there.

Guy glanced into each cell but saw no sign of Kit. The gaoler had his back to him, leaning against the wall, poking something with his foot. The agitated trill of a quail gave away his activity.

The gaoler turned and spoke in Spanish, something Guy roughly translated as why on earth are there quails here, though it may have contained some choice profanity that Guy had not experienced in his time in Spain. When he realised the approaching man was not his servant, the gaoler's face from annoyance to anger to fear.

Guy swung with his sword, but the gaoler dodged the blow. He barged into Guy, knocking him into the wall. The gaoler grabbed the nearest weapon available, a length of chain. He swung it at Guy, who twisted away. The chain caught his side and stopped him from swinging his sword in attack. Guy stepped forward, placing his foot on the end of the chain. The gaoler moved to swing with it again, not realising Guy's foot pinned its end, and before he could react, Guy butted him in the side of the head with his sword. The gaoler's legs buckled beneath him, and he collapsed to the floor. Guy finished him in the same manner as he'd ended the life of the gaoler's assistant.

Guy plucked the bunch of keys from the gaoler's belt.

There were several doors at the far end of the dungeon opposite the last of the cells. Guy checked these cells first. A couple at the end were empty. Perhaps the prisoners there were being held in the rooms. Guy had to hope they kept Kit in one of them—the alternative unbearable to consider.

He listened at the first door. No sound came from within. He tried the door, but it rattled against the lock. He tried a few keys, eventually finding one click. Inside he found a metal chair with spikes on the seat and armrest. The dark stains on the floor indicated its frequent use. From the next room, came the distinct sound of a voice.

Guy listened at the wall. Aye, someone questioning another within. He could only hear one voice, a familiar, grating voice. The prisoner (assuming the torturer spoke to one other than himself) spoke not.

Guy moved to the door and listened again. Still, only the solitary voice threatening greater violence. Guy yanked the door open. A larger room than that with the chair in it, a lantern burnt on the wall, revealing two figures familiar to Guy. Kit sat in the chair, his face racked by pain. Even from the back, Guy recognised the other man. Iker had come so close to killing him, and now the opportunity for revenge presented itself. Guy pressed his sword to his back.

"I could do as you did to me," Guy said.

Kit peered up and opened his mouth in shock. A string of bloody drool slopped out.

"But I'll not be so cowardly as to stab you in the back."

Iker turned, eyes blazing after being disturbed during his favourite activity.

Guy glanced at the array of implements on the table and the blood on them.

"You're a fool to not take the opportunity to finish me." Iker drew his sword. He stared at Guy. "Your stance has changed. You hold the sword in your left hand, now?"

"Aye, I could beat you with one hand tied behind my back."

Iker slashed downward. Guy twisted his sword to deflect the blow. He stepped back, but only to come under attack from another blow. Guy needed to reverse his thinking. Blocking Iker's blows only left him open to another attack. Guy took a step back. As Iker's lunge fell short, Guy leapt in with a blow. Iker deflected it and smirked.

"I thought, for a moment, this could be a challenge."

Guy slashed again, but Iker blocked it. He kicked out, knocking Guy off balance. He slashed forward again. Guy ducked out of the way.

Iker grinned. He held his arms out wide. "Come on, strike at me."

Guy noted the position of Kit in the chair and side-stepped.

Iker grinned. "Trying to find a better angle of attack?"

Guy glanced at Kit. The lantern reflected in his eyes. Kit nodded.

Guy lunged. Iker deflected the blow, took a step back, and stumbled on Kit's outstretched leg. Guy leapt forward again, striking harder. While Iker raised his sword in time to protect himself, his balance shifted further, and he collapsed to the ground, his sword bouncing from his grip.

Guy stood on Iker's sword arm and pointed his sword at Iker's throat. "The reason I didn't stab you in the back is because I want you to look vengeance in the eye. I want to see the moment when you realise providence has forsaken you."

Iker opened his mouth, but no words came.

"Aye, there it is." Guy plunged his sword into Iker's throat, leaving him gasping for air. He waited for the struggle to cease before he turned his attention to Kit.

"You came for me." Kit's voice emerged as a fragile whisper.

"Aye, I said I would."

Kit shook his head. "I told them nothing."

Guy undid the straps at Kit's wrists. That's when he noticed his hand. "What did they do to you?"

"Crushed my finger in that thing." Kit nodded to an implement on the table. "When I wouldn't tell them anything, they cut it off."

Guy took the skin of wine from his belt, offering Kit a drink.

Kit gulped at the liquid, letting some dribble down his chin. "Sorry. It's hard to drink now." Kit opened his mouth to show where they'd pulled some of his teeth out.

Guy glanced back down the corridor. "We've got to get out of here."

"But I've heard Cecil's coming."

"He's here."

Kit gazed at Guy, his eyes wide, full of hope. "We can't waste this chance. Take out him and Fernando while we're here."

"I don't know if you noticed, Kit, but I cannot fight like I once did."

Kit glanced at Iker's body. "We dealt with him together."

"Aye, now multiply him by a dozen, add guards with muskets, and archers in elevated positions and consider our chances."

Kit wheezed. "Come on, Guy. You remember our school days? Arithmetic was never my strong point."

Guy rubbed at his left shoulder, hoping to alleviate some of the post-fight tightness. "What I'm saying is we've no chance against this many."

"We can't let them get away with this, though." Kit's voice had a slight whistle as result of his missing teeth.

Guy shook his head. "We have to. If we get out of here, it'll be a miracle."

"So, drop back and strike again another day?"

Guy hugged Kit and let him go when he groaned in pain. "You don't change, do you? We drop back, and we go home. We return to England. That flame of hope we've kept in our sights for so long will extinguish the second they sign the agreement."

"So, they've not signed it yet?"

"It's imminent. We can't stop it. Our attention turns to getting out of here."

"How do you plan on doing that?"

Guy glanced at Iker's body. "I have an idea."

First, Guy stripped Iker and put on his red robe. Next, he searched the dungeon for suitable manacles and put Kit in them loose enough so he could slip out. Kit had already been dressed in a sanbenito, a white tunic painted with devils.

Next, Guy unlocked all the cells, making a request to the prisoners to remain where they were for a few minutes, warning them of the slaughter that awaited if they did not time their escape right. They had little chance of making it out of the Alcázar. But little chance or no chance, they'd not surrender.

Guy already had a set of manacles for Gonzalo when he opened his cell and another sanbenito.

"Guido Fawkes."

Kit smirked. "Not much of a disguise, then?"

"And Kit Wright. Saviours of Cordoba."

Whether or not Gonzalo had seen through the disguise, Guy could not tell. Perhaps his mind was too broken. He did, however, take a few panicked steps back upon sight of the red robe of the Spanish Inquisition.

"Guido Fawkes," his voice had raised in pitch as he panicked. "And Kit Wright: Saviours of Cordoba."

Guy moved closer to him. "Duke, it is us. We're here to help you."

"Duke," Gonzalo whispered. "Yes. That's me."

"Let us take you out of here."

Gonzalo's eyes narrowed. "Guido Fawkes?"

Guy put the manacles on Gonzalo, and, having to lift him up each step, they made their way out of the dungeon. Even Kit had to take it slow after his period suffering torture and malnutrition. How long had it been since the duke had last seen the light of day?

As they neared the top, a great hubbub came from below, the prisoner's patience for their freedom extinguished.

"Where are you going?" the guard asked. He'd restored order within the holding cell.

Guy pointed to the tunic, hoping the guard would recognise the clothing of a man condemned to death by flame.

The guard grumbled, but as the noise from below grew, that gained his attention. "What's happening down there?"

"Your gaoler's lost control."

The guard's attention turned to the step, and Guy manoeuvred his prisoners towards the gatehouse. To allow for deliveries the portcullis remained open, freedom only a few steps away.

A great cry came from behind then as the escaped prisoners reached the top of the stairs.

"Lockdown!" called the guard. "Prison break."

The guard at the portcullis moved over to the mechanism.

"If that closes, we're finished," Guy said, glancing one way, then the other, seeking a solution.

He hurried toward the exit, guiding Kit with one arm, Gonzalo with the other. Gonzalo stumbled, yelping as Guy steadied him.

A guard, hearing the yelp, pointed a musket in Gonzalo's face. He spoke in a gravelly voice, which took Guy longer to decipher. The closing portcullis held too much of his attention, but then, as the portcullis met the stone, the Spanish word for 'execution' came to Guy and he explained why he had the two prisoners.

The guard pointed the end of his musket at Gonzalo and then Kit. "Do you want me to save you the effort?"

Guy hunted his mind for the motto of the Inquisition, the phrase Iker said repeatedly to his comrades. No, it wouldn't come.

The guard indicated with his head. "Back to the cells."

Other fleeing prisoners drew his attention, and Guy turned Gonzalo and Kit around. The chaos of the escaped prisoners made people spread in all directions. Muskets fired causing smoke to swirl around the courtyard. The familiar whistle of an arrow flying through the air preceded the thump of an escaped prisoner's body hitting the marbled floor. Guy knew few other routes—via the King's bedchamber or Ricard had spoken of a route through the kitchens. He followed the crowds moving back across the courtyard, marching his prisoners before him, feigning authority. Another arrow flew, and a prisoner fell to the ground to Guy's left. He dragged Gonzalo, whose eyes fell on the dead prisoner, back into line, and they continued toward the banqueting hall.

Guy had dined there many years ago, when Spain still offered so much hope. The decoration hadn't changed either: the same patterned tapestries, the same weapons on the walls. Guy scanned the room. In all the confusion, no one looked his way. Behind him were a few weapons. He helped his prisoners slide off their manacles. He checked again, then removed the Egyptian khopesh and the Assyrian sickle swords, handing the smaller Egyptian weapon to Gonzalo, and the pair of swords to Kit.

"Keep these hidden; only use them if there is no other option."

A pair of guards entered the banqueting hall. Their stance demanded silence. They issued an order. "Remain here. We shall have order restored shortly."

"What do we do?" Kit muttered.

"We need to find another exit. If we head back across the courtyard, they'll divert you two back to the dungeon."

"From here, we can get to the kitchen. We can exit through the staff quarters."

"Lead the way."

Kit waited until the two guards moved back towards the courtyard. "Follow me."

Kit moved through the corridors. Guy knew this hallway. The throne room lay at the end.

"Kit," Guy said.

"The servant's passageway is a little farther along." Kit gazed at Guy, then down the corridor. "You didn't think I'd lead you into—"

"We're close. And sometimes you don't know when to retreat."

Kit leant forward and found the opening for the door that led into the passage.

"*Parar!*"

Guy knew the Spanish word for stop. He turned. Fernando strode towards them, a guard on either side.

Guy questioned his ability to outwit Fernando in Spanish and to explain why he'd brought two condemned prisoners deep within the palace.

Fernando strode toward them and stopped. He spoke, and as Guy struggled to recall the Spanish words to explain, Gonzalo intervened. The former Duke of Cordoba retained little strength. His memory was shattered. Fear of further torture must have overwhelmed him, for he lifted his sickle into the groin of the nearest soldier, who collapsed in screaming agony.

Fernando, the remaining guard, Guy, and Kit all reacted, raising weapons in defence.

Perhaps they didn't have to leave Spain unsuccessful. If he could take down Fernando, King Philip III would see sense once more.

Using the pair of sickle swords, Kit took on the guard, while Guy locked swords with Fernando. From the Spaniard's moves, Guy knew he'd had lessons in sword-fighting, but he clearly had little experience in actual battle, and when Guy stepped forward and stamped on his foot, he let his guard down.

Guy raised his sword, ready to deliver a finishing strike, when nails raked down the side of his face.

In agony, he dropped his sword and turned to see Sofia before him, the deadness in her eyes replaced with livid flame.

Fernando raised his sword, ready to swing at Guy.

"Guido Fawkes and Kit Wright!" yelled Gonzalo, "saviours of Cordoba!" he drew his sword across Sofia's neck.

Fernando altered his strike, bringing his sword down into the Duke of Cordoba's shoulder.

As Gonzalo fell, Fernando followed him down, placing his hands around his throat and squeezing the rest of his life out of him.

"Come!" Guy looked at the passage. Ricard stood, urging him inside. Kit dispensed with his guard and hurried over.

Fernando, lost in rage, continued to assault the dead body of Gonzalo. Footsteps echoed as further soldiers reacted to the sound of bloodshed.

"Quick!" called Ricard.

It would only take a second to grab a weapon, to finish Fernando. But that same second would let the guards see which passage they headed down, a second that would lead to a chase and, ultimately, their capture. No, Guy followed Kit into the servants' passage and let Ricard slam the door behind them.

They'd lost the opportunity to save Spain.

Chapter 27—In Which Guy Fawkes Returns to England and a Plot is Hatched

Without pause, Ricard led Guy and Kit through the passage into the kitchen and beyond, down into the subterranean passages where the staff of the Royal Alcázar disposed of their liquid waste. Ricard left them at the entrance to the passage, advising which route to take and how to remove the grate that led to the river. The duo trudged most of the way in silence, dropping into the water where necessary without remark. Exhaustion consumed them. They diverted every bit of energy into continuing along the path. Only when the tunnel narrowed and water lapped at their waists did they speak, mutually cursing their misfortune. A little further the grate stopped their progress and they spoke again, but only for a simple count to ensure they pulled in tandem.

With the grate displaced, they continued until the tunnel opened onto the stream. There, Guy and Kit ditched the red cloak of the Spanish Inquisition and the sanbenito. They had to get away from Madrid. Only danger awaited if they returned to the city. They kept their heads down and trudged onward.

By the time darkness fell, they were several miles from Madrid.

Over the following weeks, Guy and Kit kept moving, sheltering in orchards and in abandoned farm buildings, surviving on the fruits of the land. They headed north to return to Bilbao, where they secured passage to England.

As Guy boarded the boat, failure struck him, a physical manifestation gnawing at his bones, and a mental one agonising every though. For years he'd been in Europe fighting in France, the Netherlands, Spain, visiting distant lands to keep demons at bay so that the powers of Europe would join to purge England of its demon sickness. The infestation of evil had grown stronger in Europe to such a point that corruption had taken the King of Spain. The union between the demon-infested island of his birth and the nation in which he'd put so much hope to help cleanse it told him that dream was over. Instead of returning to England with an army behind him, he had but one companion. But that one companion was his best friend. It could have been a lot worse.

From Portsmouth, where their ship landed, Guy and Kit travelled to Cowdray House. As they rode along the entranceway, Guy glanced over to the topiary. As he identified the place where a crossbow bolt pierced his shoulder, pain revisited him. When they knocked at the door of Cowdray House, at first, they were not permitted entrance, the servants informing them of Anthony Browne's engagement in a meeting. The head housekeeper refused to allow strangers in.

"We will wait outside. When the Viscount is free, tell him Guy Fawkes is here."

Less than an hour later, the viscount himself welcomed Guy Fawkes into the house. The years had been kind. He had grown some fine facial hair that had the tiniest hint of red in it, and his locks flowed to his shoulders. He took Guy into his embrace and shook hands with Kit, his eyes falling to Kit's missing little finger.

Anthony Browne led them through to the parlour—the room that Guy had considered the nicest in the house when he had met with the playwright Christopher Marlowe there.

Young Browne had always been fond of Guy's tales of demon hunting, and even after his own experiences, he remained keen to hear of Guy's latest exploits. Guy shared the tale of the cathedral which rose from the sea and the hulking elephant/fish demon which had tried to consume him. Alas, like all stories, it culminated in failing to save Spain from the grip of demons.

"When we heard of this union, it blackened our days," Browne said.

"And how have things been in England under the boy king?"

The Viscount sighed. "And to think we had hope of purging the demon threat under his rule. He is abusing his power all over the country. He stirs hatred of anyone involved in the occult, but that means demon hunters are being dragged to the scaffold everywhere we turn. He failed to stand by his promise of tolerance of those with other beliefs, too. If you don't sing the same hymn as the Royal Family, you're likely to have your throat torn out."

Guy massaged the back of his neck in an attempt to keep the throbbing in his head from turning into a headache. "Is he manipulating people's fear of witchcraft, or is he in earnest?"

Browne shrugged. "It's hard to say. Some say he talks of the white horse of Revelation riding through the country to signal the end of days."

"So, if we can make him see who the demons really are, he might turn in our direction?" Kit asked.

"He has so many whisperers around him pointing in the wrong direction. They've stirred the people into a frenzy. People are taking the law into their own hands and performing swimmings in every lake, river, and pond deep enough to dunk someone under."

"What's the answer?" Guy asked.

"I appeal to parliament for a moderate and measured approach, but they won't listen. It isn't helped that my reputation isn't wholly untarnished by the devilish antics that took place in your time here, Guy."

Guy gazed at the pattern on the carpet. The guilt about being unable to save Catherine Stanley still pained him.

Browne tapped Guy on the knee to draw eye contact. "Those of pure hearts are free of demonic influence thanks to your efforts."

"It's not all my doing."

"Hello, Guy. Hello Kit," came a voice from behind them.

Guy had not heard that voice since he guided the Jesuit priest onto the boat at Calais all those years ago.

Oswald Tesimond took a seat in the parlour. While he'd lost some of the colour he'd gained in his time in Europe, he still looked healthy and had maintained the weight gain which had stopped him looking skeletal. Instead of his grey beard making him look old, it gave him an air of wisdom. "I'm sure the viscount has informed you of how the wheel has turned here."

Guy shook his head. "It's crumbling beneath us wherever we turn. What hope do we have left?"

"We place the same hope in each other as we always have. That hasn't waned, has it?"

"No." Guy shrugged. "But what can we do?"

Oswald grasped Guy's hand. "Continue to believe that the good shall rise from all this ill."

Guy forced a smile, and Oswald left.

Anthony Browne looked over his shoulder, watching Oswald leave. He leant in toward Guy and Kit. "If it's action you're after and not sentiment, I can tell you where some of your old associates are meeting."

The next day, Guy and Kit headed for London.

London remained largely unchanged, as far as Guy could tell. Aye, a few more houses further crowded the streets and even more tradespeople sold their wares on any spot large enough to set up a table. Kit had visited the capital on far fewer occasions, and Guy had to drag his friend through the crowds whenever his eye caught another sight that stopped him in his tracks, whether that be a tall building, or a statue erected to celebrate some ancient event. They hurried along the perimeter of Hyde Park—the royal hunting ground. At Charing Cross, Kit needed a moment to admire the Eleanor Cross monument at Charing, and soon, they were on The Strand seeking the sign of The Duck and Drake.

They entered the inn, a busy place with a long bar, merchants and traders perched along it.

"Is he in here?" Kit craned his head, even though he'd never met Catesby before.

"Let us get some ale. We'll take a seat in the far corner. We may see him on the way."

Guy bought the drinks, and they headed through the busy bar, brushing shoulders with other patrons and taking careful steps to avoid spilling a drop of ale.

Before they reached the table in the corner, Guy spotted his old associate, Robert Catesby, and with him another whose presence brought a scowl to his face: Francis Tresham.

Guy placed his hand on Catesby's shoulder.

Catesby spun around, his eyes full of fear. The years had been unkind: his eyes were sunken, his skin leathery, his beard showing the first signs of grey. The fright left him as soon as he recognised Guy. He stood and they embraced. Guy introduced Kit.

"Brother of Jack Wright?" Catesby asked.

"You know my brother?"

"We were hoping he would join us in our endeavour."

"What endeavour is that?" Guy cut in.

Catesby glanced around the inn again. "Now is not the time to speak of it. We await some companions. There is a private room out the back where we shall speak."

Guy and Kit sat at the table. Guy stared across at Tresham.

Francis Tresham retained that habit of playing with his knuckles, and he continued to do so as he spoke. "Guy, I hope we can leave our past right there where it belongs."

Guy took a sip of his ale. "I confess, your presence here has not filled me with joy. I would have been content to have never set eyes on you again."

Tresham stared at Guy. "And yet here we are. So, can you let it go?"

Catesby put his hand on the table to draw their attention. "We can't have any animosity come between us if we are to succeed. What say you, Guy?"

Guy kept his eyes on Tresham as he addressed Catesby. "I'll listen to your plot. Then I'll decide whether I can work with him."

Evening came. Guy and Kit moderated their ale intake, while Catesby and Tresham drank liberally, their tongues becoming looser, their tales more outrageous.

"Here they are!" Tresham called across the inn as two men entered.

"My cousins," Catesby said. "Robert and Thomas Wintour."

The men were similar looking: dark, shaggy hair, pointed beards. While Robert had heavier eyelids, Thomas had thicker lips.

"To the back room." Catesby stood, causing the table to wobble. A few of the inn's patrons glanced their way, but quickly returned to their own business.

The back room of the Duck and Drake had two dark wooden tables that ran almost the length of the room. Catesby pushed the door closed and the six men gathered around the table farthest from the door. He introduced Guy and Kit to his cousins and began.

"My cousins, in all our recent discussions, we reached the same conclusion. We can no longer tolerate a country governed in the interest of demons. Attempts to infiltrate the court and spread good have failed. Our hope that James I would be an honest man may or may not be lost, but one thing is for sure—the masters of demons have his ear. It would be easier to make the sunrise from the other direction than to turn his head. Does anybody in this room not believe that now is the time for drastic action?" Catesby gazed around the room for a show of dissent. Guy eyed his neighbours, a group of men worn out by the fight, exhaustion drawn on by lack of hope.

Robert Wintour raised a hand. "What of Europe? I could travel back there to stir up some assistance."

Guy cleared his throat. "My friend and I," he indicated Kit, "have only recently returned from Europe. We will find no help from the Spanish throne."

"And in Flanders?" Robert Wintour asked.

"You will find many good men, but believe me, they are up to their neck in their own devil mess."

Thomas Wintour leant forward. "What can we six do against a whole nation?"

Catesby smiled. "Did I not speak of the need for drastic action? When change is needed, there are two methods. Everyone gives a little to show the weight of opposition. Alas, too many people will buy the lies, dunking their neighbours under the water and digging into their pockets to hand over more and more coin to the demon masters under the ruse of taxes. When that doesn't work, you need a small group of people to do something enormous."

The gathered party examined each other before nodding in agreement.

"Guy, Kit, before I continue, this is your chance to leave. If you can't understand that we need drastic action to shake this country, if you have no interest in being the ones doing the shaking," Catesby pointed, "the door is that way. All I ask is that you speak nothing of this meeting."

Guy didn't need to hear Kit's answer to know his heart. His face had yet to regain its fullness following his time imprisoned in the Royal Alcázar of Madrid. His eyes had carried a sadness ever since they boarded the boat in Bilbao, ever since they'd had to abandon Francis Ingleby's motto, which they'd grown up with—hope lies in Spain.

They spoke together. "I'm in."

"Parliament is controlled by those in league with demons, of that we are certain?"

Nods of agreement came from all at the table.

"When parliament opens after the summer recess, we blow it up. We assassinate the King, his councillors, puritans, and bishops. All those that have persecuted us for wanting rid of the evil that blights this land can be removed in a single act."

Robert Wintour's brow furrowed. "What then?"

"We follow the path of succession and James's son, Henry, becomes Henry IX."

Thomas Wintour moistened his lips. "What's to stop him from becoming as bad? Like father, like son, don't they say?"

"I'm counting on it. James became king of Scotland at a young age. He's never spoken his own mind. He's had advisers around him telling him what to say, what to think. We fill his mind only with good. We make sure he understands who is truly responsible for the scourge of demons on this isle, and we make sure it's his number one priority to vanquish every damned one of them."

Time stood still. Guy had always believed there was no point in destroying a structure without a plan in place for what to do to follow it. But Catesby had a plan, a plan that would lead to brighter days after that first hideous act. But could he be involved in something so destructive? Surely, not every man in parliament deserved death. Was the loss of their lives a price worth paying?

Guy wished he could return to that tiny room at the bottom of the secret staircase in Saint Peter's, where his headmaster, John Pulleyn, could give him the wisdom he needed. Perhaps a return to Cowdray House would be in order to converse with Oswald. He always helped Guy understand the reasons behind people's actions.

Guy realised that everyone else in the room experienced that same sensation of time having frozen to allow them to explore their thoughts. Guy had tried all his life to stop those demons. All those little pushes had failed to topple the tower of evil because too few people pushed together. This action would dig out the foundation and leave that tower to tumble down. This would give them the chance to rebuild something better.

Tresham thumped the table. "So, what say we? Do you have a conspiracy here?"

A rousing response came from the table.

Catesby stood, wandering around to shake hands with the other members of his party. He stopped by Kit. "Your brother, Jack would be a real asset to us in this endeavour. Could you speak to him for us?"

Kit nodded.

Catesby turned to Guy. "And if you're aware of anyone who has a little influence or property within the city of London, that could also benefit our cause."

Guy thought of his old friend Thomas Percy, who had made a name for himself as a tailor among the elite (and something of a toerag among the commoners for the way he'd left Kit and Jack's sister). Surely, he too would be keen on lending a hand.

With the birth of a new endeavour, some of the misery over the Spanish failure dissipated.

Chapter 28—In Which Guy Fawkes is Reunited with Family

Before the plot could move on any further, each of the conspirators had personal business to attend to. While not explicitly stated, the implication was that this was an act from which there was no turning back, and if one didn't make their peace, the opportunity could forever be lost.

Kit said a brief goodbye to Guy before heading off to seek his brother. Guy travelled first to York. Having passed through multiple communities consumed by fear, many of which promised the swimming of witches or hangings in the coming days, Guy feared returning to the city of his birth. York, however, had a different air. At Pavement, traders chatted with their customers. An air of community and trust lingered. Guy even checked the notice boards for news of forthcoming executions, but they were free of such horrors. There would be no further death through false accusations of witchcraft; instead, the spirit of freedom elevated the city above the mire all others wallowed in.

Most of Guy's business, however, was with the dead, not the living. He first visited the house in which he'd spent his earliest years in Stonegate. Of course, the house itself had burnt to the ground, but given that they'd built an identical one in its place, Guy considered this abode an apt replacement.

Standing in the street, he addressed his first ghost. "I hope you understand why I made the decisions I did, father, and I hope you appreciate why I must do the thing I'm going to do."

Guy walked on through the streets of York, past the James William Wilson Bakery at which Anne had once worked, along The Shambles where he had learned so much from Margaret Clitherow, stopping again at the place of her death, the Toll Bridge over the River Ouse. Here, Guy addressed his second ghost. "Margaret, I learned so much from you. You taught me to inspire people to be better. The peace in this city is testament to that. I hope you understand why I must do what I am going to do."

He had one last stop in the city: York Minster. Here, Guy had no intention of making peace with ghosts or renewing acquaintances with demons. He was there to make peace with the building itself. From the outside, the cathedral remained as intimidating as ever, perhaps because he'd seen this view from the outside so many times before. Once he stepped inside, he found it much smaller than he remembered. In his dreams, York Minster had often grown to epic proportions, the nave lengthening as he ran across it, the ceiling rising as hellfire dripped from it. Now he saw the truth of the place once more, and hope overwhelmed him. This building would heal. Devotion would trump corruption. York Minster could become a place of worship once more.

He spoke to his third ghost. "Sandys, you betrayed the spirit of this place, and I hope your kin can never return. This place deserves better."

Guy exited York Minster for the last time. He had one last ghost to speak to before he conducted his business with the living.

Guy left the city through that much-used road, passing through Bootham Bar for what he expected to be the last time. This journey would take him not to Saint Peter's School, but onto the road that led to Scotton.

Guy stopped a few miles from the village and slept in the open air, marvelling at the stars.

The second Guy rested his head, the old guardian rebel appeared before him, drawing light from the stars to grow ever brighter.

"What guidance have you for me, now? Would you counsel me against Catesby's plot?"

Percy's skull swooped down. "Do you forget what put me in this position in the first place? The revolt of the northern earls. We took on the might of monarchy."

"Aye, and given that you were such a pathetic failure, would you caution me against walking in your footsteps?"

Percy ignored the barb. "The chance of success in a plot to remove the monarchy is slim. Taking parliament with them as well? Pure folly."

"So, you would council against it?"

"A slim chance is better than no chance."

"You're really helping to build my confidence here, Percy. Thanks."

"Or perhaps this plot's purpose is to serve as a lesson to others. An example of how not to do it."

Guy stretched forward, trying to turn Percy away, but he eased back out of Guy's grasp.

"Aye, you know how to build someone up, don't you?"

"And maybe you, Guy Fawkes, will be in my position this time next year. Maybe you will swoop on a young man full of promise, guiding him towards his own acts of rebellion."

"Did you come to me tonight only to mock me? You've been there to guide me every step of the way, and now you're suggesting failure is my destiny."

Percy spun around, turning upside-down. "Perhaps we need to consider this differently. Perhaps we need to redefine what success is. If James I is still on the throne after this plot is over, does that mean you've failed?"

"Aye."

"What if the hearts and minds of those around him have changed?"

"Will that be enough?"

"You'd have to ask Margaret Clitherow about the effectiveness of her stand against authority when it ended in her death."

"If nothing else, Percy, you've given me a skull ache thinking about it all. For that, I thank you and bid you goodnight."

Percy's skull dimmed, leaving only the light of the stars, and Guy in the grip of sleep once more.

As soon as the sun rose, Guy woke and completed his journey to Scotton. He passed Percy House, intending to visit later, and stopped on the land in which his house once stood. Guy felt relieved that his step-father Dionis Bainbrigge had torn down the house he built with his own hands. He remembered a promise he had made and bowed on the spot where his bed once sat. "My darling Maria. I shall be with you soon. Give John a kiss for me."

A couple of villagers stood outside their houses, staring at him. He recognised one as a farmer he'd once gone to market with many years prior, when he was foolhardy enough to believe he deserved a life of peace. His expression suggested he didn't recognise the man weeping in the field as a former villager. Guy turned away from their glances and hurried to Percy House, taking a moment to dry his eyes before he knocked on the door.

A moment later, the door swung open. A man of Guy's age stood on the other side, staring at him. "Yes?"

Was Guy too late? Had his mother and Dionis moved away, or worse, passed away in his absence?

"Is Mrs Bainbrigge home?" Guy asked. He took a step back, steeling himself against a possible negative answer.

"Who shall I say is calling?"

Relief. "It's Guy Fawkes. Her son."

The man showed Guy through to the parlour, where his mother sat sewing, alone. She looked much the same as when he had left at the age of twenty-one. Thirteen years had seen little change in her.

"Mother," Guy called from the doorway.

Edith Bainbrigge (nee Fawkes) craned her neck forward and narrowed her eyes. Her vision had clearly weakened. "That's not... my boy? That's not you, is it, Guy?"

Guy hurried across the room and fell on one knee by his mother's chair. He took hold of her hand. "Aye, mother. It's me."

Edith wiped a tear from her eye. "I didn't think I'd ever see you again." She leaned in and studied his face closer. "The years have been tough?"

"I have been in Europe, mother. Things are... not well there. But what of you? What of my sisters? What of Dionis?"

Guy and his mother spent some time discussing their lives (Guy sticking to the places he'd been and people he'd met and avoided talk of the demons he'd faced). Guy remained vague about his life, and his mother oblique about Dionis's activities. Guy knew Dionis hid Jesuit priests, and his mother's silence, even to him kept everyone safer.

At the point at which their conversation stilted, partly because of the secrets held back by both, partly because they'd rarely engaged in prolonged conversation, another visitor arrived.

Guy barely recognised his sister Elizabeth. His mother had told him she had married the Rimer boy and had two children, and yet Guy expected to see a girl still, not a grown woman. She had been fourteen when Guy left. Thirteen years took her well into adulthood. Elizabeth had always mimicked her mother in terms of her activities (so many times, he'd watched them sitting side by side, sewing, their arms moving in tandem), but now she even looked like her mother had, wearing her hair the same way, wearing similar clothes.

She had brought her two boys with her. Edward, aged six and named after her father, and four-year-old Tom. The youngster had that shock of flame in his hair, and a lash of mischief in his eyes. They spoke, long enough for Guy to realise a chasm had grown between them in his absence. When he said goodbye, he promised to visit again soon. He saw no need to advise that they'd never see him again.

Guy next stopped at an address in Brearton, given to him by his mother. When he reached the village, he found it even more sparse than Scotton. He approached the first cottage on the right-hand side of the road, as he'd been told. The cottage itself appeared on the lean, the chimney looking like a good gust would knock it off. A couple of wooden outbuildings had planks hanging off the side, exposing the contents to the elements. Surely, it would need fixing before the weather turned.

Guy knocked on the door. Shouts came from inside, and a moment later, the door swung open. Anne dusted her hands on a floury apron and tucked a strand of hair behind her ear. Recognition came. She pulled Guy to her and hugged him. Then she pushed him away and slapped his face.

Guy rubbed his cheek. "A pleasure to see you too, sister."

Anne placed her hands on her hips. "When I told you I wanted no further part in your demon-hunting exploits, I didn't expect you to go off for thirteen years."

"I know, but—"

"Thirteen years, Guy. With nothing but the occasional letter or Jack Wright dropping by to tell me he's seen you, and you're well."

A child approached Anne and hugged her legs.

"Who's this?" Guy asked, relieved the young arrival had taken the focus away from him.

"This bag of wind is Christopher Croft." Anne stepped back from the door. "You might as well come in, that is, if you have any intention of staying a while."

Inside, Anne introduced Guy to her daughter, Catherine. She had much of her mother's look and demeanour, which reminded him of the other young Catherine he'd once known, Catherine Stanley, and her horrible fate. Perhaps Guy was better off leaving and keeping his family out of any further tragedy.

"John and Francis are out in the field, helping their father."

"And he is a good man?"

"I wouldn't have married him otherwise."

Anne went into the kitchen and fetched some cakes, offering one to her brother.

Guy took the cake in his left hand.

"You've been injured."

"Stabbed in the back and left to die."

Anne shook her head. "Why do you keep doing it, Guy?"

"Same reason as always. It's the right thing to do."

Anne moved to sit next to Guy. She shuffled up his sleeve and inspected the wounds on his arm. "But when does it end?"

"Soon." Guy sighed. "Anne, I can't tell you what's going to happen, but you need to understand, when the stories spread, I'm doing this for the right reasons."

"Is there anything I can do? Do you need me to join you?"

"You made it clear you wanted no part of this life." Guy nodded towards Catherine. "And you've got a whole life of your own worth living here."

"Have you seen what's on the mantle?"

Guy stood and picked up the golden angel, studying the intricately carved wings.

"I've still got the whistle, too," Anne added.

"Keep them. I hope there's never a time you or your sons need to use them."

"Or my daughter."

"Nay, her neither."

Anne placed her hands on her hips. "If you are involved in something big, and I find out you didn't tell me, I'll resent you for the rest of my days."

"Some things it's better not to know."

Anne sighed. "It's been nice to see you again, Guy. But the last thirteen years of my life have been so much easier. Thanks for making me feel like I'm not good enough all over again."

Anne returned to the kitchen. Guy followed her, watching as she busied herself in the cupboards. There was no more to say.

Outside, he glanced at the loose boards on the shed, wondering if he should repair them on the way past. Deep down, he knew his interference would not be valued. He mounted his horse ready for a return journey to

London. He glanced at the hill decorated with sheep, at the rock formations on which nothing grew. Guy doubted he'd see such sights again.

Chapter 29—In Which Guy Fawkes Enlists a Drunken Thomas Percy

Upon his return to London, Guy made for Fleet Street. While some of the other shops around it had changed, Percy's tailor shop remained the same as ever: lavish outfits displayed on hangers hung in the window.

With a pang of excitement about seeing his old friend, Guy pushed open the door.

A small man in a tangerine doublet with matching breeches and long socks glared from behind a pile of fabric. "Can I help you?"

Guy peered around the piles of cloth. "Is Thomas Percy here?"

The little man cleared his throat. "I'm afraid he's not at these premises."

"Where might I find him?"

The man smoothed a piece of fabric. "He could be at any of his shops."

"Any one? How many does he have?"

The little man tutted. "A dozen at last count."

"Could you give me the address of each one so I can locate him?"

"At this hour, though, it's likely you'll find him in one of the establishments near The Globe."

Guy furrowed his brow. "The Globe?"

"Are you not a Londoner, Sir?" The little man folded his arms.

"It's been some time since I've been in the great city."

"The Globe is a theatre. You can watch Othello."

Guy stroked his beard. "Who's Othello?"

The little man rolled his eyes. "Othello is a play by William Shakespeare." Guy's blank expression drew another sigh from the little man. "Head for the Thames and ask someone nearby."

Guy travelled through London, eventually arriving outside the amazing structure known as The Globe. A nearby pub called The Swan heaved with activity. Guy entered and pushed through the customers to approach the bar. He ordered an ale. "And I don't suppose you know the tailor, Thomas Percy?"

The barman harrumphed. He poured Guy's ale and slammed his tankard on the bar, letting ale slop over the side.

Another drinker with a fashionable beard who had stood next to Guy at the bar followed him to the one empty table in the rear corner of the establishment.

"Can I help you, friend?" Guy asked. His right hand groped at the space his sword hilt used to be. Of course, it was on the other side.

"Few around here would use the epithet 'the tailor' for Thomas Percy."

"No?" Guy supped at his tankard and placed it back on the table.

"Philanderer is about the cleanest name I've heard given him. What's he owe you?"

"Nothing. He's a friend."

Like the barman before him, the patron harrumphed. He called across the tavern. "Oi, Tanner, this one calls Thomas Percy a friend."

The man leant forward into Guy's eyeline and pulled his face into an expression of bewilderment. He started through the people toward Guy.

Guy glanced up to check the location of the door. "I take it he's not popular around these parts?"

"Not unless you're a daft young lady, and they don't like him for long once he shows his true colours."

Guy supped his ale. "Would you be so kind as to suggest where I might find him?"

The man turned to his friend again. "Tanner, where d'you reckon Percy'll be this evening?"

Tanner pushed past a couple more people and emerged at the side of his friend. "He's not barred from the Ox. They don't get many of his type in there, but he has to drink somewhere."

Guy cleared his throat. "And where might I find this Ox?"

"If you're a friend of Percy's, you must be a resourceful man. Go on. Off you go. I'll take this for my trouble." He grabbed Guy's drink. "And if you find him, tell him Tanner and DeQuincy want a word."

"Thank you for your assistance." Guy bowed his head, avoiding eye contact, and made for The Swan's exit. For all his adventures taking on demon-infested buildings, he knew few more hostile environments than the average English pub to a stranger.

Guy stood out in the late afternoon air for a moment, wondering which way to head. The most popular establishments were along the riverside. If

Tanner and DeQuincy were to be believed, Percy would not be found in those. Instead, Guy headed away from the Thames, soon spotting a pub named the Black Boar. A glance through the window put him off checking there. A couple of hundred yards farther along the road, another pub sign came into view: The Ox.

As he reached for the door, it flew open, and a figure came bundling out, collapsing onto the hard pavement.

"And stay out," came a cry from within the bar as the door slammed closed.

Guy turned to the man sprawled on the floor. The salmon-coloured hat, carrying a little extra dirt from the pavement, told Guy he'd found his man. A mustard-coloured doublet and matching breeches completed his old friend's outfit.

Guy crouched. "Thomas." Guy tried to turn the tailor over.

Thomas jerked at the touch, squirming, and pulling his legs into a ball.

Guy said in his softest, most comforting voice, "Thomas, it's me."

Thomas rubbed his eyes. "Do my eyes deceive me, or are there two Guy Fawkes before me?"

"It's me."

"You must tell me how you managed to make a double." Thomas held out a hand. "We can put you on the stage!"

"No, Thomas, there's only one."

Thomas sighed. "I'm afraid to blink in case both of you disappear."

"Blink, Thomas Percy, and you'll find me here in the singular."

Percy blinked several times and leant forward. "As I live and breathe."

A moment of silence passed as Thomas composed himself. A large scab on his nose looked to be more severe that the effect of being flung from a tavern. Several raised lumps covered the side of his face. A large, black sore festered lower on his neck and a few bald patches made his beard look uneven.

"Guy Fawkes," Thomas muttered again. He patted the pavement beside himself.

"While I'd love to join you there, do you have an abode in which we could speak in private?"

Thomas held out a hand, and Guy helped him, with some difficulty, back to his unsteady feet. He tottered forward a few steps, then took a couple back. "Follow me. I have a few fine bottles to keep us very merry indeed."

After a journey lengthened by Thomas's inability to walk in a straight line and his insistence on trying to go into every bar en route (only a couple would permit him), it was well into the evening by the time they reached Thomas's house.

Guy had to take the keys from Thomas to unlock the door. A smell of whiskey hit Guy the second he entered.

Thomas stumbled through the corridor and sat at the table in a room barely large enough for a table and a couple of chairs. A bottle of whiskey sat open upon the table with a single glass beside it.

"Let me get another glass." Thomas stumbled off once more, giving Guy time to notice the sordid negligence in his house which matched the lack of care of his person. Guy opened a box on the table. Inside were pills.

Thomas returned a moment later with another glass. He placed it on the table and sat, pouring three equal shares of whiskey, one for himself, one for Guy, and one for the table.

"So, tell me, Guy, what is it that brings you back to England?"

Guy recounted tales from Europe, hurrying through to get to his request. "Perchance, Thomas, do you know of a method in which we can acquire a property close to the House of Parliament?"

Thomas eyed his drink. He shoved it along the table, away from himself. "Guy, I might be able to help you out, and this might be the opportunity I need to bring some stability into my life right now."

"When I stopped by your Fleet Street shop, I thought things were going well, that you'd opened several new premises."

Thomas slumped in his chair. "There's success." Thomas lifted his hands in the air. "And there's success." He fell back deeper into his chair. "Yes, people love the clothes, and I thought I deserved more. I threw away the only worthwhile thing I ever had with Martha by chasing other pleasures, and none of them were worth a damn compared to her. With the debauchery came the drink, and with the drink came some poor choices." Thomas opened the box on the table, grabbed a pill and swallowed it, letting a sip of whiskey chase it down. "And one of those poor choices gave me the ruddy pox."

Guy stared at Thomas wide eyed. "So, what are the pills?"

"Oh, a dose of mercury will fix me. Enough of my problems. What is it you need me for?"

"We spoke about this a moment ago... Can you get me a property close to the Houses of Parliament?"

Thomas blinked several times. "Guy, I might be able to help you out, and this might be the opportunity I need to bring some stability into my life right now." He leant forward and kept going until his head touched the table. He snored.

Guy sighed and leant back in the chair, hoping to grab some sleep himself. He'd explain all to Thomas in the morning.

Chapter 30—In Which Guy Fawkes and Thomas Percy Visit a Suitable Property

A further meeting at the Duck and Drake brought the conspirators together again, the original six, alongside Thomas Percy and Jack Wright, who Kit had located. Prior to the meeting, Guy had met Thomas at his tailor shop in Fleet Street, and they had arrived together at the pub.

As soon as Thomas set eyes on the Wright brothers, he winced. "Are you sure you need me here, Guy? Can't I be one of those silent partners?"

"I need you to show everyone that we can trust you. Part of that is making amends."

Kit glanced towards the door and spotted Guy. He smiled, but that faded when he saw who accompanied him. He pushed through the tavern's patrons and met Thomas with a fist to the jaw. His scowl turned to a smile. "Hello, Guy."

Thomas turned his head to one side and licked blood from his lip. "I earned that. Your sister deserved better."

Kit shook his head. "Don't even talk about her."

Thomas held out his hands in surrender.

Kit led the way deeper into the tavern, and they moved into the back room.

Jack approached. He first went to Guy, embracing him. "It's so good to see you again, friend."

"And you, too."

Jack released Guy, turned to Thomas, and struck him with a straight right to the nose.

Thomas stumbled back into the wall, blinking rapidly. He took out a handkerchief and dabbed at his nose, soaking a trickle of blood from one nostril. When he opened his mouth, Jack held up a hand.

"Least said, soonest mended." Jack sat.

Guy took a seat next to Jack and Thomas sat on the other side, also a safe distance from Kit. "Jack, do you think any more of our old allies from Saint Peter's would join us."

Jack screwed up his face. "I'd struggle to find any."

"What about Gaunt's party in Leeds?"

Jack shook his head. "King James's dogs sniffed them out."

"And Fairfax?"

"Through him they found Gaunt. Wasn't his fault. Careless. That's all." Jack shook his head.

Guy glanced at Kit. "There's few of us left from those days."

Jack shook his head. "They've damn near wiped us out. That's why we have to do this."

Catesby cleared his throat and started the meeting. He revealed that he'd added others to their number, primarily for financial reasons. While he kept many of the names to himself, he couldn't help but let slip the name of Sir Everard Digby, a man with some influence that could raise a small army to protect them all after the deed while they established a new order.

During the meeting, Catesby welcomed Thomas, suggesting that he would prove a useful addition to the band. While he had failed to care for himself on a physical or indeed mental level, his business brain and eye for fashion meant he remained a tailor considered in high regard. As a tailor to the elite, Thomas had access to influential people, and that influence he would use to his advantage. Many of those in attendance at the state opening of parliament would indeed be in Thomas Percy's attire. Thomas showed he felt at home among the group when he cracked a joke: "The greatest loss when parliament falls will be some fine doublets."

Even Kit managed a smile at that one.

After a meeting, in which Thomas assured his co-conspirators that he'd be able to secure apt premises, he took Guy aside.

"I'm going to need you to attend a party with me tonight."

"A party? Thomas, I'm not the right person to attend a social gathering with you."

"Nonsense. I attended Queen Elizabeth's get-together with you at Richmond Palace. This is the least you can do for me."

Guy stood close to Thomas and spoke in a loud whisper. "If you remember rightly, I held a knife within stabbing range of the Queen and sliced open my hand with a broken goblet."

"Well, it's not ideal, but I'm going to need a foil."

"Robert Cecil won't be there?"

"He remains in Europe meeting with Juan de Velasco collecting names of English traitors, so he'll not trouble you."

"I guess I'm all out of excuses. What's the plan?"

Thomas touched the side of the nose, close to the scab. "I have it on good authority that some warehouse space within spitting distance of the Houses of Parliament is available. If we put in a fine performance, it's as good as ours."

"In that case, I can't say no. What time shall I meet you?"

"Meet me? Good gracious, no, Guy. You must come with me immediately. You need dressing, and you must put some make-up on me to cover this dreaded black spot. If they think I've got the blasted pox, they'll never want to do business with me."

Guy and Thomas returned to the Fleet Street tailor shop, where Thomas rifled through his stock.

"There's obviously insufficient time to get you measured up, so we'll have to find something a client has returned or rejected."

Guy watched his friend, bemused. "Why don't you make a range of doublets in all sorts of sizes, so people can come in and grab one that fits without all this need to measure?"

Thomas sighed. "What a preposterous business proposition. People come in many shapes and sizes. If you did that, the people on the streets would look hideous. And think of the waste! No, Guy, you clearly have no idea about either business or fashion."

"It would be so much quicker for the customer."

Thomas rifled through a stack of folded clothes. "Quicker? Customers don't want quick! They want to come here and have an experience. They don't come to throw on a doublet, not caring if it's baggy at the armpits, and dash out into the streets wearing it. No, they like the feel of the tape on their thighs. They like someone to appreciate the tightness of their chests. And most of all, they enjoy conversation with their tailor. In your world Guy, the horrific world in that messed-up mind of yours, people would shop without so much as a word from the vendor."

Guy jutted out his bottom lip and nodded. "What the problem with that?"

Thomas gave Guy a gentle clip of his ear. "Too much continental weather has addled what business sense you ever had." Thomas thrust his arm out, holding two doublets, one in lime green with tangerine stitching, the other a tawny brown with no decorative features whatsoever. "Try these on. You'll have to go with whichever fits better."

In the privacy of the back room, Guy tried on the tawny doublet. It was a little tight across the chest, and the arms came up short. The lime green and tangerine doublet, however, fit perfectly. Guy gazed at his chest in that remarkable colour, and removed the doublet once more, leaving himself in his best, only slightly stained jerkin. He returned to Thomas.

"Are either any good?"

Guy raised the tawny doublet. "This is the best of the two."

Thomas's eyes narrowed. "Are you sure?"

Guy put his hand to his chest. "When have I ever been anything less than honest with you?"

Thomas sighed. "I hoped to see you in lime. Maybe I can have it altered for our next endeavour."

Guy rolled his eyes. "Let's get this one out of the way first."

Guy and Thomas hurried through the streets to Percy's abode. It had been some time since Guy's first visit, and the change struck him. The whiskey stink had faded. The place itself looked almost tidy, respectable even. Thomas left Guy at the table and marched into his bedroom. He returned a moment later, slamming a drawer on the table.

"We have a carriage coming for us in an hour. You need to make me presentable to the elite."

Guy glanced in the drawer at a range of powders, pastes, and brushes.

"What do I need to do?"

"It's make-up, Guy. Any fool can do this. They train chimps to put make-up on the ladies on the continent, Guy."

Guy remembered Thomas's similar claim about chimpanzee servers many years prior, something which had turned out to be true in the Royal Alcázar of Madrid. Were they also adept with make-up, or was it another tall tale from Thomas, who had accidentally found gold with the previous strike of his rhetorical pickaxe?

"If I had the same training as a chimp, Thomas, I'm sure I could do an adequate job."

Thomas sighed. He took several concoctions from a drawer. "First, cover the worst of the dark spot with this." He pushed a small pot towards Guy and handed him a brush. "After that, it's all about using enough power to blend in the colour."

By the time Guy had finished, he couldn't make out either the dark spots on Thomas's neck or the scab that refused to fall from his nose. His face was a uniform colour—a pale shade, but consistent, nonetheless.

Thomas grabbed what looked like a pencil from the drawer. With it, he drew a small dot on his cheek.

Guy stared at him, bemused. "I made all that effort to cover your neck only for you to draw a spot on your cheek?"

Thomas pointed to his neck. "Well, that indicates a great disgrace. This," he pointed to his drawn speck, "is a natural blemish on my otherwise pure skin. The impurity helps the rest of the beauty to radiate from me!" Thomas smiled.

Guy dusted powder from his hands. "Are we ready?"

"Almost. You've got your alias? The name Guy Fawkes still carries a stink around here."

"An alias?"

"You'll think of something. Let's go."

Within thirty minutes, they were inside Westminster Hall. The gathering offered a secondary purpose of business networking with wealthy landowners, nobles, and successful merchants. Shipwrights liaised with traders formulating great plots to sail across the Atlantic. Deeds traded hands as merchants attempted to expand their empires.

The primary purpose, however, seemed to be to drink to excess and gorge on the range of food spread on tables all over the great hall. As Guy and Thomas wandered, engaging in conversation with all and sundry, sampling a range of treats, both liquid and solid, Guy realised Thomas's reputation was untarnished among the elite. Of course, he'd never tried to take any of their daughters or wives home with him.

Half an hour after their arrival, a great hubbub came, signalling the entrance of a special visitor. Alongside his group of guards, King James I strode through the hall. Even Guy admired his attire, his hose making his legs look like they were made entirely of silver. He wore a doublet of the same colour, heavy gold jewellery hanging over it.

Thomas put a hand over his heart. "That robe is divine! To make a robe so exquisite worn by a member of the royal family would be a dream come true."

The robe, a material that shimmered like gold, had intricate patterns embroidered onto it.

"If events unfold as we wish, one day you shall, my good man." Guy pictured his old friend in a palace discussing fabrics with a young monarch. Aye, he hoped he'd see such a day come to pass.

Guy and Thomas watched King James move through the hall. He stopped nearby, pulling his hand through his ginger beard. "Nay, lad," he said. "Ye cannae permit a witch t' live. Aye, it says so in the good book."

The King remained in conversation, allowing Guy to eavesdrop for a moment longer.

A serious look overcame King James. "Overcome to the pleasures of the flesh, that's their problem. We cannae have them spreading their perversion to the masses."

Even below the layers of make-up, Thomas's cheeks pinkened at the periphery. "I guess His Majesty doesn't know the capital as I do."

As the king walked away, Guy considered the plot. He'd known his share of deceivers. Were the king's words part of his own act of deception, or were the king's actions against demon hunters the result of the deception of others? Before Guy could consider for long a question that would trouble him for the rest of his days two gentlemen sidled over to them.

The gentleman on the left wore a red robe which raised Guy's suspicion given his recent engagements with the Spanish Inquisition. He appeared feeble enough to be a familiar, albeit a well-fed one. The pointed teeth and beady eyes of this small man led Guy to believe he was anything but pious.

The other gentleman acted as if in charge, a tall, thin man with a pointy beard and thin facial features—thin lips, narrow nose, and miniscule eyebrows.

"Duke, so kind of you to give me the honour of your presence," Thomas shook the man's hand. "This looks good on you." Thomas stroked the fabric of a purple doublet embroidered with a thick, black thread.

"It should do, the amount you charged me for it." The Duke smiled, a grin that made his lips narrow to such a degree they almost disappeared.

"Only the finest materials will suffice."

"Is this the gentleman you told me about?" The Duke slapped Guy hard on the shoulder.

"Aren't you going to introduce yourself?" Thomas stared at Guy and mouthed *use the alias.*

Guy, however, had forgotten about the need to have one and blurted out the first name that came to him. "John." He paused, realising he needed a sur-name. "Johnson. John Johnson."

"So, John Johnson," Thomas narrowed his eyes at Guy. "This is the Duke of Buckingham."

The Duke of Buckingham placed his arm around Thomas and guided him toward the exit. "Shall we visit the property I mentioned?"

Together, the four men left Westminster Hall and headed in the opposite direction from the Houses of Parliament, but not more than two hundred yards away.

The little man in red took out a key and opened a door at the end of a row of small buildings.

"As you see," said the duke, "it's more than sufficient for the storage of your materials. It's dry and easily accessible."

The little man circled round to the back of the group, standing by the door. "The real treasure of this space, though, is the cellar."

As soon as the duke opened the cellar door, heat radiated from the floor below. A red light, indicative of flame, glowed.

Guy turned to Thomas, asking a thousand questions with his stare.

Thomas nodded in return, a nod that Guy had seen so often before, a nod that said 'trust me' when Thomas had so rarely proved himself to be worthy of trust.

The duke placed his hand on Guy's shoulder, guiding him towards the staircase.

Guy took a few steps. As he reached the corner of the stairs, the source of the red light became apparent, a flame burning in a brazier in the centre of a spacious cellar. Around the brazier stood three men in red attire, much like that of the little man who stood behind them at the cellar door, locking them inside.

"Thank you, Thomas Percy, for bringing us this sacrifice." The duke grinned. "You have truly earned your place at my side in the new world we shall build together."

Chapter 31—In Which Guy Fawkes Makes the Cellar Fit for Purpose

Since Guy had rescued Kit from the dungeon of the Royal Alcázar of Madrid, he had hoped his days of calculating odds of survival and wielding a sword in anger were over. Alas, the layout of the room before him, the attire of the gathered men, and his moniker of sacrifice revealed those days were very much not behind him. Guy would have struggled with overcoming six human enemies in his prime. He didn't fancy himself having to fight with his weaker arm. But Guy didn't know the meaning of surrender. While his arm still had the strength to fight, fight he would.

Guy glanced at the Duke of Buckingham, his arm around Thomas Percy, who grinned at his new noble friend.

The three men in red came for Guy, each holding a dagger. Meanwhile, the fourth drew his weapon as he walked down the stairs. Guy suspected he'd find no better opportunity to fight and drew his sword. The four men eyed one another as they formed a plan of attack.

Guy retreated to the wall, scrutinizing each of the men, wondering which would flinch first.

The duke strode forward, hurrying to the bottom of the steps. "I thought he was a willing sacrifice!"

Thomas shoved the duke. "Get him, Guy!"

The duke stumbled towards the brazier. Flame leapt at the doublet, consuming the black thread in an instant, spreading flame all over the rest of the material. He threw himself to the ground, screaming as he clawed at his burning threads.

Guy took advantage of the moment of confusion and lunged at the man closest to him, stabbing through his red robe to spill his belly.

Thomas drew his sword and stood by Guy's side. "I can't believe they fell for it! Imagine! Me offering you as a sacrifice."

Guy elbowed Thomas. "You can't believe *they* fell for it?"

Thomas's mouth dropped open. "You thought I'd sell you out after all these years? Really, Guy?"

The remaining three men glanced between Guy and Thomas, and the flaming brazier, to the duke who had stopped rolling around on the floor.

A creak came and dust dropped from the ceiling.

The flame in the brazier grew brighter, and with a creak, the steps collapsed. The slats of wood flew against the far wall, which fell inwards, opening a huge cavern, flame dancing at its edge. At first, visible only as a silhouette, a crouching figure approached with a staff, horns atop its head, and a tail darting from one side to the other.

"You know you offered the duke a sacrifice?" Guy said, looking from Thomas to the creature.

Thomas's eyes fixed on the closing beast. "But we never completed it."

Guy pointed at the smouldering dead body of the duke on the floor. "When you pushed him into the flame, you offered the duke *as* a sacrifice."

The creature moved into the light, revealing the white fur on its face, the cloven hooves, and the fact it carried a spear, not a staff. Guy stared at the creature in dismay, noting the black eyes bulging on the side of its head and the twisted beard at the end of its chin. The three remaining robed men dropped onto their knees and bowed.

The goat demon bleated.

Guy plunged his sword into the back of one worshipper whose eye had been drawn to the hell beast.

Thomas moved to a second, whacking him on the back with the flat of his sword.

The third stood as Guy approached. As Guy slashed at him with the sword, he dodged the blow.

While Guy remained occupied with one man, the other remaining red-robed man stood and faced Thomas, no doubt annoyed at being slapped on the back with a sword. Instead, he should have been relieved that Thomas's incompetence had spared his life. Thomas lunged with his sword, random swipes through the air, causing the man to step back. The grin on his face showed he knew he faced a poor swordsman. He planned to wait him out. Let him exhaust himself.

Alas, he and the goat demon were not on the same page. As the robed man stepped back, the goat demon plunged his spear through his back. He lifted the skewer to his mouth and bit a chunk out of the man's shoulder.

A spray of blood decorated Thomas's face.

Guy, meanwhile, had dispatched of his adversary. Thomas darted to the other side of the room, away from the marching demon. Blood stained its white fur. It bleated: a feeble sound more suited to a pygmy goat rather than a hulking demon. Still, the robed man (or what remained of him) remained on the spear, having slid down to where the goat demon gripped the weapon.

"Why is it still coming?" Thomas called.

"What do you mean?"

"We killed the demon master. The familiar is dead. Shouldn't that send the demon back?"

"Aye, that's normally how it works, except *you're* the one who made the sacrifice."

Thomas gulped and took a step forward. "Excuse me, hello!" He waved to the goat demon.

The goat demon bleated again.

Thomas spoke in a loud, clear voice. "I did the sacrifice by mistake."

Guy rolled his eyes and tightened his grip on the hilt of his sword. He ran myriad possibilities through his head, plans of attack to distract the creature and get the upper hand. He considered the rubble of the collapsed staircase and the danger of fire. This would be a fight in which he'd need all his cunning, all of his skill to survive.

Thomas cupped his hands around his mouth. "Didn't you hear me? I said I did the sacrifice by mistake. You can go now."

Again, the goat demon bleated. It stopped marching. It pointed its spear to the ground. The dead body slid down the spear and flopped off onto the floor, sending a plume of dust into the air. The goat demon belched, the sound echoing around the cellar. It bowed to Thomas, turned, and sauntered back along the flaming tunnel. As it disappeared from view, the flames departed, and most of the tunnel sealed again, leaving a chasm under where the steps once were.

Guy stared at Thomas in shock.

"Sometimes, Guy, diplomacy is a far superior tool than a sword." Thomas lifted his sleeve to his face and wiped away the blood.

Guy walked into the open cavern. He stared at the door above and calculated his position. "Looks like we've got the start of our tunnel towards the Houses of Parliament."

Thomas gazed into the tunnel and then at the door. "So, which is the quicker way out: tunnelling or climbing?"

Chapter 32—In Which Guy Fawkes's Dislike of Cecil Intensifies and the Conspirators Start Digging

Weeks passed. A talking point for a few days, the social elite soon forgot about the disappearance of the Duke of Buckingham. When someone known for dabbling with demons disappears, speculation rarely lasts long. To avoid getting caught up in any investigation, the conspirators stayed well away from Thomas's new property. Nobody raised any suspicion about the transfer of an unimportant building into the hands of a reputable tailor, for many had seen him concluding the deal at Westminster Hall prior to Buckingham's disappearance. People spoke of a mysterious stranger though, John Johnson, who spoke his name aloud on the night of the duke's disappearance.

To ready themselves for the coming manual labour, the conspirators set about securing pickaxes and lengths of wood to construct supporting struts. The conspiracy would go nowhere if they were trapped in a collapsed shaft midway between their storage room and the Houses of Parliament. They procured pickaxes from various places outside London and only moved them to the building under the cover of darkness.

Thomas used another approach to get the wood in, ordering other conspirators to carry it into the building in the middle of the day while complaining to anyone who'd listen about the weak ceiling in the building he'd been tricked into buying.

With all in place, the tunnelling could commence. Great excitement in the streets of London, however, delayed their start further. Banners appeared in prominent places in the city requesting an audience at the Holbein Gate of the Palace of Whitehall. People spoke of a great proclamation, of the King's intent to address his people.

Despite all his unsatisfactory experiences of hope, Guy held on to the belief that this announcement would bring an end to all of his troubles. He dared to dream that James I would reveal that he had ousted the demon masters from government and bring a time of celebration in their great nation. As often as he told himself how ridiculous that was, hope continued to burn.

Guy gathered as part of the crowd of thousands of people close to the royal palace. While his friends were in the crowd, they had split up. Part of their conspiracy agreement meant limiting time together in public. That way, if one was compromised, witnesses couldn't link them.

Robert Cecil emerged first, blowing a gust onto Guy's flame of hope. Close behind followed Juan de Velasco, there to cement that peace agreement with the Spanish. James I then emerged, striding with purpose.

Cecil spoke to a silent crowd. "Treachery is among the greatest crimes in this world of ours. Witchcraft is another. When one stands not only against their country, but in support of witches, too, it is a truly heinous act." Cecil stepped away.

Through the gate came several men who constructed a platform. They placed three blocks and a basket beneath each one.

Next, guards manhandled three men through the gates, forcing them to kneel over the blocks. Guy face dropped as he recognised one of the men: Sir Henry. The complexions of the other two suggested they too had been captured on the continent.

Three executioners stomped through the gate wielding great axes.

From behind the gatehouse, drummers played, and when they stopped, the axes plummeted through the air, cleaving the prisoners' heads from their shoulders. Many in the crowd gasped.

Cecil walked through the gate. He plucked the head of Sir Henry out of the basket by his hair and held it aloft to the shocked crowd. Their surprise soon gave way to cheers.

"These heads shall decorate the gate to the Tower of London to serve as a reminder of your duty to your king."

King James I strode out to stand in front of the platform. "Thou shall not permit a witch to live. The devil, that simple illusionist, will make a hundred things seem both to our eyes and ears other ways than they are."

Guy turned away before James did. The King continued to speak of witches and demons and their evil. He knew how to identify deceivers. How could he not see those around him deceived him? Could he not see they were false? Guy hurried to Thomas's property and took the repaired stairs. Guy grabbed a pickaxe, entered the alcove the demon had left for them, and smashed at the rock with the pickaxe. Each strike became an act of punishment as bits of rubble sprayed into his face. Unpractised in such action, his shoulders and arms burned, particularly his right shoulder.

He'd not made more than three dozen strikes when another clash of pick-axe and rock came beside him. Guy set down his tool and watched Kit strike at the wall. Jack stood beside him, too, pickaxe in hand.

"Poor Sir Henry," Guy said as Kit recoiled from the strike.

Kit shook his head. "He didn't deserve that."

"Father Dijon, too." Jack added, "He trained Oswald and a bunch of the other Jesuits I brought to this country."

"You know what that means, don't you?" Guy asked.

"No one's safe. If you stand against demons, they'll lop your head off." Kit swung the pickaxe at the rock again.

Guy took his pickaxe in hand again and struck the wall. "So, we have to do this. We have to find a way under the Houses of Parliament and blow every demon-loving one of them to bits."

Catesby raced down the stairs, waving his hands about. "Stop!"

That flame of hope stirred in Guy once more before he shook off the feeling.

"We can hear you banging from the street. We'll have all sorts coming around asking questions about what's going on."

"Tell them there's building work to repair the cellar roof," Kit said, preparing to swing his pickaxe again.

Jack grabbed Kit's arm to stop him striking the rock again.

"That's only going to be feasible for a couple of weeks." Catesby leant against the wall and held his head in his hands. "This is going to take months. We need to disguise the noise somehow."

One by one, the conspirators appeared in the cellar, drawn by a need to do something in reaction to the horror of the executions. When each man entered, Catesby asked the same question: "How can we disguise the noise of our digging?"

They needed Thomas Percy to arrive before anyone made a workable sug-gestion, and for Thomas, it tripped from his tongue like the most obvious an-swer in the world: "A printing press."

"Are they noisy?" asked Catesby.

"When operated by a brute, they are." Thomas put his arm around Francis Tresham, who shook it off and shoved him away.

"Where are we going to get the equipment to start one of those?"

"I have a friend of a friend who may be able to put me in touch with someone."

"Even if we get hold of a printing press, whatever are we going to print?" Catesby asked.

Thomas weaved between people until he stood beside Catesby. He put his arm around him. "How about we start with a little title called *Daemonologie* by a certain King James I?"

"Brilliant," said Jack. "Surely no one will suspect us of misdeeds if we're showing devotion to the king by printing his work."

Thomas tapped his temple. "Not just a pretty face." A scab drifted from the side of his face to the floor.

Thomas's friend of a friend proved reliable and put him in touch with someone replacing an old printing press. A successful publisher wanted an upgrade from their work machinery, and they were sick of all the clattering of their aged equipment. The day the new one arrived, Thomas enlisted Guy's help to dismantle the old one and take it to the building in Westminster. Within a couple of days, they'd made it operational once more. Upon testing it, Thomas brought the top plate down with a clatter.

Guy stood outside and asked Thomas to do it again. Aye, it was perfect. The action of the printing press meant no one would think twice about the noise coming from the building. Back inside, Guy had Thomas repeat the process, counting how long it would take before he could slam the upper plate down once more.

"Okay, maintain that precise rhythm," Guy said before rushing into the cellar, counting in his head.

Above, the printing press clattered. Guy grabbed the pickaxe. He waited for it to clatter again, and counted, swinging the axe so he collided with the wall. He continued to count, striking it again, and again, and again.

After several minutes, Guy turned around.

Catesby watched him.

"What's the verdict?" Guy asked, panting.

"It's perfect. I couldn't distinguish the sound of digging from the printing press from above. I didn't know you were here until Thomas told me to look downstairs."

"So, we continue."

"That's right and I'm putting you in charge of this operation. Use everyone. You have Bates too."

"Bates?" He often worked on Catesby's behalf. "Can we trust him?"

"If I couldn't, I imagine we'd already be imprisoned in the tower. He overheard Wintour and me in discussion, and as cautious as we were, he read between the lines..."

"And he wanted in?"

"Indeed. Stick to short shifts throughout the day." Catesby glanced down. "Overnight, we can work on removing the rubble."

Guy stared at the rock wall, seeing through it to the Houses of Parliament. "Is this going to work?"

Catesby put his hand on Guy's shoulder. "With every inch we carve through this rock, we're getting closer to a better world."

Chapter 33—In Which Guy Fawkes is Troubled in the Tunnels by Unquiet Spirits

The digging continued to the rhythm of the printing press for the next few weeks, with the first struts in the tunnel put in place to secure it. After business hours, after sunset, they removed the rubble in small amounts, dumping it into the Thames.

The combined efforts of their digging had resulted in several yards of progress, but an unexpected problem arose. Despite not digging any deeper, and despite going away from the river, the bottom of the tunnel filled with water.

Only when Kit came in for a digging shift did anyone come close to a reason. "There might be an underground river nearby, a tributary from the Thames."

"What can we do about it?" Guy asked.

"We can put the rocks back." Kit stared at Guy, blank.

"Any other bright ideas?"

"We might have to put up with it. We can hardly bail it out in buckets. But if it is an underground river, it might save us some time."

Guy leant against the rock, then pulled himself away from the cold. "How?"

"If there are secret caverns, we don't have to dig all the way through."

Guy, Kit, and Jack set to work at the rock, and after a couple of hours, Kit came away from the rock, spitting and fanning at his face.

"What is it?"

"Water, coming through the rock."

Guy entered the tunnel. Under the light of a lantern, the rock glistened. He touched the cold water dribbling down it. Guy returned to the cellar to grab a pickaxe. He struck the wall close to the spot where the water came out. It ebbed out of the hole a little faster, then slowed back to a trickle once more.

Guy struck the rock again, and the pickaxe embedded further into the rock. It had to have found a hollow behind it.

Guy yanked out the tool and struck the rock several more times until he'd made a gap wide enough to squeeze his fingers through. Water splashed onto his hand.

"Kit, Jack, have a look and tell me what you think."

Kit and Jack headed into the tunnel. Guy listened to surprised coos and then a few strikes of the pickaxe came.

Kit and Jack wandered back out, Jack's face dripping wet.

"What do you make of it?"

"We've found a spring. We'll have to dig our way in to be sure."

Given the danger of working outside of usual business hours, they had to wait until the next day before they could dig out a hole big enough to fit through. Kit climbed through first. Guy handed him a lantern, which he shielded from the dripping water with his arm.

"We've got a spring, all right," Kit yelled. "There's water squirting through the rock."

"Where does it go?" Guy called.

"Up."

Guy bit his lip. "I'm coming in."

In some ways, Kit was right. The water sprung from the ground and shot out. From there, it dripped over him. Shivering as drops ran down his spine, he took the lantern from Kit and crouched. The water had worn several rivulets and disappeared through gaps in the bottom of the rock. Guy held his ear to the rock and stood.

"Kit, listen there."

Guy shuffled out of the way and Kit moved into place. A few seconds later, Kit stood. "There's water. We found an underground river."

"Did you hear anything else?"

Kit shrugged. "No."

"I heard bells."

Kit lowered his head again. "Oh, yeah."

Guy tried to listen while standing up, but his head filled with whispers. He covered his ears. The restless dead always spoke to him most while church bells rang. That call to worship alerted the restless dead, made them cry out in anger at their injustices. He squeezed through the gap and returned to the cellar.

Jack followed behind. "What is it?"

"The voices of the dead. They're calling inside."

"What are they saying?"

Guy shrugged. "There are so many talking at once, I can't make sense of it."

"What do we do?"

"Continue. Help Kit clear out the entrance to the spring. We'll tunnel past it."

It took a couple of days to excavate the area. The cavern had been formed by the spring, and they could continue to tunnel straight towards the Houses of Parliament without too much fear of falling into an underground river, for the water exited to the right of the chamber. Kit had little doubt that the water flowed in that direction and had even walked above ground on a route which he believed connected that underground stream to the Thames.

Only once they opened up more of the cavern did Guy return. Everyone else reported hearing a shallow ringing sound. Only Guy heard the voices. Guy tried to maintain his focus on the job, examining the chamber, suggesting where struts needed to be placed, and offering a slight correction about where the digging needed to continue.

Guy had readied himself for this moment. It had been a long time since the restless dead spoke in mass to him. He had learned to filter out the voices, only tuning them in at times of need. But this great ringing bell insisted he listen. He closed his eyes. They all came at once, voices shouting, indistinguishable from one another. He tried to pick up a certain pitch, tuning out all others. Now words were distinguishable. One voice called his name over and over. He tuned out the rest to listen:

"*Guy, Guy, Guy, Doctor Faustus was a tremendous success. Thanks for all your advice on demons, my good man. So, this doesn't feel like a complete waste of your time, I'll leave you with a spot of drama! Avenge me, Guy Fawkes! Avenge me."*

Guy bathed in a confused sense of satisfaction. When he learned of Christopher Marlowe's passing, a deep sadness hit him. Hearing from him again brought back only happy memories, albeit of difficult days.

Hoping another voice would bring similar warmth, he tuned in another voice.

"I lost everything, believing a small sacrifice would give me it all. What a fool."

Was that the Duke of Buckingham? He listened in again to similar voices sharing tales of woe: so many people drawn to devilry, only to be betrayed by it. Never had he needed to put an end to the misery and suffering more.

A strong female voice called out, drowning out all others.

"You're the one I blamed for the death of Catherine Stanley. How wrong I was about the sycophants around me. Do your worst!"

Guy clearly recognised the voice of Queen Elizabeth, though they'd conversed only once. If only Guy had spoken to her honestly, if only he had fought harder to gain her trust, he could have persuaded her to cleanse her court.

The voices quietened. Many only needed someone to hear their last words before they passed on to an everlasting peace. The ringing sound itself, Guy presumed, came from the way the water forced through the rocks, causing a vibration the spirits had mistaken for the ringing of bells.

Finding the small chamber meant there were a couple of square yards they no longer had to chip their way through, so they were ahead of schedule. Listening to the dead, though, had disturbed Guy, and he longed to leave London for a short period. That evening, he visited the Catherine Wheel Inn to meet with Robert Catesby. Nervous about meeting in the same place all the time, Catesby decided on several other appropriate venues, places where spies of Cecil were not known to dwell.

"How goes the printing business?" Catesby winked.

"We had a huge breakthrough this week. Progress is going better than expected." Guy too winked. "And what of your latest endeavour?"

"I have accrued sufficient finance to allow the project to enter its final stage."

"That's wonderful." Guy quaffed ale. "As we are ahead of schedule, I'd appreciate a chance to collect the goods from the docks."

"But who shall continue the fine work on your project?"

"I have many eager to take a turn at the wheel. The brothers, for instance."

"Wright?"

"What about Wintour?"

Catesby nodded. "So that might mean we need to make some extra allowances. You can set off tomorrow if that is..." Catesby altered his tone, "all Wright with you."

"Aye, I appreciate the company. Another drink?"

Guy and Catesby smiled smugly and ordered more ale.

Chapter 34—In Which Guy Fawkes Revisits a Wise Old Friend En Route to Collect the Gunpowder

As discussed with Catesby, Guy left the Wintour brothers in charge of the digging, and they promised to work Tresham hard. Guy hoped that by the time they returned (likely late December) the bulk of the digging would be complete. Percy had a tailor shop on the south of the Thames with a large storage room next to it. Until such a time they needed it in the tunnels, the gunpowder would be secure there.

They were to collect their shipments of gunpowder in Portsmouth. Beyond the desire to escape the capital, Guy had an ulterior motive for collecting the gunpowder. En route, he could call in on an old friend. Guy wanted Kit and Jack beside him because he trusted them the most should the gunpowder collection turn ugly, but they would also be part of the conversation he needed to have.

Rain had fallen every day over the last week, making the journey away from London miserable. They stopped in various inns but found their choice of suitable towns in which they could stay depleted. They arrived at some walled towns to find signs on the gate warning of plague. Others were eerily quiet as they passed through, curfews enforced to stop the spread of the foul infection. Guy feared this demonic plague, and worried about the hellish spores farmed in Morocco and sent out in barrels by the Children of Mizraim. How he wished he'd had an update from Samra! Since leaving the Spanish Netherlands, though, he'd lost contact.

One night, when close to their destination, they found a town free of plague familiar to Guy. He'd stopped in Haslemere the night Marlowe had pulled him into his carriage, and a surgeon had yanked a crossbow bolt out of his shoulder. We wondered if the old surgeon (and his even older mother) were still operating but thought better of making his face known in too many places. The trio remained in the inn, keeping their talk clean and their ears open.

Only when patrons spoke of the plague, did Guy's ears prick up. "Hideous yellow eyes," he heard one gentleman say. Another spoke of his relative, "shuffling mindlessly in the streets."

Kit lifted his shirt to cover his mouth, glad when the men moved on.

Early the next day, the trio arrived at Cowdray House. This time, the housekeeper ushered them inside and into the parlour with no delay. The Viscount, they were told, was away on business. As much as Guy would have liked to have seen his friend again, Anthony Browne's absence meant he needed to know no part of the plot, a desirable outcome until such a time they needed a noble to support their puppet monarch who would reign over a demon-free land.

After passing coded messages through servants, Oswald Tesimond joined them. As he entered, he gazed at his three former pupils of Saint Peter's. "When were we last gathered together with the light of the Lord shining upon us?" Oswald indicated the window where, after days of grey skies and drizzling rain, the sun shone once more.

Guy wondered if Oswald had added this last clause to avoid reference to the time they were last together in that secret area beneath Saint Peter's. Scarred by the hand of a demon, his faith shattered, then, Oswald desired only to escape that life before it destroyed him.

As Guy looked at Oswald, he realised his change of life had saved him. While he still bore the scars, his healthy complexion rendered them insignificant. While his eyes had sunk and his face was full of shadow, the light sought it out to radiate upon, and that light beaconed out, bringing goodwill to others.

"As much joy as it brings me to spend time in your company, I suspect you are here to do more than reminisce." Oswald folded his arms in the manner of Pulleyn during their days at Saint Peter's. "If you wish to unburden yourself of your troubles, please believe I have the strength of an ox and can impart some guidance that will leave you sure the Lord has placed you on this path for a good reason."

Guy gazed at Kit and then at Jack.

Only when the silence became palatable did the first twinge of concern appeared on Oswald's face.

Guy broke the silence. "Tell us your opinion of the reign of King James I."

Oswald sighed. "He has broken every covenant he has ever made to men of our faith." He stared at Guy, Kit, and Jack. "We had hope for his mother, Mary Queen of Scots. She vowed to put faith at the centre of her reign and chase the demon scourge from our land."

"But Queen Elizabeth had her killed." Guy stared at the floor.

"So, we assumed King James would oppose the past monarch. He even wrote letters to other leaders in Europe, to Pope Clement VIII promising to put piety at the centre of his every action."

"Has there been any change in policy?" Guy asked.

"Only for the worst. Queen Elizabeth always kept a close eye on the papists, believing they harboured the last remnants of the Knights Templar. She controlled them with fines and house searches. King James has increased fines and called in all arrears, taking livestock and property instead of payment, leaving families destitute."

Jack leant forward. "Do you believe him to be a wicked man?"

"His actions have, unquestionably, been wicked. But can a good man be manipulated into doing evil? Is that not Satan's purpose? A victory over a good man is so much better than bringing another ill soul to the table."

Kit leant forward, too. "If we could replace him, would there be a chance for this nation?"

Oswald shook his head. "A King reigns by divine right. I cannot condone any action to remove a monarch."

Guy linked his hands. "You know what King James thinks of us. He considers all that follow the Catholic creed as treacherous already. Our sect, we who hunt demons following the covenant of the Knights Templar, is part of that. If he already considers us traitors, what further punishment can there be if we commit acts of treason?"

Oswald turned pale. "You are getting into dangerous territory."

Guy moved from his chair, onto his knees. "Forgive me, Father, for I have sinned."

Behind him, Kit and Jack moved into similar positions, the palms of their hands pressed together.

Oswald's eyes grew wide. "Remember your teachings. Remember what Pulleyn said about those that strike out in wrath. What do you want to become?"

"We are plotting against our King to bring one to the throne who will confront the plague of demons in the palace."

"I cannot hear this." Oswald turned and left.

Guy, Kit, and Jack continued to confess their sins. Once they had finished, the trio stood.

Outside, light continued to shine despite the gathering clouds.

Chapter 35—In Which Guy Fawkes Finds a Problem with the Gunpowder

Guy Fawkes and his friends rejected the offer of a bed for the night at Cowdray House. Their intended actions sat uneasy with Oswald, and spending a night under the same roof felt disrespectful. All, however, agreed that his words about King James I only made their plot more necessary. They stopped instead in Harting and continued the next day to stop at an inn on the outskirts of Portsmouth.

Tresham had already visited the docks to arrange the purchase. Likewise, he had purchased a series of wagons to transport the gunpowder to London. They, too, awaited near the docks.

Guy hoped to be far from Portsmouth, with the goods in transit by the time night fell. They collected the wagons and rode to the docks, where they were to meet a trader by the name of Matthew Gordon. When they arrived, Gordon awaited with the goods ready for loading. Optimism hit Guy, a strange notion that he'd rarely encountered before.

Gordon showed them into the warehouse, one of his employees carrying a lantern before them. "These are the barrels we have set aside for you." Gordon leant against his wares.

As the lantern shone on the barrels, Guy saw something which stopped the breath in his chest: the pierced star symbol of the Children of Mizraim.

Guy shook his head. "Do you have any from a different supplier?"

Gordon glared at Guy. His eyes narrowed as his cogs turned.

Guy suspected he'd rather avoid a confrontation with a customer whose money he'd already taken and knew how to grease the wheels of the transaction. "We'd be happy to pay a supplementary charge if there is any inconvenience."

Gordon nodded and beckoned them deeper into the warehouse. He indicated several more barrels. "Would these be adequate?"

Guy checked the barrel for signs of the tainted mark. He asked Gordon to lift the lid so he could examine the product. He had Kit and Jack check it over, too.

"Aye, this is perfect." Guy took out a handful of coins. "I hope this will cover your troubles."

Gordon's eyes fixated on the pile of gleaming coins. "There will be a delay. If you return in two hours, we'll have loaded your wagons and you'll be ready to roll."

Guy thanked Gordon, and the trio made for a nearby tavern.

"What was that about?" Jack asked once they'd settled at a table with their ale and a bite to eat.

"Did you see it, Kit?" Guy asked.

Kit nodded and turned to his brother. "Remember what I told you about Morocco?"

"The contaminated gunpowder?"

"Aye."

"It's here."

Guy checked over his shoulder for unwanted company. "Every town we passed through that had the plague has a large barracks. None of the clean towns had mass gatherings of soldiers."

"So, where soldiers have that gunpowder, the plague spreads?" Jack asked.

"We have to destroy it," Kit said.

"Aye, but we can't set the building alight. That'll release the poison."

"Then what?"

"We sink the barrels to the bottom of the sea."

When the trio returned to Gordon's warehouse, they kept conversation to a minimum. Each checked their wagon to ensure the correct supply of gunpowder had been loaded. They thanked Gordon for his efforts and left. The deal was as unproblematic as a transaction could be. Gordon could not have noticed that while Guy checked the distance between the warehouse and the sea, Jack inspected the quality of the doors, and Kit investigated the neighbouring premises. When they stopped at a tavern north of Portsmouth, they shared their thoughts.

"We'll be able to bust through the door, no problem," Jack said.

"Once we get past the first couple of yards, we can roll the gunpowder into the water. It'll land on the jetty, but I'd wager it'll smash right through."

Kit joined in. "Most of the business premises will be empty, but there were signs that someone lives above the one opposite."

Guy leant forward. "So, we may have a witness. Chances are they'll either come out and confront us or send word to Gordon."

"We're doing this then?" Jack asked. "We're going back to destroy the gunpowder."

Guy shrugged. "I don't see that we have a choice. There's no point over-throwing a corrupt monarchy to preside over a land decimated by disease."

After securing their stock, the party made their way back to Portsmouth, and when night fell, they crept toward Gordon's warehouse. The tavern in which they'd earlier supped remained lively but far enough away that no one would hear their noise. No lanterns illuminated any windows in the area. Even the dwelling Kit had identified as a risk seemed quiet.

First, they surveyed the area between the warehouse and the water. Aye, after hefting the barrels out of the warehouse and shuffling them only a few yards, they could be rolled to the jetty to crash into the sea.

Jack set about gaining access to the premises. A rudimentary lock proved no match for brute strength. The trio covered their faces and slipped inside, pulling the door closed behind them.

Guy had surveyed the stock in the warehouse when selecting barrels; the questionable stock lay behind the door, and in the barrels kept in the area around to the left.

"If we move all the barrels close to the door to begin with," Guy suggested, "we'll be able to roll them out and to the water quicker."

Over the next half hour, they shuffled barrels closer to the door, moving the good stock back further, not wishing to waste any of the decent stuff. They took a moment to catch their breath, and Kit pushed the door open.

Guy rolled a barrel towards the door, but Kit remained standing in the way.

"Kit, move," Guy called as he continued to push the barrel forward.

"We have a problem," Kit said.

Guy steadied his barrel and moved to the door. Jack joined him.

A group of six men stood outside the warehouse, three of them holding clubs. "Go tell Gordy we've got a rat problem," one man said, and another hurried off.

Guy gazed at Kit and Jack. Their hands were on the hilts of their swords. They had more confidence than he did about their ability to fight their way out of trouble. There had to be another way. What had Thomas taught him about diplomacy?

Guy eased past Kit and stood with his hands raised. "Gentlemen, we are not thieves. We are here because these barrels are contaminated."

"Liar," shouted one of the gathered men.

Guy took another step forward as Kit retreated into the shadows of the warehouse. "The plague affecting the cities, towns, and villages all around us is spread by something mixed with this gunpowder." Guy turned to pat the nearest barrel. "They harvest it from the filth-infested streams of Hell."

"Nah, I'm not having it. You're jus' trying to thieve it."

Guy stepped forward, opening his hands to show his palms as he'd seen Thomas do. "This entire land is under the control of demon worshippers. They're farming your souls. Help us! Take back your freedom by dumping this gunpowder into the sea."

Applause sounded. The young man who had run off returned with Gordon behind him, clapping. "That's quite the speech. It's a wonder you're not in parliament."

Guy gritted his teeth. "Parliament is home to demon masters and toads."

"That may or may not be, but it don't give you the right to steal my stock."

Guy's whole body shook. "It's contaminated with evil!"

"If you have a problem with the quality of my goods, I suggest you speak to my supplier."

A figure six and a half foot tall stepped from the darkness, a man Guy had not seen for many years. Thick, dark facial hair framed his face, a small gap only at the chin. He wore a gauntlet, his familiar, a Pharoah eagle-owl clinging to it. Zidan al-Saqar's booming laugh brought bats screeching out of nearby buildings.

"My business associate told me to be wary of people questioning my stock." Gordon grinned. "And look at us now."

Zidan raised his arm, bidding his owl to fly. "You're the maggot who tried to shut down our mine! Another failure. Countless barrels have been shipped to ports all around your little island. You think your intervention here will make a difference? You will die for a pointless endeavour." Clutching the stone on his necklace, Zidan dragged his arm up, shaking as if the air offered great resistance.

The owl screeched. Buildings quaked. Wood splintered as the nearby jetty collapsed. As Zidan squeezed his fist, the dirt between him and Guy split, letting a blast of hot and fetid air gush out.

Within seconds, clawed hands appeared at the top of the rift.

Guy drew his sword, muttering the words to bring it greater power. Jack stepped beside him and did the same. Guy turned, expecting Kit to step forward too, but he'd disappeared. While Kit's absence caused concern, for not a second did Guy fear Kit had abandoned him.

The creatures' bodies were halfway out of the pit. Several men who'd gathered to confront potential thieves fled, and the others took nervous steps back, not sure if they should ready themselves with their clubs in case the creatures came for them.

Guy and Jack slashed at Hell's furies, the blades scorching through the weak flesh, and sending them back into the chasm below, knocking some of their climbing brethren down with them. They swarmed in the pit below, eager to cause chaos and destruction. They would continue to spill out until Zidan closed the rift, an act he'd not do voluntarily. His death, or the death of his familiar, was the only other solution.

With the familiar out of reach above, Zidan offered their best option. Alas, Zidan had no intention of succumbing to death, and, as if to prove this, withdrew his sword, a golden falchion, a glowing jewel in the hilt. As he slashed through the air with it, angry flames burned along its blade. He touched it to the ground, drawing a line, scorching the earth. He darted towards Guy, swinging his sword.

Guy blocked with his blue-flaming sabre. Even if he had his full strength, even if he could use his once stronger sword arm, he would not wish to get into a slashing contest with a taller, stronger enemy armed with a falchion.

Guy had liked the mobility of his lighter sabre in his nimbler days. He'd not adjusted to his lost pace, to switching sword arm, and he struggled to hold off the blow with his weapon close to his body, the heat of Zidan's cruel flame radiating through his flesh.

Jack moved in from the right, kicking Zidan in the leg and forcing him to one knee.

A creature leapt out of the pit. Guy twisted away from its lunging claw and slashed with his sabre, opening the creature's gut, spilling steaming slop onto the ground.

Jack came with his sword at Zidan, but he blocked it with his weapon before rolling away.

More creatures emerged from the pit. Their hungry mouths filled with razor-sharp fangs, and their claws, like daggers, demanded immediate attention.

Zidan eyed opportunities to strike when Guy and Jack were most occupied, lunging forward or diving in with his weapon. His long reach enabled him to strike and recoil while remaining safe from reprisal, and Guy considered himself fortunate that only his clothes had suffered the blade's fury. Emboldened, Gordon's thugs swung their clubs too, striking Guy and Jack before falling back to allow the furies to attack again.

Guy had felled his seventh or eighth creature and taken a number of lumps from clubs, when a distant blast and burst of light drew the men's attention.

Guy and Jack knew better than to let distractions draw them from their cause, for demons lusted only blood and could not be distracted by light shows.

"My ship!" Zidan cried.

While the men stood dumbfounded, Guy and Jack continued to chop away at furies, until Jack shoved Guy close to the ridge.

"Stop any more climbing out. I'll deal with this lot."

Guy regained his balance and set to lopping off the hands of the creatures that reached the earth. He checked that Jack had a handle on the landed furies, but as he blocked one and kicked out with another, Guy realised Jack could handle himself. Guy glanced too at Zidan, who issued orders to the remaining men. Gordon (who had been watching with his arms folded from the side) and a couple of others raced towards the dock, where flames continued to illuminate the night.

Zidan and the remaining club-wielding thug turned their attention to Jack and Guy.

"Don't let any more reach the surface," Jack cried as the last of the furies fell to the dirt. He took a deep breath and raised his sword, ready to take on Zidan and the other man.

So focused were they on Jack, they didn't hear the thud from farther along the road of one of their men falling to the ground.

Guy barely noticed, for every time he knocked a creature into the rift at one end, another closed on the top at the other. The constant running back and forth, the bending down to slash, the panic at every creature's cry, started to take its toll. Guy's arms and legs burned, but he couldn't stop.

Jack held off his opponents, kicking out at Zidan to force him back before turning to the man with a now-flaming club. Jack lunged, pushing his sword into the club-man's shoulder. He dropped his weapon, but before Jack could finish him, Zidan came again. Jack dodged to the side. The wounded man dived forward, grabbing Jack's shoulders, pulling him off balance.

Guy moved away from the rift, towards Jack, towards Zidan who raised his falchion high, ready to terminate Jack.

From so far away, Guy couldn't intervene.

But when Zidan's sword reached its apex, a whistle sounded, followed by a pained screech. From above, something plummeted, landing on Zidan and knocking him to the ground.

The earth groaned as the rift pulled together, the remaining furies tumbling back into Hell's fire.

Zidan shook the fallen owl, his familiar, from his body, but before he could clamber back to his feet, Jack plunged his blade into his neck.

The remaining man scrambled for his flaming club and glanced at Guy and Jack. His body heaved as he considered the fight. Outnumbered by men he'd seen slaughter demons and badly injured, he fled into the warehouse.

"Don't go into there with that..." Guy cried.

The panicked man ignored them, his act of life preservation ultimately doing the opposite. Guy and Jack hurried away from the warehouse, pulling their scarves back over their mouths.

Kit hurried toward them. Jack grabbed his arm, turned him around, and before they'd gone another hundred yards, the warehouse behind them exploded, the sickness escaping the barrels and drifting on the wind.

Only when they stopped, many miles away, did Kit reveal the weapon he'd used to dispatch Zidan's familiar. A crossbow modified to attach to an arm stump.

"We don't *know* it's Samra's," Kit said.

"How many other people had a crossbow they could attach to their arm?"

"Aye, but it doesn't mean he's dead, does it?"

No one spoke in reply.

If they'd succeeded in Morocco, Zidan would not have slaughtered Samra. He would not have shipped countless infected barrels to England. The disease wouldn't be spreading all over the country. Now, with diseased embers falling on Portsmouth, Guy had failed again. He'd grown sick of the feeling. Alas, he'd experience it again before the end.

Chapter 36—In Which Guy Fawkes Takes a Break from Demons to Attend a Wedding

Guy, Kit, and Jack slept for only a few hours where they'd secured the wagons full of gunpowder before heading off once more. They stopped at Cowdray House to warn Anthony Browne (who had returned from his business) to avoid Portsmouth and guard against the plague. After days of travelling, they reached the outskirts of London where they waited until nightfall, when the streets were quieter, to take the gunpowder into the city. The guards at the gate waved them through, checking only to ensure no additional people hid in the back of the wagons, not even asking for an explanation for the explosives. They delivered the gunpowder to Thomas Percy's storeroom on the south of the river, planning to sneak it across the river and into the tunnels nearer to the time of the state opening of parliament.

Guy woke Thomas to open his storeroom and take the delivery, and once they'd finished shifting the barrels from the wagons inside, Thomas asked Guy to remain.

"What is it, Thomas? I could do with getting my head down."

Thomas smiled. "I won't keep you long. I'd like your presence at another social engagement."

Guy huffed. "You've not pimped me out as a sacrifice again?"

Thomas's jaw dropped. "Now, really, Guy Fawkes, do you think so low of me? I only did that to obtain the deeds to the property we required."

Guy placed a hand on his temple. "So, what is it this time?"

"A wedding."

Guy massaged the side of his head. "Why do you want to go to a wedding?"

"Because I have been invited."

Guy pointed to himself. "But why should I wish to go to a wedding?"

Thomas's brows closed. "Do you recall nothing of our earliest endeavour?"

"Aye, I remember meeting my wife, getting locked up, fighting demons, and fleeing the streets. A typical day out with you, my old friend."

Thomas sighed. "But why did we go to King's Manor in the first place?"

237

"To spy. So, you're still in the information trade?"

Thomas placed his hands on his hips. "No one ever truly leaves it, Guy. So, while I'm listening for official secrets worth a little coin, you can get some of the general impression nobles have of our king and our parliament, sow the seeds of dissent, and suggest a chance of a better world."

"Oh, aye, as simple as that, right?"

Thomas placed his hands on his hips. "Do you want to attend this wedding or not?"

Guy answered quickly. "Not."

"Tough. You're coming. I've already got that lime green and tangerine doublet altered to fit you."

Guy rolled his eyes. "When is it?"

"Tomorrow. Meet me at my abode at midday."

The wedding was that of the twenty-year-old Sir Philip Herbert, recently elected the member of parliament for Glamorgan, and the seventeen-year-old Susan de Vere, the daughter of the 17th Earl of Oxford and famed poet Edward de Vere. How did two such youngsters get to have a wedding at the royal court at Whitehall? The poet had passed away earlier that year, and as Susan worked as a lady-in-waiting for James I's wife, the Queen Consort, Anne of Denmark, the king wished to provide for her. He grew fond of Philip Herbert after he proved himself capable on their hunting and hawking exploits. James and his wife, Anne, ever the eager matchmakers, decided the two were to be wed. What choice did they have? That said, on the day of their wedding, both looked ecstatic.

As Guy wandered around the royal court, nodding politely and engaging in informal conversation under the guise of John Blake (returning to his mother's maiden name), a pang of guilt about the plan to blow up the majority of the men in the building hit him. Even King James appeared amiable as he wandered around his court, wielding a turkey leg, taking bites as he greeted people. However, Guy remembered that affability, particularly among those surrounding him, was often only a façade, proven when James slipped the phrase "heinous papists" into a conversation.

"And to think there were rumours I'd show favour to the recusants," the king said, laughing. He took another bite of his turkey leg and guffawed, showering his eager courtiers with bits of shredded meat. "If I thought my son would grow up to be Catholic, or even sympathetic toward those heretics, I'd smother him with a pillow!"

How easy it would be to assassinate him as he roamed around his palace. Guy could ram that turkey leg down his throat until he choked.

King James continued to talk. "I'd argue only witches are worse than papists, but there's not much in it!" Some laughed, others shared nervous glances. Aye, he could end the life of the King, but with a court rammed full of demon masters, they'd soon corrupt his son too. Henry IX would never reign in his own mind. Catesby's way, however barbaric, ultimately seemed better. Wipe the lot of them out and put wholesome influences in place instead.

During the banquet, Guy had a deep desire to switch positions with the servers who swept in to deliver food and clear plates with the utmost efficiency. Thomas couldn't help but whisper his disappointment to Guy that the King had yet to buy into the Spanish court's chimpanzee server method. At dinner, Guy gazed around the room. He recognised few people from his past encounters with nobles. Few of Elizabeth's favourites remained. One notable sycophant remained, however, in a position close to the King. Robert Cecil sat sneering, picking at his food, and eating only a little, as if too good for a royal banquet.

If Guy had any fears that Cecil recognised him, he dismissed them when the spymaster cast his eyes over Guy with the same disdain as he did everyone but the King. Studying Cecil across the room, Guy saw the years had not been kind. Too much time spent drawing power from the depths of Hell had further pinched his face, leaving his cheeks hollow. Where his hair had receded, his forehead became prominent, but with the thin skin of a much older man.

After the feast had concluded, Guy ventured near to Cecil, finding a place to sit close to him as the actors performed their masque. The actors entered and announced they would perform *Juno and Hymenaus*. Typically, Cecil paid little regard to the performers, talking and demanding the attention of servers who remained nearby to replenish his goblet.

An equally rude gentleman joined him. Through Thomas, Guy later discovered his name: Richard Sackville. Their conversation suggested he served Cecil regarding clandestine matters. If he weren't a spy, he had his network of them. Small, though better built than a typical familiar, he bore an impressive black moustache, but his neckbeard looked patchy. He'd combed his dark hair to one side, swooping over his forehead as if trying to disguise a blemish. They spoke first of the Jesuits they had sought in Kent before speaking of signs of a Templar Knight's activity in East Anglia—they had intercepted an artefact in Ely Cathedral, much to Cecil's chagrin.

"And what of the plague?" Cecil asked.

"It continues to spread. A pigeon arrived stating Portsmouth had fallen, and I have sent riders to investigate."

"Any news on our plotters in the capital?" Cecil said.

Guy's ears pricked up and the muscles in his neck stiffened as he resisted turning to face Cecil.

"My informant suggests being vigilant around a new printing press that has opened at Buckingham's old property."

"Pay close attention to the site." Cecil's sneer even came through in his voice.

"Would you like me to continue to pay my source?"

"Tell him he's surplus to requirements. He'll give us the information and beg to remain on the same rate."

Guy risked a glance as the rat-like Cecil showed his teeth.

"Do you want me to send someone to investigate the property? We could pay a visit to collect taxes, or make claims of rumours they're hiding papists," Sackville said.

"No need. I may have a surprise for them."

The performance of *Juno and Hymenaus* drew to a close. The lute music stopped, and the lead performer delivered a soliloquy that left even Cecil's speechless. During the rapturous applause at the show's conclusion, Guy slipped away. During Cecil's conversation, he'd sensed the King's spymaster's eyes boring into the back of his head. Perhaps he imagined it, but the residual feeling of Cecil former influence, when Walsingham held sway in Guy's mind, troubled him.

Guy scanned the room, seeking Thomas. A ruckus on the other side of the chamber drew Guy's attention. Some of the palace guards had hold of a man's arm. For a second, Guy feared Thomas had got himself into trouble, but as he moved closer, he realised the man looked nothing like his friend.

Someone prodded Guy's shoulder. Thomas, his cheeks pink from excess, smiled at him and tottered forward. "This, Guy, is as good as the masque." He pointed to the man now being dragged away by the guards.

"What's going on?"

"See that chap there?" Thomas pointed.

"Aye."

"During the masque, he saw fit to lift some jewels right from around the neck of the young lady before him. When she realised, she kicked up a stink."

"Of course. Why'd he do it?"

"Guy, there are two reasons a man does anything, and this wasn't for love."

"Money." Guy sighed.

"Got it in one. Bravo. You really are beginning to understand how the world works. It's only taken some thirty years of your life, but bravo all the same."

Guy pondered only for a moment. He knew of Thomas's dire financial state at home, but if he needed money, he had plenty in his businesses to juggle around. Beyond that, he'd known Thomas long enough to trust him in such matters. "On the subject of money, one of our number may be taking Cecil's coin and is more than willing to sell us out."

Thomas's eyes grew large. "Any suspicions?"

Guy pictured Catesby's favourite. "Aye, I do."

Chapter 37—In Which Guy Fawkes Confronts Catesby in the Tunnels

After the revelation of treachery within their group of conspirators, Guy needed to speak to Catesby. Guy had scheduled Catesby to be onsite that morning alongside the Wintour brothers while Tresham operated the press. He hurried there, determined to resolve the issue.

As Guy entered the building, he gave Tresham a cursory glance. If anyone would sell out their friends for a little coin, it was him. When he had heard Cecil speaking of the snivelling toad who'd surrendered information with the simplest manipulation, he'd pictured Tresham's face. Guy considered confronting him, forcing him between the plates of the printing press and bringing it down until he confessed.

Instead, Guy headed below and grabbed a lantern. With the tunnel barely wider than a barrel of gunpowder, only one could dig at a time at the far end. It took a couple of minutes to reach the end of the tunnel. The Wintour brothers busied themselves in the cavern where the spring rose, adding support struts. With the opening of parliament only six weeks away, they were on schedule. But if Cecil already knew, why continue?

At the end of the tunnel, Guy waited for Catesby to complete his swing of his pickaxe and grabbed his arm.

Catesby's body jolted.

"We need to talk."

Catesby put down the pickaxe. "What is it?"

"Cecil knows about us."

The lantern flickered, casting strange shadows on Catesby's face. "What do you mean?"

"We need to pull everyone together and get to the bottom of it."

A grinding noise came from above. "What's that?" Guy asked.

"We're underneath the entrance to the storeroom." Catesby touched the pickaxe, turned back to Guy and then looked at the exit. "Shall we..."

They headed back into the spring chamber. Catesby crouched and rubbed his hands over the water. "Do you two want to disappear? We're stopping for the day."

The Wintour brothers nodded and made their way out of the tunnel.

"Tell Tresham to close up, too."

"Wait..." Guy's desire to confront Tresham had not receded.

"Tell Tresham to go." Catesby stared at Guy, holding his gaze until the brothers were out of the tunnel and up the stairs.

Catesby busied himself, moving tools in the cellar while Guy stood with his arms crossed. Once he heard the door upstairs close, he spoke. "Tell me what's going on."

Guy explained what he'd heard Cecil discussing, his anger building with each sentence, until he reached the end of his frustration. "And you let Tresham go!"

"It's not Tresham." Catesby put his hand on Guy's shoulder.

Guy shrugged Catesby off. "How can you be so sure?"

"I trust him. Thomas Percy's the more likely leak. The man can't keep his trap shut after he's had a drink or two."

"This wasn't an accidental leak. This is someone giving Cecil's spy information about what we're doing."

"How do you know it's not talk designed to scare plotters? I know how Cecil operates. He pretends to be aware of something, hoping the anxiety will cause something to slip."

"He mentioned this building. What about the Wintours?"

Catesby shook his head. "The Wrights?"

"This is not time for tit-for-tat."

"Well, it has to be someone, and I know who I trust."

"Aye, as do I." Guy sighed. "So, what do we do?"

"Continue."

An uneasy feeling grew in Guy's gut. "If they know about this, why haven't they stopped us?"

A squeak came from the far end of the tunnel.

Guy glanced into the blackness. "What was that?"

"I told you, we've dug to beneath the storeroom."

"No, it sounded different."

Another squeak came. This time, Catesby stared at the tunnel, too. "You're right. Come on."

Guy relit the lantern. The squeaks came more frequently. "We may have a rat."

They ventured along the tunnel until they reached the cavern. The squeaks came again, more distant, echoing from below.

Catesby nodded at the gap through which the spring water ran. "Didn't Kit say a river flowed beneath us?"

"You trust him on that, do you?"

Catesby grumbled.

The tunnel shook. Both Guy and Catesby groped for the walls for balance.

"Get out," Catesby cried.

A great scrabbling came from behind them, scratching and clawing and gnawing. The squeaking became a constant, a high-pitched wave rising and crashing.

Catesby and Guy raced into the cellar and peered back at the tunnel. A cloud of dust stirred in the entrance. It swirled, then broke as a brown shape burst through it, a rat, slick, and wet, with a body a foot long and a tail the same size.

Guy yelped before grabbing a spade and whacking the creature away. Its head looked wrong, somehow misshapen. Guy had no time to figure out what, as a second, third, and fourth rat burst into the cellar.

Catesby too grabbed a spade and swung for the creatures, but more replaced them until the volume of weird-headed rats in the tunnel left nowhere to stand. With each step, something squirmed beneath Guy's feet, threatening to tip him off balance. Rats nipped at his boots, and stretched on their hind legs toward his hose, making him kick out with one foot, then the other. Catesby performed a similar dance, throwing in an additional move in which he smashed the floor with the spade, splattering some rats and sending others scurrying away.

Guy kicked out again, then stepped in a weird jig towards the lantern. He hurled it into the tunnel, where the floorboards gave way to rock. The glass shattered, and burning oil spread over the rock, covering the entrance, licking at one of the supporting struts.

The rats' squealing became a panicked chorus of greater intensity as they fled the flames. Guy made first for the steps, glancing back to check Catesby followed. At that point, as he spotted a rat sitting on its hind legs and with his body upright. As Guy stopped to stare at the create, Catesby bolted past him. Guy realised what was wrong with the rat. No fur covered its face. It had no snout and a small mouth with lips. No wonder they hadn't bitten him with the ease he'd feared. These rats had tiny human faces, and as Guy glanced at another, it became clear that each bore the face of Robert Cecil.

Guy bolted out of the cellar door to find Catesby standing dumbstruck, facing a six-foot-tall rat standing on its hind legs. This one also had the face of Cecil, the forehead even longer that the real thing. It lunged at Catesby, who leant back, lucky to lose only a button from his shirt.

Guy drew his sword, blessing it, but not quite believing the abomination before him.

The rat twisted, its tail lashing out and knocking Catesby's feet from under him.

The rat remained on two legs, mocking a human stance as it shuffled toward Catesby.

Guy grabbed Catesby's arm and dragged him out of the way as the creature flopped onto its belly. Having missed its target, it squealed. It shimmied along the ground before rising onto its hind legs again.

Guy and Catesby moved round to the rear of the printing press as the creature tottered toward them again.

"You got your weapon?" Guy asked.

"No, I can't dig with a sword by my side."

"That settles it."

Mistrust grew in Catesby's. "What?"

"You're the bait."

Catesby's bottom lip curled, but he made no protest. He stepped into the view of the Cecil-faced giant rat.

The rat's human nose wrinkled, and he came for Catesby again.

Guy circled the printing press, coming out behind the rat, but as he lunged, the tail flicked up, knocking his sword from his hand.

The rat twitched. The back of its head bulged, and a second face of Robert Cecil appeared. Its eyes blazed and its teeth gnashed together. The rat shuffled forward after Catesby as the tail continued to slash at Guy.

As it chased Catesby, Guy's sword no longer remained under threat of a tail wallop. He grabbed it, and pursued the rat, trying to lure the tail into a slash.

Catesby continued to back off, keeping the rat-creature moving until it stopped once more, twitching again.

Catesby called out in revulsion.

"Another head?" Guy asked as he continued to step towards the tail.

"Yes, it burst out of the gut."

Guy took the creature's shudder as an opportunity and stood on the tail.

The rat screeched and twisted towards him, flexing its claws.

Guy slashed, severing the end of the tail.

The creature turned to Guy, shuffling towards him. The head in the rat's gut had Cecil's eyes, but with yellow irises. A tendril of flesh hung in front of the face.

Guy backed away, studying the pattern of its awkward movement. He lunged, and the creature shuddered once more. As a face poked out of its side, Guy thrust his sword into the gut face, piercing Cecil's eye.

The creature squealed and turned away from the threat. Guy lunged for the face on the back of the rat's head, puncturing the cheek, which leaked a yellow bilious liquid.

The creature slumped onto the plate on the printing press.

Catesby yanked the top plate down. It continued to move through the creature as its body exploded, sending great torrents of rat-swill over the room, the equipment, but most of all over Guy and Catesby.

They wiped the slop from their faces and leaned against the lop-sided printing press.

"Okay, so Cecil knows," Catesby said.

Guy wiped his sword and sheathed it. "Aye, the question is, why send something like that and not the King's guard? Why hasn't he arrested us?"

"That might be his plan—pin us down with that thing and send the guards. We go cold for five days, keep eyes on this place, then meet back at the Catherine Wheel?"

Guy agreed, and they went their separate ways. Guy left the property and hurried for the river to wash the worst of the mess from him. The whole time he wondered if this signalled the end for their gunpowder plot.

Chapter 38—In Which Guy Fawkes Goes Rowing

For days, Guy lay low, passing by the Whitehall property only to check for any sign of activity. He spoke only to Thomas Percy, who continued selling as many secrets as he did doublets. There were no rumours of any kind of plot, no talk of tunnels. Cecil always bragged about plots uncovered to help raise his status among the elite. Guy remembered how he had used the Dudley plot to worm his way into the position of spymaster. Perhaps, he intended to exploit this further. Maybe he wanted the conspirators to continue so he could gather more intel on traitors, inviting them to slip their own heads into the nooses lined up for them.

The day of the meeting at The Catherine Wheel came. Slush covered the streets after light snowfall the previous night, on that day in early 1605. Guy arrived at the tavern half an hour before the scheduled meeting time. He bought some ale, and instead of heading for the back room they usually met in, he sat in the shadows with the door in his eyeline. Several minutes passed before another member of the conspiracy arrived, still some time before the designated meeting. It was Tresham. A soldier dressed in the colours of the royal guard followed him in. Did Tresham plan to betray them at the meeting?

While Tresham went to the bar, the guard probed the opposite side of the tavern.

Tresham took his drink and headed for the meeting room.

Guy hissed, drawing his attention.

Tresham glanced toward the back room before heading over to Guy. "What are you doing, sitting there in the dark?"

"Keeping my eyes open for signs of treachery."

Tresham rolled his eyes. He took a sip of his ale. "You seen any?"

Guy stood. "Aye, I saw you enter with that soldier."

The soldier questioned a couple of drinkers on the other side of the tavern.

Tresham waved a dismissive hand. "He followed me in here."

"You'd like me to believe that, wouldn't you?"

Tresham placed his drink on the table. "If you've got something to say, say it. Stop tiptoeing around it like some tiddy child with a head full of nonsense."

Guy lunged forward and balled up the front of Tresham's shirt, pulling him closer. "There's evidence of a traitor in our midst, and I'd wager your fingers are stained with the crooked coin of the spymaster."

Guy released Tresham, who straightened his clothes.

Tresham took a half step closer to Guy, their noses almost touching. "Calm down. You're the one drawing attention."

The soldier stared at them from across the tavern.

"If I get any proof that you've sold us out, I'll spill your guts."

Tresham took a step back to study Guy. "Please. Don't think I ain't spotted your switch in sword arm. Don't think I ain't seen your awkward gait. Spill my guts? You can barely twist your hand to spill your drink."

Guy glanced over at the soldier. He remained fixed upon them, ready to intervene and engage in the sport of head cracking if the opportunity arose.

"If you'll excuse me," Tresham grabbed his drink with such vigour some slopped onto the floor, "I'll be waiting for the others in the back."

Guy headed to the bar to refill his ale. He tried to take the tankard with his right hand, but he couldn't grip the handle. Annoyed with himself, he sat once more. Guy scanned the bar. The soldier had left. When a few sips into his drink, Thomas Wintour entered. Guy let him pass and only stood when, a couple of minutes later, Catesby entered.

When Guy sat at the table—as far away from Tresham as possible, Tresham eyed the other two. "Did you get the Guy Fawkes accusatory welcome too, or did he reserve that for me?"

Catesby stared at Guy, his eyes narrow. Over the next couple of minutes, more of the party arrived: Robert Wintour, Kit Wright, Thomas Percy, and finally, Jack Wright. The other members of the conspiracy remained distant, Bates on an errand for Catesby, Digby and the newly recruited Rookwood, Grant, and Keyes supporting financially rather than in person, and more likely to be involved in the days that followed the fall of the King.

They started the meeting by talking about their experiences of the last few days. No one reported being followed or watched. Catesby recounted the events that led to them stepping back. Those that had passed the Whitehall property noted no soldiers. The door remained locked, and no one had been inside.

"I've come from there," Jack said. "It's why I'm late."

Catesby puffed out his cheeks. "What's it like?"

Jack shook his head.

Guy pictured the gore on the walls, the mess of the rats in the cellar.

"None of what you said is there. The printing press needs repair, and there's a scorch mark and broken glass from the smashed lantern, but no blood, no bones, no rats."

Catesby scratched his head. "But, how, if—"

Guy had experienced this trickery before. "Typical demonic behaviour. Remove all evidence of their horrors—leave the inflicted feeling like they're losing their minds."

Robert Wintour stood. "If Cecil has wind of our plot, why are we still here? Our lives are forfeit if he catches us."

Jack rose and cleared his throat. "Over the last few years, I've spent a great deal of time with," he checked over his shoulder, "Jesuit priests. They suspect Cecil is making a play for all-out religious war. He's hoping to decimate any genuine spirituality to leave the population prone to demonic possession. If Cecil knows about the plot, there's a good chance he wishes to let it happen to pin it on the Catholics—he'll claim it's a directive from the Vatican."

"So, we cease," Guy said.

Catesby stood and urged everyone to sit before doing likewise. "On the contrary. I say we call his bluff. If he's willing to let parliament fall as part of his game, we play that card, but we make sure we have every one of the king's children in our grasp. He needs an heir to wield any power."

Kit shook his head. "How are we even going to get close to them?"

"We'll worry about that when the time comes. Our next priority is to shift the gunpowder."

"When do you plan to do that?"

"Tonight."

Tresham guffawed. "Tonight? It's freezing out there."

"Which means fewer people out and about, and guards unwilling to do their patrols. Bates should have positioned the vessels by the time we reach the docks."

The members of the table glanced at each other.

"If anyone wants out, now's the time."

No one left.

A couple of hours later, with night at its darkest and the temperature at its coldest, the operation began. With his weakened arm, Guy could not row, so Catesby stationed him at the north of the river to help unload the barrels.

On the other side, loading, were Thomas Percy, Robert Wintour, and Bates.

Jack, Tresham, and Thomas Wintour had the joy of rowing across the Thames.

While waiting for the rowers to arrive, Catesby, Kit, and Guy popped back into the Whitehall property. The damage to the printing press remained, as Jack had said, but they were still in disbelief about the otherwise clean state of the building. They returned to the riverside, listening to the splash of oars in the water. And more splashing. Altogether more splashing than three boats rowing across the river necessitated.

The trio hurried to the riverside as the first of the rowboats thumped against the jetty.

"There's devilry afoot in those waters," Tresham said as he disembarked. He continued away from the boat, with Catesby following.

Jack landed next.

"What's going on?" Kit asked after tying Jack's boat.

Jack shook his head. "Fish leaping out of the water."

Wintour arrived.

Kit helped drag his boat close enough to tie up. "Did you have fish jump out of the water at you too?"

Wintour raised his eyebrows. "Fish! They were more like rats with fins and wings, smacking into us all the way across."

They unloaded the barrels and kept them by the water's edge.

Catesby returned. "The coast is clear. Speed the barrels into the building. We'll move them into the cellar later. We need a change of plan for the next load."

After they had emptied the boats, they gathered once more at the waterside.

"We're doubling up on the boats," Catesby said. "One to row, one to fend off whatever monstrosities are leaping from the water."

They nodded.

"I'm going with Thomas," Catesby said. "Jack and Kit, pair up. That leaves Guy and Tresham." Catesby put his hand on Guy's shoulder, which Guy shrugged off. "Consider it a trust exercise."

They boarded the boats and rowed back toward the south side where Thomas, Bates, and Robert Wintour waited to load them.

"Pairing us together, Catesby must want us to fail," Tresham quipped.

Guy ignored him.

"What good are you going to do when a flying rat lands in the boat? Next to useless."

"Maybe I'll lend them a hand to do you in."

"Not much of a hand, though, is it?"

Guy remained quiet as they continued across the river, focusing instead on the sound of the oars plunging into the water and the subsequent ripples and the icy chill of the night air. They rowed to the other side undisturbed by flying rat-fish and loaded more barrels into the rowing boat.

They headed for the north shore again, Guy sitting astride a barrel to allow a sufficient load on board. "How far across were you when they attacked?"

Tresham pulled on the oars, exhaling noisily, indicating the strain. "Before halfway."

Guy held his sabre, ready. And there was Tresham, arms occupied opposite him. While he had no intention of murdering the man, he couldn't keep the smile from his face.

A splash in the water came that differed from the other sounds, with a screech following it. A creature landed on top of a barrel. Aye, the others were right when they described it as a rat with wings and fins, a weird hybrid of mammal, bird, and fish. Guy didn't study it for long and ran it through with his sabre. He clambered over to the next barrel, closer to the middle of the boat.

"Don't upset the balance, you damned fool," Tresham barked.

Guy caught sight of a creature flying towards him. He slashed with his sword and chopped it into the water.

Tresham grunted.

When the next one came flying, Guy let it crash into Tresham's head, slashing it between his legs when it landed.

"Do your job!"

A second later, they bumped against the jetty.

They unloaded the barrels and made a repeat journey with few problems. They needed one last trip.

Once they'd loaded the boat, Tresham rowed once more, with Guy balancing on a barrel.

"You've not done a bad job, you know, with the left hand," Tresham said.

Guy waited for a barb that didn't come.

"It's not easy when you lose your primary sword arm."

"And you'd know?"

"Aye, I couldn't wield a sword with my right hand for months."

Guy remembered the way Tresham touched his knuckles. Hadn't Catesby mentioned some prior injury? A splash came, and Guy sliced the creature in two.

"I know you don't trust me, and I'm not too keen on you either."

"Get to the point." Guy eyed the dark water, waiting for the sound of a flying fish-rat.

"Perhaps the one you should be wary of is Robert."

"Wintour?" Guy glanced back over his shoulder into the darkness.

"No."

"Catesby?"

"Say no more."

While considering Tresham's words, a creature slapped into the back of Guy's head. It clawed at his hair, as it struggled for purchase then sank its teeth into his ear.

"I'll get it," called Tresham. He raised the oar and smacked the creature and Guy's head. Guy grabbed the side of the boat to stop himself from toppling over. The boat rocked, and Tresham chuckled.

Guy put his hand to his ear, feeling blood run over his fingers.

Another creature landed on the nearest barrel. Guy slashed at it and flicked the carcass into the river. Again, he considered Tresham's claim that Catesby had led them astray. It made no sense. Catesby was the architect of the scheme. Another creature came, and Guy slashed at it before it landed. Did Catesby have an ulterior motive? If so, what?

As they thumped into the jetty and started unloading the last of the barrels, another possibility came to Guy. Tresham had given him this information to sow the seeds of discord to distract from his own misdeeds. He'd have to keep a close eye on everyone.

Chapter 39—In Which Guy Fawkes Goes Wassailing and Yulesinging

At Catesby's request, the conspirators continued to keep their distance from the Whitehall property until after the winter festivities. Each took turns passing the building and watching for suspicious activity, but after they moved the barrels into the cellar, they did not return.

Thomas Percy secured Guy an invitation to a lavish Twelfth Night party, one free of the antics of children which often occurred at the end of the period of celebration. Cecil would be at the gathering, alongside Sir Edward Coke, the Attorney-General, and Richard Sackville, the young man who had reported to Cecil at the wedding. For Guy, this offered another opportunity to spy. The King would not attend, for he planned to remain at Whitehall Palace for their traditional Twelfth Night party in which the children acted the role of adult, something James' sons Henry and Charles would enjoy, while his daughter Elizabeth would witness the revelry from a sophisticated distance beside her mother after her return from the care of Lord and Lady Harington at Combe Abbey.

Guy met with Catesby alone at the Duck and Drake prior to the party. Catesby had beat him there, and by his demeanour, Guy suspected he's already had more than a couple of ales.

"What troubles you, friend?" Guy sat at the table opposite Catesby after buying ale.

"Oh, nothing. The weight of the nation on my shoulders." Catesby took a heavy draught of his drink.

"Tonight, at the party, our enemy shall be present. Should the opportunity arise..."

"Do nothing." Catesby took a sip of his drink.

"But we might not get another opportunity to get close to him for some time."

Catesby sighed.

Was that the sigh of a man caught in a twisted web of betrayal?

Catesby finished his drink. "I need to understand the game he's playing. If he knows but does nothing, what does it mean? Does he want us to succeed? If so, for what purpose? Is it as Jack supposed? He wants to use our plan to bring holy war upon our country? Or is he monitoring our plot from afar, toying with us, only so he can swoop in at the last moment to stop us? He'll be a hero. Is that what he wants? And yet, there may be some unseen angle."

While Guy understood Catesby's concerns, nothing he said convinced him it wouldn't be a good idea to get Cecil out of the way.

"We need to let him think he has the upper hand. When we swoop in to secure the royal heirs, that's when we'll have him."

"I'd feel a lot more content if he were out of the way."

Catesby lifted his tankard to his mouth again, but found it empty when it touched his lips. "Does it not trouble you, Guy, that some men in parliament may also be Catholics? That we might wilfully kill our allies?"

"Aye, it struck me as a rotten consequence."

"How about we draw them away?"

"How?"

"Guy, what I'm about to tell you may shock you to your core."

Guy's internal organs stiffened. The blood froze within his veins.

"I have been in contact with Cecil."

Guy touched the spot on the side of the head where Tresham had whacked him with an oar after suggesting Catesby was the traitor. Guy rose. "How could you?"

Catesby stood too, grabbing Guy by the arm and staring into his eyes. "It's a diversionary tactic. I'm arranging a force of Catholics to fight in Flanders. It will pull good men from parliament. Cecil will be glad to be rid of a disruptive force, but I can't do it if he's in his coffin. Do you know how long it takes to organise that kind of thing without the right people?"

"This is a dangerous game you're playing. Stand too close to the fire, and you're likely to get burned."

"A little burn is not a great cost for doing the right thing."

"Nay, but you're letting it consume you."

"Maybe, I am, Guy. Maybe, I am."

Guy left the Catherine Wheel and headed for The Strand, the venue for the party. Guy, however, had no thirst for revelry. The doubts, once settled, arose again. They were close to being in a position in which they *could* blow up the Houses of Parliament. Did that mean that they *should*?

Guy met the splendidly attired Thomas Percy at their designated meeting place. The blemishes on his face had cleared over the past few months, though the worrisome black spot remained. He did, however, develop a habit of dabbing the corners of his mouth with a handkerchief as result of producing too much saliva.

The hosts had provided a lavish buffet in the great hall on The Strand. Guy didn't know who lived there. Thomas did not know either. A friend of a friend had passed on the invitation, and when they arrived, they were welcomed in for some wassailing and yule-singing. They gathered a cup of hot cider, and instead of socialising, Guy urged Thomas into a quiet corner.

"What think you of our endeavour? After our recent troubles, should we continue?"

Thomas took a sip of his drink, winced, and licked his lips. He blew on the steaming liquid. "Did I ever tell you about my trip to Scotland?"

Guy shook his head.

"There's no reason I should have done. You were gadding about Europe. Everyone expected James would succeed Elizabeth by then. He didn't want to come here resembling some Scotch barbarian, so he called on the best tailor in London—"

"And when he wasn't available, they asked you?" Guy hid his smile behind his mug as he took a sip of his drink. The sharpness made him clench his teeth.

Thomas rolled his eyes. "And as London's most eminent tailor, I jumped at the chance. I found the King of Scotland to be an affable chap—deeply passionate about religion. When he spoke of the demon scourge and the dangers of witchcraft, I hoped we were onto a winner."

"If only."

"Indeed. As I measured him up, conversation moved on to Elizabeth's treatment of Catholics. Again, he frowned and talked about the importance of faith, his inclination to let man go to God in his own way. As long as he eschewed the kingdom of evil, he didn't much mind how they reached Heaven."

"So why..."

"Time has proven his words false. Shortly after his coronation here in London I first heard whispers contrary to our conversation. Do you know what he said?"

"I can imagine."

Thomas puffed out his chest and jutted out his lower lip. "He said, 'The time is coming, and I hope it is soon, when all papists' throats shall be cut'. Can you believe that Guy?"

Guy sipped his drink. "From what else I've heard, aye, I can. But what has caused this change? This is the crux of the matter for me, Thomas. Is there something we can do to turn the tide back the other way?"

Thomas gulped his drink and raised his eyebrows in appreciation. "That's the thing about tides, isn't it?"

"What?"

"They change. We work on James, he switches his view, we celebrate, but then some damned devil turns him back the other way."

Guy sighed.

"Do you know what happened when I told all and sundry that James brought great hope, that he'd free us Catholics from our bondage, only for him to be worse than Elizabeth in that regard? It ruined my reputation. That, more than anything, caused the rift between Martha and me; it put me on the drink and had me leaping into any warm and welcoming bed." Thomas sucked the saliva that collected in his mouth back and swallowed it before dabbing his mouth with his saturated handkerchief. "It's my ruin, Guy. I don't have a lot more wassailing in me."

"Don't say that."

"It's true. So, when you ask if we should continue in our venture, I say, one thousand times, yes. If we're going to have a monarch as malleable as tin, we may as well have one we can bash into shape, and we rid ourselves of all the others who hold hammers."

"Aye, I think you're right."

"Of course I am. And as my days of wassailing are near gone, I'll make the most of this opportunity."

Guy, however, was in no mood for celebration. By the time another yuletide came, England could be a different place, and while he agreed with Thomas about the necessity of change, Catesby had been right too—the weight was heavy.

Further burden fell on Guy when he eyed Cecil conversing with Coke. As a group broke into song, he moved around their perimeter, joining in as he tried to eavesdrop on the King's spymaster and chief judge.

"In that respect," Cecil said with a sneer, "One has to envy Fernando de Andalusia."

The carollers raised their voices, drowning out Coke's response. Guy thought it probable that Cecil spoke of the slumbering situation of King Philip III, which allowed the Chief Advisor full control of Spain. Cecil had hold of King James I's strings, but controlling him took some effort. Fernando had it easy. To all he suggested, King Philip III gave the nod. This gave Guy another good reason to rid the country of Cecil.

Coke wandered off, and Sackville joined Cecil.

"What word from the wilds?" Cecil gazed at his young spy.

"Plague rife in the north. From the south, it's spreading closer."

Cecil grinned.

"Is there any more you need from me?"

"Let me know when there are significant cases in the capital. Once it is here, we shall close the city down. We'll enforce a curfew, close the theatres and the public houses. By the time we return people's freedom, they'll be so relieved they'll be begging us to take more taxes."

Guy continued to listen into the conversation, hoping they'd change the topic to the printing press in Whitehall, but they failed to mention it.

Cecil knew. He had to. His silence on it suggested he wanted the plot to continue.

What else could Guy do?

Chapter 40—In Which Guy Fawkes Seeks Plague Answers

The plague descended upon London only days later. Reports spread of yellow-eyed folk with pustules pulsing on their faces, shuffling along the streets, coughing their sickness onto anyone stupid enough not to cover up or stay indoors.

Since Morocco, Guy had tried his hardest to avoid the plague. He could scarcely believe that anyone could be evil enough to inflict this on people, generating fear and mistrust in their population only so they could better control them in a miserable future. Guy longed for parliament to open, so they could rid themselves of the menace. The digging had progressed to the required position somewhere beneath the Houses of Parliament. The gunpowder sat in position, waiting to do its duty.

With only days remaining, Guy stood over the barrels. He'd deliberated over this time and again. Soon, the time for worry would pass. Or so he thought. Catesby ran into the building and hurried through the tunnel to announce the latest news to Guy. "They're proroguing parliament."

"What?" Relief washed over Guy. They didn't have to do this. "Until when?"

"Summer at the soonest."

"Then what? We wait?"

Catesby leant against the tunnel wall. "What more can we do?"

What more could they do, indeed? Staying alive became their priority, a job best done by avoiding all others. As the weeks passed and spring arrived, with every ban and every closure, Cecil's fingers wrapped around the throat of the country. How many would he let die before he let the people breathe again?

Guy recalled how infection had spread in Fez all those years ago. The Children of Mizraim had poisoned the water supply. Was Zidan's presence in Portsmouth more than a supplier meeting with a client? Had Cecil or his cronies met with him to share ideas? Was Cecil following Zidan's plague plan to bring chaos to London? Guy trusted one person more than any other, particularly for mapping rivers and subterranean passages. He wrote to Kit and asked if he'd be willing to meet him.

Kit, of course, agreed, and when they met at the Whitehall property (risking a fine for mixing with other people), he had been thinking along the same lines.

After some discussion, Kit suggested a plan. "If we find out where the first cases were, it would give us an idea of where they corrupted the water supply."

"I might have a source of that information."

Rumours stated that many politicians, lords, and nobles had taken refuge in the country in their self-sufficient manor houses, leaving London to suffer. King James I had relocated to Windsor Castle, and Robert Cecil to Burghley House in Lincolnshire. Both households were inaccessible, for they took on no new staff to keep them free of plague. The likes of Richard Sackville, however, remained low on the greasy pole to noble status and didn't have such luxurious country homes to fall back upon. He had an abode on Knyght Ryder Street. Guy and Kit waited until nightfall to pay the property a visit. His home was in the middle of a row of townhouses. He had no family with him, but he would have household staff. Guy had no intention of hurting them and would only do so if necessary. Sackville, however, would suffer if he didn't cooperate.

Given the dearth of people on the streets, Guy and Kit stayed in the shadows and moved quietly. Any noise would draw people desperate for some kind of action to the window. When they were close to Sackville's house they shared a plan.

"As our fighting days are numbered," Guy said, failing to stop a smile from creeping to his lips, "we should do a Kit special."

"Run in like a storm descending from the heavens and deal with the problems as they arise?"

"Aye, that's the one. I'll knock. When they answer the door, we shove our way in, take the butler out. You contain him, and I'll rush Sackville."

From outside the building, they noted a fire burning through one window. That gave them a good idea of which way to head.

Guy climbed the three steps to the door and knocked hard. Guy supposed Sackville's position made visitors common, so it was no surprise when the butler, an elderly gentleman with short white hair and no beard, answered without so much as a mote of suspicion. The butler's innocent face gave Guy a moment's pause. Kit, however, had not seen him and barged into the door, knocking it into the old man, who collapsed to the floor.

Kit glanced at the old man. He bit his lip.

"Tie him up," Guy said.

"What in blazes do you think you're doing?" the old man cried.

"I don't want to hurt him," Kit muttered.

Guy glanced at the old man's swollen lip. "Might be a bit late for that."

The old man spat a bloody tooth onto the floor.

Kit pulled out a rag and shoved it in his mouth as Guy shut the front door.

"I'll rush the front room. Bring him through in a moment once I've got the situation under control."

Guy drew his sword. He turned the door handle and eased it open. A figure sat by the fire, reading.

Guy took several cautious steps inside and when in range, lifted his sword and pointed it at Sackville's neck. "Don't move," Guy said.

Instinct made Sackville turn his head, forcing the tip of the sword into his flesh. He yelped and put a hand to the wound. He gaped at the blood on his hand and whimpered.

"I told you not to move." Guy placed the tip of the sword back on Sackville's neck, to the north of the previous wound.

Sackville learned quickly: he continued staring forward, unblinking. "Who are you?"

"I'm not here to make friends, so there's no need for introductions."

Kit bundled through the door, dragging the butler behind him.

Sackville tried to turn his head, but received another prick for his efforts.

Guy placed the sword at a third point. "Don't worry. We brought your butler in here so he couldn't go for help. Is there anyone else in the house?"

"Annie has a room upstairs."

"Who's Annie?"

Sackville gulped. "My maid."

"And are you expecting to see Annie tonight?"

Sackville clenched his teeth. "I'm sorry."

Kit stood next to Guy. "That's a development. What's he sorry for?"

"What are you sorry for?"

Sackville tried to shift his eyes as far to one side as he could to see Guy. "What are you, her brothers or something?"

Guy nudged Kit. "Sounds like our friend here has been climbing those stairs to help pass the time."

Kit moved to the other side of Sackville's chair and placed his sword between Sackville's legs. "Sounds like he's got a lot to lose."

"My friend has an unsteady hand. It gets worse when he suspects someone's not telling the truth."

"I react badly to liars and time-wasters." Kit let his sword brush against Sackville's inner leg.

"Do you want money? I can give you money."

"Do we want money, Kit?"

"Sounds like he's wasting our time." Kit pressed his sword against Sackville's crotch. The material there darkened. "Oh look." Kit prodded again. "He's had an accident."

"You'll spill worse than a drop of piss if you're not honest," Guy said.

Sackville whimpered.

"I know you were tracking the plague as it entered London."

Sackville's brow furrowed and confusion spread on his face. How many mucky pies did he have his grubby fingers in?

"Where were the first cases you noticed?"

Sackville's lip trembled. "There were three at the orchards in Ealing."

"And next?"

"Hanwell."

"Go on."

"Osterley."

Guy turned to Kit. "Does that make any sense to you? Sounds like they're running against the river."

"Osterley's on the River Brent."

"Any cases in Brentford?"

"Several." Sackville's voice rose by a few octaves.

"And after that?"

"Everywhere. That's when they decided to prorogue parliament."

"Kit, remind him these questions are serious."

Kit plunged his sword into the armchair and pulled it out again before resting it between Sackville's legs.

"What's the origin of this disease?" Guy asked.

"It's spread on rats or fleas on rats. The rats give it to people and they pass it to each other."

Guy glanced at Kit. "Do you believe him?"

Kit's grip tightened on the hilt of his sword. "Sounds like he's talking rubbish to me."

"No!" Sackville elongated the word into a pitiful cry.

Kit glanced at Guy. "But he believes it." Kit pulled his sword away.

Guy pressed the tip into Sackville's neck a little harder, to where the skin threatened to give once more. "Your employer has planted the disease in the country. He's let it take hold; did you know that?"

"I didn't."

"You said you had money in the house."

"Yes, please, take it. Leave me alone."

"Oh, I don't want it. You're going to gather all the money, gold, jewellery, anything of value you can find, and tomorrow, you're going to give it to Annie, and you're going to send her on her way. You will not go upstairs tonight; do you understand?"

"Yes, I do. I'm sorry."

"It's not us you should apologise to. We'll be back to make sure you've followed our instructions. If that's clear, nod your head."

Sackville nodded, breaking the skin on his neck for a third time.

Guy withdrew his sword. "One more thing. Give your butler a raise."

Guy and Kit sped from the house, waiting until they were a couple of streets away before speaking. "So tomorrow, we check out Ealing?" Kit asked.

"You bet on it."

Ealing's orchards were full of blossoms on that fine March morning. Life was lacking everywhere else.

Kit approached a tree and pulled a branch to eye level, examining the leaves and the blossom.

"What do you see?" Kit asked. He pulled the branch closer to Guy.

Guy shrugged. He knew little about trees.

"Note the dark edge on these leaves?"

Guy peered at a leaf. "What's that tell you?"

"The disease is in the trees."

"Did they get infected by the fruit?"

Kit concentrated, his hand plunging into his pouch where his runes were. "The season's wrong. This is an effect of the poisoning, not the cause."

"So where now?"

Kit scanned the orchards, studying the spread of the trees. "Why do you think there are so many trees planted here?"

Guy shrugged. "I guess the soil is fertile and suited to the growth of trees."

"Aye, but what makes it particularly suited?"

"You tell me."

"It needs goodness from the soil. It needs water. I'd wager there's a spring here and an underground river running southwest towards the Thames."

"So, we head to where this underground river meets the Brent in Osterley, right?"

Kit shook his head. "If we go to Osterley, we'd have to find where this water gets into the Brent, which is probably filtering through rocks in the bottom. So, we excavate the river and swim miles this way. Underground. Underwater. Does that sound like a good idea to you?"

Guy raised his hands in surrender. "You haven't socialised much in the last few months, have you?"

Kit stared dead-eyed at Guy. "It's been maddening, but what does that have to do with anything?"

"Never mind. What do we need to do?"

"The first cases were here. The trees are suffering. We find a well nearby, one that runs into that underwater river to the north-east, and that'll be our source."

"We'll cover more ground if we split up."

Kit glared at Guy with wide eyes.

"Or we could stick together for safety reasons."

Together, they moved to the nearest property. A board across the door, *plague house* written in crude letters, turned them away from it. It didn't take long to move from one abode to the next, each revealing a similar sorry tale of sickness. In some houses, the sick shuffled around on the floorboards and leaned against doors, waiting for death to take them. They found a well in the back garden of one, but someone had filled it with rocks. Those responsible for infecting the water may have covered their tracks. But the abandoned house suggested a family had hastily fled the plague.

Even from a distance, the next building looked a better place from which to hatch a shady plot. Trees and shrubs hid the building from the outside, and once they got close, they discovered a barn beside the house. They waited nearby for a moment, but no sound came from the property. The front door had no plague warning. From closer, no sound of shuffling came. They knocked on the door and backed away. No answer came. They tried the door, but it was locked. Around the back of the house, they discovered another well. They peered in.

"It's a well all right," Guy said. "Could it be our place?"

Kit peered in. He grabbed a stone from the ground and dropped it in. After the plonk came, he gazed up. "There's water. It could be. Check the barn."

As soon as Guy and Kit entered, they knew they were in the right place. The remains of splintered barrels of gunpowder filled the store, the sign of the children of Mizraim branded on the side. Several full barrels remained.

"You think they'll be back?" Kit asked.

"I'd wager they're returning periodically to spread the poison."

"So, we wait here for them?"

"Aye, but let's get rid of this first."

Kit remained within spying distance of the property while Guy rode to collect a wagon.

Within a couple of hours, he'd returned. They loaded the wagon and took it to the orchard, out of sight.

They returned to the now-empty barn. "We might be in for a long wait, so I brought food."

Kit's mouth dropped open in relief. Together, they ate and reminisced about some of their past adventures.

"If Cecil gets his way," Guy said, "kids won't do the things we did again. They won't go off looking for trouble, following suspicious people around towns."

"Can you imagine how awful it would be for them?"

"That's what I'm trying to focus on. As bad as it is, if we can act to stop Cecil's plan, if we can put an end to his unholy plot, then people can live again. They can let go of the fear."

"If you think it's the right idea, I'm with you."

"And what do your runes say?"

As Kit reached into his pouch, the sound of hooves on the road came.

"Plan?" Kit whispered.

"If they're back to add more poison, we should wait here, in the shadows. Wait for their shock when they see the barrels are gone and wipe them out."

From their position, they heard footsteps growing louder and a whispered conversation. It played out as Guy had suggested. First, one man entered the barn. He stared into the empty corner.

"Cooper!" he cried.

Guy glanced at Kit. Together they counted the footsteps of the other man. As Guy attacked the one in sight, Kit burst into the light and stabbed the second man in the belly.

"You think there will be more of them?" Kit asked.

Guy shook his head. "No, simple operation to keep the plague going."

"What now?"

"Collapse the well so they can't do it again. Check the house for anything useful."

"But what about the plague?"

"There's not much else we can do other than wait it out."

After throwing as much rubble into the well as they could, they entered the house, but finding nothing useful, they made their return to central London.

"How long will we have to wait?" Kit asked.

Guy shrugged. "A lot of that depends on how sensible people are."

A shout from the end of the street drew their attention. Two people hurled abuse at each other, getting closer and closer until words changed to blows.

"We might be in for a long wait," Guy said.

Chapter 41—In Which Guy Fawkes Prepares the Gunpowder

Each conspirator had a role to play in the build up to the event. Members of the party had each visited different stately homes to identify the locations of the royal children, ensuring they knew where to swoop on the day parliament opened.

Thomas made himself useful in combatting the disease, using his self-repaired printing press to produce a pamphlet promoting washing activities that would help reduce the risk of infection. "Education," he argued, "is our best weapon against this."

Month after frustrating month passed, though the effects of plague lessened throughout the summer. A parliament opening in October had long been mooted. In July, the government again put this back to November 5th. "More time to prepare," Catesby said. It gave Guy only more time to doubt.

Opportunity, however, arose to develop the plot in a different way. The storeroom above the tunnel, from where they'd heard shuffling while digging, became available for rent: one of the Houses of Parliament's cellar rooms.

Thomas Percy used his position to take on the lease, filling it with reams of fabric.

Excavation work began again, but not to lengthen the tunnel. No, they dug up, breaking into the bottom of that storeroom. And as November approached with restrictions lifted, the conspirators met to put final plans into place. They returned to where the conspiracy started, the Duck and Drake. People behaved as if the plague never happened, with plenty of drinkers filling the seats of those that had fallen. Instead of wallowing in the year's misery, they revelled in their freedom. Aye, surely Cecil expected this carefree mood among the population, a mood that would allow him to slap all sorts of restrictions, levies, and taxes upon their homes and businesses the second parliament reopened. Given the simple joy of being able to leave their houses once more, they'd not flinch before sticking their hand in their pocket to support their glorious nation.

The months of delay had left the conspirators frail. The Wintour brothers had a constant look of having missed too much sleep. Thomas Percy had lost a considerable amount of weight and, on top of the incessant drooling, had developed a twitch. Tresham complained endlessly, either banging on about what he deserved from the new world or suggesting various people should be warned. He claimed his relative, Baron Monteagle, didn't deserve to die.

Catesby had been back in touch with Cecil and obtained permission to take a force to the continent as planned. In truth, he would never make the dock and circle back to London. Not only would his action keep several Catholics from parliament, but that force would be the one to protect the young royals.

On the day parliament was to open, November 5th, 1605, Guy would light the fuse to set off the gunpowder. Their intel had told them Prince Henry remained at the Palace of Whitehall, while Prince Charles resided in Lincolnshire, and Princess Elizabeth in Combe Abbey. Catesby (after turning his army around in readiness) would swoop into Whitehall Palace alongside Tresham and Bates to pluck Prince Henry from the confusion under the guise of taking him to a safe place while London came under attack from foreign invaders. This lie, Catesby believed, would bring the greatest panic to the palace and make them more likely to relinquish the Prince.

Thomas Percy would remain in London to stir confusion and point fingers.

The Wintours were to travel to Lincolnshire to keep an eye on Charles while the Wrights would take charge of the Haringtons of Coombe Abbey to keep Elizabeth safe. Rookwood provided fine horses for these endeavours, while Digby prepared another small army, ready to protect their interests when the time came. Other parties, they expected, would swoop for the royal family when the power grab took place. But of course, the conspirators of the gunpowder plot were the only ones forearmed with the knowledge of the coming destruction. They'd fortify themselves with their quarry before the others had so much as recovered from their dismay at the news.

With the plans settled, the conspirators went their separate ways. "Next time we meet," Catesby said as they parted, "it shall be as free men with the power to make this land anew."

Kit stopped Guy before he headed along The Strand. "Do you need a hand tonight, getting things ready?"

Guy had already moved most of the barrels into the storeroom, but he welcomed the company. They entered the property in Whitehall, for it was less suspicious to visit there at night than the room attached to the Houses of Parliament.

They moved through the tunnel and up the ladder into the store.

Kit nodded at each of the barrels, disguised by Thomas's fabric. "So, how are you going to do it?"

"There are a few barrels in the tunnel still. I'll set a long fuse on those first, climb in here, and set the shorter fuse on these. I'll run to a safe place before it all crumbles."

Kit whistled. "That's going to be some sight."

"Won't it?"

Kit stared at Guy, holding his gaze before he spoke. "Do you believe it can be different after?"

Guy took a deep breath. "Aye, I do."

"You're uncertain, though?"

Guy put his hands to his face and rubbed his eyes before dragging his fingers down his cheeks. "If we had an idea about what waited on the other side, if we could act with clear knowledge of the consequences, we'd all be different people, would have done different things. We have to have the courage of our convictions. We have to believe we're making it better, or why try anything?"

Kit sighed. Time had taken its toll on them all. Kit seemed to defy it best, but even he looked worn at this moment. "Our whole lives, we've been in this fight."

"Doesn't that make it more likely we'll see it through to a finish?"

"When you put it like that, Guy, I believe you."

"How often do you think about our time back at school?"

Kit smiled. "All the time."

"Do you remember the adventures or the lessons?"

"Both. Sometimes things Pulleyn or Uncle Francis said swirl around my head, and I try to make sense of them. Sometimes I wonder what they would do."

Guy pictured his old mentors. "And what would they do?"

Kit paused.

Guy took a deep breath. "They wouldn't go through with it, would they?"

Kit shook his head. "They didn't teach us to do this. They taught us to fight for good, and to defend ourselves against our enemies."

"And this is different."

Kit gazed at the floor. "Aye."

"But what happened to them in the end? Standing their ground wasn't enough."

"Maybe." Kit placed a hand on his chest. "But I wish they were here."

"Aye. They could tell us what to do. There aren't many days when I haven't wanted guidance from someone. The time comes, though, when we have to shoulder the burden."

Kit looked down and rubbed the stump of his missing finger. "When this is done, when we get to start the world over, we'll still see each other, won't we?"

Guy smiled. "Aye, but I'm hoping the time will come when we can ride upon an orchard without a sword by our sides, without having to peer into windows seeking enemies."

"Maybe it is all worth it." Kit sighed. "Well, I guess I'll see you on the other side."

Guy went to the door. "Aye, see you on the other side."

Once Kit left, Guy locked the door. He took the top off the nearest barrel and stared at the gunpowder inside. To think something like that could cause such destruction. He placed the lid back on and leaned against it. In a few days' time, all that would be gone, and everything around it, too.

Guy considered the myriad consequences of their actions. Most of their party, even those Catesby had brought in late for either financial purposes or to provide other necessities to the plot, were pious men. He did not doubt that they wanted the better world Catesby spoke of. But did they only want it better for themselves? Would Catesby, when he held power, inflict torture upon those that wished to maintain the Protestant way of life? Would the Puritans be driven from the shores or forced to hide in within allies' homes?

Tresham could not be trusted. Bitterness consumed him and Guy suspected he'd use any power to commit acts of cruelty. When he spoke to Catesby in the past, he found Tresham's vengeful streak a blind spot, reassuring Guy that he'd keep him in check, but would Catesby leave himself in a position to do that?

A light grew in the room, and at first, Guy feared capture, that the plot had faltered, that he had been discovered. He turned, expecting the lamps of the night watch crowding at the door, accusing faces staring at him.

When he turned, however, only one face hung before him. The glowing skull of Thomas Percy drifted from the corner. "But, Guy, the real question is whether you can trust yourself?"

Could he? Of course, he believed himself to be incorruptible, but did Catesby not believe that of himself too? Even Tresham would paint a picture of himself free of that blemish if he were the one holding the brush.

"What would you have done, Percy, if your rebellion of the northern earls had such an opportunity?"

Percy drifted around the top of the barrels of gunpowder. "I have little doubt that had the chance arisen, we would have taken it."

"Oh," said Guy.

"But I didn't know then what I know now."

Guy tracked Percy's movement, turning as he drifted around the room. "That's little help."

Percy stopped. "Without drastic action, nothing is likely to change in this land."

"And yet you stop short of telling me to light the fuse."

Percy drifted closer but let his light wane. "My purpose is not to make decisions for you."

"Tell me, why am I here? Why have you followed me along this path if it is not to commit this dreadful, terrible, incredible act?"

Percy twisted one way, then the other. "Perhaps the path itself is more important than the destination."

Guy sighed. "I've thought about all the people I've met, all who I've learned from and still, I cannot see the way forward."

"And what of nature and natural order?"

Guy thought back to the lessons he'd learned at school. "The King has his place in the great chain of being, beneath only God and the angels. If we break that chain, the effects will resonate to the bottom. The skies will revolt, and the ground will shake, with all things in between in turmoil."

Percy dashed to Guy's side. "Is this a reason to stop this plot?"

"Chaos is only temporary. The chain of oppression needs to be broken so we can all live in peace."

Percy glowed brighter. "But who appoints a King?"

"They say a King represents God on Earth. He is there by God's appointment."

Percy came so close to Guy that white light blinded him. "You once asked your headmaster a question about God."

Percy's white light consumed all, and the scene around Guy transformed, removing him from the storeroom of the Houses of Parliament and placing him beneath Saint Peter's in the secret chambers where he learned his earliest lessons on demonology.

Guy stared at his young self, a boy that had yet to witness any death in his family. Grief to him remained a blessed unknown. His only experience with demons was his encounter at the farmhouse, something like a strange dream rather than the beginning of a lifelong struggle.

He watched his young, eager self raise his hand, the fingers twitching.

Guy watched as Pulleyn nodded, fondly studying those enormous arching eyebrows.

As young Guy spoke, his older self spoke the words, too. "And God is all-powerful, too, right?"

The older Guy focused on his headmaster, knowing what he would say: "Also correct."

He studied his youthful face, scrutinizing the lines that grew as he struggled to work something out and again, he spoke in tandem with his young self: "So, he's stronger than all demons? He's stronger than the devil?"

Pulleyn answered as he had done all those years ago. "Infinitely so."

Old Guy again watched his younger self struggle with theology. "So why doesn't he kill all demons?"

As Pulleyn raised his index finger, old Guy did the same. "For this is the very thing that the Dark Lord desires. If God shows his wrath, if God defeats his enemy, then has God not become every bit as dark as they are? If our God smites like this, using his superior and infinite power, it would not be a fair fight. Morality is dead. Heavenliness dies. In effect, God becomes the devil."

The white light faded and Guy returned to the storeroom, barrels of destruction all around him.

He hurried from the storeroom, checking the street first and headed to his abode. He had a letter to write.

Chapter 42—In Which Guy Fawkes Blows It

With the conspirators having taken off to perform their parts in the plot, many riding away on Ambrose Rookwood's beautiful horses, Guy was alone with his guilt. They had sworn a pact to tell no one of their intentions. While Guy had perhaps kept that promise in the strictest definition of those words, if anyone intercepted his letter, he'd hinted at enough to damn him. He had to hope the others would not suffer as a result of his actions. Maybe if they captured the king's children, the king would listen. It would be enough of a turning point for the English Catholics that they could forever change their perception in England. Perhaps this would be one turn James I would not flip back on. This act could give them the platform they needed to reveal the demons in James I's court. Guy, of course, knew these hopes were ridiculous. His letter had purged him of no great sin. His words would not stop the hurt to come or the suffering of his kin.

Guy walked alone at midnight. When day came, parliament would convene for the first time since 1604. Whether Guy intended to walk to Westminster, or whether the habit of his boots took him there without conscious thought, by the time he got there, he could no longer say. He stared at the mighty building and imagined the skyline without it. Still, it brought a sense of freedom. If the building fell, and with it the structure of their society, no one would remain to issue cruel orders. The orchestrated spread of the demon plague throughout the land would end, and the country would thrive once more. But the words of Pulleyn kept coming back to him. An act of such evil would delight Satan.

He wandered back to the storeroom and slipped inside. Everything was ready. They'd positioned the gunpowder to cause maximum devastation. Guy had laid the fuses and cut them to the right length. He only had to commit one act of evil, and he could change the world forever.

Again, that light came into the corner.

Guy turned, expecting to find Thomas Percy's shining skull swooping in front of him to provide some last guidance, some final words of wisdom to sway him from the path he feared to treat. Alas, Thomas Percy was not there. The light grew closer, brighter, and the door flew open. Four guards in royal colours stood at the door, Robert Cecil's hunched form behind them. The men entered the room and flanked the door, allowing Cecil to enter. He leered at Guy, fire burning in his eyes.

Guy knew not if Cecil recognised him. The King's Spymaster had no doubt trodden on so many people to manipulate the world into the way he wanted it, that one steppingstone looked much like any other. "Seize him." Cecil sneered.

Guy's chances of fighting off four trained soldiers in a contained space were slim with his weaker sword arm. He considered dropping into the tunnel and fleeing that way. However, if the men followed to Thomas Percy's printing press, that would put his friend under suspicion. No, better to fight to the finish there in the storeroom with the barrels of gunpowder to witness his stand. Perhaps they would never inspect that tunnel, or at the least, news of the gunpowder being discovered would spread, and Thomas Percy would have time to disappear before they came for him.

In drawing his sword, Guy made a lavish sweeping motion, knocking struts of wood over, partially covering that hole over the tunnel and letting reams of fabric fall to hide it further.

As soon as Guy drew his sword, the soldiers acted. A glance into each of their eyes showed Guy the level of control Cecil had over them. They were seeded with the demon, the tell-tale yellow ringing their eyes. They drew on the power of the underworld to give them strength. And yet, these were not the crazed possessed Guy had faced in the past. When the likes of Dudley had demons possess his men, it was in entirety. Cecil had only let the demons get a taste of these men's souls, and as such, they regained their composure and strategy in a fight.

The first blow came from the left. Guy raised his sabre to deflect it, but the soldier stepped back, and a second attacked from the right. A quick twist of his wrist deflected this strike, too. He kicked out, knocking the man away, and slashed at the first soldier.

A lunging strike came from beyond this man, a third soldier joining the fight. They would not take turns to be felled by him.

For so long, Guy had remained composed in the fight, considering poise and balance, and even in the most desperate situations, he had not left himself vulnerable. But while he could only fight with his left hand, he had not those years of training and experience to fall back upon. He let rage take over and targeted Cecil.

Drawing his right arm up for protection, he threw himself into the soldier on his left. He swung his sword in defence, but Guy moved inside his arc. The soldier battered the hilt into Guy's back, but Guy pushed on, knocking him into a barrel of gunpowder. Guy slashed at the soldier behind him—the one holding the lantern. He leapt back and dropped it where it smashed on the floor, leaving a burning patch of oil. The flames licked out, desperate to ignite the fuses. One piece of fabric took.

Cecil was in sight.

Guy raised his sword, but a boot in the back dropped him to his knees, the fire dancing mere inches away. Guy made unpredictability his ally. He plunged his arm into the fire, letting his sleeve catch the stone floor, hoping the oil would soak in.

His action had the desired effect, for the soldiers stood off, unsure what to do.

While the agony of fire ate at Guy's right hand, he focused all of his remaining effort on destruction. He could end Cecil here. If he lit the fuse, if the gunpowder exploded, Cecil would die. His days of dark influence would end. Aye, Guy knew he too would die, a small price to pay for ridding the country of so heinous a villain. Aye, Parliament would be turned to rubble, but during the night it wouldn't result in the terrible loss of life that destroying it during the day would cause. He threw himself forward, aiming for the nearest barrel of gunpowder.

One soldier must have foreseen the danger and threw himself onto Guy's legs, and as Guy's arm came close to the barrel, it fell short, brushing only the fuse.

Another man fell upon Guy's shoulder. A third stamped on his flaming hand.

The fuse continued to burn. In the doorway, fabric burned. It was only a matter of time before one of the barrels ignited.

With a click of his fingers, Cecil's eyes glowed. Lightning flashed and thunder cracked as rain assaulted the ground outside. Cecil pointed into the building and an ill wind, carrying a tide of rainwater blew into the room, extinguishing all flame.

Hope died. The men on top of Guy dug in with fists and knees, battering him with the hardest parts of their bodies. They couldn't hurt him anymore than those dying flames had.

Chapter 43—In Which Guy Fawkes Visits the Tower of London

The history books will tell you what happened in the aftermath of Guy's capture. The fate of the remaining conspirators, and all linked to them, is widely documented. But for many weeks, Guy was oblivious to anything other than his own suffering.

Outside the Houses of Parliament, the soldiers clapped Guy into manacles. Cecil stationed a soldier outside the storeroom to stop anyone else from concluding the ambitions of the plot. Cecil dismissed another soldier, leaving Guy with two to contain him, an undemanding job, for all the fight had left Guy the second the flame on the fuse extinguished.

A sword at his neck kept Guy on his knees. He tilted his head back to avoid the blade which snagged in his beard with every movement.

The storm departed as quickly as it arrived, leaving a clear sky. Night was at its darkest. He gazed at the stars. He'd see them no more. Were these the same stars that lit up the sky on the night he fought on Uncle Thomas's barn roof against the furies raised from Hell by Sandys and Hastings? Were these the same stars that looked upon him when he had raced from his barn to his home only to find a hideous tentacled beast assaulting it, murdering his wife and child, and ruining any chance of happiness he ever had? Were these the same stars that shone upon him in Morocco and in Spain, when he'd tried to do the right thing only to fail again, and again, and again? Aye, the stars had witnessed the worst of Guy Fawkes.

While the soldiers beside him braced themselves against that cold and blustery November night, Guy felt thankful for its ravages that kept his mind alert, thankful for the chill it brought to his blackened right hand. Perhaps that wind could travel to his friends and warn them of yet another failure, give them a chance to flee and let him alone pay the penalty for taking on the weight of monarchy and losing.

After some time, a wagon arrived. The soldier hitched Guy into it with cruel fingers prodding into his armpits. More soldiers waited in the back, who dragged him inside. They placed a sack over his head, and connected his

chains to one in the wagon. From that position, he could not escape. He had
no desire to.

The wagon's movement, coupled with the disorientation of the lack of vision, made Guy focus on his injuries. The pain in his burnt hand compared
only to the agony of soaking in Master Leonard's acidic demon blood. But
each time the wagon wheels bumped over a stone, the soldiers' blows pained
him again. The torturous journey could have taken minutes or hours. Guy
had lost all sense of time. For on top of the physical pain came the accusations
of failure, guilt about letting the rest of the conspirators down, and a strange
sense of relief that he would no longer commit an act of mass murder.

When the wagon came to a stop, the guards dragged Guy out. For a moment, the cool of the night air relieved him. The bag over his head distorted
the words of the soldiers, but shouts came in angry voices, followed by more
blows to the arms. A heavy door creaked open, and after the soldiers manhandled him through, it slammed shut. Guy wondered if he would ever see
beyond that door again.

The soldiers forced Guy along a corridor, through another heavy door,
and his feet scrambled beneath him until he realised they were taking him
down steps. He had suspected they would take him to the Tower of London;
now, as he descended, he recognised the familiar stink of a dungeon, that
human stew of suffering and torture. After a few minutes, the ground lev-
elled. Someone barked more muffled orders. The guards held Guy still. A
key rattled in a lock and an iron door swung open. The guards dragged him
inside. They shifted position to get him through the narrower door. They
wrenched his arms up and released him, for the wall had him now. The
guards trussed Guy's shackles to a heavy bolt embedded in the stone wall. His
tiptoes touched the floor. He took a second to adjust to this new position, to
this new torture, and the iron door swung shut once more.

Time ceased to be measurable in perpetual darkness. Through his sack, sometimes he saw the colour of the blur of the Lieutenant of the Tower's lantern.
Thomas Percy had once pointed the man out to Guy, a barbarous gentleman
named Sir William Waad. When he or one of his gaolers fed Guy a few

spoons of slop, they never lifted the sack above his nose. Guy's only source of liquid was when they threw cold water over his head. He sucked moisture from the saturated fibres. Sometimes, the contents of the bucket struck hard. Left outside in November, sometimes an ice crust had formed. On other occasions, the acrid taste suggested his torturers doused him in something other than water, and yet, this bitter liquid sustained life.

Why did Guy desire to hang on to life? He could not quit; he knew not how. Even in this dire situation, hope lingered. In those long hours, to forget about the agony in his shoulders, the burning in his constantly stretched leg muscles, he remembered his friends. Attempts to call on Thomas Percy failed. He drew hope instead from another prisoner: Margaret Clitherow. He wondered if anyone would find a way in to see him, as he had found a way into York Castle to visit her prior to her execution. Margaret's hope never died, even as she did, even as they placed rocks upon her that crushed her ribs and burst her lungs. Her resilience, her defiance in her last moments, had saved a city from darkness. If Guy could hold on long enough even to make the smallest ripple, it was worth it.

Guy's cell door creaked open. He opened his mouth, expecting the slop, but someone yanked the sack from his head. A confusion of colours danced before him. The sack's fibres had scratched his eyes, and even as his vision stabilised, blurry edges remained. The light of a lantern became clear, then Waad holding it, followed by the figure of Cecil, hunched over and grinning.

"Tell us your name, and we shall free you from these chains."

Guy opened his mouth to speak, but his mouth was too dry to make the sound.

Cecil glanced at the gaoler who dipped a rag into a bucket and shoved it in Guy's mouth. Guy sucked the water from the rag, relief trickling down his throat, though when it hit his gut a cruel stir made his stomach muscles tense, sending spasms up his legs and into his arms causing him to stretch onto his toes to relieve that pain, only for his calf muscles to scream out once more.

Waad yanked the rag from Guy's mouth with little regard for Guy's teeth. "Name," repeated Cecil.

A mess of jumbled memories swirled around Guy's mind. He muttered, "John Johnson."

"Johnson, it's time you knew what put you here. Monteagle forwarded me a letter."

Cecil pulled a folded piece of paper from within his doublet. He scanned it for a particular part. "I would advise you as you tender your life to devise some excuse to shift your attendance at this parliament, for God and man hath concurred to punish the wickedness of this time."

Monteagle: Guy had heard Tresham speak of him. So, Tresham bore the skill of holding a pen to craft such a letter. The Wintours and Digby all knew Monteagle, but hatred for Tresham burned inside Guy. Of course, it had to be he that betrayed them.

"In part, this letter led to the search of the parliament buildings. And yet we knew of your tunnelling exploits long ago. We wondered how long it would take before you would incriminate yourselves, how many more traitors your exploits would draw out of the mire. We could have put you to death long ago."

Cecil moved in closer, turning his head on its side to scrutinise Guy. "So will you confess to your treason and name your co-conspirators?"

"No!" cried Guy.

Cecil turned to the gaoler and whispered in his ear. The gaoler left the cell. Cecil grabbed Guy's hips and pushed them down.

Guy's shoulder burned. The chains bit into his wrists. Blisters burst on his burned right arm.

Once alone, Cecil crept closer to Guy, so close, he could feel his breath on his cheek, and yet, he moved closer still, lips brushing against his cheek. Cecil sunk his teeth into the flesh, drawing blood. He backed away, wiping blood from his lower lip. "A part of me wanted to let you do it. I would have taken such a grip on the fallen kingdom. But that damned letter forced my hand. I couldn't stand by once others knew of the plot. Instead, I shall make your suffering my reward."

Waad returned wearing a gauntlet in which he held a hot poker, the end glowing orange.

Cecil grabbed the material of Guy's clothes and tore his shirt open.

Waad prodded Guy's chest with the poker, his face twisted in perverse delight as skin hissed.

Guy gritted his teeth.

Waad jabbed the poker into Guy's right nipple and dragged it down his sizzling flesh.

"Thank you, that's enough." Cecil dismissed the gaoler and faced Guy. "Remember, only I have the power to bring you a speedy death."

Cecil left, with Guy almost willing to take his offer.

The pattern of slop feeding and icy water baths resumed until Cecil again disturbed Guy's routine.

"Tell us about Thomas Percy," Cecil said.

Guy first thought of his spiritual guide.

Pre-empting his inability to speak, Waad once again stuffed a moistened rag into Guy's mouth, yanking it out once Guy had sucked fluid from it.

As much as Guy wanted to speak of the Northern Revolt and the Rebellion of the Northern Earls, his fractured mind could not string a coherent narrative together, and he managed only a simple refusal.

"Before you make the poor decision to protect your master, let it be known that we have the dribbling fool, and he has signed a confession. When we asked of John Johnson, he had quite the account of your lack of decorum."

"I know no Thomas Percy."

Cecil gestured to Waad, who nodded, then left. "And he said you couldn't tell a doublet from a jerkin either. What else? The worst kind of servant—incompetent and yet egotistical, with ideas above his station. Is this a man you wish to protect?"

Guy gritted his teeth. "I know no Thomas Percy."

Waad returned with a metal contraption. He clamped it onto Guy's thumb and twisted a screw. The metal pressed what little flesh Guy had left on his thumb into the bone.

"The building from which you tunnelled came into Percy's possession after an event in Westminster. Witnesses heard the name John Johnson spoken. The Duke of Buckingham has been missing since. I am certain that Percy will tell us you are responsible for this. Do you wish to protect your master?"

"Percy's a fool!" Guy cried out as the gaoler tightened the thumb screw.

"At least I understand we speak of the same man."

"Was Percy a key architect of this plan?"

Guy shook his head as further pressure crushed his bone. "That man couldn't organise his wardrobe."

"Was Thomas Percy planning to destroy the Houses of Parliament and replace the King with his own man?"

"Percy couldn't plan breakfast. He was a fool, manipulated and used by others to get what they wanted."

"Who manipulated Percy? He was your master; he forced you to do his bidding, but who controlled him?"

Guy took a few hurried breaths and tried to form a smile. "I know no Thomas Percy."

Waad tightened the thumb screw further. Bile filled Guy's mouth as the bone cracked.

"Take him down," Cecil left the cell. "He needs a smaller cell."

Once Cecil had left the dungeon, the gaoler summoned his assistants. One grabbed each arm as the gaoler freed Guy. The pressure in Guy's shoulders shifted, and a whole new level of pain hit him as the muscles stretched in different ways. The gaoler's assistants dragged Guy out of his cell to a different part of the dungeon. Guy lifted his head, trying to spy other captives, hoping none of his friends were present. Alas, even with his poor eyesight, and the trauma he too had faced, Guy recognised Francis Tresham chained to the wall, great weights hanging from his ankles. While he'd never call Tresham a friend, his presence, his suffering, still pained Guy.

Waad turned Guy away from Tresham to face his new cell.

Guy glanced down at the barred cube, no bigger than a yard square.

Waad opened the door, and the assistant gaolers shoved Guy inside, kicking at his limbs until he contorted into a position in which he could bring them inside. They locked the door and left him to his suffering, Tresham visible in his peripheral vision. The traitor's suffering brought Guy no pleasure.

Chapter 44—In Which Guy Fawkes Takes on the Traitor and has an Audience with the King

For several meals the gaolers left Guy in the cage, his muscles spasming, his body crying out to stretch. They held pieces of stale bread to the outside of the cage, forcing Guy to gnaw at them like a rat. Gaolers frequently flung liquid at the cage. Guy opened his mouth each time, ready to drink, not knowing whether the contents would be icy or boiling, not knowing whether the substance was fit for human consumption. Fluids of every colour and viscosity had drenched him time and again, and he'd tasted them all.

At one point (Guy assumed night because of the lack of activity), a light appeared, like fire, but only burning as a pair of tiny orbs. They moved along and stopped at Tresham. Guy had witnessed much of the traitor's torture, had heard him spill names more readily than drops of blood, though to his credit, none were names Guy knew. Guy suspected Tresham's mind had been broken beyond all repair and babbled whatever name came into his head, real or imaginary. What good further torture would achieve, Guy had no idea.

The height of those burning orbs indicated eyes, and as they neared, the hunched form bearing them became clear. Guy had not seen Cecil in the dungeon without Waad.

He stood before Tresham who had long been silent, hanging like broken meat. When Cecil stood before him, lucidity returned, for he cried out a scream of great anguish.

"Tresham, I'd like to thank you for your service, your reward, a release from your suffering." Cecil pulled a vial from his belt, uncorked it, and held it beneath Tresham's nose.

The traitor cried out before a raking cough took over. His head fell forward, and his body hung limp. Cecil reached above him and unlocked his chains, letting the body drop to the stone.

Cecil turned to Guy, fire burning in his eyes.

A great throbbing pulse ate into the air, pushing at Guy's temples, the pressure in his head growing. Red light emitted from behind Cecil, and heat suffocated the dungeon.

Guy gripped the bars of his tiny cage as Cecil edged toward him. Guy eyed Cecil's belt, looking for another vial.

Cecil grinned. "Oh, you think you're getting the release of death, too? Not without greater agony."

Cecil bent to unlock the cage, then retreated beyond the barred doors.

Guy contorted his body to twist out of his tiny prison. His muscles screamed out at their new freedom, and neither his arms nor his legs acted as they were supposed to.

He stood upright and stretched out the pain. Before he had time to consider why Cecil had granted him release, Tresham's body twitched.

Whether he realised something was wrong, or if his intense dislike of Francis Tresham swayed him, Guy did not rush to his fallen co-conspirator. As Tresham's joints cracked and he rose to his feet, Guy backed away. He looked over his shoulder, but saw nowhere to hide. Tresham's eyes glowed with the yellow of the plague victims. The skin on his face bubbled, pustules rising to the surface and bursting, the pus dripping down his cheek and off his chin. Those diseased eyes fell on Guy, and he shuffled forward.

From behind the safety of the bars, Cecil laughed.

Tresham continued for Guy, raising his arms as he walked, stretching out, grasping.

Guy scanned the ground for any kind of weapon, but the gaolers were not foolish enough to leave any of their implements of torture lying around. Guy crouched and hurried towards Tresham, wrapping his arms around his middle and pushing forward.

Both crashed to the floor, Tresham onto his bottom, Guy with his arms still on his foe.

Tresham clubbed at Guy's back. The blow, and the earlier exertion, sapped Guy's strength. When Tresham put his hands into Guy's hair and lifted him, Guy allowed himself to be dragged toward the villain's mouth. Tresham's jaw dropped and saliva dripped from his teeth. Guy reached out, his hand feeling at Tresham's face until his forefinger fell on the eye.

Tresham continued to manipulate Guy's head, twisting it to access the flesh at the neck.

Guy prodded at Tresham's eye, but the act failed to deter him. When Tresham's hot and diseased breath moistened Guy's neck, Guy jabbed harder, breaching the eyeball's resistance, pushing through the vitreous body to release a slew of gooey liquid.

Still, Tresham continued, teeth scraping Guy's neck.

With all his remaining strength, Guy pushed his finger further, deep into Tresham's skull, until he found something that ended Tresham's fight. Tresham's legs shot out, rigid, and he released Guy from his grip.

Guy pushed himself up and backed away from Tresham. If he rose again, he didn't think he'd have the strength to stop him.

Cecil huffed and walked away, leaving Guy alone with the stinking, twitching monster.

A few minutes later, a gaoler arrived. Guy needed little prompting to crawl back into his tiny cell. Guy watched as the gaoler dragged the body of Tresham away. Perhaps fortune favoured Tresham, for his torment was over.

When Cecil returned the next day, he walked a little more upright, the events of the previous night having had a restorative effect. Waad followed with a lantern to provide light, and yet Cecil held a candle, nonetheless.

"Good day, Johnson." Cecil smiled the smile of a man who thought he held the trump card. "You would tell me if that wasn't your name, wouldn't you?"

Guy muttered that moniker back: "John Johnson."

Cecil sighed, faking reluctance as he tipped the candle up, pouring wax over Guy. It hit the back of his neck and ran part way down his back before it dried.

Cecil crouched, his teeth clenched. "You're Guy Fawkes. You're the worm that helped rid me of Dudley and murdered Catherine Stanley instead of using her as you were supposed to. Tell me where you wriggled to, worm."

"John Johnson," Guy muttered again.

Cecil stood and drizzled more hot wax into the cage and handed the candle to Waad. "Perhaps these will help jog your memory and bring a little sense back into you."

Cecil grabbed a pouch. He considered the cage and the position of Guy's head and emptied the contents of the pouch onto the stone floor. The items clattered against the stone, some falling face down, but those that fell face up revealed what they were: Kit's runes.

"Where?" Guy could only form part of the question.

"Your associate at Coombe Abbey had no further need of them after he spilled his guts."

"No!" Guy stared at the runes.

"They succeeded in their part of the plan. They had the young princess. If it wasn't for your failure to detonate the gunpowder, the country would be in your hands."

Guy gazed only at the runes.

"They tell me, the younger of the brothers, when he discovered your failure, wept." Cecil grinned.

Guy ignored him.

"Do you know what we found that fiend of a friend of yours doing?" Cecil bent down to face Guy. "He'd ravaged the princess's chambermaid, left her bloody in the bed, her throat slit. He made the Princess watch and told her she'd get it next. He sickened the soldier who caught him, so he opened his belly the second he stopped blubbing about your failure. An animal like that doesn't deserve to live."

Despite the cramped cell, despite the trauma in every one of Guy's bones and muscles, Cecil's words freed Guy's mind from similar bondage. Demons at the lowest level were always deceivers. That's all Cecil was. And evil men always imparted their values on others, assumed, given the opportunity, anyone would act in the same way they would. Cecil's lies were a mirror. No one knew Kit like Guy did, and to paint a picture of him so false destroyed the deception. Guy shuffled as far as he could to turn away from Cecil.

Cecil, misreading the movement, smiled. "All your friends are dead or captured. Sign the confession and welcome your fate at trial."

Guy gritted his teeth. "I shall speak only to the King."

Time passed. As Waad placed him on devices to separate his joints, trauma-tise his muscles, and break his bones, Guy responded only with that same statement: "I shall speak only to the King." When the gaolers tore out his hair, flayed his skin and ripped off his fingernails, he said the same thing: "I shall speak only to the King."

Whether Cecil made a request to His Majesty or if word of the prisoner's defiance reached King James in a different way, it is not known. All that is known is that sometime after Yuletide, when a trial date had been set for Guy Fawkes and the other surviving conspirators, King James met with Guy Fawkes.

Of course, the dungeons themselves were no place for royalty. Two gaol-ers freed Guy from his latest torturous prison and, led by Waad, dragged him back up the stairs. Given his feeble weight, a single gaoler could have carried him up those stairs and taken him to the small windowless room with no fur-niture other than a large oak table that dominated the room and three chairs. At least the air tasted less of death and deprivation there. Cecil sat waiting in the room, a victorious smile pasted on his lips. As the gaolers made to leave, Guy leant to one side and toppled to the floor. He tried to push himself up, but putting any pressure on his broken arms brought only agony.

Waad gestured to the gaolers, who lifted Guy and placed him on the chair once more. Waad stayed to hold Guy in position and dismissed his as-sistants. Guy's feeble frame and inability to remain in the seat made him look like a toddler among adults, though his without face looked like that of a man exceeding his years by a generation.

Heavy footsteps came from the corridor. A soldier wearing the armour of the King's Guard opened the door and stood aside, allowing King James to enter.

He wore his royal robe, a deep maroon colour, which only helped to bring out the traces of red in his hair at the temples and in his beard.

Any hint of that hair colour Guy Fawkes had once shared was lost among the filth which encrusted every part of his body.

King James strutted to the table and thumped it. "Is this the English dog that wished to blow up parliament?" He glanced at Cecil before crouching to look Guy in the eyes. "Are you the Papist worm that tried to kill me?"

Guy managed a weak nod.

"And what do you desire to share with me? Your excuses? Your apology? Your confession?"

Guy opened his mouth, but again found the words would not come.

King James pointed to a guard. "Bring this man some water."

The guard at the door hurried off, returning a second later with a pitcher and some wooden cups. Waad helped Guy to a sip of the water.

"More," Guy whispered.

Waad cuffed him on the side of the head. "You're in no position to make demands."

"Let him have more," King James said.

Waad held the cup once more, allowing Guy another gulp.

"You are Guy Fawkes, are you not?"

Guy nodded. "Aye."

"And you were part of this gunpowder plot against me?"

"Aye."

"That is your confession. Is there anything else you wish to say?"

Guy peered into the King's eyes, trying to ascertain what kind of man he spoke to. Was this a deceptive demon lover, one who claimed to be cleansing the country while feeding on the powers of evil? Was this man a fool, an empty shell sitting on the throne delivering the wishes of deceivers? Or was this a man trying to do the right thing, blinded by years of misinformation, corrupted by advisors that had been drawing from the demon well long before his birth?

"We have a written confession here." King James indicated a piece of paper. "All you need to do is sign it."

His eyes lacked the tell-tale colouring, the aura of malevolence that the truly evil men Guy had encountered possessed.

"The devil..." Guy muttered.

"'Twas the devil made you do it?" King James glanced at Cecil.

Cecil grinned. "A true confession from a suspected Catholic. It is they that are in league with the devil, and as such, you are right to continue to drive them from our shores."

King James cleared his throat, a sound like a siren. "All Catholics are liars, so easily tempted and prone to the corruption of necromancy."

Guy shook his head, the effort threatening to throw him off balance, requiring Waad to hold him steady.

"You Majesty, you need spend no further time with this low life." Cecil sneered.

"The devil..." Guy said again.

Cecil waved a dismissive hand at Guy. "He wishes to profess his allegiance to the dark lord."

Guy placed his hand on the table, too weak for the defiant thump he intended.

King James sat. "No, I," he leant in closer, "suspect there is more."

Cecil's eyes narrowed. In him, the dark aura was clear.

Guy took a few rasping breaths. He eyed the water, and Waad let him have another drink.

Guy spoke slowly, pausing after every couple of words, the effort exhausting. "The devil... holds sway... in your court."

King James licked his lips as if tasting the words. He mimicked Guy's stuttered rhythm. "The devil... holds sway... in *my* court."

King James smiled, though Guy had an idea he was less amused than he suggested. Cecil's eyes burned with anger.

"So, this is less a case of Catholic rebellion and more one of madness." Cecil rolled his eyes. "Shall we sign the execution order and be done with it? No trial is required for one such as he."

Cecil edged a piece of paper towards the king.

"Daemonologie." Guy nodded towards the King, again having to be supported by the assistant.

King James' cheeks rose ever so slightly. "You are a literate man?"

Cecil again edged the paper towards King James. "Long have we argued that education is too much for those not of noble blood. This confused fellow proves that."

King James ignored his spymaster. "What know you of demons?"

A flood of memories so extreme swamped Guy. Every creature he had faced, every corrupt man stood before him. They all bore Cecil's face. Every fight had led to this moment, and he was so weak he couldn't even hold himself in his seat. He could barely string the words together to speak.

He lifted his hand, pointed at Cecil, and quoted King James' own words on demons: "That simple illusionist... will make a hundred things... seem both to our eyes... and ears... other ways... than they are."

Cecil's face erupted with anger, bright fire burning in his eyes, sharp fangs growing from his face, his frame expanding. But as soon as it had come over him, it disappeared again.

The king shuddered, but by the time he turned to Cecil, his spymaster had regained his human form.

"You think this gentleman who had guided me on every step of my reign is corrupt? You really are quite mad. Let me sign to say I have heard his confession."

King James chuckled. He took the quill from the inkwell and signed his name on the paper.

Cecil smiled a sickening smile of victory. "All we need is the prisoner's stamp on the confession. Are you ready for this all to be over?" Cecil slid the lies over to Guy.

"A fingerprint will suffice. You need not sign your name."

Guy held out his hand, waiting for the quill. The assistant pushed it over to him.

Both of Guy's thumbs were broken. Infection in his hands meant they wouldn't stop shaking. He shoved the quill between the index and middle fingers of his left hand. With his right hand, he stabilised the quill.

There would be no chance of salvation while in the dungeon, but even then, a last morsel of defiance stirred in his gut. With quaking hands, he signed his name, taking the moniker from his days overseas: Guido Fawkes.

Chapter 45—In Which Guy Fawkes Faces Trial

With the confession signed, Waad and Cecil left Guy alone. Aye, he remained in the dungeon, but in a different part, granted the freedom of a cell, with no chains pinning him to a wall in an awkward position. He saw no further sign of the cruel objects of torture that had been his close companions in recent weeks. Even the food was a marginal upgrade on the spoons of slop, and the water provided tasted like water, served cold and in a cup.

When Guy suggested an ale would be nice, it brought a half-smile to one gaoler's face. Alas, he did not bring ale.

What's more, in this part of the dungeon, Guy had companions in the cells opposite. Grant, Bates, and Keyes had faced the torturer's trials and signed their life away. Ambrose Rookwood, who had done little more than supply horses, also faced trial.

A voice sounded from the cell next door; though broken, Guy recognised it as one he'd heard many times at the Duck and Drake.

"Wintour," Guy took in a raspy breath. "Is that you?"

"Yes, it's Robert. Thomas is in the next cell over."

"What news have you," Guy took another breath, "of our friends?"

"Did you hear of the fate of the Wrights?"

Guy felt a heaviness in his chest. He'd feared as much when Cecil had produced the runes, but hoped it was a ruse.

"Aye" He swallowed hard.

"And Catesby and Percy fell together. Took a stand against soldiers armed with muskets."

Guy's overwhelming sadness at the fate of his friends was tempered only slightly by the stand Thomas Percy had made at the last, facing his foes head-on. At least the pox didn't get him.

"And how came you to be captured?"

Robert Wintour sighed. "We rode to Lincolnshire and had taken a position ready to swoop in for Charles once the panic started, but when that never came, we fled. We thought we had found a friend to keep up safe, but his damned cook turned us in."

"Is anyone else... imprisoned with us here?"

"Digby has a cell next to Thomas. But Guy, what stopped you doing your part?"

Guy sat in silence for a moment. Could he admit to his reluctance? "Tresham," he said. "He wrote a letter to Monteagle... warning him... to avoid the opening of parliament." Guy paused to let the pain in his chest ease. "Cecil got hold of it. He searched of the premises."

"The damned fool."

Guy couldn't help but agree.

With the torture over, and provisions increased, Guy found a little of his strength returning over the following days, not so much that he could walk unaided, but he could at least speak entire sentences without stopping for breath. With no new trauma to his body, some of the old wounds started to heal, though the sores at every burn refused to stop weeping.

On the 27th January, the trial of the gunpowder plotters took place at Westminster, with Francis Coke presiding. Guy recognised him for a man he'd seen in Cecil's company at the Twelfth Night party and knew at once they were doomed, as they had been since they dug the first part of the tunnel, since they met in the Duck and the Drake, and since he had been for his whole damned life.

Coke invited each party to enter their plea. Only Digby pleaded guilty, and as such, Coke challenged him to speak first.

"Something had to be done about the damned injustices rife in this land." Digby sat, satisfied he had said his part.

With his guilty plea entered, Coke issued his sentence: to be hanged, drawn, and quartered, the standard punishment for those guilty of high treason.

Coke asked each member of the accused to explain their actions. Some claimed the court unfit to judge them. Others complained of the unfair treatment they had suffered for their creed. With the Wright brothers, Thomas Percy, Francis Tresham, and Robert Catesby all dead, only Guy could speak the truth.

When called to answer his crimes, he stood. "I stand before you today as a Templar Knight."

Expressions shifted around the room, some to confusion, others to more intense hatred.

"All my life, I have fought demons and the evil men that use demons to gain power, strength, and perverted wisdom. Some of these men are present today."

Someone booed.

Coke held out a hand to silence the crowd. "Tell us, Fawkes, how one fights a demon."

Shocked by the question, Guy stuttered. "You must bless a sword to injure a demon."

Waad stepped forward and handed Coke a sheet of paper. He pointed to a passage. Coke read aloud. "Guy Fawkes stalked through the trees, his blade glowing with a blue flame. Warthill did not return that evening."

"Do you recall this night?"

Guy peered up, puzzled. "Where did you get that?"

Coke ignored Guy's question. "Do you recall this night?"

Guy recalled the night. He rolled his eyes. "I did not kill Warthill."

"That is not what I am asking."

"Then aye, I remember the night. We stopped a plot, vanquishing a demon that sought the death of Queen Elizabeth."

"And how does one kill a demon?"

Guy's brow furrowed. "To kill demons, one must bless a weapon to empower it with the ability to sear demon flesh. I am not ashamed to say I have slaughtered many demons."

"Enter the confession of Francis Tresham as evidence against Guy Fawkes."

Guy Fawkes felt bile rising in his belly. Even from beyond the grave, Tresham pained him.

Coke cleared his throat. "Fawkes, where did one learn to fight a demon?"

"I cannot say."

"You have used power beyond that of man, power, one could argue, that comes from Satan himself."

The crowd gasped.

Guy thumped the stand before him with as much strength as he could muster. "That's a lie."

Coke held a book aloft. "From His Majesty's *Daemonologie*: 'He will oblige himself to teach them arts and sciences.'"

"We did good. We saved hundreds of lives."

"A counterargument typical of downward-going men is that one, Fawkes." Coke read again from the book: 'Pleasing God as he did, consequently, that act professed by so godly a man could not be unlawful.'"

Guy concurred.

Coke licked his lips. "It is also written in Daemonology that 'Evil is *never* to be done.' Only that way good happens."

"But without blessing the weapons, you cannot defeat a demon."

"Let Guy Fawkes' testimony be stricken from the records. We are here to try him for high treason, a greater crime than his confessed witchcraft.

"Guy Fawkes, did you plot with diverse others to commit regicide and destroy our Houses of Parliament?"

Guy sighed. "Only to rid this Isle of its demonic influence."

"Once more, strike all mention of demons from the records. Your admission here, regardless of reason, confirms your guilt."

"Is this not a place of justice?" Guy cried.

Coke's eyes blazed. "Sit down!"

"You will listen to my testimony!"

Guards ran at Guy, one grabbing each arm, dragging him back into a seated position.

Pinned to his chair, defeat washed over him. How could telling his truth make no difference? How could his truth not matter?

Once Coke had finished questioning all parties, their guilt assured, he moved on to their sentencing. A look of glee spread over his face. "Having been found guilty, you shall be first drawn backwards at a horse-tail, and being unworthy of either heaven or earth, thou shalt be strangled by the neck between the two where your fellow man can witness your depravity. After which, you shall be cut down, alive and have your genitals cut off and burnt before you as thou art unfit to leave any generation after you. Your bowels and inlayed parts shall be taken out and burnt. Your head shall be cut off, your body quartered, and the quarters set in high and eminent places to the view and detestation of man and to become prey for the fowls of the air."

The Wintour brothers hung their heads low. Whether in shame, sorrow, or fear, Guy did not know. He had accepted his fate. Things were coming round full circle.

Chapter 46—In Which Guy Fawkes Faces the Scaffold

After the trial, back in their cells, silence reigned. What more could they say? Guy reflected upon his fate. Perhaps he followed Thomas Percy's path, his existence a warning to others. When Coke had spoken of a feast for the crows, he had gone back to his earliest, innocent memories of the walks with his father and of the traitors' heads on spikes at the city's gates. Was it always his destiny to end up there from the moment he saw those decapitated heads and asked his father what they were?

While Guy did not converse with the living, one of the dead came to him, Thomas Percy, his only visitor, arriving on the night before Guy's execution. The first set of executions had emptied half of the cells. Only Thomas Wintour, Ambrose Rookwood, and Robert Keyes remained.

In the corner of the cell, Percy hovered, his glow dull. Guy half expected him to gaze upon him with those impossible eyes burning and laugh at his pathetic fate.

"It's not over," Thomas Percy said.

Guy raised his eyebrows. "Nay? Is my sword handy? Perhaps I can grip it between my toes and fight my way out of here."

"Still thinking it's about the physical fight after everything? Maybe I have failed you."

Guy shook his head. "If it's your guidance we have to blame for putting me here, then aye, you have failed me."

"Think back to the decision you made by the barrels. You haven't failed. You turned away from wrath and anger. You rejected mass murder. You called on something else; you called on someone else."

Aye, he'd written the letter. "All I hope my words will provide is understanding. That failed in court. What hope lies beyond that?"

Percy swooped closer, his glow intensifying. "I have failed you if you believe hope ever dies."

Guy touched his face, probing the lack of flesh. "Am I to follow you? Am I to plague the nights of another young man and follow him along a path to destruction?"

"Not if you've done enough. Not if you believe there is hope for this nation to change."

A bitter laugh caught Guy by surprise. "Maybe in the morning, it'll come back to me."

"Aye," Percy mocked Guy. "Maybe it will."

Sleep came. With that sleep came dreams once more. He dreamed of his wife, Maria and his son, John. He dreamed of his father and Uncle Thomas. He dreamed of riding Pewter and leaping over puddles. He dreamed of St Peter's, where Pulleyn and Ingleby shared their wisdom and of the Shambles where Margaret Clitherow taught him how to butcher a pig, sharpen a knife, and fight evil with more than a blade. He dreamed of Kit and Jack and Ralph and Ghost. He dreamed of Thomas Percy mocking him for his poor choice of sleep attire, of General Bartolomé de Sevilla calling him "Guido" for the first time. He dreamed of practising his crossbow skills with Samra. He dreamed of all those moments in which he faced death and had little other than hope, the training of good people, and his friends by his side.

And when Guy woke, a kind of hope resided in him, not for his survival, but a survival of the spirit that meant he never gave up. That spirit lived in all he loved most, and if it existed in so many people he had shared time with, how many others had that spark? How many others would fight on for a second longer to withstand the blows until their friends came to their aid? How many others would stand before the giant and refuse to bow to their threats, risk getting stomped on if they knew it would make that giant show his true colours?

Aye, the crown and the court intended for his death to serve as a warning to others, to keep them oppressed, to quash their ridiculous notions of rebellion. But there could be another outcome. If he refused to play their game at that dying moment, maybe it could show others they, too, did not need to be led to their deaths by dishonest men.

Guy had to be woken when the hour of execution came.

One of Waad's gaolers shook him into consciousness. As Guy blinked awake, the gaoler spoke. "It's rare anyone sleeps so well in their last hours." He prodded Guy until he stood.

Guards guided the four shackled prisoners out of the tower and to the dock. They shoved them onto a barge already occupied by a dozen more guards, one of whom barked an order to sit. No one told them not to speak, but they had nothing left to say. The only remaining words any of them had were for God as they prepared to face him.

Guy tasted the cool air on that frosty January morning. While he could only take shallow breaths, the fresh air in his lungs reminded him of days spent out in the open, camping in the wild, riding through the forests. For Guy, time was awry. His limited future collided with the past and present mingling so he could not tell one moment from another.

The barge stopped. The guards led the prisoners up the steps to where four strong horses stood.

Ambrose Rookwood whimpered.

Guy understood. Ambrose had spent his life rearing horses, now one would lead him to his death—a particularly cruel aspect of the sentence for him.

Guy offered no resistance as the guards strapped his limbs to the wooden frame even though his muscles cried out with the memory of their history of torture. Once the guards had strapped all the men to the hurdles, they pushed them to the ground, letting each of the prisoners fall face down into the dirt beneath the frame. Their faces were further ground into the earth when they lifted the rear of the frames to attach them to the horses' harnesses.

Guy waited as the first of the horses set off under the command of its rider. A scream sounded for a second before being muffled by the earth.

The second horse set off. No scream came from whoever rode behind the second horse. Guy, too, had no desire to give the executioners the pleasure of showing the pain of this first torture. The horse shifted as its rider mounted, scratching Guy's face on the ground, and seconds later, it took off.

At first, warmth grew in Guy's cheek as it scraped against the ground, but as the friction increased and the horse galloped faster, the first layer of skin peeled away. Guy gritted his teeth, but this shifted the position of contact with the ground, and a new pain emerged. As the horse continued to gallop, a stone embedded in Guy's cheek. Each yard pushed the stone further into his flesh until a great flap opened. Stone and mud pushed into the flesh, grating it away from the bone. Guy wanted to turn his face to save that cheek from further agony, but at the cost of his nose, his teeth, and the greater hurt that would bring, he stilled his neck.

The horse slowed and came to a stop next to its kin. Guy lay on the hurdle. He twisted his head, peeling the remains of his disintegrated cheek from the dirt. A flap of flesh hung from his cheek, and blood poured from a wound on his forehead into his eye. Once they stopped, he heard the crowd gathered in Old Palace Yard. Some cheered: not cheers for the conspirators, but for their punishment. Many more booed, directing their ire at Guy and his remaining co-conspirators.

The final horse arrived a second later. The executioners played on the cheers of the crowd, lifting, one at a time, the hurdles the four bloody men lay on. Guy glanced across to Ambrose. Half of his nose was missing, and blood dripped from a deep gash in his chin.

The executioners took Wintour from his hurdle first. Blood pulsed in Guy's ears, so could not make out the executioner's words. The event had a degree of ceremony, and while waiting for action, some of Guy's lucidity returned. In his official role as Secretary of State, Robert Cecil attended public execution. Funny how evil men are always drawn to positions where they can legitimately witness horrors. He strode along the platform where the second stage of the execution would take place: the hanging.

On a platform opposite with the best view of the spectacle sat King James I, with his wife and children. The king folded his arms and stared with a solemn expression.

A strangled yelp came again from the platform as the executioner shoved Thomas Wintour from the ladder. He kicked his feet in the air and clawed at his neck. Only when his feet gave up the fight did his executioner cut through the rope.

Wintour suffered the next part of his ordeal, culminating in his beheading and his body being split into quarters, away from Guy's view. Each excited squeal from the crowd signalled the next barbaric event in Wintour's end.

The executions dragged Robert Keyes to the scaffold next. The executioner helped him to the top of the ladder, but rather than waiting for them to swing him from the rope, he jumped, yelling, "God damns all..." Alas, the rope cut off his last word when it tightened around his neck. As he swung, struggling to claw the rope from his neck, Guy understood his purpose, but it had failed.

As he looked to have breathed his last, the executioner cut the rope, and Keyes collapsed to the floor, breaking limbs he no longer had use for.

Realising they'd missed a trick with Wintour's torture, the guards shifted the hurdles, forcing them to watch Keyes' final moments.

While Guy did not know Keyes well, he owed him his compassion. He did not hide from the view, but witnessed every act with the knowledge his turn approached.

With Keyes' body separated, Guy's guard cut him from the hurdle. He stumbled forward, causing jeers from the crowd. His legs were no longer his own. The guard dragged him up the steps onto the platform. His co-conspirators spilled blood stained the ground and continued to drip from the platform to the dirt below. The stink of blood and the effects of disembowelment hung in the air. A guard pushed Guy to the ladder. The executioner had to stand behind him to stop him from toppling back.

He climbed awkwardly up a few steps when the executioner placed the noose around his neck. "Look up," he whispered, "for this is as close to Heaven as you're ever going to get."

From nearby, church bells rang. Guy had come into the world to a clangour of bells. It felt fitting he should leave to the same herald. At such times, Guy could always hear voices. Now he heard one crying, "Stop."

This voice, however, spoke not from that plane between the living and the dead. No restless spirit cried out. The crowd parted to allow a rider on a white horse through. Was this the white horse of revelation that King James had spoken of? But when the rider called again, Guy's eye focused on his sister, Anne. She put something to her lips.

Guy could not see from such a distance, but he knew what she held: his grandmother's best whistle, carved from bone and with the power to shake demons. On the platform, Robert Cecil's face contorted into that of a demon as his evil could no longer be concealed.

Guy watched King James. His face contorted into dismay as he pointed at his demon spymaster.

The crowd roared in terror, all pointing at the demon on the scaffold. They knew what lurked among them now. They'd watched the torture done by these evil men. Now was the time to reject evil once and for all.

Guy gazed at Anne again; his sister had received his letter, had come to London to finish the job for him. As he gazed at her, she blew that whistle again, casting further members of the elite into their true forms. Guy glanced at the horrified crowd. Some ran. Some stared up, horrified, their disgust sowing a seed of future rebellion.

He watched the chaos. As hope stirred in his chest, his legs buckled. He fell with the weight of the noose around him, his neck snapping.

He would not suffer the indignity of the others.

And why should he?

That's no fate for a hero.

Epilogue

Jamie leans forward in his chair. "That can't be it."

Sidney takes a drink. "What do you mean, it can't be it? The story's over. Guy Fawkes is dead."

"But then what?"

Sidney glances at Jamie. "They did what they said they would. They pulled out his innards. The executioner cut off his head. Then he chopped him to bits. His premature death saved him that torture."

"But what happened to Cecil? How did it change things?"

"Politically and spiritually, the changes were at the same time massive and yet imperceptible. The King was no fool. He didn't confront so obvious an evil head-on. Instead, he side-lined Cecil, taking away that role of spymaster, to make him Lord Treasurer."

"Isn't that an even greater power?"

"Not when James also burdened him with managing the difficult relationship with the Kingdom of Ireland. King James loaded his court with men he could trust. What's more, he sought an end to the Catholics' persecution. While the Popish Recusants Act required Catholics to deny the pope's authority over the king, it started the ball rolling to an uneasy acceptance of Catholicism on this isle."

A nurse enters to warn visiting hours are drawing to a close. She's carrying a newspaper, a picture of the Prime Minister on its front page.

"Was it enough? Did that get rid of all the demons?"

Sidney huffs and rolls his eyes. "You're a smart lad. You know what's going on. They're everywhere. Cromwell tried to take it further, but he had no kind of legacy, and over the years, they crept back in."

Jamie glances at Sidney's chart and notices his full name. Croft, Sidney Guy.

"Croft? Are you—"

"Aye, can trace the line back to Anne. Here, give me that box."

The nurse huffs, but Jamie passes Sidney the box containing that whistle which Anne had blown in Guy's dying moments.

"Take this." Sidney drops the whistle into Jamie's hand.

Jamie examines the ancient artefact, feeling the coldness and smoothness of the bone. He places it in his pocket.

Sidney, meanwhile, is twisting the box. He yelps as it gives way, and a splinter of wood enters his hand.

The nurse rushes over to check his fresh injury, turning to give Jamie an accusatory glare.

"Hold on," Sidney says, pulling his arm away from the concerned nurse. "You," he waves the broken box at Jamie, "take this."

Jamie takes the broken box while the nurse attends to Sidney's wound. From the bottom of the box, between two pieces of wood that comprised a hidden section, is a yellowed sheet of paper. Jamie plucks it from the wood, unfolding it in such a way that it is the signature he reads first: *From your ever-loving brother, Guy.*

Jamie scans the letter, written on the night Guy realised he could never ignite those barrels while the Houses of Parliament were occupied. It's true, every word of it.

Once the nurse leaves, Sidney sits forward. "There's something I need to ask you."

Jamie stares at Sidney, the descendant of Guy Fawkes' sister, Anne, now wearing an additional bandage.

"What is it?"

Sidney beckons Guy over to whisper in his ear.

At home, Jamie turns the bone whistle over and examines it. His fears of it being brittle are unfounded. The words of Guy Fawkes' letter echo around his head. More prominent in his mind is Sidney's request.

The message icon on his phone is showing, and while twirling the bone whistle in one hand, he checks the message. Yes, it's confirmed, the Prime Minister, Alistair Barclay-Fitzwilliam, is giving a speech at the Innovate North-East event in Hartlepool at the end of the week and is once more likely to promise greater investment in the region, with better travel links to the capital, more lies about reinvigorating the docklands. With the threat of a general election looming, the Prime Minister and his cronies are going all-out on a charm offensive in the north. Jamie imagines his weaselly face contorting as he proposes a Council of the North to ensure greater autonomy and opportunity for the region.

Jamie sends messages to his contacts, proposing an account of the Prime Minister's speech. It's hardly the assignment any experienced journalist is likely to be thrilled to be sent on, so he hopes an editor will bite his hand off.

Not expecting an immediate response given the time of day, Jamie instead calls Michael to tell him about the end of Sidney's story, the end of Guy's story, and of Sidney's request.

"It's madness," Michael says.

"But what if..."

"You're buying into the fantasy of a madman."

"You didn't hear the story..."

"No, but I can hear you. At first, I worried about the damage you were doing to that poor, old man, buying into his nonsense, but now I'm worried about the damage it's doing to you."

Jamie sighs and disconnects the call, his chest tightening. He switches off the phone and gives the whistle his full attention. Where had it been for the last four hundred years? He raises it to his lips and blows. Despite all he knows about the whistle, he's surprised when it makes no sound.

It's the morning of the Prime Minister's speech at the Hillcarter Hotel, Hartlepool, and Jamie prepares for the day at the budget hotel at the marina in which he stayed the night. He has committed to two journalistic assignments which have given him access to the conference itself and the Prime Minister's itinerary. For *Business North,* he is to summarise Barclay-Fitzwilliam's speech with a positive spin, focusing on how it can develop the region. For the *County Durham Weekly Press,* he is to recount the entire visit to Hartlepool, covering the Prime Minister's arrival by train and engagements at the marina and at a small business based on the docks before focusing on the press conference at the hotel. Jamie checks his phone for sufficient storage space and opens the appropriate apps. He checks out of the hotel, slings his overnight bag in the back of his car, and heads for the train station.

Gathered outside are equal numbers of supporters and protesters. Jamie recalls the part of Sidney's story when he spoke of the separate factions Guy encountered upon his arrival in Cordoba. He photographs placards both in support of the Prime Minister's policies and those demanding he resign for his controversies. While he has no intention of interviewing any of the spectators, Jamie falls back to that old journalistic train of eavesdropping on the pair talking politics behind him.

"It's the same old tired ideas, recycled again and again. It's time for change, right?"

"Politicians have always lied and stolen. The other lot is as bad. Stick to what you know, I reckon."

Time passes, and the crowd become impatient. From inside the station, the sound of the loudspeaker system announces a problem for those travelling to Middlesbrough. There's a delay on the Prime Minister's train. Jamie checks his phone, reads a tip-off that the train has had to terminate at the previous station because of people on the track between there and Hartlepool. Jamie recalls the parts of Sidney's story in which worshippers threw themselves in the path of speeding horses. He heads for the marina, expecting Barclay-Fitzwilliam and his ever-present adviser Kristian Byrne to arrive by car instead.

Beside Hartlepool's infamous monkey statue, Jamie awaits the Prime Minister. As the minutes tick by, more and more arrive at the marina, some chanting as they wave their placards. No doubt news of Barclay-Fitzwilliam's alternative arrival plans has spread. News cameras from at least two different stations are already positioned facing a podium placed for a brief interview.

It's not long before the black car pulls up, followed by another. A few men in long coats and wearing earpieces have already positioned themselves. Jamie recognises the usual attire of the Prime Minister's security team. First out of the car is a group of the Prime Minister's aides. They swarm around the second car, ready for Barclay-Fitzwilliam to emerge. Jamie fingers the whistle in his pocket, wonders how many of them would react if he were to blow it now, but it's not the right time. Sidney had told him he'd know when.

Instead, he snaps a few more pictures of the crowd, records a few notes on his phone and waits for the speech. It's derivative: thanking voters for their support, weak praise of a town he names with barely a drop of his eyes as he checks his notes to confirm where he is. It's over without a fuss or a single moment of interest, and then the Prime Minister is back in the car. The protestors can't get close, and their yelled questions remain ignored.

Jamie breaks into a fast walk, taking a shortcut he tested the previous evening to arrive at the docks and the premises where the Prime Minister is scheduled to have a brief tour for more publicity shots. This time, when he emerges from the car, Barclay-Fitzwilliam wears a yellow high-vis jacket. Someone hands him and his advisor white hard hats. The hat is too large on Kristian Byrne. None of the protestors have followed, this part of his day a much better-kept secret. Of course, the cameras are on hand to capture the moment. Jamie spots a refrigeration unit in the corner and ponders blowing the whistle to see if it would force the Prime Minister to scuttle toward its security, but that's surely not Sidney's desired outcome. Again, business is conducted quickly, with the few questions from the press dispatched with more false promises and statistics which the opposition will later refute.

Next up is the conference itself. It is due to start shortly, but the Prime Minister won't be speaking until later. Alas, Jamie must be there for its duration to report to *Business North*. That's what's going to put food on the table, not this favour he's doing for Sidney. Jamie resents leaving Barclay-Fitzwilliam, but there is a gap on the itinerary, no doubt while the Prime Minister lunches somewhere lavish at the tax-payers expense. Instead, Jamie has to listen to a couple of CEOs debate the challenges posed by the current economic climate and the demands of labour.

There's a brief break in which Jamie grabs a bag of crisps from the bar. During this time, the media presence swells, and before the arrival of the Prime Minister, his security team grows too. Kristian Byrne loiters at the edge of the stage.

The audience returns to their seats, fresh drinks in hand. Alistair Barclay-Fitzwilliam's name is called, and he comes out, music blaring in the background as he waves his hands in the air.

No sooner has he thanked the crowd than a blast echoes around the chamber, a blast which Jamie immediately recognises as a shotgun. Fear drives many for cover, but Jamie's journalistic instinct keeps him alert. The nearby pillar will suffice should he need to get out of the way. Jamie is one of the few men to see the gunman pointing his weapon at Barclay-Fitzwilliam, and almost certainly the only one to recognise him: Sidney Guy Croft. He'd not had word from the old man since he'd finished his tale and had no idea he'd been discharged from hospital. Jamie's eyes dart around the room, and he sees several things at once. Members of the Prime Minister's security team that aren't at the barrel-end of the gun navigate around the room to get into a position to protect their boss. A cameraman continues to film the action. Kristian Byrne dashes onto the stage to take Barclay-Fitzwilliam's hand. The barman has fled out of the conference room into the main foyer, where the general hubbub grows ever louder as rumours about the blast spread. From behind overturned tables and chairs, a legion of mobile phones glow, their cameras pointing at the action on stage, hoping to capture the moment when this vigilante shooter fires his shotgun at the Prime Minister, hoping to sell their footage to the wealthiest news station.

That's when Jamie understands. He reaches into his pocket. He places the whistle between his lips, and he blows. Except the security guards, no one is watching Sidney as he's hit with a taser, and fifty-thousand volts jolt his body, stopping his heart. Most eyes are hiding, but the cameras capture it. They capture the moment Barclay-Fitzwilliam and Kristian Byrne react to the bone whistle, the sound only the demonic can hear. They capture the contortion of the Prime Minister's face, his failure to stop his mask from slipping. Within minutes, a hundred-thousand people have shared the video and one million viewers around the world have watched it. Everyone knows the Prime Minister of the United Kingdom is a demon. All his actions, so often called malice by the opposition but deemed necessary evils by his supporters, can be reappraised. He'd designed each act to drag the country into the gutter and leave its people susceptible to demonic possession. Alistair Barclay-Fitzwilliam's every desire was to make Britain Demon Isle once more.

Surely this is too much for people to take, regardless of political allegiance. With the moment caught on camera, this will reverberate further than it did four hundred years prior and echo in every chamber of power. With the proof being shared the world over, people will question whether they, too, are ruled by demons. This time, people will rise, unite, and fight as one against the demon scourge; the world won't tolerate being governed by the denizens of Hell.

It has to be better this time, right? People won't put up with it. Now is the time for change.

Or will the Prime Minister, Alistair Barclay-Fitzwilliam, have the gall to run his re-election campaign with a simple slogan: It's Better the Devil You Know?

Acknowledgements

After an intense period of planning, writing, and editing for the last eighteen months, the trilogy is complete. I've committed an awful lot of time to writing these three books over that time period, with my laptop joining me on most of the overnight breaks we had, and a notepad came along every time I left the house. Thanks to everyone who has put up with me during this period of time!

Real events in Guy Fawkes' life are touched upon here, and *The Real Guy Fawkes* by Nick Holland was again invaluable in terms of keeping some of the history real. When it's gone awry, that's me taking in on my slightly different path. There was plenty of other research needed. Looking at maps of Europe and north Africa from that period is fascinating, and who know there really was an Anglo-Moroccan Alliance? I've loved using these pieces of history give a spot of verisimilitude to the whole thing. Even the names of demons and some of the beliefs are very much based on what can be found in real grimoires written during the period. Rev Montague Summers' book *Witchcraft and Black Magic* was incredibly informative. A reprint of James I's *Daemonologie* was also useful in capturing the fictional version of the king. Oswald Tesimond's account of the event, *The Gunpowder Plot The Narrative of Oswald Tesimond alias Greenway* was also fascinating, offering incite into the religious situation in England and contemporary impressions of James I's reign. It also included lots of information about the trials and torture of the conspirators, and as such it was an invaluable resource.

Again, to make sure no one is in doubt about this, many of the characters in this series really existed, and some of the events in history really occurred, but my interest is not, and has never been in creating a realistic historical portrayal of them and their lives. It is not a reflection on their actual lives and characters.

The team at Shadow Spark Publishing continue to be incredibly supportive from editing passes to cover design to promotion and social media. Thank you for believing in the project and supporting me with it. It's a much better series for your input.

Thank you also to all the support of my friends, and all of those that have taken the time to read and review the book and share news about it. We're lucky to have sites like Ginger Nuts of Horror and Happy Goat Horror – go check them out. I was also privileged to be able to read from Guy Fawkes: Demon Hunter at two amazing events: ChillerCon and FantasyCon. There's a remarkable community of people out there making sure these events continue to happen, and I am so grateful for the opportunity to be a part of them.

So, this is the end of the Guy Fawkes: Demon Hunter trilogy. Thanks for reading, and keep an eye out for what's next!